REBECCA WEST

(1892–1983) was born Cicily ... er father had come from Count... her early education in Edinb... pen name, Rebecca West, from the strong ... character of that name in Ibsen's social drama, *Rosmersholm*, in which she once acted in her late teens. She began to appear in print as a journalist and political writer in London as early as 1911, in *The Freewoman*, and was soon deeply involved in the causes of feminism and social reform.

Rebecca West's first book, *Henry James*, was published in 1916; she went on to write novels, criticism, satire, biography, travel and history. Her works of fiction include *The Return of the Soldier* (1918) – a major British film), *The Judge* (1922), *Harriet Hume: A London Fantasy* (1929), *The Harsh Voice* (1956), *The Thinking Reed* (1936), *The Fountain Overflows* (1956), *The Birds Fall Down* (1966) and the posthumously published *Sunflower* (1986). Other notable works include *The Strange Necessity* (1928), her biography of St Augustine (1933), her two-volume magnum opus, *Black Lamb and Grey Falcon* (1937), *The Meaning of Treason* (1949), *A Train of Powder* (1955) and *The Court and the Castle* (1957).

Her only child, Anthony West (b. 1914), is the son of the novelist H. G. Wells. In 1930 she married Henry Maxwell Andrews, the banker, and began a lifelong companionship at their country house at Ibstone, in Buckinghamshire, with visits to London and many travels together, including her journey to Yugoslavia that inspired *Black Lamb and Grey Falcon*. Rebecca West was created a Dame Commander of the British Empire in 1959. After her husband's death in 1968 she returned to London where she lived until her death in March 1983.

Virago publish two of Rebecca West's works of non-fiction and eleven works of fiction, including *The Only Poet and Short Stories*, published in 1992 to celebrate the centenary of her birth.

VIRAGO
MODERN
CLASSIC
NUMBER
143

Rebecca West

THE
FOUNTAIN
OVERFLOWS

With a New Introduction by
VICTORIA GLENDINNING

The cistern contains: the fountain overflows
WILLIAM BLAKE

To my sister

LETITIA FAIRFIELD

Published by VIRAGO PRESS Limited 1984
20–23 Mandela Street, Camden Town, London NW1 0HQ

Reprinted 1987, 1988, 1992

First published in Great Britain by Macmillan & Co. Ltd 1957

*A CIP catalogue record for this book is
available from the British Library.*

Reproduced, printed and bound in Great Britain by
BPCC Hazells Ltd
Member of BPCC Ltd

INTRODUCTION

The Fountain Overflows is a novel of childhood. Adult problems
are seen through the child Rose's eyes, and made explicit only in
so far as Rose can understand them. It is known as Rebecca
West's most autobiographical novel, and for that reason it is
important to spell out the ways in which it is fiction. It is
autobiographical in spirit, though not always in fact.

It is the first volume of a family saga—'a saga of the century',
she called it in her synopsis—that was never completed. The
Aubrey family in the book consists of the parents, three
daughters, and a son. Rebecca West—or Cicily Fairfield, as she
was born—did not have a little brother. Rose and Mary Aubrey
are close in age, and Cordelia not much older, whereas Letitia
and Winifred Fairfield were eight and six years older,
respectively, than Cicily/Rebecca, and were away being
educated for most of the middle years of her childhood.

The house in the story, called 21 Lovegrove Place, is based
on Rebecca West's early childhood memories of 21 Streatham
Place, Brixton Hill, in South London, where the Fairfield
family lived from 1894 to early 1898; when they left,
Cicily/Rebecca was only six years old, much younger than Rose
Aubrey is even at the beginning of *The Fountain Overflows*,
which is also pitched a decade or so later in time. The Streatham
house, Rebecca West wrote in her unpublished 'Parental
Memoirs', was 'very much like the one I described as the home
of the Aubrey family in *The Fountain Overflows*, except that it
had no coachhouse. It was one of a line of semi-detached
Regency villas which formed one side of a charming street . .'
It also had, as described in the novel, an unkempt back garden

ending in a grove of chestnut trees, where Papa would pace when depressed or preoccupied.

Streatham then was still more or less in the country, 'a green suburb', as the novel lyrically stresses. Rebecca West remained loyal to her preference for South London long after it was thoroughly urbanised; in the very last summer of her long life she was driven by a friend round the built-up area of her early childhood, and wrote in her diary afterwards: 'The superiority of the south side of the river is extraordinary—the trees were gorgeous; the leaves so perfect, so green . . .'

However green, Streatham was not a 'smart' place to live. The cultivated, literary Fairfields, who lived by books, ideas and talk, like the Aubreys in the story, were chronically poor by middle-class standards and socially 'in a vacuum' in the class-stratified society of their times. The girls in the novel never expect to find husbands: 'We are not part of any world.' Charles Fairfield, alienated by his erratic life from most of his Anglo-Irish relations still had, like Piers Aubrey, 'a spectral aristocracy, the ghost of privilege'. What money he made came from the articles he wrote for two Melbourne papers, the *Argus* and the *Review* (the family had returned from a sojourn in Australia, where the Fairfields had married, not long before Cicily/Rebecca's birth), and the *Glasgow Herald*. Charles Fairfield, a chronic gambler and speculator, was 'continually and frenetically' unfaithful to his wife; the same is suggested of Piers Aubrey, whose financial unreliability, polemical passion and anti-socialist politics also tally with Charles Fairfield's. Yet Rebecca West later insisted that Papa in the book is only 'vaguely' a portrait of her own Papa. And how could it be otherwise, when her own Papa left home when she was about eight, and died a year or two later?

Piers Aubrey in *The Fountain Overflows* is a dream father and a nightmare father, 'a shabby Prospero', idolised, idealised, intoxicatingly attractive, but not to be relied upon. As Rose Aubrey says, 'I had a glorious father, I had no father at all.' (In the 'Parental Memoirs' Rebecca West writes about 'the detachment of my father from the consequences of his actions'; everything in him 'was turned in a direction that led him away from his wife and children'.) To all intents and purposes, Rose says in the novel, there was 'no man in the house'. She herself, in defence of her mother, feels she has to 'supply the need' from time to time. Yet Rose describes herself as a child who was temperamentally 'born to acquiesce in patriarchy', even though 'feminism too was in the air, even in the nursery air'. These conflicts inform and enrich the novel, even as they informed and enriched—at great cost to herself—all Rebecca West's life and work.

In spite of financial and emotional insecurity, Rebecca West's babyish memories of the Streatham years were 'happy, even ecstatic'. This was largely because of her own passionate, life-embracing personality, and that of her Scottish mother, who was unlike other people to the point of seeming strange. Rebecca West wrote to close friends in America, the year after *The Fountain Overflows* was published, 'My mother is of course the mother [in the novel]'; and in her 'Parental Memoirs' describes her as 'an ugly, witty, fascinating, intelligent and sensitive woman'. The mother in the novel had in her youth been a famous concert pianist: Mrs Fairfield, Rebecca's mother, had 'the air of a professional musician, which she had never been', though she was a good amateur pianist, as in her youth was Rebecca herself. Letitia and Winifred Fairfield, however, unlike Cordelia and Mary Aubrey, had no musical gifts.

Music plays a huge part in the novel, and serves as a metaphor for all spiritual and artistic aspiration, as well as performing a narrative function in the characterisation and development of the intensely musical Aubrey children. Rebecca West wrote to A.O.R. Cockshutt in August 1957:

It is always difficult for a writer to say what the theme of a book may be, but I think you are right and the subject of *The Fountain*

Overflows is the difficulty of leading the artist's life. That artist has to practise an inhuman industry and has to see more of the truth than is convenient—the father, who was not an artist, happened to see the truth as if he had been one, and the result was that he could not live at all.

Rose and Mary, in the story, are potentially artists; their elder sister, the complacent, conformist Cordelia, though a skilled technician on the violin, emphatically is not.

It is no good pretending, as Rebecca West very understandably sometimes did, that poor Cordelia is not a portrait of Rebecca's eldest sister Letitia Fairfield, even though Letitia played no instrument at all. (Rebecca West even dedicated the novel to Letitia, a supreme act of bravado or conciliation.) In later life Rebecca West spoke all too often of how Lettie's malice and disapproval had, she felt, poisoned her childhood. In the 'Parental Memoirs' she writes that Lettie was 'a very pretty little girl with golden hair and blue grey eyes, and an exquisite complexion, a sweet and serious voice, and a gentle air of dutifulness which captivated adults.' She describes watching Lettie dance—'so lovely, so cool, so innocent'—at a school entertainment (as Rose and Mary in the book watch Cordelia playing at a concert) and remembers uneasily her private cruelty: 'If she denounced me she must be right.'

Rebecca West conceded in later life that Lettie, being the eldest, suffered the most strain when the Fairfield marriage was in difficulties. The stress in Rebecca West's childhood home may have been more intense even than she describes in the Aubrey household. The middle sister, Winifred, wrote after reading *The Fountain Overflows* that Rebecca had 'minimised' that sadness, in the novel, 'as no one could read the truth'. In the novel, the warmth and light of the hearths and gaslamps and love of home are continually contrasted with the threatening outer darkness of which glorious Papa, inexplicably, was an ally.

Horrible Aunt Theodora in the novel is Rebecca West's idea

of a hated aunt in real life, Sophia Blew-Jones; and one of the most extravagant episodes in the book—the poltergeist in Cousin Rosamund's house—appears to be founded on fact too. Rosamund's mean and vulgar father is based on a relative of Mrs Fairfield's: 'Thomas Mackenzie, an exquisite flautist and an efficient commercial traveller in paper, but an odious man, I described as Rosamund's father in *The Fountain Overflows*, and there I flattered him.' Cousin Thomas spent a lot of his spare time at seances; and as for the poltergeist in his house, Rebecca West wrote in 1975 that 'I blush to confess that my family actually had experience of one. I had cousins who lived in a large and gloomy old house in South London. They had a terrible period of furniture being thrown about and saucepans revolving round clotheslines.'

All the Aubrey children in the novel have access to the supernatural, though their mother, a psychic herself, discourages it. Rebecca West, alongside her lifelong hunger for information and documentation of real events, had a strong and often disturbing impression of supernatural forces working in her own life; her eldest sister, as Dr Letitia Fairfield, qualified in medicine and the law, was a member of the Society for Psychical Research and an expert on exorcism.

The murder case in which the Aubreys' Papa takes such an interest—being capable on occasion of self-sacrificial generosity and expenditure of energy—is perhaps based on the Mrs Maybrick case of 1889; late nineteenth-century murders figured largely in the folklore of children of Rebecca West's generation, as is reflected vividly in this novel, where they are part of the 'forces of darkness'. But the book is also full of small, domestic reminiscence. The Aubreys' old red leather chairs, from which curls of leather were peeling away, were the Fairfields'; the Fairfields, like the Aubreys, had a loved servant called Kate, and family portraits really did hang over the Fairfield girls' beds, as described in *The Fountain Overflows*.

Rebecca West in her 'saga of the century' also conveys almost didactically, the texture of life in the years before the First World War. The comic-pathetic characters of Miss Beevor and Aunt Lily are vintage Rebecca West creations, but they are also authentically 'period'. She describes in humorous detail not only Miss Beevor's 'artistic' draperies but the huge feathered hats of the servant class, the glamour and terror of steam trains, the exquisite delicacy of gas-lighting, the red bicycles of telegraph boys, the smokier air, the more corpulent men, of her childhood. She reminds us how a childish illness could with terrifying swiftness became terminal, she describes Rose's first sight of a fountain pen, and her first drive in a motor-car: 'the miracle of not being pulled by anything, of the nothingness in front of the driver', To surrender to *The Fountain Overflows* is to experience a time-warp.

Rebecca West had by 1956 written twenty-three draft chapters of her family saga. The 17 chapters of *The Fountain Overflows* are a slightly reworked version of the first 14 chapters of this draft. Chapters 15 to 23 exist in typescript, as does the beginning of the second volume in a more thoroughly worked form, and there are many disconnected scraps belonging to later sections in her manuscript notebooks. This second volume was to be called *This Real Night*; she worked on one chapter of it as late as 1977, when it was published in *Rebecca West: A Celebration*—the visit to Mr Morpurgo. But by that time, the completion of the whole was a lost cause.

In the late 1950s it seemed simply a matter of expanding and making a 'fair copy' of her draft; in the early 1960s, she was still struggling with the sequel to *Fountain*, feeling increasingly that circumstances and her own state of mind were conspiring to doom it. Then she turned aside to work on something quite different—a novel conceived in the 1940s, which became *The Birds Fall Down*, published in 1966. Yet the draft of *This Real Night* shows no falling off in intensity or purpose, rather the reverse. It is full of vitality, and contains some of her best writing and some extraordinary scenes and set-pieces. It should be published.

There also exists, in synopsis form, the outline of what was to come after *This Real Night*, in a third volume (sometimes she said there were going to be four). The themes of darkness and loss were to grow ever stronger. It is no accident that delicious little Richard Quin in *Fountain* chants that there's *not* 'all the time in the world', because for him there is not; it is no accident that Mr Aubrey in *Fountain* carves for Rosamund an angel copied from one at Nuremberg.

The overall working title of the whole project was 'Cousin Rosamund', which may seem strange to readers of *The Fountain Overflows*. But in the unpublished phases of the work she grows in stature and significance. In the novel that we have, she is the trusted friend, tranquil, undemanding, with a special affinity with little Richard Quin; unlike the Aubrey girls, she has no special talent or ambition, she fulfills herself simply by existing. Rebecca West wrote that Rosamund was 'religion'— she is capable of doing what art alone cannot do, she is that which music seeks to express. Rebecca West's 'saga of the century', her magnum opus *manqué*, exists and does not exist, the known but unachieved conclusion reaching out like a dream landscape, or an amputated limb that responds to the severed nerves.

Rose Aubrey's mother impresses on her children that life is 'as extraordinary as music says it is'. What Rebecca West wanted to do was to transpose this heightened vision into narrative, to convey the 'fountains of rage and pain' and of love, and 'the strong flood of life of which I was a part', as Rose says at the end of *The Fountain Overflows*. On page 1011 of her unpublished draft typescript, Rose says: 'I was impatient because I always feared to be overtaken by the darkness, and was not arrogant but pitiable.' Someone who fails in a self-appointed task is pitiable; the ambitious project was overtaken by the darkness. But *The Fountain Overflows* retains its first freshness.

Within the structure of a traditional 'realistic' novel Rebecca West made poetic sense of the central drama of her childhood, and bore witness to the fierce avowal she made in 'A Visit to my Grandmother' (1963):

> My work expresses an infatuation with human beings. I don't believe that to understand is necessarily to pardon, but I feel that to understand makes one forget that one cannot pardon.

Victoria Glendinning, London 1983

I

THERE was such a long pause that I wondered whether my Mamma and my Papa were ever going to speak to one another again. Not that I feared they had quarrelled, only we children had quarrels, but they had each fallen into a dream. Then Papa said hesitantly, 'You know, I am very sorry about all this, my dear.'

Mamma answered almost before he had finished. 'It will not matter at all, provided that everything goes right this time. And it will go all right, won't it?'

'Yes, yes, I am sure it will,' said Papa. A sneer came into his voice. 'I should be able to do all that is asked of me. I should be able to edit a small suburban newspaper.'

'Oh, my dear Piers, I know the work is not worthy of you,' said Mamma warmly. 'Yet what a godsend it is, how lucky it is that Mr. Morpurgo should happen to own such a paper, and how good it is of him to want to help you ——' She faltered before she came to the end of her sentence.

'Again,' said Papa absently, simply supplying the word. 'Yes, it is odd that such a rich man as Morpurgo should bother himself with a thing like the *Lovegrove Gazette*. It brings in a fair profit for what it is, so they tell me, but it is very small beer for a man with those enormous interests. But I suppose if one accumulates a great fortune all sorts of rags and bones get mixed with the diamonds and the nuggets.' He retired once more into his dream. His grey eyes, bright under his straight black brows, pierced the walls of the farmhouse parlour. Even though I was a very little girl I knew that he was imagining what it was like to be a millionaire.

Mamma lifted the brown teapot and refilled his cup and hers, and sighed, and his eyes went back to her. 'You hate being left here in this lonely place?'

'No, no, I am happy anywhere,' she said, 'and I have always wanted the children to have a holiday on the Pentland Hills as I did when I was their age. And there is nothing better for children than life on a farm; at least people always say so. I can't imagine why. But letting the flat furnished, that I do not like. Such a thing to have to do.'

'I know, I know,' said Papa, sadly but impatiently.

All this happened more than fifty years ago, and my parents were not making a fuss about nothing. In those days few respectable people were willing to let their homes furnished, and no respectable people ever wanted to take them.

'I know these people have a good reason for wanting somewhere to stay for the summer, coming over from Australia to see this daughter of theirs in Dr. Philip's Sanatorium,' Mamma murmured, 'but such a risk, leaving strangers in the flat with all that good furniture.'

'I suppose it is valuable,' said Papa, thoughtfully.

'Well, of course, it is only Empire,' said Mamma, 'but of its kind it is the best. Aunt Clara bought it all in France and Italy when she was married to the French violinist, and it is all solid and comfortable, and, though I know it is not Chippendale, the chairs with the swans and the others with the dolphins' heads are really very pretty, and the silk seats with the bees and the stars are quite handsome. We shall be thankful to have all that furniture when we start afresh at Lovegrove.'

'At Lovegrove,' said Papa. 'Really, it is very strange that I should be going back to Lovegrove. Isn't it strange, Rose,' he said, giving me a lump of sugar from the bowl, 'that I should be taking you back to a place where I used to stay when I was little, like you?'

'Was Uncle Richard Quin there too?' I asked. Papa's brother, who had died in India of fever when he was twenty-one, had been christened Richard Quinbury to distinguish him from another Richard in the family and Papa had loved him so much that he had called our little brother by his name. We regarded our little brother as much the nicest of us four children, so we thought of our dead uncle as a joy stolen from us, and were always trying to recover him in our father's stories.

'Richard Quin was there too,' said Papa, 'or I should not remember it so well. The places I visited without him are never so distinct.'

'Try to find us a house near the house where you stayed,' said Mamma, 'it will be an interest for the children.'

'What was the name, I wonder? Oh, yes, Caroline Lodge. But of course it will have been pulled down long ago. It was quite a small house but very charming.'

Suddenly Mamma laughed. 'Why should it have been pulled down? You are so gloomy about everything except the future of copper mines.'

'Copper will come right in the long run,' said Papa, cold with sudden anger.

'My dear, you must not mind what I say!' she protested. She and I looked at him anxiously, and after a minute he smiled. All the same he then glanced at the clock and said that it was time he was getting back to the station, if he were to catch the six-o'clock train to Edinburgh; and the light had gone out of him, he had that shabby, beggar look that even we children some-times had to remark in him. Tenderly Mamma told him, 'Very well, we don't want you to miss your train and have to hang about that draughty little station for hours, though Heaven knows we want to keep you with us till the last moment. Oh, it is good of you, indeed it is, when you have so much on your mind, to help me bring the children down here.'

'It is the least I could do,' he answered heavily.

While the trap was being brought round we went out and stood on the holystoned steps of the farmhouse. The paddock in front of us stretched down to the shores of the loch, which was a dark shining circle, perfectly round, under the grey-green walls of the valley. Midway to the water we could see two white scraps that were my sisters Cordelia and Mary, a blue scrap that was my little brother Richard Quin. He was just old enough now to run about very fast and fall down, always without hurting himself, and to babble and laugh and tease us; we played with him all day and never grew tired of him.

My mother threw back her head and called to them, her voice going straight out like the cry of a bird, 'Children, come and say goodbye to your father!'

My sisters were for one moment frozen where they stood. In this new lovely place they had forgotten what overhung us. Then Cordelia picked up Richard Quin and hurried as fast as was safe; and then the four of us stood and looked up at Papa, looking hard so that we would remember him perfectly while he was away these dreadful six weeks. It was perhaps a mistake to look

3

so hard at him, he was so wonderful. This was no childish delusion, we were objective enough about certain things. We all knew that Mamma was not good-looking. She was too thin, her nose and forehead were shiny like bone, and her features were disordered because her tortured nerves were always drawing a rake over her face. Also we were so poor that she never had new clothes. But we were conscious that our Papa was far handsomer than anybody else's. He was not tall, but he was slender and graceful, he stood like a fencer in a picture, and he was romantically dark; his hair and his moustache were true black, and his skin was tanned, with a faint rose under the tan on his cheeks; and he had high cheekbones, which made his face sharp like the muzzle of a cat, it was the least stupid face one could imagine. Also he knew everything, he had been all over the world, even to China, he could draw and could carve wood and make little figures and dolls' houses. Sometimes he would play games with us and tell stories, and it was almost impossible to bear it, every moment brought forth such an intense delight, quite unpredictable, so that one could not prepare for it. It was true that sometimes he would take no notice of us for days and that too was almost unbearable. But it was part of our grief that we were not going to suffer that woe either for six weeks.

'Children, children, we will soon be together again,' said Papa, 'and you will enjoy being here!' He pointed to the hills beyond the loch. 'Before the holidays are over they will all turn purple. You will like that.'

'Purple?' We could not think what he meant. All four of us had been born in South Africa and had left it less than a year before.

When he had described the flowering of the heather Cordelia, who was older than Mary and me by two years and made the most of it, sighed noisily, 'Oh, dear! This is going to be a dreadful holiday for me. The children will be wandering off all the time to look at it, and getting lost on the hills, and I will always have to be running after them and bringing them back. And the loch, they are sure to fall into that too.'

'Idiot, we can both swim as well as you can,' muttered Mary, and indeed all of us girls had learned when we were babies on the South African beaches. Mamma heard her and said, 'Oh, do not quarrel with Cordelia now, Mary,' and Mary said, teasing

4

her, 'Then when?' and Cordelia made an exaggerated grimace of despair, as of one who cannot succeed in drawing the world's attention to the huge burden she is bearing, and I murmured to Mary, 'We will box her ears afterwards.' But then we were distracted by what Mamma was saying.

'I have got it clear then, you travel to London tomorrow, and at once go, I suppose, to see Mr. Morpurgo.'

'No,' said Papa. 'No, I go straight to the office at Lovegrove.'

'Not to see Mr. Morpurgo? Not to thank him? Oh, but surely he will expect you to do that first of all.'

'No,' said Papa. 'He says he does not want to see me.' As Mamma's stare hardened on him he gave a little sneering laugh. 'He was always a timid little fellow. Something has put him out for the moment, and he says he is glad that I should edit his paper for him, but he thinks it better that I should only deal with one of his directors who sees to that sort of minor thing, and that we should not meet. Let him have his way, though I cannot see the point of it.'

Mamma perhaps could. She drew a shuddering breath and said, 'Oh, well. You go straight to the office at Lovegrove and settle all about your work, and look for a house for us, and then you go to Ireland and see your uncle and then I come down with the children and the furniture in good time to have all ready for the children to go to school at the beginning of the term and you to start work on the first of October. That is how it is to be, isn't it?'

'Yes, yes, my dear,' he said, 'that is how it is to be.' He kissed us all, beginning with Cordelia and ending with Richard Quin, an order he always observed, for he was a just man. This had at one time distressed Mary and me, for we were all against primogeniture, until it occurred to Mary that we ourselves always ate the dullest food on our plates and kept what we liked to the last. Then he dropped his mustachioed mouth to Mamma's cheek and as he raised his head again asked lightly, 'How long can you stay here?'

Mamma's face became convulsed. 'But I have told you. I took the money the Australians gave me for the flat, I paid the landlord our arrears of rent and settled all the tradesmen's books, and with what I have left we can stay here till the third week in September. But no longer. No longer. But why do

5

you ask? Are your plans not settled? Is it not to be as we have just arranged?'

'Yes, yes,' said my father.

'Tell me if it is not to be so,' she begged him fiercely. 'I can face anything. But I must know.'

We watched them with curiosity which referred to much more than this moment. Why were we leaving Edinburgh so soon? Mamma had told us when we left South Africa that, because Papa was to be assistant editor of *The Caledonian*, we would live in Edinburgh till we were nearly grown-up and had to go to London to study at one of the great Schools of Music, as she had done. And in South Africa, why had we left Cape Town so suddenly for Durban? And why was Mamma always so distressed when these calls to movement came, while Papa remained calm, but spoke absently, as if all this were happening to someone else, and often laughed to himself, quietly and contemptuously. That was what he was doing as he walked towards the trap. 'There is nothing to know, my dear Clare,' he said, and jumped up to his seat beside the driver.

'Goodbye,' Mamma cried to him. 'And write! Write! Only a postcard, if you are too busy for a letter. But write!'

We watched the trap take off and cover the stretch of road which ran to the end of the valley, and go over the pass and vanish. That did not take long. The boy who drove was getting the best out of his horse, people always showed off in front of Papa. Then Richard Quin pulled at Mamma's skirts and told her in his babble that she was not to cry and that he wanted a drink. We all went back to the parlour and adored him while he sat on Mamma's lap and gulped down some milk, shaking all over with the effort and pleasure of gulping, like a puppy at a saucer.

'Who is Mr. Morpurgo?' asked Mary. 'It is a funny name. It sounds like a conjuror. "The Great Morpurgo."' She realised quite well that Mamma had been disturbed by something this unknown man had done, but she was not simply being tactless. We were quite little but we were already cunning as foxes. We had to be. We had to sniff the wind and decide from which quarter the next misfortune was coming, and make our own provisions against it, which were often not quite what our parents would have approved. When the trouble began

6

in *The Caledonian*, whatever it might be, Mary and I thought it prudent to tell the children of the people in the next flat that Papa had had an offer to go to a better post somewhere else. Thus we secured that at a time when Mamma was unhappy she was not treated by her neighbours with less respect but with more; and anyway, as we pointed out to each other, it turned out to be true, for here he was going to the *Lovegrove Gazette*. We had found out a sensible way of behaving, and we were not going to drop it because of adult fussiness.

'Mr. Morpurgo,' said Mamma, 'is someone we should bless all our lives. He is a very rich man, a banker, I think, and ever since he met your Papa, on a ship somewhere, he has done everything he could for him. He gave your Papa his position in Durban after the proprietors of his paper in Cape Town behaved so strangely. They made no allowances whatsoever. And now that *The Caledonian* has proved such a disappointment to your Papa, Mr. Morpurgo has made him editor of this paper he owns in South London. I do not know what would have happened to us all if he had not come forward. Though I should not say that. You must never think that your Papa would not find some way of providing for us all. He will never,' she said, tilting the cup so that Richard Quin would get the last drop, 'fail us.'

'What does Mr. Morpurgo look like?' I asked.

'I don't know,' said Mamma. 'I don't think I ever met him. But your Papa has known him for a long time. He admires your Papa very much. Everybody does except people who are envious of him.'

Cordelia asked, 'Why should anybody envy him? We have so little money.'

'Oh, they envy him his brains, his appearance, everything about him,' sighed Mamma, 'and then, he is always right when everybody else is wrong. A situation,' she said, sternly, fixing her blazing black eyes on each of us in turn, 'in which none of you are likely to find yourselves.' Then she grew soft again, and looked down on Richard Quin, as he held the cup almost upside down in an effort to get the last drops. 'No, my lamb. When you make a great noise eating you must stop, you are doing it the wrong way; unless you stop and do it without making a noise you will turn into a little pig, and then you will have to

7

go and live in a sty, and though you might like it your poor sisters would be distracted. They would want to be with you, there would be no room for them and you must consider them, they are so good to you. Oh, my little lamb, I wonder what instrument you are going to play. It is irritating not to know.'

For of course we all played something. Just as all the people in Papa's family in Ireland were soldiers or soldiers' wives, so everybody in Mamma's West Highland family were musicians, and always had been for at least five generations back. They had left no great names in music, perhaps because they had always died quite young; but Mamma's grandfather had gone to Austria and played in the orchestra of the Viennese opera, and had spoken to Beethoven and Schubert, and her father had been Kapellmeister at a small German ducal court, her dead brother had been quite a well-known conductor and composer, and she would have been a famous pianist, indeed she was already well-known by her middle twenties, when one night, just as she was going on the platform at a concert in Geneva, she had been handed a telegram which told her that her favourite brother had died of sunstroke in India. She had played the programme out and then had gone back to her hotel and fallen into a sort of fever, which had lasted for weeks and left her so melancholy that she had gone on a journey round the world to recover, as companion to an elderly woman who had admired her playing. In Ceylon she had met Papa, who was just then leaving a good position on a tea-plantation. They had married, and had gone to South Africa where some relative of his had found him another good position. But he was unfortunate there too, Mamma had never told us exactly how. It did not matter, however, he had been writing for some time, and had discovered a talent for it, and he very easily got a post as leader-writer in a Cape Town newspaper. And Mamma had had all of us, and had been very worried, and now she was past forty, and her fingers were getting stiff, and her nerves were bad, and she would never go back to playing again. But she was teaching us to play, and though Cordelia was no good and she had given her up as hopeless when she was seven, Mary and I were, she thought, all right. And somehow we knew Richard Quin was going to be all right too. He managed the triangle, on which we always were started, quite well.

8

'I don't believe it will be the piano,' Mamma said, scrutinising him narrowly, as if it were written in the grain of one's skin what instrument one would play. And there was some sense in it. Even then one could not imagine Richard Quin sitting down in front of a piano, which is a forthright, monumental instrument, bigger than the person who plays it, and resistant to all relationships except those effected through the keyboard, though one could imagine him picking up a violin or a clarionet. 'And you, Mary and Rose,' she went on, 'the Erard in the corner is old but it is in tune. There is a man comes out from Pennycuick every six months and tunes it. Fate is on our side. The Keiths say that you can play it when you like except on Sundays. Let there be no excuses, you must practise just as regularly as you do at home. And while we are here I will give you lessons five times a week instead of three. I will have more time.'

'And what about me?' said Cordelia.

Mary and I looked at her tenderly, though we so often hated her, and there was a pause before Mamma answered, 'Oh, you will have your lessons like the others, never fear.'

Cordelia had no idea that she was not musical. When Mamma had stopped giving her piano lessons, a little girl in the house next door was having violin lessons, and she had insisted on learning too, and had ever since then shown an extreme and mistaken industry. She had a true ear, indeed she had absolute pitch, which neither Mamma nor Mary nor I had, which was a terrible waste, and she had supple fingers, she could bend them right back to the wrist, and she could read anything at sight. But Mamma's face crumpled, first with rage, and then, just in time, with pity, every time she heard Cordelia laying the bow over the strings. Her tone was horribly greasy, and her phrasing always sounded like a stupid grown-up explaining something to a child. Also she did not know good music from bad, as we did, as we had always done.

It was not Cordelia's fault that she was unmusical. Mamma had often explained that to us. Children were like their father's family or their mother's, and Cordelia had taken her inheritance from Papa. That gave her some advantages, it did indeed. Mary had black hair and I had brown, and so had many other little girls. But though Papa was so dark there was red hair in his family, and Cordelia's head was covered with short red-gold curls, which shone in the light and made people turn round in the street. There was something more to that than mere heredity, too, which made it harder to bear. It was at Papa's insistence that Mamma kept Cordelia's hair short at a time when that was a long-forgotten fashion, not to be renewed for years. At his home in Ireland there had been a portrait of his Aunt Lucy, who went to Paris just after the Napoleonic wars and had herself painted by Baron Gérard in a chiton and a leopard-skin, with her hair dressed in the fashion known as *à la Bacchante*, and as Cordelia was very like her he got Mamma to get her curls cut in as nearly the same style as puzzled hairdressers in South Africa and Edinburgh could manage.

Mary and I were not pleased about this. It made us feel that Cordelia was not only closer to Papa than we were, owing to an unfair decision of Nature, but that she was also an object on which he had worked to bring her up to the standards of his taste. He had not done that to us. Nor were we worked on by anybody else. With all this piano-playing, Mary and I had no time, and Mamma had no time either, to subject us to any process which would turn us into finished articles, we were raw material. It really was cruel that we had to play the piano as well as do so much, that Mamma had to go shopping and help with the housework and deal with Papa's worries so that she was never composed and dressed like other Mammas, that we had to go to school and always struck our teachers as careless and hurried. Yet it was piano-playing that set our accounts right. For though there was red hair in Papa's family, there was not a shred of musical talent, and we would rather be musical with Mamma than have red-gold curls and make utter fools of ourselves by playing the violin as Cordelia did. We were sorry for Cordelia, particularly now, when Papa, from whom she derived such interest as she possessed, had gone away for six weeks. But all the same she was an ass to think she could play the violin, it was as if Mary and I thought we had red-gold curls.

The air of the room swayed with the tides of liking and dislike, forgiveness and resentment, and then the farmer's wife came in and asked if we would like to see the mare and foal which her husband had just brought back from a sale at a hill farm, and we passed over into the world of the animals. But here too there were tides, nothing was stable. First of all we were introduced to the collie dogs, who were made to sniff us and lick us, so that they would recognise us as members of the household and give us neither bark nor bite. This we did not enjoy because we disapproved of animals so abandoned to ill-will that cere-monies had to be performed before they would consent to show common civility to inoffensive people, like Mamma and us. 'But they are watch-dogs,' Mamma reminded us, 'they protect the farm from thieves,' but we jeered, 'What thieves?' and looked round the amphitheatre of the clear green hills trium-phantly, as if the innocence of the stage setting proved the innocence of the drama. It is strange how it was in the air in those days, the belief that war crime and all cruelty were about to vanish from the face of the earth, even little girls knew it to be a promise that was going to be kept.

Then the farmer's wife pointed to some fields on the hillside, spotted brown with cattle, and told us not to go there, because a bull was running with the cows. We had no quarrel with that, we must have felt that the mysterious safe conduct we had been given by the universe did not extend to bulls, our mouths went dry when we thought of what it would be like to be caught in those fields, particularly if we had Richard Quin with us. But in the byres the young stock stood, the calves that were not yet yearlings, as civilised and friendly as we could have wished to be ourselves; and there was a two-day-old calf, lax on the ground like a great skein of fawn-coloured silk, which was as frightened of us as we would have been of the dogs and the bull, had we not anaesthetised fear in us, from fear that we might give support to the lie that girls are not so brave as boys. Feminism too was in the air, even in the nursery air. But the farm cats spat at us, and we had to draw back our hands, brave or not, while they glared at us, coarse as burglars, coarse as Charles Peace, not like cats at all. 'Remember,' cried Mamma, 'the poor things have to fight rats, they could not do it if they let themselves be gentle. It would be a luxury they cannot have.' Was the world kind or was it not, was the farm going to be a safe place for Richard Quin?

But in a loose-box we found the new mare and her foal and knew there was hope. Her long straight forelock falling between her two big ears gave her the look of a plain woman wearing an ugly hat, her gaze was anxious as if she were human and could count, she towered over us but it was not imaginable that she would organise her strength against us, her long-legged foal was shy as if it had been warned not to make a noise and irritate the people in this new place where their lot must lie. She made me think of a widow with her orphan child, unresentful and willing to serve, but sad, whom I had once seen in one of the registry offices which my mother sometimes visited. (For though we had so little money we had a servant, in those days even poor households had servants, they shared their poverty with some girl quite destitute.) We went on into the stables, and could see nothing through the darkness except the white stars on the standing horses' foreheads, the long white blazes on their faces, their white stockings and a white pattern of light traced high on the wall by a mullioned window. This farm had been built among the ruins of a medieval castle which had been a meeting-place of the Knights Templar, and this stable was where they had dined. After a time we could see the rolling of the horses' nervous eyes that showed they had wills if they chose to use them, the barrel-bulk of their girdled bodies, the tree-trunk-straightness of their forelegs, the cunning elastic spring of their hind legs, the huge spread of their round feet, all the strength that stirred so little and so much more mildly than it needed. These were kind creatures. We saw two mice dallying in the litter underneath one giant, and knew it was proved.

The journey, and parting from Papa, and meeting all these animals, made us so tired that we went to bed only a little later than Richard Quin, while it was still light, though usually we stayed up to the last moment that we were allowed. Cordelia and Mary and I slept in the same room, Mary and I in a double bed with a high mahogany headboard carved with plump fruit and flowers, and Cordelia in a camp-bed at its foot. Nobody could sleep with Cordelia, she so often threw herself about in her dreams, calling out orders. Mary and I were very comfortable at night, we used to snuggle down with one of us burying her face in the other's back and pressing her tummy against the other's behind, and both knowing nothing more till morning. Mary was tall and slim, in a way she looked grown-up though she was a child, she was collected and calculating, at the piano she could work out any problem of fingering quite easily while I would rush at it and get excited and cry; but with me she was always soft and yielding, we were like two little bears together.

When Mamma said good night to us I noticed that since she had been talking to the farm people her Scots accent had become much broader than usual, the line of her sentences had only to be exaggerated for them to be like the phrases of a song. It sounded very pretty. She told us that if we wanted anything in the night we were to rouse her, and we need not even go out into the passage, the door by the window was not a cupboard door as we might think, it led into the room where she and Richard Quin were sleeping. She was always saying things like that, but we never wanted any help, we were so independent, so old for our age. But it was very nice of her, we thought, as we sank into our sleep.

Suddenly we were all awake. I was as alert as if I had never slept. I put out my hand and I found that Mary was sitting erect with her back braced against the headboard; and the camp-bed creaked under Cordelia as she started up. It was quite dark, and there was a terrible noise. It was as if the night were frightened of itself. Someone or something was beating on a drum. The noise was not very loud, but the resonance was total, it was as if the drum were the earth itself. It made us feel as sad as Papa's departure, as Mamma's occasional tears. It meant nothing but sadness, it stated it again and again.

It stopped. Mary's hand came into mine. I moistened my lips and breathed, 'I wonder what that was.' After all Cordelia was older than we were, she might know something we did not.

Cordelia said, 'It is nothing. It can't be anything. The farm people must hear it too. They would come and warn us if it were anything dangerous.'

'But it might be something that has never happened before,' said Mary.

'Yes, this may be part of the end of the world,' I said.

'Nonsense,' said Cordelia, "the world won't come to an end in our time.'

'Why shouldn't it?' I asked. 'It will have to come to an end in somebody's time.'

'And in a way it would be exciting to be there,' said Mary.

'Go to sleep,' said Cordelia.

'We will, if we want to,' said Mary, 'but do not tell us to.'

13

'I am the eldest,' said Cordelia.

It started again, this beating on the huge drum.

'Mary, Mamma said there was a candle by your side,' I said. 'Light it, and then we can get to the window and see if anything is happening.'

Through the darkness we heard the rasp of matches on the box, but no light came. 'I cannot think,' said Cordelia, 'why Mamma didn't leave the candle with me.'

'Because there isn't a table by you, you ass,' said Mary. 'And I think the matches are wet, they won't strike.'

'You are making excuses because you are clumsy,' said Cordelia.

'You are getting cross because you are frightened,' said Mary.

The noise swelled up to a wild proclamation of loss and doom; but suddenly the darkness melted into pale and wavering light, for the door in the wall opened, and Mamma came in, holding a candlestick in one hand and rubbing her eyes with the other. 'Children, what are you doing, talking so loud at this time of night?' she asked. 'We are not alone as we are at home, you might waken the Weirs, and they work so hard.'

'Mamma, what is that terrible noise?'

'A terrible noise! What terrible noise?' she asked, her eyes and mouth stupid with sleep.

'Why, what we are hearing now,' said Mary.

Mamma murmured, 'Can something else extraordinary be happening?' With an effort she set herself to listen, and her face lightened. 'Why, children, that is the horses stamping in their stalls.'

We were astonished. 'What, just those horses that we saw this afternoon?'

'Yes, those. Why, now I listen, I do not wonder you were frightened. It is astonishing what a tremendous noise horses make with their hooves.'

'But why does it sound so sad?'

Yawning, she answered, 'Well so does thunder, sad as if everything had gone wrong for the last time. And the sea often sounds sad, and the wind in the trees nearly always. Go to sleep, my lambs.'

'But how can a horse's hoof stamping down on a stable floor sound so sad?' I asked.

14

'Well, why should Mamma's fingers coming down on piano keys sometimes sound sad and sometimes all right?' asked Mary.

'We will think of that tomorrow, please,' said Mamma, 'though really I do not know why I should promise you that we will think to any purpose. If you ask me tomorrow or any other day why some sounds are sad and others glad I shall not be able to tell you. Not even your Papa could tell you that. Why, what a thing to ask, my pets! If you knew that, you would know everything. Good night, my dears, good night.'

All of us were happy at that farm for the first ten days or so. We children were drunk on the hill air, for till then we had never spent more than a few hours above sea-level. 'And it is better still in the real mountains,' Mamma told us. 'Oh, children, when you have made your way in the world, you must go to Switzerland. Up there at Davos, the air is so clear that everything looks as if it had been polished with a soft cloth.' We said, doubtfully, 'Switzerland?' and declared it our intention to go further to Kilimanjaro, to Popocatepetl, to Mount Everest. Yes, we would wait until Richard Quin was old enough, and we would be the first party to climb Mount Everest. 'No, no,' said Mamma, not at all pleased, 'not Everest. Once you are doing well, you will find you have enough on your hands with your concerts, and indeed too much.' That answer, given gravely, was of a kind commonly made by her, which caused one of the main inconveniences of our lives. Ordinary people often spoke to Mamma for a short time and then went away, thinking her silly and even mad, because of just such remarks. But she was showing the most splendid sense. She knew she would have climbed Mount Everest if she had had the chance, and she supposed, with the world changing as quickly as it was, that the chance might come to us; she had nearly become a famous pianist and she thought it probable that with our talents we might succeed where only ill luck had given her failure; and in any case she was talking to children, and so she talked as a child, as one played Bach in the manner of Bach, and Brahms in the manner of Brahms.

We made this holiday a rehearsal for Everest, a trial of strength, and again she was sympathetic, but applied a principle of moderation. We had supposed we would spend the part of the day left over from our practising in taking long walks over the

15

moors, but we found it more amusing to help on the farm, doing things that the farmer and his wife would not have thought we were strong enough or grown-up enough to do. We would take a forgotten basket of bannocks down to the men working on the furthest field, away beyond the pass; we would polish the horse-brasses the day before the cart was to go down to the market; we stripped the lavender flowers from the bushes in the garden and laid them on boards to dry in the sun under muslin. Mamma let us do what we liked, provided we got in our proper hours at the piano; and that was no hardship, for we always played better during the holidays, when there was not all that idiotic home-work, and now that we were so well our fingers were twice as intelligent as usual. But as soon as we had all had our lessons Mamma joined us in this lovely, boastful, new, exciting work on the farm, though at first the farmer and his wife had kept her at a distance. We had seen her make another of those mistakes that made people think her odd, the morning after we got there. Gaily she had spilled on the kitchen table, in a jumble of Bank of Scotland notes and sovereigns, the whole amount she had contracted to pay for the six weeks of our holiday. The Weirs, bony, sandy, grave people, had looked at her with narrow and imbecile glances of suspicion. They could not understand why anybody should want to pay in advance when there was no need; and still less could they understand why a middle-aged woman should laugh like a young girl going to a ball when she did this uncalled-for thing. We understood. It was a delight for her to snatch this money from the mysterious force that acted on all money in our family, annulling it as if it had never been; it was such an indulgence as she had not enjoyed for years to make a payment and prevent it from being even for a moment a debt. But that could not be explained. We could see the Weirs thinking that she was probably a silly, feckless woman, who had only herself to blame for being so shabby. Soon it was all right. She helped Mrs. Weir one day in the dairy, she had learned to make butter when she was a child and it came back to her; and the rightness of her hands, which was as remarkable anywhere else as it was on the keyboard, proved to the countrywoman that she had been wrong. They began to like her even better than they liked us, and every day she seemed younger, and ate more, and her eyes did not stare so much.

But it did not last. Soon she looked ill again, and did not enjoy her food, and was milder with us when she gave us our lessons.

'What do you think is worrying her?' Mary asked me one day, when we were picking runner beans in the kitchen garden. She had passed us with Richard Quin in her arms; I did not say so, but she had made me think of the new mare and its foal, though she was still fierce and quick.

'Well, Papa has not written,' I said.

'I feel it's that too,' said Mary. 'But what I can't understand is, why she ever thought he would.'

'Did you know he wouldn't?' I asked.

'I thought he would probably forget.'

I did not like her having known better than myself what he was going to do.

'What I can't understand,' Mary went on, 'is that they never seem to get used to each other. Mamma is always surprised when Papa does things like not writing. And Papa is always surprised when Mamma wants to pay bills.'

'Yes, and Mamma minds so,' I said.

'That's extraordinary,' said Mary.

But we were touching on a long-standing perplexity. We could see that Papa would take an intense interest in us, and that we would take an intense interest in him, because we belonged to the same family. And we could see that Mamma would take another sort of intense interest in us, and that we would give it to her back. But we could not see that Mamma and Papa could matter very much to each other, because they were not related.

'But, Mary, I have been rather wondering. What happens if Papa never writes?'

'If he doesn't come back?'

'Yes.'

'I should die,' said Mary.

'So would I,' I said. I stood back from the beans and looked at the circle of green hills, which fused and wavered glassily through my tears. But they were there, they remained solid when I wiped away my tears. 'But what would we do?' I asked.

'Oh, we could work, we could go into factories or shops or offices, or we could be servants, and between us we could make enough to keep Mamma and Richard Quin till he grows up,' said Mary.

17

'But I rather think there is a law forbidding people as young as us from working,' I said.

'We could cheat and say we were older than we are,' said Mary, 'everybody is always surprised when they hear our ages.'

'There is that,' I said.

'Anyway it will be all right,' said Mary. 'Really all right. You see, we would go on working at the piano in the evenings and someday we would switch to being pianists, and after that it is going to be all right.'

'Oh, yes, of course, I'm not worrying,' I said, 'and now I think we have picked enough beans.'

Mamma had not seen us at work in the bean-row when she passed through the kitchen-garden, or she would not have looked desolate. Instead she would have looked as if she were a sick woman, posing for a photograph she meant to send to someone whom she intended to deceive concerning her health. She was thinking and staring again, but she smiled perpetually, she called out cheerful greetings to everybody she met as she went about the farm, 'Another bright day again', or 'Not so sunny, but we can do with a little coolness for a change', often greeting the same person twice. The weather was calm around us; it was an unusually fine summer. The hills were calm around us; this was the highest farm on that spur of the Pentlands, nobody climbed to us, the August ramblers took a footpath that cut south of us to the main range, we saw them no nearer than the skyline. This calm made an unkindly frame to my mother's restlessness, the people about the farm began to scrutinise her doubtfully again.

One afternoon I came out of the stable, a polished horse-brass blazing bright in my hand, and found her sitting on the stone dyke which separated the paddock from the garden. The postman was due in about a quarter of an hour, and she was rocking backwards and forwards, not much but more than would be natural unless she would feel herself abandoned if a letter did not come; I looked across the garden to the farmhouse and thought I saw someone watching behind the lace curtains of the Weirs' room. It was probably Mrs. Weir, whom I had hoped would praise me for the brightness of the horse-brass. I was in part distracted by pity for Mamma, in part annoyed that things did not go easy with us as they did for other children and that I would not claim the thanks that I deserved. The great thing and the little thing were together in my mind, I wondered if I ought to be ashamed of that. I put the horse-brass down on the dyke, and then, remembering how apt I was to lose things, picked it up and slipped it inside one of the knee-elastics of my knickers. I put my arms round Mamma's neck and kissed her wild hair and whispered, 'If you are worried because Papa has not written, why do you not telegraph to the newspaper offices in Lovegrove or to his uncles and people in Ireland? He must be at one of those two places.'

She whispered her answer. It was easier for us to pretend that none of this was happening if we did not speak aloud. 'Rose, you are a thoughtful child.'

'Do you mean,' I asked bravely, 'that we have not got the sixpence?'

'Oh, yes, we have the sixpence, thank God. But, you see, I do not want to let them know that Papa has not let us know where he is. They would think it strange.'

'Well, so it is,' I said.

'But not,' she contended hopefully, 'strange in the way they would think it. Oh, there is nothing we can do, we must wait. And give him time, he will write. A letter may come this very afternoon.'

We kissed. She drew her lips away from mine to say, still whispering, 'Do not tell the others.'

I was amazed at her simplicity.

Mary came out of the stable and looked across the yard and saw that something was wrong, and joined us. She said, 'Mamma, do not wait for the post, it is Tuesday, nothing nice ever happens on a Tuesday,' and then stopped. Cordelia had begun to practise in her bedroom. We all three listened in silence while she played some scales. Then she broke off and repeated some bars of a melody. 'It isn't even like cats,' said Mary. 'Cats don't scoop.'

'Oh, children, children,' said Mamma. 'You should not be so impatient with your poor sister. It might have been far worse, she might have been born deaf or blind.'

'That would not have been worse even for her,' said Mary; 'she never would have known what was wrong with her, any more than she does now, and she would have gone to one of

19

those big places with gardens for the deaf and blind one sees out of trains, and she would have been looked after by people who like being kind to the deaf and the blind. But there are no homes for bad violinists.'

'Homes for bad musicians, what a terrible idea,' said Mamma. 'The home for bad contraltos would be the worst. People would be afraid to go near it at night, the sounds coming from it would be so terrible, particularly when the moon was full. And you children are unnecessarily unkind about your sister, really if I did not know you I would think you were spiteful. And really she is not so bad. She is not bad at all, this afternoon. She is much better than she used to be. Heavens, how horrible that was! This is intolerable, I must go and try to help her, the poor child.'

She rushed up the garden path towards the farmhouse, wringing her hands. A stranger would have supposed that so distraught a mother had just realised that her baby had been left alone in a room with an unguarded fire or a dangerous dog. Mary and I sat down on the dyke, and when we began to swing our legs I became suddenly conscious of the horse-brass in my knickers. I found it had grown dim in its hiding-place, and I fell to rubbing it again.

'Listen, it is too silly,' said Mary coldly. There was sometimes nothing to listen to; Mamma could not play the violin, so she had to talk or sing her precepts. Between these patches of silence came Cordelia's repetitions of her melody, always without improvement, but each time offering instead a new variation of error. 'How can you laugh?' asked Mary through her teeth.

'Of course I'm laughing,' I said. 'It's funny when someone keeps on falling down on the ice, and this doesn't even hurt Cordelia.'

I knew Mary through and through, I could feel her pondering over the possibility of scoring a point over me by pretending as she knew the teachers at school would have done, that she was too grown-up to think that someone falling down on the ice was funny, but I went on polishing my horse-brass, I could trust her to decide that was not honest, she did think that someone falling down on the ice was funny, and anyway she did not want to score off me, not really much.

She said softly, suddenly, 'Mrs. Weir is coming down the path. With that cousin of hers from Glasgow. They're going to ask us questions.'

We knew that look. I kept my head down and went on polishing. Mary bent over me and pointed her finger at the brass as if she had just noticed the design. Mrs. Weir had to speak to us twice before we realised the two of them were there. 'Excuse us!' we said, quite confused, standing up politely, and simpering a little. We realised we were not the type which can dare to simper much, but what we could get of that particular advantage we seized.

'Your big sister's a bonny fiddler,' said Mrs. Weir.

We said in sugared accents that she was.

'These bairns,' said Mrs. Weir, turning to her cousin, 'are no so bad with the pianny. But they're wee yet, they spend most of the time grinding away at exercises.'

All summer we had been infatuated with arpeggios. They dripped from our fingers, we had hoped, like oil.

'Maircy, do you let these bairns play your pianny?' asked the cousin from Glasgow. Her voice became hollow and alluded to the tomb. 'Elspeth's pianny?'

'Oh, they play weel eneuch,' said Mrs. Weir. 'I canna play the thing. Though I had lessons with Elspeth from the old body who cam oot from Edinburgh to teach the laird's daughters, my hands were aye like hams. Elspeth left me the thing weel knowing that, just for a matter of sentiment. That,' she added, speaking as one who turns the knife in a wound, 'and the apostle spoons.'

'She'd little else to leave that was worth having,' said the cousin from Glasgow sourly.

'I wouldna say that,' said Mrs. Weir. 'I'm sure you think of the Coats shares she left every time you put a reel of cotton on your sewing-machine. But she left them neither to you nor to me but to poor Lizzie who had four bairns and a man killed at Omdurman.' Her eyes turned to the farmhouse window from which Cordelia's contention with her art was emitting an unsteady and polluted melodic line. 'Has your Mamma wearied of waiting for her letter?'

We noted stoically that the consideration of Lizzie's plight had immediately made her think of Mamma. We got into position, like two tennis players waiting for a serve, with knees slightly bent, racket held across the body, eyes ready for the ball. 'No. She just went in to help Cordelia. Our music,' said Mary, smiling, 'seems more important to her than anything.'

'But she'll be fretting to hear from your Paw,' said the cousin from Glasgow, quite without finesse.

'Oh, yes,' we said, carelessly. 'Mamma,' I said, 'isn't used to being without Papa. He never goes away from home.' 'Except,' said Mary, 'to speak at political meetings, and then he is back the next day.'

'I wonder your Maw's so anxious, then,' said the cousin from Glasgow.

We smiled again. 'Well, she feels worried because she isn't there to look after him,' I said. 'He's absent-minded, because he's a great author.'

'Oh, your Paw's a great author, is he?' said the cousin from Glasgow. 'Tee hee. Tee hee. A great author like Robbie Burns?'

'No, like Carlyle,' said Mary.

'Imphm,' said the cousin from Glasgow.

'I'll explain how he's like Carlyle if you would like to hear,' said Mary. This was a frightful lie, and I was terrified lest her bluff was called.

'No, it can wait,' said the cousin from Glasgow. 'But he's absent-minded. I see. So he's not written to your Maw. Does he often not write?'

'Well, as he isn't often away from home it isn't us he wouldn't write to, so we don't know,' said Mary flatly, with the tired look of a child talking to a stupid grown-up.

'I must say we've never had a soul on the place that can get the horse-brasses so bright as these bairns,' said Mrs. Weir.

'I don't know your Maw,' said the cousin from Glasgow, 'but I'd think she was looking awful worried. About something.'

'Oh, she is worried,' I said. 'She's always worried about Papa.'

There was a silence, and Mrs. Weir began to say something more about the horse-brass on my lap, but the cousin from Glasgow said, with a grin dripping of sweetness, 'And why is your Maw worried about your Paw?'

'He is so terrible about money,' I said with the utmost simplicity. I felt Mary draw a deep breath, I felt Mrs. Weir stir

22

uneasily, I kept my eyes steady on the eyes of the cousin from Glasgow.

'And how is your Paw terrible about money?' enquired the cousin from Glasgow, as light-hearted as might be, almost hilariously.

'Och, Jeanie, now,' Mrs. Weir began, but I cut in. 'People send him cheques and he forgets to pay them into the bank. He leaves them all over the house.' I was not altogether lying. It had happened once.

'Or he does not open the envelope, and he puts it in his pocket, and there it stays,' said Mary. I felt great admiration for her. That had never happened. Not with a cheque.

'Once quite a big cheque came and Mamma found it in the wastepaper basket,' I said. 'Papa had thought it was a circular.'

'A big cheque in the wastepaper basket! Losh save us! The puir woman!' said Mrs. Weir.

'A big cheque,' said the cousin from Glasgow, 'now how much would that be?'

'We wouldn't ever know,' said Mary. 'Papa and Mamma never talk to us about money. They don't like being bothered with it. They think it's vulgar.'

'Yes, they would like to give it away, if it were not for us,' I said.

Mrs. Weir and the cousin from Glasgow uttered cries of distress. 'Give it away! Losh, what a fancy! And who would they give it to?'

'Why,' said Mary again assuming the tired look of a child talking to a stupid grown-up, 'to people who are poor.'

We had really done quite well, considering we had had no time for preparation. They hung over us in silent bewilderment, while I went on rubbing the horse-brass and Mary picked a long grass and sucked it and looked up at the white pillow clouds in the blue sky. Suddenly there was the whirr of a bicycle bell and the two women exclaimed and wheeled about. We took a quick look while their backs were turned and saw that the postman had ridden into the yard. My eyes went back to the horse-brass, Mary stared up at the sky again.

'Oh, has the postman been!' Mary exclaimed when Mrs. Weir touched her on the arm and held before her a telegram addressed to my mother. We were careful to walk quite slowly with it to the farmhouse, and we heard what the cousin from Glasgow said: 'Well, a telegram costs sixpence and a letter costs a penny. . . .' Her shrill voice trailed away, she could not think how to link on this consideration to the puzzling glimpse of our family which she had been given by two children who were surely, too young to lie.

In the little bedroom Mamma was standing in an attitude of despair which struck me as excessive. Of course Cordelia could not play the violin, but Mary and I could play the piano. Surely that should be enough for her? But she was standing with her hands crossed on her bosom and her eyes staring wildly about her while she cried, 'But anybody not an idiot must understand that tahatahatahahahahata is not the same thing as ta-ta-ta-ta-ta, which is what the composer wrote?' with a passion that would have been appropriate had she been a person in Shakespeare's world declaring that she was going to tell the yet unknowing world how these things came about, so shall you hear of carnal, bloody and unnatural acts, of accidental judgments, casual slaughters, of deaths put on by cunning and forced cause. But her disorder was excused by the intact appearance of Cordelia, who was standing with her violin firmly held in her hand, a patient expression on her face. To her it seemed that she had been quietly practising in her room when Mamma had come into the room, and had been quite unable to understand what she was trying to do, for of course the composer would have preferred tahatahatahahahahata to ta-ta-ta-ta-ta, because it sounded prettier. I thought how nice it would be if I were a street child and could take a piece of chalk and write on a wall, 'Cordelia is a fool.' It would do no good really, but it would be something.

Talking through Mamma's cries, Mary said, 'Papa has sent a telegram.'

Mamma was instantly still. She did not move to take it from Mary's hand. 'How do you know it is from Papa?' she asked in a thin voice.

'There isn't anyone else, is there, who would send us a telegram?' I asked.

'No, you are right. We are quite alone,' she said, and took the telegram and opened it and, reading the first words, was flooded by radiance, by hope, by certainty. 'He is well, he has found us a house, he likes the office at Lovegrove—but he has gone to Manchester to settle important business with Mr. Langham.' The radiance, the hope, the certainty, receded, they were not there. 'To Manchester! To settle important business! With Mr. Langham! To Manchester, when he should be in Ireland, seeing his family! How will they ever take an interest in your children? To settle important business, but it will come to nothing! And with Mr. Langham! With Mr. Langham!'

'Who is Mr. Langham?' we asked.

'A little, little man,' she said. Then radiance and hope and certainty came back into her face, and she cried, 'But your Papa has found us a house! I do wish I could have taken that trouble off him, with all he has to think of! I wonder what it will be like! There are some very nice houses in the London suburbs, your Papa has very good taste.'

'What, nice houses in London?' one of us said. We thought of it as a black, geometric place. But we were happy, we knew that she would contradict us, that she and Papa had created another place for us, as they had created Cape Town and Durban and Edinburgh and the Pentlands, where we were.

'Why, of course there are nice houses in London!' she cried. 'There are nice houses in Paris, in Vienna, in Copenhagen, you will see them all, but first we will live in a nice house in London. You must not be disappointed if the rooms are not as big as they are in the Edinburgh flat, it is different in the south, but down there the brick houses are very pretty. And it will be nice not to be in a flat but to be in a house, it will have its own garden or be in a square, and that will be so good for Richard Quin, he will be able to sleep out as he is sleeping now — is he all right? I had forgotten him.'

'Yes, yes,' said Cordelia, proudly, 'I have looked out of the window several times and he is lying quite quiet.'

'I wish your Papa had told us more,' she looked at the telegram and wailed, 'he has not said where he is staying in Manchester. And he has not given the address of the new house. How will I be able to get the furniture sent on from the flat if I cannot tell the removal man where to send it? But he will write. Your Papa is always very much occupied, but he will write.'

We all knew that Papa would not write, yet for some days we believed that he would. It was the time when the heather flowered

25

and the grey-green hills turned purple, and every hour a different purple. 'It is like wine,' my mother used to say, her eyes strained upwards, Richard Quin running by her side and pointing and laughing. We grew neglectful of our work on the farm, and ran up the footpaths to the moorland heights where we could walk and walk and see nothing from horizon to horizon but this flood of colour which was at once dry and resonant. Our hands could rub the heather to dust, it was poor starved fibre, yet the dyed field of it was rich like a bass chord sustained by the pedal. One day we took charge of Richard Quin as soon as our practising was over and let Mamma go up and walk on the moors alone. She stayed up there so long that we grew frightened, but she came down through dusk, voluble with happiness, her hands full of grasses which we had not seen before. Then we found a shoulder of moorland so low that we were able to get Richard Quin up to it, and several times we took our lunch with us and lay on a purple ledge, pitted with a wet green circle where the bog-cotton was white like narcissus, and looked down on the checkered farmlands stretching north towards Edinburgh. Once when we were all up there it was really hot, and Mary called to us, 'We have not seen such sunshine since we left South Africa,' and Mamma, who had been bending over Richard Quin, giving back his laughter and tickling him with a stalk of heather, suddenly was rigid. At Durban she had not cared to hear us speak of Cape Town, and now we were in Scotland she did not care to hear us speak of South Africa. Without doubt, when we got to London she would like it better if we never spoke of Edinburgh. But were we going to London? If we did not know where Papa was, we could not simply take a train to London and look for him, particularly in view of the possibility that he might, compelled by his strangeness, have stopped in Manchester. But if we did not go to him, what were we to do in Edinburgh? The flat would not be ours after the quarter-day, the landlord was taking it back, and somebody else was moving in; and anyway we would have no money. We lay on the ledge in silence, looking down on the plain, which in the strong noonlight looked insubstantial as a cloud, not solid earth at all, while Richard Quin kicked and laughed, and Mamma forced herself, stiff as a soldier, back to the game again.

One night about that time, I woke and saw my sister Mary a

26

white shape in the moonlit room, kneeling beside the door that led into Mamma's bedroom, her ear close to the wood. I got up and joined her. We did not eavesdrop when things were going well, but there were times in our life when we had to know where we were. We heard the boards creak, Mamma was walking up and down, we heard her sigh. She muttered, 'Dear Mr. Morpurgo, I wonder if you will ever. Dear Mr. Morpurgo. I do not think we have met, but I am sure you will forgive me if I write to you to ask. No. No. That is not the proper way. The great thing is to keep it light.'

We heard her pull a chair towards her. She settled into it and gave a little careless laugh. 'Dear Mr. Morpurgo. You know that my husband is a genius. No. No. Dear Mr. Morpurgo. I know from your kindness to my husband that you must hold him in special esteem, and I dare to hope that, like me, you think him to be a genius. I dare to think that, like me, you believe him to be a genius.'

Now she was writing it down, that we knew from the way she spaced out the words. She was writing it in the half-light, so that she would not wake Richard Quin. It worried me very much that she must be doing what I was always being told I must not do, and spoiling her eyes.

'The ways of genius are not the ways of ordinary mortals, and so you will not be surprised to hear.' Now she spoke to herself. 'Oh, why do I always have to bother, why is nothing ever simple. To think that there are women who when they move just have the things put in a van and go.' Now her other voice was used. 'So you will not be surprised to hear that my husband' — she gave again that careless little laugh — 'has gone to Manchester and has forgotten to send me his address, so though he constantly sends me telegrams I cannot reply. If you should know his address I should be obliged if . . . But it sounds so strange.'

She began to walk about the room again.

'Do I end "yours sincerely" or "yours truly"? I cannot remember if I ever met the poor man. But anyway it sounds so strange. It will be dreadful if the people in the office know that he is strange before he starts. At least everywhere else it has taken them time to find out.'

Her whisper sounded as if she had a sore throat.

'Oh, I must leave it till the morning. And then perhaps a letter will come. Oh, I am like the children.'

When Mary and I got back into bed I was more worried about Mamma's eyes and her throat than about our future. Indeed, I noted it against her, as a weakness which I looked on tenderly but had to recognise as a weakness, that she failed to realise that we were going to be all right. Cordelia might represent a difficulty. All teachers liked her, and that was ominous. Mary and I did not dislike school but we knew it was the opposite of the world outside, it was the grown-up's error of errors, they imagined they prepared children for life by shutting them up in a place where nothing happened as it did anywhere else. It might be hard for Cordelia to find her feet, but Mary and I would be all right. Only very rarely did we feel the panic we had felt on the purple ledge. The rest of the time we realised quite well that it was only a question of keeping going till we were able to earn a lot of money as pianists, and somehow we could manage till then. If Papa had not got us into the workhouse by this time, it was probable that he never would, and all that distressed me was Mamma's failure to consider this cheering point, and her folly in sitting up at night getting unhappy and spoiling her eyes by writing in the half-dark, probably with nothing over her night-dress, though she seemed to have a sore throat. I do not think I stayed awake very long, I know Mary fell asleep quite soon.

The next day it struck Mary and me, when we were carrying some hot tea up to some men working in a field below the pass, that it might be easier for Mamma to communicate with Mr. Morpurgo by telegram. It would at any rate cut out that adult nonsense about 'yours sincerely' and 'yours truly.' So at tea-time we dropped some artless questions, asking Mamma how the removal man was to know where to send our furniture if she could not tell him our address in London. At that she sighed deeply, and Cordelia shook her head at us and frowned and hushed us, as well as kicking us under the table. It was like Cordelia to use both grown-up and childish means of expressing disapprobation, she was always on both sides if she could be. Afterwards she caught us in a passage and hissed at us, 'Can't you see poor Mamma is worried to death?' It was almost impossible to pull her hair, as her red-gold curls were so short and tight, and we knew all about the dangers of blood-poisoning, because Mamma's brother had died of tetanus, so we never scratched, but practice had made us quite good at hitting her, and we got in several telling blows that time.

'And Mamma's much too worried to be told we hit you,' said Mary, unctuously.

'How mean!' breathed Cordelia.

'Isn't it?' said Mary. 'It is the sort of thing you would say.'

Cordelia made the gesture of despair which we had often seen her make before, and went away, saying vaguely, 'I am the only one.'

The next afternoon Mary hung about Mamma, who was sitting in the garden while Richard Quin slept, till she heard the sound of the violin, and then said, 'You know, Mamma, Rose is much more of a baby than you think.' We had thought it out together, so it was all right her saying that. 'We all think of her being sensible, but she is really very childish, and it is showing now.' She went on to tell Mamma that I was worrying about what was going to happen to our furniture. She said that I knew that we had given up the flat and that we could not go on living there because someone else was going to move in, and that I thought the removal man would just take the furniture to London and dump it down somewhere and that we would never find it. Mamma became agitated and said that she must speak to me about it, and explain it was all right, and Mary said that that would not do because I had told her what was worrying me in confidence. Mamma accepted that. Mary and I had known she would. Also, passing her hand over her forehead, she had said: 'Besides, what can I say to the child?'

'Well, can't you think of anything to do?' said Mary. 'She cried all night, you know.'

'Oh, no!' wailed Mamma. 'Oh, no! Not Rose!'

'Why don't you send Mr. Morpurgo a telegram?' asked Mary.

'A telegram?' said Mamma. 'Why that would seem even stranger than a letter, and that will seem strange enough to Mr. Morpurgo when he reads it. But no. Why do I not try the newspaper office? Surely he will have told them where the house was when he took it. And I could say that the removal man wanted to know the address. And that I wanted plenty of time for them to turn on the gas. Yes. And the water. Then if they are in touch with your Papa they will tell him that I have telegraphed

29

and we will know where he is too. And Rose will be all right anyway about the furniture. Yes, I will send the telegram today, I will give it to the postman. Answer prepaid. My husband in Manchester has omitted give me address house he has taken please send must instruct removal man and gas and water immediately. Get me some paper and a pencil.'

When Mary brought them she began writing, then threw them on the grass. 'This telegram would seem so much less strange if I could say your Papa was in Tibet.'

'Surely it would be strange if he was there, as the Tibetans don't let anybody in?' said Mary, picking up the paper and the pencil. She really thought it was all being too much for Mamma.

'It is more difficult to communicate with your wife and family from Tibet than it is from Manchester,' said Mamma.

It all went very well, except that Mamma looked at me in bewilderment all that evening, and made Mary very uncomfortable by asking her if she was quite sure I had been crying at night, if she had not dreamed it all. 'Oh, no, Mamma,' Mary said, her oval face as smooth as a silver teaspoon filled with cream, 'I could not dream it night after night.' Of course it was no good, really. Mamma knew there was a lie somewhere. She knew the style of each of her children as she knew the style of all the great composers. But at the same time she would never pose herself unnecessary questions about her children, any more than she ever cared to read much about the personal lives of the great composers. She judged us by our sum, and in any case the whole episode passed out of our minds the next day, when the postman brought the answer to the telegram. Papa had, it appeared, taken for us No. 21, Lovegrove Place, and Mamma need not see about the gas and water, for Mr. Morpurgo had given instructions that the house was to be cleaned and got ready so that the furniture could be moved straight into it. This news was supposed to give me back my unbroken nights, and it certainly did my mother that favour. She spoke of it every day. 'But this is exceptional treatment. They did nothing like this for us when we came here, or when we went to Durban. Your father said that he did not think that Mr. Morpurgo wanted to see him. But that must have been a mistake. After what has happened at *The Caledonian* your father might well be sensitive. But he must be wrong over this, Mr. Morpurgo is being so very kind, and he can have no reason except that he is well disposed towards your father.' Absorbed in her development of this not unreasonable idea, she was no longer distressed by Papa's continued failure to write to her.

There came a night when our story came true. I lay awake in the darkness and cried. But not because I was anxious about our furniture. I had toothache. At first Mary and I were concerned lest this should be a divine judgment on me for deceiving Mamma, but as nothing had happened to Mary, and she had played the major part in the deception, we dismissed the thought. When we told Mamma in the morning she called me all the broad Scots pet names which always came from the back of her mind when we were ill or had hurt ourselves, and then she hurried out of the room and came back very quickly, for she moved faster than anybody I have ever known, stirring a bowlful of honey and hot milk. It was her panacea of every ailment, and it did in fact anaesthetise by distraction. She sent Cordelia and Mary down to breakfast, and sat down on my bed, and I enjoyed being alone with her, feeling the warm invisible fluid of her love flowing out towards me, comforting me as the warm sweetness of the milk and honey comforted my mouth. She told me that she was sorry, she could not let me lie, I must soon get up and dress, for she had already arranged to hire the trap and we would drive down to the station and take the train to Edinburgh, and our dentist, who was sure to be back at work now it was September, would make time to see me.

'Your playing,' she sighed, 'must just stand aside for the day.'

That was not what was worrying me. 'Will this all cost a lot?' I asked.

'Oh, my poor lamb,' she answered, 'what a thing for you to say! I talk too openly before you, I suppose. But do not think of that. An aching tooth is an aching tooth, and we will find the money for that. Do not think of the cost again. And indeed I will profit by this. The Australians left the flat last Monday, and I will take this opportunity to go in and see that everything is ready for the removal man. I would have gone and done this all alone, now I will have my lamb for company. How I wish I had smarter clothes, it is such a fine day! It will be nice for us when Richard Quin is grown, we will always have a man to go about with us. Though of course he will marry and we must let him live his own life. But you girls will have husbands by then, I hope. But anyway do not worry about the money, we have enough to get to London and a little over, and after that it will be all right, we will be better off than we have ever been before, as Mr. Morpurgo thinks so much of your father.'

I had slept so little in the night that I slept in the train, nuzzling against my mother's shoulder. Though it was a mild autumn day she had wrapped me in a tartan shawl which was always brought out when we were ill. Milk and honey and that tartan shawl, they were our ju-jus, I had felt relief at the sight of it on her arm as she got into the trap. When we reached Edinburgh I awoke, feeling warm and babyish and contented, and the pain was so much less that I could hop with joy as we went along Princes Street, because of the splendour of the Castle high on its rock over the trough of the green gardens, all the majesty of the city that lives more masterfully among its hills than Rome itself. But when I said, 'Isn't it beautiful? Isn't it beautiful?' Mamma made no answer. She had always liked the two classical buildings that lie under the hill called the Mound which falls from the Old Town to Princes Street, the National Gallery and the School of Sculpture; she had once said that each was as neat as the new moon. I really did not know where I was. 'Don't you like the town any more?' I asked. 'Don't you think it's looking beautiful today?' She answered, meekly, as if I had accused her of a fault, 'Oh, yes, Rose, of course it is beautiful. But you must excuse me, they have been so horrid to your Papa that I want to go away and never see it again.' I remembered she had not even liked going down to the beach during the last few weeks we were at Durban.

But she got better at the dentist's. He liked her very much. We had all realised that long ago because each time we were shown into his surgery he was always standing in the middle of the room, well away from the chair, as if he were trying to look as unprofessional as possible, and his eyes always went to her face and never strayed to us. He always talked to her first, sometimes for quite a long time, and always laughed a lot, often repeating over and over again something she had said, although it did not strike us as funny and I usually found out afterwards that she had not meant it to be funny. And when we got into the chair he would always sigh as he bent over us and say, 'Well, bairn, you'll never be the man your mother is.' It struck me as a measure of

32

my mother's distressed state that for the first time she seemed to take pleasure in his company. It was as if she found it re-assuring to be with someone who admired her. I supposed she was worried because her clothes were old. But she dutifully hurried him on till he had me in the chair, and when it was found that the source of my pain was an abscess under a tooth that needed just the faintest encouragement to come out, and I stood up again, as well as I had ever been in my life, she thanked him and paid him his fee and took me out as quickly as might be.

She had, indeed, something on her mind. In the passage she bent down and kissed me, and said humbly: 'It must have shaken you, my poor lamb. You were very brave. But you must forgive me. I have not enough money left to take a cab all the way to the flat. We will have to take the tram up the Mound. Do you feel able for that? If you cannot do it we can rest here in the waiting-room and take the early train back. Would you not rather do that? Tell Mamma.'

'I am all right,' I said, quite truthfully.

'You are sure?' she pressed me, and sighed with relief when I nodded. 'I have to think of every penny,' she explained. 'But,' she continued, when we were out in the street, 'you children must not worry. We will not starve, whatever happens. I promise you that. But just now I must scrape and save. It is difficult to explain, but you must trust Mamma.'

'Yes,' I said, 'yes, Mamma.' But I did not trust her. I loved her. Still I could see that she had been tripped by the snare of being grown-up, she lay bound and struggling and helpless.

The tramcar rocked up the Mound with the free, camelish motion of trolley-cars, swung round the curve at the top, and shambled over George the Fourth Bridge, the bridge which fascinated us children because it crossed no river but canyons of slums. Cordelia and Mary and I would be sorry to leave Edinburgh. The Castle on its rock made us feel we were living in a fairy-tale, we liked climbing the slopes of Arthur's Seat, which was so like a couchant lion that it seemed quite unscientific to suppose it could be a natural mountain, and it had to be admitted that it was probably wizard's work. Also these dark slums below the bridge ran under the open stately city to Holy-rood Palace, where darkness and light met, and the white star of Mary Queen of Scots was for ever in opposition to the black

33

star of John Knox. My heart swelled at the thought that we must presently leave all this, simply because it was our doom always to leave. I could have wept. I stroked Mamma's hand and smiled up at her as grown-ups like children to smile, and I knew from her face that she was thinking, 'Rose is a contented child.' We got out at the head of Meadow Walk, and as we went down it we saw the dark blocks of the Infirmary among the reddening trees. We knew a woman medical student who talked of it with awe, as a cathedral of healing. Cordelia sometimes wanted to be a nurse and train there, and when she thought of that her face grew noble and stupid, but stupid in a nicer way than it was when she played the violin. Cordelia would mind leaving Edinburgh more than any of us. All her teachers admired her, they did at every school she went to, they made plans for her, they told her she had only to go on in a straight line and she would be where they wanted her to be, which was where she, with her intense desire for approval, would want to be. Our doom was hardest on her. I turned to Mamma and said, 'Next winter we will not be as cold as we were here last Christmas!' Delighted, she said, 'Why, I believe you are eager to go to London!' 'We all are,' I said. It was strange, Mamma was said to have second sight. A Scottish nurse we had in South Africa had said so; on the beach at Durban Mamma had once lifted up her voice because on a blank sea she had seen a small steamer go up in flames and boats row out towards the shore, and it had all happened as she had seen, twenty-four hours later. But we children could always deceive her. Had it not been so we could not have provided for her happiness half as well as we did.

We came to the grey terrace where we lived, and walked past the house where we had a flat, because we had to make some purchases in the shops round the corner. 'It is odd to pass our own front door without going in,' I said, and Mamma said, 'I feel like that about leaving the city where I was born.' But she went on. 'How happy I am. Your pain is over and the dentist said that all your other teeth were good, and I am doing something I dreaded, I did not want to come in from the Pentlands all alone and do this sad thing about going away from our flat, but now it does not seem sad at all.' She was happy in the shops, too. She liked the act of spending in itself, and although we bought very little that day, just enough to give us something

34

of a midday meal, the smallest tin of cocoa for me, a quarter of a pound of tea for her, a quarter of a pound of sugar, some milk which our dairy gave us in a little metal can with a hoop handle, even so there were parcels, there was a sense that there was more on our side of the line than there had been before, and there were civilities with the shopkeepers. 'I do not owe a penny anywhere,' she said proudly, as we came out of the grocer's, and then came to a halt by a bakery window. After loitering for a while she said timidly, 'Rose, would you think me very greedy if I bought a doughnut? I have not had one for such a long time. And these look so very light.' This modest demand touched me by its contrast with the wonderful things to eat which Mary and I would give her when we had become famous pianists. I urged her to have one, and got her to add to it a cake of another kind that had mincemeat in it and a Christmas look.

As we went up the stairs to our flat we saw that the door of the flat on the other side of the landing was open, and that our caretaker, nice fat Mrs. McKechnie, was standing on the threshold, between her bucket and broom, unwrapping a bar of soap. She came forward to greet us, and in the dark well of the staircase, as she was a bundle of sacking and was wearing a black bonnet, nothing of her was visible except the white patches of her round face and her huge hands. I stood and stared at her, fascinated by the chiaroscuro, while she and Mamma exchanged amiabilities. It was like looking at the Man in the Moon, her features were vast and only vaguely illuminated, but one could recognise the expression. She seemed to be regarding Mamma very tenderly, and her rich voice, an oatmealy contralto which always gave us great pleasure, was telling us that she was redding up the Menzies' flat against their return from Rothesay and would be there all the afternoon, and if Mamma wanted her she had only to tirl the bell.

'A nice woman,' said Mamma, letting herself into the hall. 'I will send her a good present after a month or two in London when I see how the accounts stand.'

We dropped the parcels down on the kitchen-table, and Mamma lit the gas-ring, and poured some milk into a saucepan for my cocoa, and I put her doughnut and the other cake on a plate. 'I knew it,' said Mamma, 'they have left everything

35

beautifully clean. I was sure they were nice people. But look. The mice are terrible. These old houses are all the same. But how lovely they are. These high rooms take in every bit of fineness the day will give them. I must just go to the drawing-room and see if they have been polishing Aunt Clara's furniture.'

Some minutes passed before she came back and sat down with her elbow on the table, her head on her hand. My milk had boiled, and I had made my cocoa, I was putting on the kettle for her tea.

'I will not want all that water,' she said. 'Pour some away. It will never boil. I was not born to have much of anything. Even an excess of water would be grudged me. It would never boil.'

She was very pale and she was trembling.

When I had put the kettle back on the gas she said. 'What has happened does not really matter to us. I cannot explain that to you now. But in a way it is of no consequence at all, although it matters more than you can imagine. Aunt Clara's furniture has gone.'

I left her and went into the drawing-room. It was on the side of the house away from the street, and its two tall windows looked south over the public park known as the Meadows. There was now nothing in the room but our Broadwood upright piano, dragged out to the middle of the floor, and the worn rose-coloured carpet which had come from my mother's home, and three big copies of family portraits on the walls, and millions upon millions of motes dancing in the bright emptiness. There had gone the round table supported by the three entwined dolphins, the chairs upholstered in green silk patterned with gold bees, the high desk with the swan mounts. I went into the dining-room and saw that the sideboard flanked with the two swaddled nymphs and the chairs with the brass inlay had gone too. Those were just the things I at once remembered. Probably I had forgotten a lot of other things.

I ran back to the kitchen, crying, 'Mamma, shall I run round to the police station and tell them we have been burgled.'

'But perhaps we have not been burgled, dear,' she said stupidly.

'They must have taken the things away in a van,' I said, 'Mrs. McKechnie may know something about it.'

'She will know,' said my mother, 'I am wondering how to ask her.'

'How to ask her?' I repeated.

My mother got out of her chair, very stiffly, and went out into the hall, and stood for a time with her hand on the knob of the front door, her other hand across her mouth. Suddenly she opened the door and went out and crossed the landing to the still open door of the opposite flat and called, in mimicry of a happy woman, 'Mrs. McKechnie! Mrs. McKechnie! When did the man come for the furniture?'

The rich voice answered from within that the man from Soames in George Street had sent for it the very day and hour he had said he would, when he came with Papa to buy it, just after we had left for the Pentlands.

'Then that's all right!' Mamma said heartily. 'I thought there might have been a mistake but my husband's managed it all most efficiently.'

When we got back into the flat we closed the door softly and Mamma stood shuddering in the hall. She muttered to herself. 'He will have sold it for a fraction of its value. Oh, I am getting old and ugly, but it is not that. I cannot compete with debt and disgrace, which is what he really loves.' She lifted her arms to embrace a phantom, but they fell by her side.

II

APARCEL came from a second-hand bookshop in Manchester, containing a book about Brazil in three volumes by a Frenchman called Debret, who had been there in the early years of the nineteenth century. We all liked it very much, it was full of lovely coloured lithographs. But Papa did not write to Mamma, so we got into the train at the Waverley Station without knowing what was going to happen to us when we got to London. It was our theory that we did not mind but positively enjoyed this uncertainty, and it was not too wildly untrue. In the night I woke up and looked across the carriage and saw that Mamma was in an ecstasy of courage. It was the fashion of the day for women to wear hats which, though not large, rode on their heads like boats and were moored by veils drawn over the face and made taut by a mysteriously contrived twist under the chin. Her veil was torn here and there, and the holes fell at awkward places. Her nose, which now she was so thin, was very beaky, kept on poking through one of these holes, and she kept on jerking her veil into a different position by altering, never successfully, the knot under her chin. I suppose she had almost no feminine graces. But her lips moved with spirit, from time to time she tossed her head majestically, there was lightning in her eyes. She was rehearsing some scene of triumph that awaited us in London, and she looked like a gay eagle. Presently she took off her hat, she had kept it on so long only because it was part of the costume she was wearing in her dream; and she leaned back against the seat and fell asleep among her sleeping children, not tamed by her burden, interesting as a strolling player.

When we got to London Mamma managed our descent very slowly, considering how quickly it was her habit to move, and as she talked to the porter she looked about her furtively. We realised she had hoped that Papa would be waiting for us on the platform. Then she told the porter to take charge of our baggage for half an hour, because she felt she must give us tea and buns before we started our journey across the town to Lovegrove. The buffet was on the platform, and there were big glass windows. We found a table near a window and she sat with Richard Quin on her lap, giving him milk, while her eyes raked the crowd outside. Everybody looked at Richard Quin; although he had been travelling all night and the train, like all trains at that time, had been black with grime, he was not at all dirty, and he was really very beautiful, with his large grey eyes and black lashes, and his white skin, and his hair that was fair above and dark below, and his air of tranquil amusement. An old lady came up and gave him a banana, which was then a very rare fruit, and he accepted it with a lovely coquetry. I could not see why Mamma worried so much about Papa when she had him.

At last Mamma sighed and said we must be going, and we started on the second and more dolorous part of the journey. We went in a stuffy cab to another station across the Thames, which we thought looked dirty, and took a train that was very slow and ran between nasty little houses, and we got out at a little wooden station high above the ground and went down shabby steps and had to wait till a cab was fetched, and then went a long drive and stopped at the newspaper office, which was in a horrid yellow-green brick Victorian house at a crossroads. It had the name of the newspaper in pale-yellow letters on black horsehair screens across the bottom of the windows, and we thought that ugly and vulgar. Mamma went into the office, because she had arranged that the key should be left for her there, and she came out looking very tired.

'Had they heard anything about Papa?' I said.

'How could I ask?' sighed Mamma, and Cordelia frowned and shushed me. I think none of us felt brave any more.

But then the cab took us into a different sort of district, where there were trees along the roads and in the gardens, many trees, which astonished us, because we had believed that London was nothing but houses. The trees were just touched with gold, and the gardens were full of Japanese anemones and Michaelmas daisies and chrysanthemums, growing out of wet earth dark as plum cake. This was not like Scotland. It was a rich, moist, easy place. But then the cab took us into another horrid street of little red-brick houses with front doors arched with yellow plasterwork and lace curtains hanging at mean little sharp-angled bow windows. We all grumbled, we had hoped we were going to live where the trees were. But it was all right. We had always known it was going to be all right. The houses came to an end and the road widened, and there were trees and flowers again, and the cab slowed down before a white villa which instantly pleased us. It never ceased to please me. I cannot so adjust my mind that I cancel my intention of living there some day, though it was destroyed by a bomb in the Second World War.

I cannot remember what I saw that afternoon, because I saw it too often afterwards. But here the road came to an end, running to a wrought-iron gateway, flanked by pillars on which two gryphons supported coats-of-arms, and set in a high brick wall. The gates were blind, backed with tarred boards, and this might have been frightening, but reassured, it proclaimed that everybody had gone, the place was private. On the right was a neat terrace of a dozen houses. Just before the gateway, on our left, was our new house. A neat plaque on its first floor gave the figures '1810' and it had the graces of its time. It had a porch to its front door, a verandah screening its lower windows, of copper weathered to a wistful, smoke-soft blue-green, and twisted into exotic shapes to satisfy the Chinese taste. Above, the bedroom windows each had a pediment carved above them that gave them a certain distinction, and above them the attic windows were disguised by a balustrade adorned at each end with sentimental urns. But it had been newly painted, so my Mamma muttered, 'That paint, what does it mean, who can have paid for that? Will that be the first bill?' And she flung out a tragic finger at a wide gate beside the house, ghost-coloured for lack of paint, and the red-purple tiles of the roofs that showed above it, the turret with a broken weathervane and a clock which was telling a shocking lie about the time. 'What, are we to keep a carriage?' she said ironically. 'Oh, this is far too big. What shall we do? What shall we do?'

'It will be all right,' said Mary.

'Of course it will be all right,' I said. 'Let's go in.'

We three little girls ran along the paved path, and Mamma slowly followed us with Richard Quin. 'How good the boy is,' she said heavily, and put the key into the lock. She turned it and stepped inside and at once became rigid, her mouth falling open as if she were a fish, not to the advantage of her appearance. One of the doors opening into the little hall was ajar, and from the room beyond there came a scraping noise. She thought, and so did we, that a burglar had got into the house. Only for a moment did she hesitate, then she ran into the room, and Cordelia and Mary and I followed. My father was standing beside the chimney-piece, scraping with a penknife at the wallpaper where it joined the marble. For a second he persisted in this occupation, then he put down the penknife, opened his arms to my mother and kissed her on both cheeks, and we stood in a half-moon about them, Richard Quin crawling round our feet. Mamma glowed, we all felt safe, rescued from the abyss, because we had our dear Papa with us again.

'But, Piers, how did you get in without the key? They said there was only one,' said Mamma. 'This is the last thing I thought of!'

'I know a dozen ways into the house,' said Papa, in the mocking voice that people hated so much. 'This time I came in by the coach-house roof.'

'You know this house? It is — it can't be the house where you used to stay?'

'Yes,' said Papa. 'It is indeed the very same house where I used to stay with Grand-Aunt Willoughby.' He stood back from the hearth, closed his knife, and slipped it back into his pocket. 'Yes, it's there,' he told us in parenthesis, 'there used to be a flat painted panel over this chimneypiece, and they've covered it over, I can't think why. It was really good. We'll get it clear later.' Fingering the closed knife in his pocket and giving one of his dark, oblique looks round the room, he went on, 'Yes, this is Caroline Lodge, only nobody calls it that now. It was built for Grand-Aunt Willoughby by her rich son-in-law who lived in that big house behind the gates. It is a Theological College now. And this house belongs to my cousin Ralph. He has let me have it.'

'Oh, you and Ralph are friends again?' cried my mother.

'No, not noticeably,' said Papa. 'But he has let me have it.'

'How good of him,' Mamma said, making the best of it. 'But is it not very dear?'

'No, the place is falling to pieces, and nobody wants to live here now it is in the middle of a slum,' said Papa contemptuously. 'But we are paying him something.'

'We must never be a day late with the rent,' said Mamma enthusiastically. My father made no response. 'Oh,' she cried, looking about her, 'it is pleasant to be here, and find you here, and now, children, let us go round the house and see where we are going to be so happy. Is there a nice room for your study?'

There was indeed. The little square room at the back of the house was Papa's study, and the bigger room beside it was to be our sitting-room. The removal men had set down most of the furniture there, but the grace of the room was still apparent. Here Mamma flung open the French windows, and we all stood by her on the top step of the broad iron stairs leading down into the garden, which was a square of lawn edged with flower-beds and ending in a grove of chestnuts, then brightened by their first gold and scarlet leaves. I remember those wild tints, for like my sisters I was looking at the scene with an exalted vision. We were experts in disillusion, we had learned to be cynical about fresh starts even before we had ourselves made our first start, but this house gave us hope. Indeed, it gave us back our childhood. Papa came to stand behind us, swung me up on his shoulder, and I was proud, I was wrapped in delight, as if I knew no ill of him. It was not a warming pleasure, but it was glorious, it was like being cradled by the Northern Lights and swung across the skies. Mamma watched us in ecstasy, when our family life was as it is supposed to be on earth she was as if lifted to heaven.

In the room behind us Cordelia said, 'Mamma, the removal men have broken a chair.'

Mamma said absently, 'If they have left us enough to sit on, do not worry, this stuff is all rubbish.'

A chill fell. It was as if I had grown heavy in my father's arms. Of course I had had to tell Cordelia and Mary what had happened to Aunt Clara's furniture. But we all loved Papa so much that somehow Mamma saying that seemed worse than Papa selling the furniture, and Mamma felt that too. She turned to him with a desperate movement and cried in tearful gaiety, 'Show us the garden. Did you play here with the other Richard Quin?'

Papa shifted me to his other shoulder and, shambling a little as if he were old, led us out into the garden. He pointed to some straggling thickets on the wall and told us they were peach-trees. Their branches hung down like trailing curtains. Cordelia ran and pushed them back and underneath were the neat trunks given them by early care. My mother exclaimed in distress at the neglect which they had suffered and expressed the fear that they would bear no fruit for us. My father did not seem concerned. He told us how large and juicy the peaches had been, and how he and his brother had always had one each with cream and sugar for dessert with their supper. 'We called our ponies Cream and Sugar,' he said, 'they were not really our ponies, the old man in the big house lent them to us when we were staying here for our holidays. But we stabled them here.'

'In those very stables?' said Mamma.

'In those very stables,' said Papa. He put back his head and looked through his narrowed eyes at the roofs we could see over the wall, the ruined roofs. '"Change and decay in all around I see."' He gave a sneering laugh, set me down on the ground, and strolled towards a door in the wall, and sneered again because the rusty latch broke in his hand. Beyond was a courtyard feathered green underfoot with the camomile which grew thick between each cobblestone, buildings round it that stared with the blank eyes of glassless windows. My father pushed back a door which hung squint on its hinges, and sauntered into a stable where more motes danced in the sunlight than had danced in that room in Edinburgh which had been so empty, because Aunt Clara's furniture had gone out of it. The floor was strewn with pale wisps of litter, and where the walls met there were hundreds of brackets made by the dark velvet of old cobwebs. There were four stalls, and a door on which my father laid his hand and said, 'This was a loose-box. Grand-Aunt Willoughby had a son called George, he was a naval officer, his horse Sultan was stabled in here, it was a black gelding.' He wheeled about, looking very grave, and called urgently, 'Cordelia. Mary. Rose. Do you all understand that you must never go into a loose-box? You can do nothing more dangerous. The horse can get between you and the door in a second, and if he savages you, you are done. You must always remember that. Always.'

43

Every now and then he used to give us counsels of this sort, which might have been relevant to his childhood, but were not to ours, and I think, from my recollections of his bearing at such moments, that he then felt pride because for once he was properly discharging his duties as a father.

Leaving the dangerous territory, he said to Mamma in an undertone, 'By the way, I am afraid that Manchester business came to nothing.'

Softly she answered, 'I am sorry for your sake, but what does it matter? You have a good position here.'

Circling round the stalls, he said, 'Pompey and Caesar were here. They were the carriage pair. They were fat old dapple-greys and groomed like satin, they always reminded us of one of our mother's ball-gowns. This is where Cream and Sugar were. I rode Cream, Richard Quin rode Sugar, so did my brother Barry when he was here, but he hardly ever came. He had left Harrow by then and gone to the India Office. It was usually Richard Quin and I that were here by ourselves, and that was the way I liked it, we always ran well together in double harness. We had some wonderful times here. Those were the days when we had that French tutor I have told you about, my dear. . . .'

He was gone from us again, but not, as so often happened, on a dangerous journey, from which he would come back not simply empty-handed, but bearing a loss that was positive. This time he had gone back to his childhood. We listened, our mouths open as if we were singing a hymn in his praise. Mamma was watching him as people watch fireworks. About us another autumn morning was hazy, a little later in a distant year. My father and his brother had not been able to go back to Harrow at the beginning of term because they had had measles and were being allowed some convalescent weeks. They had ridden a lot with their French tutor, who had to ride Sultan. This was not the hardship that might be imagined, when it was said that a French tutor had to take the mount that belonged to the son of an English household. For this French tutor was a man of mark, member of a gentlemanly Belgian family, who had become a geographer and held a lectureship in Paris when he was expelled from France as an atheist and an anarchist by Louis Napoleon after the *coup d'état* of 1851. My grandmother met him some years later, when she was travelling to forget the pain of her widowhood, and engaged him as tutor to her orphaned sons in the mistaken belief that he had been exiled from France as a Protestant rebel against Catholicism. He had discovered her error shortly after he arrived at her home in County Kerry, and had handled the situation sensitively and honourably, for he gave no hint of his real beliefs while he was under her roof, and taught her boys the elements of the classics and the French language and scientific method, without giving his instruction any peculiar character except a certain mid-nineteenth-century humanitarianism. My father, though very cruel, was very kind.

All this I learned later. That morning Papa simply explained that the tutor knew how to ride, though he was a scholar and not a passionate horseman, and that George Willoughby, like many another naval officer, had his reasons for liking a quiet mount, and Sultan got very little exercise when his master was at sea and had grown thoroughly lazy. He waddled along, and the tutor had no trouble except when his charges got out of sight, for Cream and Sugar were very fast, they were fine spirited creatures and were well exercised during the boys' term time when they went back to their owners' stables. That day the tutor had angered the two boys by making them deal more scrupulously with their daily ten lines of Virgil than they thought fair on their holidays, so they lost him in the first few minutes of their ride, where there was a bridge and then a sharp turn and a canter up a hill. Not only were Cream and Sugar neat on their feet as ballet-dancers, they understood every word you said to them. So the two boys were able to dismount and get the two ponies to leave the road and scramble up a steep wooded bank, and keep dead quiet, at a word's command, when the tutor jogged along the lane beneath, calling his charges' names.

I have seen miniatures of my father and his brother at that age; they were very lovely with their olive skins, and their light eyes fiery under long lashes, their dark hair streaked with gold and their air of proud incompatibility with any sort of defeat. Human relations are essentially imperfect. Supposing that Papa had been the best of fathers, I would still have been hungry. Because I was his daughter I could not have known all of him, there was that continent in which I could not travel, the waste

45

of time before I was born and he already existed. I could not have been a child with him, I could not have been with him and his brother when they knelt on the dry red beech-leaves, with their laughing faces pressed against the pulsing silken necks of their crouched and panting ponies, the tree trunks rising sharp silver above them to the blue October haze.

When Sultan's hooves had clop-clopped up the lane the boys had their laughter out aloud and then led the ponies to the top. There they found some uplands which they did not know, and they followed the gates and came to a farm. An old woman wearing a mob-cap threw open a window and called them by their names, and told them to tie up their ponies in the yard and sit down to the wedding-feast. This was a farm called Pinchbeck Hall, and the farmer's daughter was marrying a London milkman. The boys obeyed her and went into one of the barns and found a long table set out, covered with food, with people sitting round it who were comfortable, ordinary people, mixed with others who had come out of a fairy-tale. There were men wearing queerly cut broad cloth suits and women wearing tall hats and plaid shawls. For the milkman, like most London milkmen then and for long after, was Welsh. Papa did not remember the bride and bridegroom at all, so entranced was he by these fairy-tale people and by the food. That had been coarser and more impressive than the refined dishes he was accustomed to eat at his widowed mother's table, or the spiced dishes enjoyed by Grand-Aunt Willoughby, who had spent most of her life in India. Here there were huge joints of beef, marbled with broad veins of fat, pork with splendid crackling, shining moulds of brawn and great tongues lolling back on themselves, golden-crusted pies, jewel-bright jellies, foamy syllabubs, pitchers of solid cream, cheeses big as mill-stones, of sorts not known today. There was a great deal of laughter: these people made more noise when they laughed than the boys could have believed possible, they used to practise in the stables afterwards. And after the food was eaten there was singing. The Surrey people sang comically, all but one very young, flat-chested girl with big eyes, out of whose bony little body there had come a strong, languid, rich voice. 'I wonder,' said Papa, 'what happened to her afterwards,' and for a moment he paused and brooded.

But then the Welsh guests stood up all together, stiff as soldiers, and sang like the sea, like the wind, like falling waters. Somebody asked if the two boys could sing. My father could not, he had from babyhood felt a fear that if he studied music he would grow up into a woman. But Richard Quin liked to sing, and was not shy, and he gave them 'I know that my Redeemer liveth,' which he had been taught by his Aunt Florence, who afterwards broke the family's heart by leaving the Low Church — like all Anglo-Irish my father's family was very Low Church — and joining Miss Sellon's Sisterhood at Plymouth. He had a beautiful voice, and of course he was a most beautiful child, and the wedding party sat and dried their eyes. He was going to sing again, when a lad ran in shouting, and everybody poured out into the farmyard just as a russet streak flashed through it, throwing up before it a spray of squawking poultry. 'It must be fun to be a fox,' said Papa, dreamily. 'To be a fox and kill poor things, and in the end be hunted.' 'Fun?' asked Mamma in wonder. 'Yes, in a way,' said Papa, but went on with his story. Then the horns were heard, while people hurried to open the gates on each side of the farmyard, and in a moment the hounds were through in a chanting white flood. Then came the thud of the hunt's hooves, louder and louder, a fine sound, like thunder, and the sweating hunters brought along the sweating men in pink, but they did not turn into the farmyard, the horses had their heads so well set on the lane running past the farmyard and were going so hard that the riders could not turn aside, and looked over their shoulders with speed-glazed eyes as they were carried past the open gates. It struck Papa and Richard Quin as strange, as a little frightening that the people in the farmyard were shaken with their own huge kind of laughter because the hunt had lost their fox and their pack. These were the gentry. It served them right to have a bit of ill luck, for once.

They were all going back to the barn to sing and drink some more when another horse came up the lane. It was rolling stiffly backwards and forwards like a rocking-horse. It was Sultan. The boys shouted and ran forward to stop him, which was not difficult, and they found their tutor unable to dismount. He went on sitting in the saddle, his eyes closed, saying, '*Je meurs, je meurs, je meurs.*' While the poor man had been

47

searching the lanes for his charges the hunt had crossed his track, and Sultan had suddenly remembered his youth, and joined the field. Nothing would stop him and he had cleared several hedges and a water-jump. It was no wonder that the French tutor, who had never hunted before, could say nothing but '*Je meurs, je meurs, je meurs.*' But it all worked out well, for the farm people had never heard of such a joke as a Frenchman who had been caught up into a hunt, and they stuffed him with food and brought him flagons of drink, and he ended by singing too. He gave them 'La Marseillaise' and 'Ca Ira,' and had the Welsh people lala-ing a fine chorus to them.

At that Papa suddenly left the past. The story stopped. He was sad, we knew it, we moved away. He sauntered about the stable, humming 'La Marseillaise,' which insensibly turned into the 'Wearing of the Green,' the only tune he was really sure of, and poking with the worn toe of his shoe at such evidence of decay as a rusted bucket without a bottom, a birch broom which had retained only a few of its twigs, but making no move to alter their position. He was always making such movements, which spoke of an intense but inactive fastidiousness. For a time we lost him, and Mamma found him in a little room where there were three saddles hanging on the walls, half transmuted into blue-green mould.

My mother slipped her arm into his. 'How lovely it will be for you to work on this newspaper,' she said. 'They have been so kind. They are sending a man to put up the beds this afternoon. The manager's wife has found us a servant.' My father said nothing. He was often kind, but he was also ungrateful. My mother went on, 'If this is a success it might lead to all sorts of things. The children,' she said after a pause, her voice rising bravely to hope, but muting its hope because she had known so much disappointment, 'the children might have ponies. You would like that.'

My father did not answer. 'Like Cream and Sugar,' she mildly persisted.

He pointed at the mouldy saddles. 'That stuff is wonderful for cuts,' he said.

'What?' exclaimed my mother.

'Yes,' said my father. 'There was an old saddle like this in the saddle-room at home, and whenever any of us boys cut

48

ourselves Micky McGuire the groom used to take us in there, and rub the mould deep into the cut, and it always healed in no time.'

My mother sighed with impatience at what was not to sound a reasonable remark until half a century had passed, and turned away. 'Children, children,' she called. 'You must have some luncheon and we must find some way of getting poor Richard Quin a place to rest. Oh, how good he has been!'

All parts of the puzzle fell into place before nightfall. The man who came in the afternoon was, as Mamma put it in the language of the day, very civil, and he hammered up our beds and put up the dining-room table and moved the bookcases into Papa's study, so Mamma was able to get him out of the way, for she told him that the best way he could help would be to unpack his books, though she knew he would only sit down and read them. But it was necessary to keep him in his study, for poor Mamma could not help groaning over the horrid furniture which was now all she had for the downstair rooms. It was too shabby, even by our standards. There was a particularly dreadful set of chairs covered with red Spanish leather so worn that the surface was flaking off and leaving bare pinkish patches. We grieved with her, and we were surprised when she said that she had decided that the three copies of family portraits which had hung in our Edinburgh drawing-room should go upstairs and that each of us girls should have one to hang over her bed. We could not imagine anything nicer, but we thought it a pity that, when she had to make a new drawing-room without her good furniture, she should choose to do without these pictures too. But she said, speaking with some distaste, that she did not want to hang them where visitors could see them, lest it should appear that she was trying to make a grand impression by passing off as originals what were only copies.

That seemed strange, for they were really very pretty, and surely Mamma could have explained what they were to anybody who seemed specially impressed. They were very good copies. Indeed, when they had been left to Mamma by a relative of Papa's who had come out to South Africa just before he died and had liked her very much, there had been some hope that they were originals, which had been dismissed forever by a dealer when we got to Edinburgh. The one that would have been most valuable had it been what it seemed was a portrait by Gainsborough of our great-great-grandmother, which made its reference to the mystery of that artist's career. She looked out of the canvas with narrowed eyes; it would have seemed natural if fine feelers had grown from her pursed little mouth; a feather head-dress gave the illusion that she had two high pricked ears set very high; and she was dressed in the faint fawns and blues a Persian cat would choose to wear if it were changed into a woman. How was a fashionable portrait-painter able to persuade his clients, in an age not given to fantasy, to let him represent all their women as looking like cats? He might have been telling the truth about our ancestress, since Papa looked so like a great cat, but really there cannot ever have existed all over England and Scotland at one time a number of women all feline in appearance and all so wealthy that they could commission Gainsborough. Mamma could never understand it. Mary and I at once proposed that Cordelia should have this portrait hanging over her bed because we knew that otherwise she would be given first choice because she was the eldest, and we always thought that was bad for her.

There was no question which picture could hang over Mary's bed. Sir Thomas Lawrence had painted my grandfather's eldest sister, Arabella, in a high-waisted gown of white satin, and with her smooth black hair, her oval face, her arched eyebrows, her undisturbed mouth, her long neck, and her air of being coolly herself within her clothes, she was exactly like Mary. She was said to have had a sad life, and it was true that she had early been left a widow, childless except for one daughter, from whom she was divided by one of those quarrels which were so frequent in my father's family. There was no wrangling in these quarrels, they were merely silent and final separations. It was as if the people involved had looked into each other's faces and been appalled by what they saw, and had turned away to walk in opposite directions. But there was no sign of sadness, no threat that she ever could be sad, she just looked like Mary, who never laughed aloud and rarely wept. That left for me Sir Martin Archer Shee's portrait of our grand-aunt, who had been a clergyman's wife, though that would not have been guessed from her costume. She wore a classical robe which left bare one arm and shoulder and shoulder-blade, and she held a gold cup of antique design, to show off the beauty of her hands. Papa said she had been a mischievous woman. She had persuaded her foolish husband, who was much older than herself, to press an imaginary claim to an extinct barony, which had been warmly supported by one of the Royal Dukes, for reasons that made Papa and Mamma shake their heads. But you could see how it all happened. The cup she held, and the bracelet she wore around her upper arm, and the fillet binding her short golden curls, were studded with enormous jewels like crystallised fruits. An extinct barony, a Royal Duke, would be to her something she might find in Aladdin's cave, and therefore hers by licence derived from a magic lamp or magic ring.

In the course of the afternoon the new servant came, a tall girl named Kate, who walked with a roll like a sailor dressed up in skirts, and she unpacked all the kitchen things, so we had tea at the usual time. We said we were not tired, and got our toys and books out of our special trunk and arranged them in our rooms, and by the time we had finished we found that it was supper-time, but we were so tired we could hardly eat anything, and we were very glad to go to bed. I was half asleep when Papa came in to kiss us good night, I could not open my eyes, he made a bright rent on the darkness behind my lids and became a person in a dream. I thought, as I sank with him into the dream, 'I should get up early tomorrow and get to my practice, we have missed a day, but I am very tired, I think I will be very late,' for we were a great family for sleep. But in the middle of the night I was surprised to find I had been awakened by a sound to which I had, during the previous few weeks, grown accustomed. The farm horses were stamping in the stables: boom, and then, after a pause, boom again went the hesitating, shifting, irregular hammer of their hooves.

'What a noise they are making tonight,' I thought. 'I wonder if Mr. Weir will go out and quiet them.' Then I started up, for I remembered that I was not at the farm. I was in a London house, and the stables were empty. I was not frightened. All the same it was as if a great door were swinging on its hinges, and the wind of its swinging blew on my face. I was not frightened, even when I sat up in bed and looked across the room at Mary, sleeping with her still smooth head on the crook of her arm, and Cordelia lying face down between her clenched fists, and

51

realised that I was awake, was where there were no horses, and was listening to the sound of horses stamping in their stalls, and presently I did not even feel lonely. Footsteps went past my closed door and creaked on the staircase. I heard the French window in the room below open after some fretting of the bolt, and there was a twang from each iron step in turn. Papa had gone out to the stables and would protect us from any danger that might be there.

I dropped back in my bed, rolled the sheets and blankets about me, and, rejoicing, told myself that I was safe, I could sleep. Then I longed to see him, and I kicked off the clothes and ran over to the window and pulled aside the curtains. But it was not Papa who was in the garden, it was Mamma. She was walking slowly, as she did when she was worried about money, across the lawn, which glistened white under a flood of moonlight so strong that the lantern she carried gave out no rays but was a calm yellow flame, self-contained within the pervading brightness. The trees beyond the lawn cast an inky lace of pattern on the lawn, and seemed part of a landscape other than was to be seen by day. Now our garden was the edge of a great park running to low wooded hills, which were furred with distant moonlight and mounted one upon another until there was only a handspan of clear pale black sky between them and the lowest star. I thought I heard the horn of the hunt that had gone by that morning in my father's story. I liked this changed world but I did not want my mother to be out in it alone.

I put on my outdoor shoes and the old coat which had once belonged to Cordelia and was now my dressing-gown and ran downstairs, partly because I wanted to help my mother if there was anything dangerous abroad, and partly because I thought of what was happening as not a danger at all, but as a tide, white as the moonlight but not the same as the moonlight, which was washing the walls of the house, which might make them rock on their foundations but would not break them down, which would suffuse one in pleasure if one bathed in it. I too had difficulty with the handle of the French window, and by the time my small hands had dragged it round my mother had passed through the door in the wall, and I was out in the moonlight and had to cross the white challenging square of the garden before I could reach her. I began to be afraid of the night, of the horses behind the wall that were stamping but were not there, of the scolding I would get from Cordelia if she woke up and missed me and came down and found me before I had got to my mother. The two fears competed, and I went forward. I dreaded Cordelia more than the night.

Mamma had left the door in the wall open, which was as well, for the handle was high. Perhaps she had known that I was following her, perhaps she had known I would follow her before I left my bed. But when I found her she had forgotten me. She had gone to the further end of the stable and set her lantern down on a window-ledge, and was looking back at the four stalls. The yellow light shone on the perfect emptiness that filled the lesser spaces of those stalls, the larger space contained by the plastered walls and the broken windows. It showed everything, the brackets of frail cobweb which cast much stouter shadows, the mangers which held nothing but dust and shadows, the pail which was cracked though its shadow looked sound enough. But in this emptiness four horses slept and dreamed after their different fashions. Now it was Pompey or Caesar that shifted a heavy and complaining hoof, now it was Cream or Sugar that moved lightly like a drowsing dancer among the thick litter which was not there. Now one of the carriage horses snorted, now Cream or Sugar delicately ground his teeth, then a carriage horse slowly blurted bubbles through his muzzle. They were not so sad as the brick and wood and plaster about them, but they sounded anxious about an issue not yet settled. My mother was looking towards them and beyond them. Her mouth was open in the bafflement of extreme stupidity, and her eyes shone with wisdom. I wondered what it was that she knew.

A silence fell, far away a clock struck two, and in the loose-box Sultan, who had been an old horse when my father was a child, whinnied loudly. My mother's eyes moved to my face. The horses in the stalls became luminous shapes. We knew that if we willed it, if we made a movement of the mind comparable with the action of throwing all one's weight on one foot, we could make them visible as ourselves. But it was my mother's choice to abstain. The horses remained faint outlines for a minute or so and then were only sound again. Mamma looked past me into the distance, at the remote sources from which she had drawn her assurance, before picking up her lamp and coming towards me, meeting the shadows and sending them jerking into a dark mass behind her. She said my name very softly and took my hand, and we went out of the stable, pausing on the threshold to give a last civil glance at the horses which we could not see. 'Hurry,' she breathed as we went through the door in the wall, and we ran together over the white grass to the house, which now seemed a small pale box, dwarfed by black trees and curiously stamped with the filigree shadows of the wrought-iron balconies and verandah. When we got into the sitting-room she knelt down and grasped me closely and whispered in Scots, asking me if my feet were not as cold as ice. Putting my arms round her neck, I told her they were not, but she said that I must be freezing, and grieved over her fear, though she herself was also clad in only a nightdress and dressing-gown, and· her flesh was far colder than mine. I rubbed my body against her to warm her, and we nestled together for a little while. Then she softly broke the grip of my arm and murmured, 'Come down very quietly to the kitchen, and I'll warm you some milk.' I remember the chill of her flesh against my fingers, and on my lips; I remember the warmth of the milk in my mouth, she made it hotter than I liked it. Surely it cannot have been a dream.

III

'AS SOON as you children go out,' said Mamma, as we stood at the French window after lunch the next day, 'I am going to write to my cousin Constance and ask her to come and see us. It cannot be a long journey for her, she lives in South London too. Oh dear, I wish we could furnish the attic room next to Kate's, so that Constance could come and stay with us, and bring her little girl Rosamund. But I cannot spare a stick of furniture from the other rooms.' She stared through the glass as if she hoped to see some overlooked chairs and tables on the lawn.

'Don't bother to have them just because you think we would like to play with the little girl,' I said.

'We have you and Papa and Richard Quin, and that is enough,' said Mary.

'But I want them,' said Mamma, her eyes wide with desire. 'Constance is not my cousin, she is married to my Cousin Jock, God help her, but she was at school with me, we were like sisters. I want to see her. Think what you two would feel like if when you were grown-up you never managed to be together. You cannot think how lonely it is,' she said, with a passion which we children sympathetically recognised as the passion of a child, 'never to be with anybody who knew you when you were little. And also I must try to make a world for you. It is not good for you never to be with other people than yourselves, and Papa's relatives are not friendly, and things may not be easy with the people here . . .' Her voice faded away.

'Oh, Mamma, we will be all right,' said Mary.

'Yes, Mamma, we will always be all right,' I said.

'I will sit down and write the letter now so that you can post it at once,' Mamma said ecstatically.

At first her fears that things might not be easy at Lovegrove seemed groundless. Papa was always happy when he was engaged in certain activities. Of these the one which gave him greatest pleasure was his lifelong wrestling match with money.

He was infatuated with it though he could not get on good terms with it. He felt towards it as a man of his type might have felt towards a gipsy mistress, he loved it and hated it, he wanted hugely to possess it and then drove it away, so that he nearly perished of his need for it. But he knew almost as great joy if he were conducting a campaign against some social injustice, particularly if it were the rights of property which had been dealt with unjustly. This was not because he himself had any property, of which he possessed not one farthingsworth, nor because he any longer numbered among his friends any property-owners, nor because he was callous about the sufferings of the poor, but because he was a disciple of Herbert Spencer and believed the right to own property to be the only instrument by which the individual could protect his freedom from the tyranny of the State. It happened that an ideal specimen of this type of campaign came his way very soon after we arrived at Lovegrove.

We heard of it first one Saturday afternoon which was so wet that we could not go out even in mackintoshes, so my mother sat down and played the whole of Schumann's Carnival to us, which was our great treat. Just as she had finished Kate put her head round the door and said, 'Madam, did you know it, there is a double rainbow,' and we all ran out into the garden, which was suffused with the grey-green end of the world light which comes after a storm, and we did the nine hops and the three curtseys that are called for by a double rainbow. Then Mother heard a muffin-bell in the distance, and gave us sixpence, and Kate ran up from the basement with some plates and we ran down the street until we overtook the man with the green baize apron and the brass bell and the heavy wooden tray on his head, and we bought lots of muffins and crumpets. We were eating them at tea-time, when Papa came in and joined us, and Mamma advised him to have some, saying that Kate could not have done them better, though she had put so much butter on them that we would have to be economical for the rest of the week.

'Butter?' said Papa, his eyes blazing. ''There should be no butter eaten in this house. Do not offer me butter. The children should not eat butter.'

'My dear, why not?' asked Mamma. She was not too perturbed, for she knew that when he spoke with this earnestness he was happy and occupied.

'We must eat margarine,' he told her.

This was an astonishing pronouncement in those days, when dietetic error flourished. Skim milk was emptied down the drains, it was the worst condemnation of jam that it contained glucose, and margarine was held to promote rickets.

'There is a conspiracy,' said Papa.

And so there was. Papa had been going through Hansard at his office and had read the text of a Bill which proposed that all margarine should be coloured purple, and which was being supported by the Government. This had struck him as strange and sinister, so he went to the House of Commons and looked up an Irish M.P. whom he knew and together they enquired into the origins of the Bill. They found that it was backed by landowning members, and that it had been drafted by the dairy-farming interest, to exploit the fact that taste is three-fourths sight, and that sight is prejudiced, and that the poorer class of customer, who would be the most likely to buy margarine, would not buy it if it were coloured purple. 'This is the attempt of a vested interest to monopolise a market by depriving the poor of a valuable article of food,' said Papa, 'and I am going to fight it.' This he did, by gathering a company of dissidents, some anarchists, some socialists, some followers of Herbert Spencer, some men of wealth and influence, some poor as himself, who protested against this measure in the press, at street-corner meetings, and by lobbying members of the House of Commons. So pure was this movement in its motives that it only accidentally came into contact with the manufacturers of margarine, who were conducting a much less effective campaign of their own and were bewildered by this curious and unsolicited championship. One astonished manufacturer showed his gratitude by sending my father a case of port and another of sherry. Alcohol meant nothing to my father. All of his being was under the control of his secret purposes, and he was content it should be so, he never wished for relaxation. So a bottle of each was kept out to be offered to visitors and the rest was sent down to the cellar. Poor though we were, it did not occur to either my father or my mother to sell the wine. In that age it would have seemed very disreputable to sell a gift.

But my mother got something better than money out of this crusade. Papa wrote some brilliant leaders on his crusade in the

Lovegrove Gazette which were quoted in the national newspapers. Mr. Morpurgo, though he still showed no desire to meet Papa, wrote to him several times congratulating him on those leaders and on the liveliness he had brought to the paper, and as Papa wholly neglected every part of his duties except his writing Mr. Morpurgo put in a technical journalist who did the editorial work instead of Papa. Also he made a speech at a public meeting which brought him friendly letters from the other speakers, who were all distinguished men. He had nothing of that beggar look about him now. The situation produced a certain conflict in my mother's heart, because she did not really like giving us children margarine instead of butter, but that was settled by our servant Kate. She pointed out to us that we liked dripping, and that we could do our Mamma a good turn if we started hollering for it all the time.

Yet my mother was not altogether happy. I had found her weeping in her room, with Constance's answer to her letter in her hand. It was a cold answer, excusing herself from a visit to Lovegrove on the ground that her daughter Rosamund was not well, and making no suggestion that my mother should visit her. With the cruelty of a child I was shocked at seeing my mother abandon herself to grief. It was as if she had let me see her in too few clothes. For the first time I felt curious about this Constance and her Rosamund. The letter gave not the faintest token of affection, but I had noticed that when people rejected the advances of my parents they usually made some pretence that they were not doing so. Papa's employers and relatives were apt to be openly disagreeable, but for the rest, 'he writes very nicely, and says that he will write again next week and suggest something definite,' was the usual formula. But Constance made no such pretences. I felt that perhaps she and her daughter were in some special case, and I wondered if they were better or worse than appeared.

My mother spoke of them several times with bewilderment and regret, but soon they were displaced by another anxiety. During the first month or so after our arrival at Lovegrove a number of ladies called on her, and she bought a new hat and dress and returned the calls, and even gave some simple tea-parties. But as the year drew on towards its close, there came a Saturday morning when a brougham drove up to our house,

and a short, stout man got out and went up to our door and asked
for my father, and on hearing from Kate that he was away for
the day, went down the steps again, wearing a very odd expression for a grown-up. His eyes were bleared and his cheeks puffy
as if he had been crying. My mother, who was in the front garden, helping me to get Richard Quin's kitten out of the laburnum
tree, caught sight of his face and ran after him, laid a hand on
his arm, and asked if there was anything she could do for him.
He lifted his head and looked at her without saying anything. I
thought he must be drunk, for in Scotland I had got used to the
sight of drunken men, and I was much surprised when Mamma,
her eyes grown huge in her thin face, led him back to the house.
Then she sent Kate out to tell us that we must not come into the
sitting-room till the man had gone, and when we asked Kate
what was happening she said that she did not know, but surely
we had recognised the man as the Mayor of Lovegrove. She was
surprised that we had not known who it was, for we had had a
good look at him wearing his badge and gold chain when she
had taken us to see Princess Beatrice open the new hospital.
Presently Cordelia came out with her violin, complaining that
she did not know how she could be expected ever to learn how
to play decently when she could not get a moment's peace to
practise. Mary and I jeered at her, and went down into the
kitchen and sat miserably in front of the range, wondering what
Mamma could sell this time. The furniture now left to us would
fetch nothing and, anyway, we needed it. Every now and then
we tried to cheer ourselves up by telling each other that there
was probably nothing really wrong, though we knew there was.

When we heard the front door close we looked out of the
basement window and saw that the man was walking out of the
garden to his brougham, openly wiping his eyes with his handkerchief, and we hoped that Mamma had simply been comforting
him for a trouble which had nothing to do with us. But Mamma's
face was white when we went upstairs, and she did not have
luncheon with us, she told us that she had a headache and must
lie down. We more or less forgot about the enigmatic incident
when we were out for our walk and at our practice, for we never
would have succeeded in getting through our childhood if we
had not cultivated the art of ignoring the unpleasant till it was
forced on our attention. She came down into the sitting-room

about four, and when Kate rang the bell to tell us that tea was ready in the dining-room we all went together into the hall, and found a strange and handsome lady talking to Kate at the open front door. When she saw Mamma she stepped past Kate into the hall and said, in an affected tone, as if she were reciting in an elocution class, 'I think my husband called on you this morning, I would be glad if you could give me a little of your time.' She had blue-black hair and big brown eyes and red cheeks, and it was all too much; and though she seemed excited she gave an impression of being fundamentally lethargic, it was like seeing a cow running fast. Her hat was too romantic for her round face. Mamma scrutinised her and sighed deeply, and told Kate to give us tea.

When we had finished Kate kept us in the dining-room; and after an hour or so Mamma came into the room, exclaiming, 'Charbovari! Charbovari! It is most extraordinary!' Though the word sounded funny she spoke it tragically.

'What is Charbovari?' we asked.

'Somebody in a book,' she explained wildly. 'His real name was Charles Bovary, they called him Charbovari at school to make fun of him, everybody was always horrible to him. And Emma too! It is all most extraordinary. I am looking for the book they are in.'

'We will find it,' said Mary. We were always finding books for Papa. 'What is it called?'

'It is called *Madame Bovary*, it is by Gustave Flaubert. Did we not put all the French books together in one of the book-cases, or did I only mean to do it?'

We found it for her, and Kate asked her if she would not like some tea, and she said that she wanted nothing, and, with the book open in her hand, went back to the sitting-room. When we halted at the door and asked her if she would rather we stayed with Kate in the kitchen, she said no, that we were never to think we were a trouble to her, but she did not lift her eyes from the page. She sat deep in an armchair, looking very small, and went on reading while we sat on the floor and built castles for Richard Quin with some German bricks she had had when she was little. She was plainly quite unconscious that we were there, which never happened; and she never remembered that it was Saturday night, and that every Saturday night she read the

60

Arabian Nights to us. At first I wondered if we ought to remind
her, for she was not enjoying her book, and from time to time
uttered exclamations which seemed to express recognition of a
distasteful object. But presently she liked it, indeed, she liked it
very much, for she uttered the same cries of pleasure we often
heard when she was playing music which she thought beautiful.
At length we heard the front door open, and Papa came into the
room. We stopped our game, and after wishing him a subdued
good evening we fell silent, expecting that Mamma would tell
us to go away, so that she could tell him about this mysterious
trouble which involved the Mayor and Mayoress of Lovegrove.

But when Papa announced his presence to Mamma by bending
over her she stared absently up at him, smiled brilliantly, and
said, '*Madame Bovary* is really a wonderful book.'

Papa casually agreed. 'Yes. Much better than *L'Education
Sentimentale*, though few French people will say so.'

'I had not read it for years,' Mamma continued happily, 'and
I had forgotten how good it is! The famous scene at the prize-
giving I find not half as remarkable as I used to think it. He
satirises things not worth satirising, but how good is the passage
describing Emma's state of mind when she took up life at home
after the visit to the château at Vaubyessard!'

'I don't remember that,' said Papa. 'What has always remained
in my mind is a chapter where he first gives you the dreams of
Charles Bovary and then Emma's dreams, and builds up their
characters quite solidly out of that.'

'I haven't come to that yet,' said Mamma. 'But this passage
about her life after the visit to the château is the same sort of
trick, an inspired list of little things, Emma takes the Vicomte's
green silk cigar-case out of a cupboard where she has hidden it
and inhales the smell, and she buys a map of Paris and goes walks
on it with her fingertips, and at the end of the chapter you're
convinced that reality has gone from the poor creature's mind for
ever, she is lost.'

'I never could make up my mind whether there is or is not
too much of the pharmacist,' said Papa. 'Well, I shall go and see
if there are any letters in my study,' said Papa, and went out of the
room.

'But there is one thing,' Mamma said to us, 'that I cannot
understand. When Emma and her husband went to stay at the

Vicomte's château a great many people came to luncheon the day after the ball, and the repast lasted ten minutes. Charles Bovary was surprised because no liqueurs were served after the meal, but apparently he wasn't surprised because it only lasted ten minutes. But don't you think that was very strange, children? I do.' She looked enquiringly round the circle of our faces, and then, smiling, lowered her eyes to the page again. But then she put her hand to her forehead. 'How did I come to start reading this book?' she asked us, and then drew a deep breath. 'Oh, I had quite forgotten. I like the book so much that I had quite forgotten. I am really very heartless,' she cried, rising to her feet. 'But art is so much more real than life. Some art is much more real than some life, I mean.'

'Well, if you don't want to go on reading it, read us the *Arabian Nights*,' suggested Mary.

'No, no,' said Mamma. 'I must go and talk to your Papa. At once.' She moved to the door, then turned back. 'It will be so difficult to start talking to him after I have done this idiotic thing,' she said, and wrung her hands, but forced herself to go. We did not see her again that day, Kate came and told us we were to have our suppers with her, and she put us to bed.

We were at first puzzled by the nature of the calamity that had struck our household. We had read a great part of Shakespeare and a good many novels but nothing in them had modified our conviction that Papa and Mamma could not have any very strong interest in each other, as they were not related by blood. I am sure that I then took it for granted that it would have been unnatural if Papa had not felt far deeper emotion for his dead brother Richard Quin, and if it had been put to me I should even have thought that Mamma might be more distressed at a final estrangement with her cousin Constance than if she lost Papa. But as the weeks went on we children were educated on this point. Sometimes it seemed as if nothing unusual were happening, and then Mamma would receive another visit from the Mayor, and, as we lay in bed at night, we would hear the voices of my father and mother grinding quietly against each other in an interminable argument. Every now and then one of them would burst into high and violent speech, and then would be hushed by the other, and for a time they would whisper. Mary and I would have to pretend to be asleep at such times, for Cordelia always seized the opportunity to be an eldest sister, and would accuse us of eavesdropping and say that she would fetch Mamma if we did not lie down and close our eyes at once. But Mary and I slept in beds that were side by side, and when we heard these outbursts and their suppressions she and I stretched out our arms over the gap and held hands in the darkness. They were very touching, these efforts of our father and mother to protect us from knowledge of their conflict, with which we were as familiar as with anything on earth. Finally we would hear my father's lazy, scornful, grating laugh, and the door of the room downstairs was shut sharply as he used to shut it. We knew that our mother was probably still standing with her arm on the chimneypiece, looking down on the fire, as she often did when she was worried. She seemed to draw fresh courage from the sight of flame. Soon we fell asleep.

But it was better when the year grew into December when an anxiety that had been gnawing her was resolved. We always had a lovely Christmas, far lovelier than would have been thought possible in our circumstances. Of the many strange things about my father one of the strangest was his gift for making toys. An old carpenter on his father's estate in Ireland had taught him the elements of his craft when he was still a little boy, and he had kept up the habit of working with wood all his life. Except for his wit, which turned things upside-down, there was no trace of fancy in his speech or his writing, but his fingers dripped with it. We children were not allowed to go into his study or his bedroom after the first week of December lest we should see what he was making for us, and we did not want to break this rule; it would have been as foolish to see the things he made before they were finished as it would have been to hear half a movement of a sonata, half a song. He had already made each of us girls a beautiful dolls' house, a Tudor palace for Cordelia, a Queen Anne mansion for Mary, a Victorian Gothic domestic abbey for me. Now he was filling them not only with furniture but with inhabitants, little wooden figures, whose names and entire lives were given to us by a common revelation delivered piece-meal through the years, after he had started it with the first hint. He would lay a finger on an archway and say to Cordelia, 'This is where young Sir Thomas Champernowne escaped from his guards and made his way to the West Country'; he would say to Mary, 'That was

Lydia Monument's bedroom'; and he would say to me, 'In that saloon Tarquin Katerfelto performed some of his most extraordinary conjuring tricks, which some say were real magic,' and what we learned later of these people was surely not invented but recovered. Even if I went today and stood among the ruins of the house on the burned spot which was our sitting-room, and looked down on the place by the hearth where we put our dolls' houses on trays, I might still learn more about Sir Thomas Champernowne, Lydia Monument, Tarquin Katerfelto.

Mamma was also a creator of this world, and indeed she performed the very important feat of making us visibly a part of it. She had kept many of the dresses she had worn when she was young, and she had found some very fine ones packed away in the drawers of Aunt Clara's furniture, and every year she opened her 'rubbish trunk' and found the material for fancy dresses which had some relation to the toys Papa was making for us, and which we wore on Christmas Day and New Year's Eve and on Twelfth Night. She was under grave handicaps as a dressmaker, for the nervous force in her fingers made it torture for her to handle needles, but she would sit down at the sewing-machine and with wild slashes of the scissors and demoniacal driving of the wheel produce romantic garments which pleased her sense of beauty and gave us happiness and brought her nearer to Papa. Now I come to think of it, this Christmas dressmaking and nothing else I can remember in their life as they had come to live it at that time gave her access to the vein of imagination in my father which he was now repudiating, but which must have been what made him fall in love with her in spite of her inconvenient genius and integrity.

She had said to us several times, 'I do not know what sort of Christmas you are going to have this year. Your poor Papa is very busy.' We had not been able to tell her outright that we thought she was wrong, and that Papa would make us our toys as usual, because that would have betrayed how much we knew. But we took care to say in front of Papa that Richard Quin had stopped breaking things very early, and we thought that if anybody gave him a fortress he would know how to play with it; and of course it was all right. By the first week in December Papa and Mamma were at work together, sharing secrets, hiding things. She looked more than happy, she was uplifted. I fancy she was not only enjoying the renewed companionship with him, she was telling herself that she had been wrong in fearing that he was wholly given over to cruelty, since he had come back to his duties rather than spoil our Christmas. But of course it was not so. I who loved him too and can see him from a better distance am sure that he had left the Mayoress of Lovegrove with an abruptness that broke the poor silly's heart, only because his fingers were itching for the pleasure they were always given at this time of year, his imprisoned imagination insisted on its annual holiday.

But my mother did not enjoy complete peace of mind. She was worried, Mary and I could see, about Cordelia. We did not wonder, for we were worried about her too. When we had been smaller we had loved her very much as a sister, although we realised that she was an eldest sister, and therefore it was our duty to kick and scratch and bite her quite often, first of all for our own sake, to defend our rights, but also for her sake, to protect her from the moral deterioration which we could see would overtake all eldest sisters who were not checked. But since we had come to Lovegrove we had realised that there was something wrong with her. We were finding it easy to be happy, for though there was this queer thing about the Mayor and Mayoress, we knew it would be all right in the end, and this new servant Kate was someone we loved at once; but Cordelia was miserable. I remember sitting up in bed one morning and looking at her while she was still asleep, and thinking how very pretty she was with her red-gold curls and her white skin, which was quite blue on her eyelids and in the delicate hollows of her temple, and then as I looked, wakefulness came into her face, and it was the same as resentment. She rolled her head from side to side, screwing up her eyes for quite a long time before she could bear to open them, and then she stared about her, seeking to find a way of turning what she saw to her advantage. When her eyes reached the clothes lying on my chair, she started up, pointed a forefinger at me, and began to scold me for my untidiness.

'Cross beast,' I said, 'your own clothes are just as untidy.' It was true; and if it had been Mary who had been in a temper with me she would have recognised the truth and stopped. But Cordelia went on scolding me.

At school, we noticed, she got on discreditably well. The wrong sort of teacher liked her in the wrong sort of way, and they were constantly giving her what they called 'little tasks' and mentioning her as an example of *esprit de corps*; and she spoke to them with an air of professed insipidity which we took seriously as a betrayal of childhood. Of course grown-ups wanted children to be blanks, but no decent child, with parents like ours, would encourage them. We saw her paying too high a price for the approval of people who were not like Papa and Mamma, and we felt about her as a soldier in a besieged citadel might feel about a comrade who is meditating desertion. Quite often we hated her. But the love of the flesh which binds a family together in its infancy was still strong. I hated the cold much more than anybody else in the family, and she used sometimes to take me into her bed if she heard me tossing and grumbling in the night, although she was a light sleeper and it was a sacrifice. Often we loved her.

But even so we recognised Cordelia as a complicated problem, and it distressed us that Mamma, though regarding her as a problem, saw it as simple. To her Cordelia was someone who could not play the violin and who insisted on doing so. She saw the problem half-solved when Cordelia took her violin to school, saying vaguely she had a chance to practise there, and ceased to ask her for evening lessons. It even appeared to her possible that this might be a subterfuge, and that Cordelia had recognised her lack of talent and had adopted this way of quietly giving up her studies. Her optimism made her find further food for hope in Cordelia's request, which was made at the beginning of December, that she should be allowed to bring one of her teachers, a Miss Beevor, home to tea. Mamma asked what subject she taught and Cordelia replied, 'Advanced French,' and Mamma was delighted, thinking that perhaps Cordelia was developing her own talent for languages. We knew well enough that Cordelia was closest to what we called the scum of the teachers, but we could not tell tales, and we knew Mamma would grasp the situation as soon as Miss Beevor would arrive. But we became alarmed when we saw how vigorously Mamma had imagined a visit and a visitor which was going to solve completely the problem of her eldest daughter. Because of the advanced French, Mamma had that morning travelled some

66

distance to a bakery which sold brioches and babas, and she put on her best clothes, in order not to be disgraced before Miss Beevor, whom she pictured as being unusually elegant for a suburban schoolmistress, as a result of long residence in Paris. As half-past four approached she walked restlessly about the sitting-room, filling the vases with Parma violets, a flower which she always associated with France, and speaking with incredible bravery her ambitious thoughts. 'If Papa goes on doing so well, we should be able to afford to send Cordelia for six months to France, and six months to Germany, and then to Girton or Newnham.'

Just then Cordelia came in, looking the perfect school-girl as our teachers would have had her, neat and submissive. She looked round the room and acted anguish; and indeed if one had not been told that my mother was wearing her best clothes one would never have guessed it. She pointed at the revolving bookcase containing our *Encyclopaedia Britannica* and asked solemnly, 'Can that not be put somewhere else?'

'Why should it, dear?' enquired Mamma.

'Miss Beevor will think it very odd to see an *Encyclopaedia Britannica* in the drawing-room,' said Cordelia.

'Would a schoolmistress not be glad to see an *Encyclopaedia Britannica* in any room?' asked Mamma.

Mary and I stuck our tongues out at Cordelia, and made quite hideous faces, she knew quite well that we had to have the *Encyclopaedia Britannica* in the drawing-room, because Papa had to have the third downstairs room for his study. We also knew Mamma grieved perpetually over the horrid furniture she had instead of Aunt Clara's. Cordelia said mechanically, 'Mamma, make Mary and Rose behave,' but just at that moment Miss Beevor arrived.

We instinctively knew that we hated her and hoped we would never see her again. She was not at all as Mamma had imagined her, being a tall and sallow woman, with a battered Pre-Raphaelite look to her, wearing a sage-green coat and dress and a wide felt hat of a darker green, and a long string of amber beads. In those days, when skirts reached the ground, a big woman in badly cut clothes sad in colour had a massively depressing effect hard to imagine today. She was carrying a white hide handbag stamped with the word 'Bayreuth' in pokerwork. She did nothing to recommend herself when we had got used to her appearance, for though she was civil enough to Mamma her eyes went at once to Cordelia and stayed there, fixed in lustre. She evidently liked her very much. It was a great effort for her to force her attention back to Mamma, and, an even greater one, make it stay there, for through no fault of hers she was perplexed by what Mamma was saying to her. She seemed puzzled why brioches and babas should have been procured for her, and it turned out that she had never lived in Paris, or in any other part of France. She did not even teach French, but she had taken some sort of diploma in the subject long ago, so that when Miss Raine, the senior French mistress, had been borne away, with the new complaint of appendicitis, she had taken some of her classes.

'But,' she said, after an exchange of humorous glances with Cordelia, 'your little girl will tell you that very often I had to fall back on Dick Tay.'

'Who is Dick Tay?' asked Mamma, stupidly.

'Dictée,' whispered Cordelia savagely.

My mother grew red with shame. 'You must excuse me,' she said. 'The children will tell you how very deaf I am.' She went on to invent some ridiculous mistakes that she said she had made, through deafness, then to explain how happy we all three seemed to be at school, and how much she and Papa liked being at Lovegrove, but then she stopped talking, because Miss Beevor was not listening to her, but kept on looking at Cordelia. With a distracted gesture she put a baba on her plate when we had nearly all finished, and had to eat it all by herself, while the silence grew more oppressive, and it became more and more obvious that Cordelia and Miss Beevor were giving each other signals. Presently Kate came in to take away the tea-things and Cordelia made an excuse to go out with her.

Miss Beevor cleared her throat and said: 'It was in the French class I first met Cordelia. I wouldn't wish poor Miss Raine to have had appendicitis on my account, but that is how I came to meet Cordelia, and I can't help being very grateful. Of course I saw at once that there was something special about her.'

'You think there is?' said Mamma, hopefully.

'I was so sure she was an exceptional child that I asked her to stay behind instead of going down to the eleven-o'clock break,' Miss Beevor continued, her eyes misted.

'Well, is she exceptional?' asked Mamma with interest.

'Oh, of course she is!' exclaimed Miss Beevor, clapping her hands, indignant and smiling at the same time. 'And what was so exciting, as you can imagine, was finding that her special talent was for my very own subject!'

'What is your subject?' asked Mamma urgently.

'Why, I teach the violin,' said Miss Beevor, with proud modesty.

Mamma was unable to speak, and presently Miss Beevor continued, 'Your little girl has remarkable musical gifts.'

'But Cordelia has no musical gift at all,' said Mamma. 'She couldn't tell the difference between Beethoven and Tchaikovsky.'

'But you are quite mistaken,' said Miss Beevor, 'it is amazing, truly amazing, how many classical compositions our little Cordelia can recognise.'

'I didn't say,' my mother corrected her waspishly, 'that poor Cordelia couldn't tell Beethoven from Tchaikovsky, I said she couldn't tell the difference between them.' She waved a tragic hand at us. 'Mary, Rose, go away.'

Miss Beevor left the house about half an hour later, and Mamma came into the dining-room, where Mary and I were doing our homework, and asked sternly, 'Did either of you know this was going on?'

'Of course not,' we protested, 'we would have told you about it, Mamma.'

'To think of Cordelia going off every morning to the school and playing the violin with that woman day after day, and I here, without the slightest suspicion,' said poor Mamma, covering her face with her hands. 'Oh, this has been a season of deceit.'

Papa came in, dazed with preoccupation, and when he saw us children hid what he had in his hand behind his back. 'That stuff doesn't take paint,' he told Mamma sadly.

'Kate thought it might not,' said Mamma, caught up into happiness by his presence. 'We will find something else.' Before she left the room she turned to us and said gravely, 'I had to be very plain with that woman, I told her she must not fill poor Cordelia's head with all that nonsense. So if your poor sister seems unhappy you must be kind to her.'

69

But Cordelia did not seem at all unhappy. Nobody seemed unhappy in our house as Christmas came towards us, bearing its sure and certain rapture. Mamma was so much restored by her communion with Papa that she dealt courageously with a grief which might have turned to something else, and been a deprivation for all of us. She said to me one day, 'Rose, you are little, but you are very sensible. I showed you the letter I had from my cousin Constance. Do you think it would do any harm if I sent presents to her and the little girl?'

I told her that I did not believe it could ever do any harm to send people presents. So she cut up a dress of some light, washable material she had worn to play at a summer concert in Berlin seventeen years before, and made it into an apron which Constance might like to wear when she was doing housework; Constance's husband did not give her much money, she had to do a lot of housework. For Rosamund she got Papa to carve a wooden angel copied from a photograph of a group in a church at Nuremberg. He said it was very difficult and he could only give a rough impression of the statue, but he made a little figure that looked as if it were bending down to save someone. Mamma mentioned Berlin and Nuremberg so often in connection with these presents that I asked her if Constance and Rosamund had lived much in Germany, but she told me that so far as she knew they had never been there. These presents had just suggested themselves as suitable, and they had associations with these two places she had known well, so she had talked of them. That was all.

In case these two presents should arrive a long time before Christmas, and Constance should feel obliged to send presents in return, Mamma arranged for the apron and the doll to be delivered at Constance's home on the other side of South London by one of those local carrier waggons which still crawled all over the suburbs, and she made the carrier promise that they should be held back till Christmas Eve itself, so that Constance would have no time to send presents in response. And while we were spending Christmas Eve as we always did, by having our hair washed and drying it before the fire while we roasted chestnuts and drank milk, my mother had one of the most intense moments of pleasure that I ever saw her experience. Suddenly we heard the clack of hooves and the jingle of bells. Instantly my mother

knew that on the other side of London an equal delicacy had been
practised on the inspiration, she at once believed, of an equal
love. Constance had sent us presents by her local carrier.
Mamma told us what she believed to have happened in a reci-
tative like a long trumpet call and rushed out to test her faith.
She was right. When we followed her to the front door, stumbling over our dressing-gowns, we found her taking in the
parcels, which looked as if they had come from a far country,
for they were tied up with a peculiar white braid with a red
cross-stitch pattern on it, very pretty and old-fashioned. Mother
would not let us open them, of course. She ran with them into
Papa's study and put them with the rest of the presents we were
to be given on Christmas morning, and then she hurried us back
to the fireside, because our hair was still damp. She sat down
beside us and wept with joy because Constance was still fond of
her. That evening we lay in our beds and listened to the voice
of our father and mother as they dressed the Christmas tree in
the room below, and my mother's voice came fresh and eager
like a thrush's song. Once or twice they laughed for quite a
long time.

IV

WE NEVER had a better Christmas up till four o'clock. We woke up quite late, of course, because we had been so long in going to sleep, and found the stockings at the end of our beds. But before we could see what Papa and Mamma had put in them, Richard Quin staggered in, holding in front of him the big stocking Mamma had lent him because his socks were too small to hold anything. He could not bear to look in to it for fear of his own delight. He asked hoarsely, 'Would there be soldiers, do you think?' He always wanted tin soldiers, for Christmas and birthdays, and whenever anybody gave him any money to spend. We told him there certainly would. But he could not bear to deal with the stocking, he was all to pieces at the prospect of exquisite pleasure piling on exquisite pleasure, all day long. We urged him to be a man and start taking out his presents, but he sat down on Mary's bed and rocked himself and gasped, his eyes glazed, 'And there are better presents downstairs, aren't there?'

We told him that there would be in the sitting-room, where the Christmas tree was, the same as there had been last year in Edinburgh.

'Then why,' he panted, 'don't we go downstairs and get those in case anything happens to them and then hurry back to these?'

'Why should we do that?' asked Mary, cuddling him to her, 'there's all the time in the world.' It was a phrase that my mother often used when we hurried a bar.

His face grew piteous and he cried, 'There's not, there's not.'

Mary hugged him closer and they rocked together, tic-toc, tic-toc, while she sang, 'There's all the time in the world,' and he sang back, 'There's not, there's not, there's not,' his downy face easing into unmalicious mischief, his grey eyes sending coquettish glances under his black lashes at his three sisters.

Cordelia and I went and knelt before him, and she kissed his left foot and I kissed the right, while Mary went on singing,

'There's all the time in the world,' and he sang back, 'There's not, there's not,' bubbles of laughter forming on his lips, which were a pale but very bright pink. We all wished the moment could last forever.

Then Kate our servant came in and bent her tall body over us, so that we could kiss her, which we did all at once, Richard Quin scrambling up her bodice from Mary's arms till she took him to her. We all loved Kate very much, and she loved us, particularly Mamma, although she seemed a little frightened of her, and we realised that there was something about Kate which grieved Mamma. She had given us lovely presents, for each of us girls a handkerchief hemstitched by herself and embroidered with our names not just initials, in raised white letters, and for Richard two sentry-boxes with two Guardsmen sentinels in busbies. We gave her hatpins; we had covered the heads with sealing-wax which Papa had helped us to make look like flowers. She ran upstairs and brought down her hat, which was enormous. In those days women of all classes wore large hats, and women like Kate, who was something a little more gypsyish than an ordinary servant, wore hats as big as cartwheels, adorned with feathers. She put the huge plumey circle on her head and pierced it with our pins, and turned round and round, still looking like a decent sailor lad dressed in skirts. I do not think there was any aspiration towards beauty expressed in her possession of that hat. She had simply got into uniform.

I said, 'Kate, how strange it is to think that last Christmas we did not know you and you did not know us!'

Looking at the image of her wooden face under the great hat in the mirror on our wardrobe, she said, 'Last Christmas I was in the town where I was born, and I'll never go there again.'

We saw that tears were slowly running down her cheeks and we said that it was a shame, and wanted to know who would not let her go back, but she replied, 'Nobody could keep me out if I wanted to go back, nor my mother neither. Only I like it better here with you and your Papa and your Mamma.' Then we realised that she was grave not because she was sad but because she was happy, like the great dogs at the Pentland farm when they sat at Mr. Weir's feet by the hearth in the evening, and, as if she had been a great dog, we patted her. But we were without condescension. We respected her deeply, for we had seen her put her hand in the oven, with a batch of pastry on the kitchen table behind her ready to be put in, and take her hand out in a second, and shake her head, and say sternly, 'Not yet,' and do it three or four times and always say, 'Not yet,' and then suddenly say, 'Now,' and the pastry was always better than anybody else's. Also her mother had been a washerwoman at Portsmouth for thirty years before, for reasons we could never quite understand, she had had to move to Wimbledon that summer; and Kate knew many mysterious secrets about laundry work. She could even wash our horrible winter underclothing so that it did not scratch. She had the same relations with everything in the kitchen that Mamma had with her piano.

We were telling Kate that we thought the hat needed still another hatpin to look really grand, and that we would make it on Boxing Day, when Mamma came in, brilliant and flashing, as if she were about to give a performance on the stage. She was not looking very well. The loss of Aunt Clara's furniture, and the embarrassing circumstances of the move from Edinburgh to Lovegrove, and the trouble about the Mayor and Mayoress, whatever that might have been, had left her very thin. Also she had been working too hard over our toys. But this was Christmas morning, and she made herself a star by her strong will. We gathered round her and kissed her with adoration, and she bade us dress quickly and hurry down to breakfast, we were already late, we would not have time to be given our presents and enjoy them before we went to church. Then she whisked out, making the queer noise which she always made when she remembered something which must be done at once, which years afterwards I recognised as very much like the sound a flock of starlings makes before it leaves the ground. Kate led away Richard Quin to wash and dress him, and we girls took turns to wash in the bathroom, the ones who were waiting their turn unpacking our stockings, which were full of the best things we had had at any Christmas yet, we thought: little dolls, for though we did not exactly play with dolls any more, we were getting too old, we liked to have dolls about, wreaths made of shells and sealing-wax to wear when we played at going to the balls father had been to at Buckingham Palace and the Hofburg in Vienna and the Winter Palace in St. Petersburg when he was young, pretty painted pencil-boxes, each of us had a new one in our stocking every Christmas, with the year on it in gold, and packets of sugar almonds in different colours. Then we put on our best clothes, which like Mamma's would not have been recognised as such by any stranger.

The rooms of course were changed to apartments in a green palace. Papa and Mamma had bedecked them with holly and mistletoe and the fuzzed branches of witch-hazel that they had found in the garden. At the head of the breakfast table sat Papa, looking very handsome. It is not considered complimentary to say that a human being resembles a horse; but sometimes a fine horse has a star in its eye, that tells of its capacity for speed, its inexhaustible spirit, and there was that sort of light in my father's eye. We all kissed him, and he lingered over the greeting of each one of us. Then Kate came into the dining-room, carrying Richard, who looked at Papa and spread out his arms and said simply 'O'. The meanest intelligence would have known at once that if that sound had to be put down on paper it would have to be spelled without an h. It was a pure circle, filled with adoration. Papa smiled back at him with the same adoration and said, 'Merry Christmas, Richard Quin.' My mother stood behind them, quite free of her habitual frenzy, soft and serene, brooding over the smiling pair.

There was nothing by our plates except the headgear we would wear in the house that day: a Lifeguard's helmet made in gilded cardboard for Richard Quin, and for us girls different-coloured stars set on hairpins. The present-giving ceremony was elaborate and followed in about half an hour, for Mamma had to clear the table and tell Kate what she wanted done to start the preparations for dinner. We went upstairs to our room and collected the presents we had made for Papa and Mamma and waited there till we were called. Then we stood outside the dining-room until Mamma began to play a piano arrangement of Bach's 'Shepherd's Christmas Music', and then we marched in in single file, followed by Kate, and stood round the Christmas tree with our backs to it and sang a carol. That year it was 'Silent Night, Holy Night'. Then we handed over our presents to Papa and Mamma. I know what they were, for Mary and I wrote them down in a little book, which somehow never got lost. Cordelia had knitted Papa a silk necktie and had made Mamma a set of muslin collars and cuffs. She was the best needlewoman of the three of us. Mary had practised considerable deception over the money given her for milk and buns at eleven, and had gone to a junk shop we passed on our way to school and bought Papa a little eighteenth-century book about the sights of Paris with pretty coloured pictures and Mamma a water-colour of Capri where she had spent a wonderful holiday when she was young. I had painted a wooden box to hold big matches for Papa to keep in his study and had made a shopping bag for Mamma out of plaited straw. Richard Quin had given the matches to put in my match-box and Mamma a bright pink cake of scented soap which he had chosen himself. We were hampered because we had almost no pocket-money, but really these presents were not quite rubbish. All except the necktie and the soap were still in the house when, many years later, we left it, and I do not think they had been preserved simply because Mamma loved us, I believe they survived because of their usefulness and prettiness. We were not specially accomplished or sensible children, but, with Papa and Mamma and Kate in the house, we were propelled along the groove of a competent tradition.

When Papa and Mamma had had their presents we had ours. They were lovely. I really cannot think, looking back over a lifetime in which I have known many quite opulent Christmases, that any children have ever had much lovelier Christmas presents. We had known that Papa was making us new furniture and inhabitants for our dolls' houses, but he had done better than that. He had given Cordelia's Tudor palace a maze and a sunk garden and a pleached walk, like the one in *Much Ado About Nothing*; he had given Mary's Queen Anne mansion a walled garden with espalier trees all around it and a vinery outside built against the south wall; and he had given my Victorian Gothic abbey a small park with a looking-glass lake with a rocky island in it surmounted by a mock hermitage. Out of her old dresses Mother had made a pale-green Mary Queen of Scots dress for Cordelia, an eighteenth-century white dress for Mary, a rose-coloured crinoline dress for me, and a Three Musketeer uniform with a cardboard sword for Richard Quin. Like everything else that Mamma did each was unique, we had never seen anything like them before, each one of them was something only she would have imagined. So enchanted were we with these big presents that we had hardly time to look at the presents Constance had sent us before we had to dress for church, except to see that for us girls she had pretty little pinafores, each with a hair-ribbon to match, and for Richard Quin a little shirt. There was an air of cool composure about the needlework which made these garments as distinctive as my mother's wilder work.

It had been decided beforehand that Richard Quin was to go to church with us for the first time on Christmas morning. But he was bemused with his toys. He had not even begun to empty his stocking, but was dragging it about with him. If anybody tried to relieve him of it, he said, 'Not yet, not yet, in a minute,' but he could not bring himself to take his eyes off the fortress Papa had made for him, a proper fortress with casemates and redoubts and glacis and a garrison numbering twenty, all in silver-foil armour. He could not bear to touch it, he liked it so much. So Mamma took pity on him and said that he need not go, perhaps he was too little, it would wait till next Christmas. But he said that if Papa was going he would like to go too. So we started out through a crisp morning, Mamma going to the steps to see us off. 'Gloves?' she said sternly to us three, for all over England little girls were starting a revolt against gloves, which was to succeed before very long, but was then discouraged by all adults. 'I wish I could come with you,' she sighed, 'I would enjoy the service.'

'Oh, come!' we cried, and Papa asked, 'Can you not come, my dear?'

'If I did, you would have no dinner,' she said. 'Kate could not do it alone, and set the table, and do the beds as well. How strange it is to think of all the women who have to stay on Christmas morning to look after the dinner, and get no Christian blessing, like so many witches.' She checked herself, we did not see why, and waved goodbye and shut the door, and we started off through a scene that, when I remember it, seems peopled by marionettes. A little white dog ran across the road under the hooves of an old horse drawing an old cab, and its master bent and gave it a gentle lash with a lead for disobedience; two men came out of a shop and let the iron rollers of the shop-front shutter fall noisily behind them; a company of Salvation Army officers, the men in their peaked caps and the women in their bonnets, passed by, carrying their musical instruments. Only the horse and dog seem real, the men seem like ill-dressed dolls in

77

their so short coats, the women in their so long skirts. All these beings moved at the bottom of a sea of happiness, an old gentleman we did not know said 'Merry Christmas' to us, we passed many other families of children that danced as they walked, as we were doing.

In church we were so contented that we did not think of the singing of the choir as music and did not approve or disapprove, but gratefully took it that it was giving tongue to what was in our hearts. 'How bright,' Mary whispered in my ear, 'the silver dishes on the altar are.' We liked the holly round the pulpit, the white chrysanthemums on the altar. Of late Mary and I had doubts about religion, we wished God had worked miracles which would have enabled Mamma to keep Aunt Clara's furniture and saved Papa from his disappointment over the deal in Manchester, but now faith was restored to us. We saw that it was good of God to send his son to earth because man had sinned, it was the opposite of keeping out of trouble, which was mean, it was the opposite of what Papa's relatives were doing in not wanting to see him just because he had been unlucky. We liked the way Richard Quin stood on the seat of the pew and, though he had been told he must be good and sit as still as a mouse in this holy place, nuzzled against Papa's shoulder and sometimes put up his face for a kiss, certain that showing love for Papa must be part of being good. There was a sermon which Mary and I approved, for it was, roughly speaking, against crossness and we thought crossness was the worst thing in the world. People were always being cross with us at school, it made the thing impossible. It broke Mamma's heart when Papa was cross to her. Cordelia was always being cross to us. But I was disappointed with Mary when she murmured, 'We must try to be less cross to Cordelia.' I did not believe there was any hope of solving our problem that way. Outside the church people offered my father greetings about which even then I recognised a special distant quality. I realise now that it showed deference without confidence. So might they have wished a merry Christmas to a shabby Prospero, exiled even from his own island, but still a magician.

We had just time to get into our fancy dresses before dinner, which was wonderful. One of Papa's relatives in Ireland who never wanted to see us always sent us a turkey and a ham, and we had both sausage and chestnut stuffing with the turkey. Mamma had worried because the removal from Scotland had meant that she could not make her Christmas puddings before October, which was later than she had ever left it before, but really the one we had could not have been better. Each of us children got a charm out of the pudding, which we thought happened by chance. Afterwards we had tangerines, and almonds and raisins, and Carlsbad plums from the box with a picture of a plum on it which Papa's City friend, Mr. Langham, sent us every Christmas. We could not have crackers, none of us could bear the bang. On the sideboard there was one of the bottles of port which the margarine manufacturer had sent Papa, and he poured out two glasses for himself and Mamma, and then he asked Mamma if it were not true that Kate's mother, who was now a washerwoman at Wimbledon, and her brother, a blue-jacket on leave, were having their dinner with her in the kitchen. Since it was so, Cordelia was sent down to ask him to come up and drink a glass of port with Papa. The brother was younger than Kate, and indeed far more fragile and girlish, and at first he was shy. But Papa and the port warmed him, and he sat for quite a while, telling us of Gibraltar and Cyprus and Malta, and hearing Papa's stories of what they had been like in his day.

When he got up to go he hesitated, and we thought his shyness had taken him again. Then he said, very gravely, 'I have to thank you for being so good to Kate and my mother when they were in trouble.'

'It is nothing,' said Papa, smiling.

'We have already been repaid many times by your sister's kindness to all the children, and all the hard work she does,' said Mamma, looking very uncomfortable.

'Yes, ma'am, but when you stood by them in their trouble she hadn't done much work for you,' said the sailor. 'Kate says she hadn't been in the house three days when the policeman came, and you stood by her from the first moment.'

'It is nothing, nothing,' Mamma broke in very hastily, with a quick look at my father.

'Of course I know that it's not as if it were a real crime they had against my poor old mother and my sister,' the sailor continued. 'It's just a way that the women of our family have had since time out of mind, and very natural in a harbour town.

They had a cheek, those magistrates, to talk of sending my mother and my sister to prison. Why, fining them the other two times was cheek too, considering how long our family's been in the town.'

'What little we could do for your mother and sister,' said Mamma, standing up and shaking the sailor's hand, 'we gladly did. Goodbye, goodbye, and may you have Christmas dinner with us every year for many years to come.'

After he had left the room Mamma sank back into her chair and covered her face with her hands, and Papa, looking much amused, poured out another glass of port and dipped a cluster of raisins in it.

Cordelia asked, 'But what did Kate do that they wanted to send her to prison for it?'

'I think you had better tell them, my dear,' Papa said. 'It is not so terrible, after all.'

'But I think it is,' said Mamma. 'I want them to go on loving Kate, for she is a good girl, but I want them to hate what she did. That is very difficult.'

'Is it?' asked Papa in a teasing way. 'I have an idea that people find that very thing quite easy to do.'

'You are mistaken if you think they find it easy,' said Mamma, with a sudden flash of temper. Papa did not answer, he looked into the distance while he took a raisin out of the port and lifted it to his mouth. I saw the fullness of his lips, the whiteness of his teeth under his moustache. I felt angry because Papa and Mamma had so many secrets from us.

Mary said, tears in her eyes, 'But tell us what it was that poor Kate did?'

'Oh, I had better tell you,' said Mamma, 'in case you think she stole, which she would never do. She had been with us for just three days, as the boy said, when a policeman came and said that they wanted Kate and her mother, because they had run away from Portsmouth when they were awaiting trial. It seemed that Kate's mother had been — oh, do not think it was not a wicked thing, though she is such a nice woman — telling fortunes. Oh, dear.'

'Why is that so wrong?' I asked defensively.

'Of course it is wrong. You see, when sailors are away for a long time their wives get frightened lest their ships should have sunk, and they go to women who say they have a gift for seeing what is far away and they fill a bucket with water, and what has happened to the ships appears to them in the water.'

'But surely,' said Mary, in the tones of an advocate, 'it is nice for the sailors' wives to know what has happened to their husbands.'

'No, it is not nice at all,' cried my mother. 'For some of the women who say they have this gift are frauds and liars, and cheat the poor creatures out of their money, and though the others may have gifts, what company must they keep, the wretched spirits who hang about this earth when they should leave it! Oh, children, never pry into hidden things, the supernatural is always so very dirty. But it seems that in Kate's family the women have always done this thing, it must have started long ago when people did not understand, so you cannot blame her and her mother. And they have promised that in this house there shall be nothing, there will not be even tea-leaf readings. And you must help them keep their promise if you have the chance.'

'I hope nobody saw the policeman come to the house,' said Cordelia. 'We had just arrived, our neighbours would not know the sort of people we were.'

'But how was it that if the policeman came to take Kate back to Portsmouth he went away without her?' asked Mary.

'Let us help Kate now by clearing the table,' said Mamma, rising from her chair, 'otherwise you will never be able to take me out before tea.'

Papa said, laughing quite loud, 'Since you ask, Mary, the policeman got it into his head from something that was said to him that Kate was not the girl he wanted.'

'How fortunate!' we exclaimed.

'Yes, yes,' said Mamma. 'Hurry now, dears.'

We changed from our fancy dresses into our outdoor clothes, and while Papa stayed with Richard Quin we took Mamma for a little walk. We passed a church and she suddenly cried out with pleasure because she saw lights behind the stained-glass windows at that unlikely hour. When we got inside the service was nearly over, but Mamma was grateful for the twenty minutes or so that she had in the half-empty church. 'Now I have not had a wholly heathen Christmas,' she said, when we came out into a world blackening before a rich gold sunset, 'it is terrible if I should be

denied Christian burial just because turkeys will not baste themselves.' A cold wind blew from the sunset, it had been warm in
the church. Mamma shuddered and said, 'Let's see if your poor
old mother can still run.' Of course she could; we ran quite a
long way, we were nearly home when she had to ask us to stop.
Before we went into the house she asked us to be careful never
to say anything to poor Kate about her trouble.

We girls all went up to our room and changed back into our
fancy dresses. These were of course very roughly made. Mamma
was so busy and so tired and could use needles with such difficulty
that there were always defects in them which we had to remedy.
This time Mamma had forgotten to put a hole for the fang of the
buckle in the belt which covered the raw seam she had left at
the waist. I asked Cordelia if she thought I could safely snip a
hole in the silk with the point of my scissors, but she was dressing
in a great hurry, and she told me with an oddly fussy, consequential air that she had no time to look at it; and Mary was not
much good at that kind of thing. So I went downstairs and asked
Mamma, who was helping Kate to set the table for tea and telling
her about Constance's presents. 'There are hours of work in
each one of them,' she was saying, happily. When I showed her
my belt she said, 'Oh, my love, you must forgive me. Look,
Kate, you see what I mean. My cousin would rather die than
give anyone such work.' She said she thought we could drill a
hole between the threads with a stiletto which Papa kept on his
desk to pierce his manuscript to take the paper-fasteners. I went
into the sitting-room to ask Papa if we might borrow it, and then
came back to tell her that Papa said we could, and that he and
Richard Quin were playing with the fortress, but that Richard
Quin had his stocking beside him not yet unpacked, and that
sometimes he turned to it, and said, 'That too.' Turning from
the table, she said, 'Everything has gone very well today,' and
then sighed and added, 'so far.' But she was humming again by
the time we had crossed the passage and opened the study door.

Then she ceased to hum. Inside the room there was standing a
woman who appeared to us for a moment as a total stranger.
Then I recognised her as Miss Beevor, the teacher whom Cordelia had once brought to tea. My wonder at her presence in my
father's study was confused and even eclipsed by wonder whether
any human being could really have such a yellow skin. This

82

jaundiced effect was the work of her dress, which was made of bright violet velveteen, and of her hat, which was only slightly softer in hue. She was obviously much embarrassed at being discovered, and dipped and cringed before us, nervously transferring a roll of music to her left hand from her right, which she then offered to my mother. She said in a flat voice, 'A little surprise,' and my mother said, 'Yes?' without taking her hand. I realised that she had entirely forgotten Miss Beevor and thought her a total stranger and was speculating whether she was a lunatic or an unusual type of burglar. Her eyes then fell on the brooch which Miss Beevor was wearing, a mosaic representing two doves drinking from a fountain. My mother was by now exhausted by her efforts to give us a good Christmas, and the shock of discovering this stranger in Papa's study deprived her of all her self-control. She stared at this brooch with a positive grimace of disapproval.

It was at this point that Cordelia entered the room, looking lovely in her Tudor dress, and holding her violin and bow. On seeing Miss Beevor confronted by my mother and myself, she uttered an exclamation of annoyance and uttered another which was quite angry, when she looked from my mother's face, on which there was fixed this extraordinary grimace, to the terrified Miss Beevor's fluttering eyes and lips. For the first time I realised that a visitor from outside might think it strange that a pretty little girl like Cordelia should be the daughter of an emaciated and shabby and nerve-jerked woman like Mamma, and would for that reason be sorry for Cordelia; and for the first time I realised that Cordelia might share that stranger's opinion.

She said, with a capable air, 'Mamma, don't you remember Miss Beevor? You know, she came to tea.'

Mamma uttered a sharp sound which she tried, too late, to render cordial and welcoming, and extended her hand to Miss Beevor, who took it tremulously, murmuring again, 'A little surprise.'

'Yes, Mamma,' said Cordelia, 'Miss Beevor has been helping me with a surprise Christmas present for you. She made a proud flourish with her bow, and Mamma, who could no longer speak, pointed at her violin with an air of readiness to take any blow.

'Yes, Mamma,' said Cordelia. 'Miss Beevor has been teaching me a piece to play to you. We have been working so hard to get it right so that even you would like it.'

'You see, I have been giving Cordelia quite a lot of lessons,' said Miss Beevor. Usually,' the poor woman added, stroking Cordelia's hair, so that the force of her rebuke should be directed solely on my mother and not be thought to extend to her favourite, 'an extra. But I am proud to make my lessons a gift to your daughter.'

My mother was silent for a second. She had drooped beneath the same lassitude she sometimes showed when she had to deal with a dunning tradesman, or a nail in the sole of one of our shoes. She got the tradesman to go away, the nail was hammered down or prised out, but one felt that however much she rested after this ordeal she would never get back to what she had been before. 'How wonderfully kind,' she said. 'You must forgive me for not recognising you, Christmas is such a rush for me that I lose my wits. So you have been teaching Cordelia and have taught her a solo?' She stooped and kissed Cordelia very tenderly. 'Now let us go to the sitting-room and hear it,' she said, and held the door open for Miss Beevor, turning her head to give me the penetrating look which we knew was her signal that she at once expected us to behave well and recognised that it would be difficult for us to do so.

In the sitting-room Papa was still explaining to Richard Quin all about the passages and chambers inside the fortress, and Mary had come downstairs in her eighteenth-century dress, with her dark hair piled on the top of her head, and was sitting in the only chair she could find with a high back, doing what school-mistresses called "lolling" in it, reading a little volume of Mrs. Radcliffe's, *The Romance of the Forest*, which Papa had given her as a Christmas-tree present. I was alarmed because neither of them seemed to understand when Mamma introduced Miss Beevor that something was going to happen even worse than her being there, though this was a terrible breach of the family tradition that no stranger came into our house on Christmas Day. Papa was wearing the look of braked perception with which he regarded any scientific problem life might bring him, such as the breakdown of a paraffin stove, or whether the swelling we once all had on our throats was mumps. It was as if he thought that he might understand what was wrong if he could restrain the tendency of his mind to rush past the problem to something more interesting. He was in fact wondering, as I had done, why a woman should have such a yellow skin. Mary's mouth had gone the way that made them say at school that they did not like to see a little girl looking like that.

Mamma told them brightly that Miss Beevor had been kind enough to teach Cordelia a new solo, and had had the even greater kindness to break into her own Christmas Day to come and play her accompaniment. Mary, who had shut *The Romance of the Forest* out of politeness, opened it again and began to read again. But such a look of misery passed over my mother's face that I myself took the book out of Mary's hand. She went on looking at the place where the page had been. Mamma waved Miss Beevor to the piano, and sat down in a chair which she had moved so that her face would be hidden from the two performers. Then Miss Beevor ran her hands over the keys in a profusion of what Mary and I scornfully called collywobbles, and Cordelia stepped out into the space beside the piano, her eye running unhappily round the room. She was wishing that our dolls' houses had been put away and hoping that Miss Beevor would not think her a baby for having one. I sank down on the floor, and Cordelia frowned at me and jerked her bow at me, to show that she wanted me to get up and sit in a chair, but I took no notice. She would have liked us to be tidied away as well as the toys.

After Cordelia turned to the piano and got the note, she set her chin down and raised her bow, but, smiling as if at some intimate and ridiculous memory, lowered it again. Turning back to Miss Beevor, she said, with the simper she always assumed when talking to a teacher, 'They all know this quite well, even the children, there was a poor old man who used to play it in the street in Edinburgh.'

My mother leaned forward in her chair and said, 'You do not mean the old man who always played outside our flat on Friday nights?'

'Yes, Mamma,' smiled Cordelia.

My mother turned her face away. The old man had been a violinist of great talent, who had once been second violin in the Scottish Orchestra, who had, as she delicately put it, 'come to grief' and lost his position, and come down to the gutter. When he played under our windows Mamma would lean out into the darkness, nodding in sad joy as she sniffed up the music, muttering, 'Poor wretch, his phrasing is as pure as ever,' and calling to our servant to take him out coffee and a sandwich. Cordelia began to play the composition he had never omitted from his serenade, Bach's "Air on the G string." That meant that she had heard it played exquisitely, time after time; she made it a juicy whine. My mother twisted round in her chair and glared at Mary and me, threatening us with her full rage if we, then or afterwards, mocked our sister's musical idiocy, which was now plainer than ever before, for Miss Beevor had made her playing at once much better and much worse, by giving her resolute fingers greater power to express her misunderstanding of sound. We glared back, trying to convey to her how much we thought she was to blame for having been so weak with Cordelia for not having forbidden her long ago to touch the violin. Then suddenly we were afraid, for she began to laugh. We watched in terror while she and her laughter contended like two desperate people wrestling on the edge of an abyss, for Cordelia and Miss Beevor really did not deserve that, nobody deserved that. She won just in time to be able to turn slowly as the last note sounded and say in an unhurried voice, 'Cordelia, what a lovely Christmas present,' and meet Miss Beevor's triumphant smile, while Cordelia clattered up to her for a kiss.

'And that,' began Miss Beevor, only to break off to wipe her eyes. 'And that,' she went on choking, 'isn't all. She's learned a lovely new piece called "Meditation" from an opera called *Thaïs*, by a French composer called Massenet. She learned it so easily. Oh, it's so wonderful to teach her. She is the pupil I have waited for all my life.'

V

THREE days after Christmas my mother brought a letter into the sitting-room, where I was sitting alone, playing with my dolls' house. The others had gone with Papa to luncheon with the Langhams, and Mamma had thought three children were too many. She said, 'Rose, my cousin Constance thanks me for our presents, but she still does not ask us to go and see her and does not say that she will come here, though God knows I asked her. There must be something wrong. I am going now. You can stay here with Kate if you like, but it would be nice if you would come. You will like Rosamund, I am sure.' I said I would go with her, because I was really so unhappy about her. She did not seem able to stop worrying about Cordelia, who ever since that disgusting invasion of our house on Christmas Day had been playing the violin all over the house with the air of somebody who is being photographed. We started off at once, and very soon we both forgot Cordelia, it was such an exciting journey. First we went in a train, there was a Lancer sitting opposite us, one of those lovely soldiers who wore scarlet jackets to the waist, very tight trousers with braid down the outer seams, and little round pill-box caps on the side of the head, and were said to be very brave. Then we went up iron steps that clanked under one's feet to a station right up in the air, on a level with the treetops, and took a train which ran high above parks in which boys were playing football, a sight which almost made me glad I was a girl and could do really interesting and adventurous things. Then the train ran nearer earth between dark, close-pressed houses with bits built out behind like ladies' bustles, and thin strips of garden, each as different as people are, some tidy, some riotous, some lovely, some nothing, and at last we came to our station. A subway was damp and echoing, and as there was nobody else going through it I was allowed to halloo there for a moment or two, and then we came up beside a grey public-house called the King of Prussia. To our right and left

87

stretched a grey road, never getting any better, though one could see quite a long way down it.

'Please,' said Mamma to a passer-by, 'could you tell us the way to Knightlily Road? What, this is it? Oh, no. Oh, surely not. Oh, I beg your pardon, I did not mean that you were wrong. I am sure you are right. But it is such a disappointment to us.'

But we were standing outside Number 250, and Constance lived at Number 475. We had to ask which way to turn of a baker's boy, who was carrying a wicker basket full of smoking and sweet-smelling loaves from a van to a shop, and when he heard the number he pointed to the right, and stood still and followed us with his eyes when we started to go there. 'Why did he stare?' asked Mamma. 'Am I looking very funny?' I told her that she did not, though of course she always looked queerly thin and nerve-ridden and shabby. She did not believe me, she paused for a minute to straighten her shoulders and cock her hat and assume the character of a smart and undefeated woman. Then we started off, while I realised without emotion that Constance lived among the kind of people which in those days were called 'common.' More fortunate children than ourselves might have called them poor, but we knew better, for most of them were no poorer than we were. They were people who live in ugly houses in ugly streets among neighbours who got drunk on Saturday nights, and who did not read books or play music or go to picture galleries and who were unnecessarily rude to each other, and, what was specially degrading, 'made face,' as well as not having baths every day. We did not despise these people, we simply felt that they did not have as amusing a time as we did, and we had understood, almost as soon as we could understand anything, that we had to rely on our own efforts if we were not to find ourselves living on that level, and I was not surprised, therefore, to find that a relative of mine had sunk to that level; I was only anxious to find out whether she found life there supportable. But I noticed that my mother was of a different mind. She was dismayed by the discovery, and though she invented a distraction from the dreariness of the road by noting the patterns of the Nottingham lace curtains in the window, some of which were indeed very pretty, she could not keep her attention on them. At last she exclaimed, 'To make

Constance live here is like keeping the crown jewels in an old tin trunk.'

By then she was getting impatient, as she easily did at all times, for when we reached the four hundred and seventies we found that the figures on the transoms were so indistinct that we could not be sure which house was Number 475. We halted in front of one which we thought must be right, and immediately there came to me the feeling that we were being watched. On the other side of the road, winter though it was, a couple of window-sashes went up. A woman putting a latch-key into the door of the next house became oddly slow in her movements and twisted herself towards us, dipping her head but surely throwing a sideways glance at us. Suddenly there broke through the overcast sky a shaft of lemon-yellow, year's-end sunshine. Everything in the street, the cornices and window-frames and porches, the railings, the lamp-posts, stood out bright and sharp and unlikeable, and so too did these furtive signs of vigilance.

'I think this must be it,' said Mamma. 'But I wonder if we might ask the lady who is just going into the next house . . .' She made a step in that direction, and the lady at once brought her face down to her latch-key and the lock, and would have been sheltered from us by the thickness of her front door in another second, had she not been, like us, suddenly frozen by shock. A poker flew straight through the glass of the ground-floor window of the house we were facing and fell at our feet. After a second the front door banged behind this woman. I pushed aside my mother's hand, which she had clapped over my face a second before the poker came arrowing through the air towards us. We both stared at the window. There was a round hole in one of the panes and no other sign of damage. On the other side of the road several more sashes were thrown up.

'I am going into the house,' said Mamma, like a splendid eagle, 'but you must stay outside.'

At all times when my mother and I were together in the presence of anything that looked like danger I had the fantasy that I was a big, tall man who was protecting her. I picked up the poker and said, 'I am going in with you.'

She did not argue with me. She often did seem to look to her daughters for protection, which was not unnatural in a very feminine woman who had not only no masculine protection but

89

was threatened by its negative. Moreover she understood children, and knew that they were adults handicapped by a humiliating disguise, and had their adult qualities within them. Also I think she knew that if she and I did not go into that house something terrible would have happened to the people in it.

As it is we went to the door and Mamma let the knocker fall on it twice. We then heard a crash inside the house; it was as if a heavy piece of furniture had been thrown over and smashed at the same time. This frightened us much more than the poker coming through the window. My grip tightened on the poker and Mamma drew a deep breath. Shortly afterwards we heard footsteps and the door was opened by a woman who made one think of a Roman statue. She had large, regular features and was pale as stone, and where her fingers gripped her apron it fell into sculptural folds. In a remote, composed voice she spoke my mother's name, and my mother cried 'Constance,' and they embraced.

Constance drew back, with large regular tears running down her face. 'You see,' she said, 'I couldn't ask you to come here.'

'Why, Constance,' said Mamma, 'as if I of all people wouldn't have understood. And you could have come to me.'

'And run the risk of bringing this trouble with me into your house? Oh, you don't know what it has been like.' Though she spoke urgently, the speed and level of her voice never varied, and I cannot now remember how it was that the effect of urgency was conveyed. 'It has been going on for eighteen months, the neighbours talked, I suppose you cannot blame them. So there were reporters and photographers until I nearly went mad, apart from the inconvenience of the thing itself. But come in. Come in. Is this Rose?' She drew us into the hall with her large gentle arm, and gave me an abstracted kiss. As she bowed over me it seemed that her eyes were blank, like the eyes of a statue. 'Come in and talk to me,' she said, taking off my mother's hat, 'while I make luncheon for you.'

'Make nothing for us,' said Mamma, whose eyes were wet. 'I'll take the child out for a bun. Oh, if I had only known.'

'Nonsense, I must make a meal for Rosamund and me anyway,' said Constance, 'I am so glad that you have come. I didn't want to make you share this awful thing, perhaps I am wicked to be glad that you are here.'

By now she had led us into the kitchen at the back of the house, and there she and my mother stood together on the coconut mat in front of the range and clung together in a curiously calm yet passionate embrace. I was very much puzzled by their imprudence. Surely the person who had thrown the poker through the window and overturned the wardrobe, or whatever it was, must still be in the house, and presumably at large. I was thinking that it was extraordinary of them to take no precautions for their defence, but to stand there crying and vulnerable, when a movement outside the window caught my eye. A few yards from the house there was a clothesline, on which there were hanging four dishcloths. Three heavy iron saucepans sailed through the air, hit the dishcloths, and fell on the ground. Evidently they had taken to the air without due preparation, for their lids were scattered on the ground below them. I put down the poker, for I realised the nature of the violence raging through this house.

'Is this what you call a poltergeist?' I asked Mamma. We had read about them in books by Andrew Lang.

'Yes, Rose,' said Mamma, her voice quivering with indignation, 'you see I am right, supernatural things are horrible.'

I was a little frightened, but not much; and I tried to remain imperturbable, because I assumed that the supernatural took this coarse form in Constance's house because she lived among common people, and I had no desire to be impolite by drawing attention to her circumstances.

'If you are old-fashioned enough to eat soup in the middle of the day,' said Constance, 'I have still some of the turkey broth, and I was thinking of frying some Christmas pudding, and there are tangerines. Oh, my dear, it has been so dreadful. There is a thing called the Society of Psychical Research — oh, watch the dresser, it's starting again.'

Out in the pantry, a jug fell off a shelf and was smashed to pieces on the floor. Through the open door we were showered with small pieces of coal. Outside a tattoo was banged on the side of a saucepan, louder and louder, so that for the time being it was useless to talk.

When the din had died away my mother breathed indignantly, looking about her with a curled lip. 'The lowest of the low.'

'The dregs,' agreed Constance, 'but this Society, it made

everything so much worse. They seemed to think poor Rosamund had something to do with it. They followed her about as if she were a pickpocket, they questioned me about her as if she were a bad child, though it happens just as much when she is not in the house or anywhere near it, and though the wretched things are harder on her than on anyone, they drag the clothes off her bed at night.'

'It is always terribly hard on the children,' sighed Mamma.

'Well, it was hard on us,' said Constance calmly, 'and we are here.'

My mother made a tragic gesture. But Constance ignored it and continued. 'The trouble is to arrange for her to have friends. You are lucky in having four, they can find company among themselves. But as Rosamund is the only one she must find friends outside and she could have done it if these people had not come bothering us, for she can keep her own secrets, but now everyone knows.' Her eyes moved from my mother to me and were benignant. 'But now you have come, Rose, she has at least one friend. Go out and fetch her. She is in the garden.'

'Do I have to go out past that clothes-line?' I asked.

She looked out of the window and saw what I meant. A large cooking pot had sailed through the air just as the saucepans had done.

'My preserving pan, which I packed away in the attic for the winter!' she said primly, as if it were a housemaid's fault that it had taken this journey through space. 'Come with me, I will show you the other way out.' She took me into the dining-room, which looked as if a lunatic had been laying about him with a hatchet, and opened the French windows, which gave on to a neatly-kept strip of garden running down to a railway cutting. At the very end were some hutches, and by these was kneeling a little girl of my sort of age. She was too far away for me to be sure of anything except that she was wearing a blue coat, but the sight of her filled me with a sudden desire to turn round and go straight home. I waited with a heavy heart while Constance called in her clear, hollow, unhurried voice, 'Rosamund, Rosamund.'

The little girl slowly raised her head, slowly straightened herself to her feet, and stood quite still, turning her face towards us but making no other sign that she had heard her mother.

'Rosamund, come at once, your cousin Rose is here,' called Constance, and then, as a very loud crash came from the kitchen, went back into the house. I held my ground for a second, then turned about, with the intention of following her back to the kitchen and finding some way of getting Mamma to leave the house. But already Constance had closed the French window with a kind, inflexible gesture. I began to walk slowly towards Rosamund, who was walking slowly towards me. She moved with a hesitancy so great, particularly when she had to follow a curve in the path, that I wondered whether she were blind.

We met halfway down the garden, where the lawn touched a vegetable patch. As soon as I could see her face my heart began to beat very fast. She was not blind. Indeed what I saw in her face was chiefly that she was seeing me and that she liked the sight. This I knew, not because she gave a friendly greeting, for it took her a moment to recall that this would be expected of her, but because her grey eyes rested on me with a wide, contented gaze, and her mouth, though hardly smiling, had a look of sweetness about it. She was not pretty like Cordelia, nor beautiful like Mary, but she was very handsome. Over her blue coat hung heavy, shining golden curls of the sort that hang to the shoulders of the court ladies in the pictures at Hampton Court, and her skin was white. She did not look at all silly, as grown-ups like children to be. She had a deeply indented upper lip, there was a faint cleft in her chin, and I knew from everything about her that she was in the same case as myself, as every child I liked, she found childhood an embarrassing state. We disliked wearing ridiculous clothes, and being ordered about by people whom we often recognised as stupid and horrid, and we could not earn our own livings or, because of our ignorance, draw fully on our own powers. But Rosamund bore her dissatisfaction mildly. There was a golden heaviness about her face, to look on it was like watching honey drop slowly from a spoon.

As we met I said, 'I am your Cousin Rose,' and she said, 'You're one of the two who play the piano, aren't you? I'm afraid I can't do anything well. Except play chess.'

'Play chess? But isn't that very difficult?' I asked. Papa played chess.

'No. I will teach you how to play if you like,' said Rosamund.

'No, no,' I said hastily. 'Thank you very much, but I don't like games. They make me feel funny.' In fact, they were a nightmare to me. I hated losing, but I could never win, because I felt an irresistible compulsion to throw the game away just as it came to its end, and then if I burst into tears at my odd folly grown-ups thought I was not being sporting.

Rosamund did not mind a bit. 'Would you like to see my rabbits? I've got six. Three of them are brown and three grey. They're very tame.'

She turned about and we walked towards the end of the garden, and presently she took a grey rabbit out of its hutch and put it in my arms, and while I realised its perfections, particularly the way it wiggled its nose, she said, 'Bert Nichols gave me this and the doe. They're the best of my rabbits. Bert was very nice. He was the son of our charwoman Mrs. Nichols, but she got frightened when a coal-scuttle chased her, and she wouldn't come any more. You can't blame her. But it's horrid because we never see them any more.'

'Isn't there any way you can see him?' I asked sympathetically. There was nothing we three children disliked more about our nomadic life than the way that people we had learned to like passed out of our knowledge.

'Well, he is a porter at Clapham Junction, and Mamma says she will take me there one day,' said Rosamund, 'but of course we don't know when he is on duty.' She turned her head very slowly as I turned mine very quickly because there had come from the house behind us a noise like a weakly and malicious factory hooter. We were in time to see the sashes of every window fly up and every pair of curtains flute into folds, as if a hand were wrenching them from their rods, then billow through the air down to the garden below where invisible hooligans, or else the wind, trampled on them and trod them into the damp ground. I wondered with the financial nervousness of a child bred in poverty whether they were insured.

Rosamund said, 'I'm afraid we'll have to put Sir Thomas Lipton back in the hutch. I must go and help Mamma start the copper. Oh, dear, it will have to be such a big wash. And of course nobody comes in to help us now.'

'You haven't anybody?' I said aghast. People of our sort had to be desperately poor to keep no servants in those days, and at home we thought of housework as something dangerous, like handling acids in a laboratory, because it spoiled our hands for piano playing.

'Well, we never had anybody but a charwoman, this Mrs. Nichols,' said Rosamund. 'Papa does not like us to spend much money. And since she went away we have had other people but they always get frightened, none of them stays.'

We were close to the house now, and we had come to a curtain lying right across the path. Rosamund bent to pick it up and I hastened to help her. I had thought that I was excited and not frightened, but I knew better when I felt the drag on the furthest corner. Surely I felt that. I know the hair stirred on my scalp. And surely Rosamund flicked the curtain from the grip of the invisible hand, and we stood face to face and folded it. 'My Mamma will be very glad that your Mamma has come,' she said as our fingers met.

'Mine is always talking about yours,' I said.

'They met when they were about as old as we are,' said Rosamund. Her eyes looked into mine over the curtain and then she turned aside, folding the curtain to a size easy to carry. Now I could be sure that she liked me, that she would always like me, as I was sure that Mamma and Mary and Richard Quin liked me and would always like me. I hoped that Papa liked me in this way too, but one could not be sure. I choked with gratitude. I began to make a promise to myself that I would always like Rosamund, but my head began to hurt. Thinking of her future, I saw a summer sky ridden by shining clouds, space rising on space above them till the blue faded brightly into pure light. All the same I could not bear to let my mind dwell on it. I found myself content to stay in the present, although a pack of demons were skylarking within a couple of yards of me. For though no more saucepans had come out to assault the clothes-line, someone was throwing about a number of pots and pans inside the house.

'There's one thing,' said Rosamund, coming to a halt. 'They never hurt us. They just break things and spoil things, so that we have to spend our lives mending and washing.' Thus she managed to say 'Don't be afraid,' without making it plain that she had noticed I was afraid, as for the last few moments, finding I had a mob of spectral monsters between my Mamma and me, I certainly had been, though not to the degree that an adult would have been. That was Rosamund's way, I was to find.

So we went in by the back door, and before we reached the kitchen heard the din that possessed it. Mamma and Constance were sitting at the table, their faces contorted as by neuralgic pain, while a flour-dredger, a tin-tray, and a spikey cloud of kitchen cutlery were thrown into the room through the other door, forks striking spoons, knives clashing on knives. But as soon as Rosamund and I entered the kitchen all this possessed ironmongery suddenly became quiet. Each fork, each spoon, knife, the flour-dredger and the tray, wavered slowly downwards and softly took the ground, after the meditative fashion of falling leaves. There they lay and stirred no more, nor were ever to stir again in all the known history of that house. To drive out the evil presence it had been needed simply that we four should be in a room together, nothing more.

We let the silence settle. Then Constance said, 'Rosamund, go and look out into the garden.'

At the curtainless window Rosamund said, 'There is not a sign of anything.'

'Wait,' said Constance, 'we will wait five minutes.' We all looked at the big kitchen clock.

Before the time was up Rosamund broke out, 'Mamma, do you suppose we won't have to go on mending things and knowing that they will be broken again at once, and washing what's made dirty as soon as it's clean?'

'I do not mind anything,' said Constance, 'if only they stop pulling the bedclothes off you at night.'

'But, Mamma, it has done me no harm,' said Rosamund, 'I am sure I feel quite well on it.'

'I have been a foolish woman,' said Constance, turning to my mother. 'I should have asked you here long ago, but I was ashamed, I knew you would never have let things get so out of hand——'

'As if one could help this sort of thing,' Mamma said warmly.

'And I lost my confidence,' Constance went on. 'I was afraid it might work either way if you came here.'

'Well, so it might,' admitted Mamma, 'and of course you didn't want the whole place burned down.'

'Yes, but I should have known it wouldn't work that way, not with you,' persisted Constance.

'Why should you think that a house would not go up in flames because I was in it?' asked my mother, so bitterly that I looked through her face at our home in Lovegrove Place and saw its blackened ruins. 'But it hasn't, has it?' I asked aghast.

There was a moment of silence which Rosamund broke by pointing at the clock and crying, 'Time's up. Time's up,' and Constance told us that not for three weeks had there been five minutes' peace and since my mother had caused this peace she knew it would last forever. 'Listen to it,' she said, piously clasping her hands. And we all listened to the silence.

'We must be the only people in London listening to nothing,' said Rosamund, and we all laughed, and began to get our meal ready.

We ate in the kitchen, because all the other rooms were even more disordered. It was a very good meal, for all the Christmas things were still about. While I was eating my turkey soup I noticed that a packet of table salt on the mantelpiece had been overturned and was soberly voiding its contents in a thin white trickle which spread out into a fine spray as it reached the hearth-stone below. I exclaimed in wonder, but without apprehension. There was nothing violent or malicious about the staid little flow, and so did Rosamund, but though our mothers looked sharply in the direction of my pointing finger, they looked away again at once. Rosamund and I thought they had not seen the salt and tried to direct their attention to it, but they kept their eyes on the tablecloth and asked us questions about our schools. It may be that they knew more than we did, that in setting the salt to pour out quietly on the hearthstone the defeated presence had performed a rite which was sad for them, and that, there-fore, it was ungenerous for us, the victors, to spy on them. I can never be sure.

When we rounded off the meal with some almonds and raisins and marzipan our mothers sat down by the fire to drink tea and Rosamund and I went off by ourselves. First we gathered up the curtains in the garden, and then I helped Rosamund to drag a tin bath into the middle of the scullery and fill it with hot soapy water, and we dropped into it as many of the curtains as it would hold. The coal-dust and greasy earth rode off them in

97

specks and smears like ants and the trail of snails, and that set Rosamund and me wondering why God had made insects. After she had left them all to soak, and had put some broken cutlery and kitchen utensils in a packet for the knife-grinder to take away to mend, we wandered about the house. It was the ugliest house I had ever visited. The walls just met the ceiling, at mean intervals. But there was lovely furniture from Scotland, made of mahogany that was really red, red as some cows are. There were wardrobes so big that we could both hide in them, dressing-tables with mirrors so large that they doubled the whole room, heavy cupboards in which very clean things lay strewn with lavender bags. But all the clean things lay awry; the wardrobes had chalk figures scrawled on them; a cake of wet soap lay on a dressing-table and its spume had drawn a cross within an O on the mirror; and underfoot there was often a hard frost of powdered glass or a fall of whittled wood.

'Tomorrow,' said Rosamund, 'we will clear up, and when we have finished, it will stay cleared up, and it will be because you and your Mamma came.'

'But they may come back,' I said.

'No, no,' said Rosamund, peering through the soap O on the mirror, as through a window, 'they have gone too far now for them ever to come back'. She opened a drawer and took out a handkerchief with a fine needle sticking into it and, sighing with contentment, hemstitched for an inch or two, then laid it down, and said, 'Let's go into the garden and give the rabbits some cabbage-leaves.'

Each helped the other into her coat. Rosamund said, 'You have a pretty coat,' and I told her that it had been Cordelia's and that as I was the shortest, I never had anything new. She said, 'I always have to have everything new, being the only one, but it's lonely. All the same, Mamma and I have nice times. We bought this coat at Whiteley's. We spent hours in the shop. There is a menagerie, and you can have tea there, and they give you meringues.' Her talk was colourless as water, she never said anything funny. But it was as pleasant to listen to her as to lean over a bridge and watch a clear stream running by.

I saw what she meant when she said that the rabbits Bert had given her were much the best. She said it was quite natural, as Bert had taken many prizes at shows, rabbits were his great interest, and after that the accordion. Mrs. Nichols had told Rosamund that she thought it a pity he was so wrapped up in them, she believed it was the reason he had not married, and neither the rabbits nor the accordion would give her grand-children.

A train puffed through the cutting, we looked at it over the ears of the rabbits in our arms. Two boys hanging out of a carriage window waved at us but we took no notice, though we would have waved back if they had been girls.

'I make up animals,' said Rosamund. 'I don't suppose you do. I do it because these rabbits can't talk, and I get lonely. But you have a brother and two sisters.'

I said that all the same we made up animals. Papa had told us about three little dogs Grand-Aunt Willoughby had had, a black-faced mushroom-coloured pug with asthma, a toy spaniel, and a lapdog of a kind Papa could not identify, which looked just like a fawn fur necklet. We were always pretending they were lying about on the chairs, or jumping up on the beds, or out in the garden, though they were all so pampered that you couldn't even pretend that they would be out in the fresh air except on the finest days. Richard Quin was very fond of them, and they were really quite nice old things, considering how spoiled they had been.

I asked what animals she had made up, and she said, 'The most important one is a hare. He has always been here. He was here before they made the railway, he stayed on when they built these houses all round him. He isn't very clever, you see. But he is very nice, I am really fonder of him than I am of the mice or the bear, and he is beautiful, I have his picture in a book, I must show it to you.'

We could not stay out long, it was so cold. On the way back along the path Rosamund stopped and gathered me some sprigs of mint and sage. Her Mamma had bought the plants at the greengrocer's and she herself had planted them. They had done well, they were still growing, the winter had not killed them. I said, 'We are not good at gardening. Papa and Mamma do not know anything about it, and sometimes we have tried to put in seeds, but nothing happened.'

She was puzzled. 'Is there anything to know about gardening? Mamma and I put things in, and they come up. We had some nice plants here, very nice roses, until those things tore them up.'

Indoors she showed me her dolls. She was at the same stage that we were, she was too old to play with dolls but she still liked having them about. Hers were not very pretty, though they were nicely dressed, and their names were not very interesting, but they all had pleasant characters. The things in the house had injured every one of them, but they had all been mended. There was a lady and her husband who lived near Clapham Common and were dolls' doctors, Rosamund said. They had got interested in the case and had charged almost nothing for the repairs. Then Constance called us because it was teatime. It was good that she was Scottish, it meant that she gave us a good tea. Our family was still shocked by the nullity of Lovegrove bakeries compared to what we had become accustomed to in Edinburgh. Constance gave us hot oatmeal scones, which we spread with butter and golden syrup, and she had some home-made Scotch bun, the rich cake in a pastry case which is known as 'black death.'

While we were still eating I heard noises which made me frightened in case the horrible things had come back. There was a slam which seemed to come from the front door, and someone wiped his feet on the mat, but with an insane amount of noise. There were two thuds, like an exaggeration of the sound people make when they take off their shoes and drop them on the floor; all these noises were not merely the sounds made by a person performing these actions; they were that and something more. They were meant to be heard and to distress. I looked at Rosamund with anxious eyes, and she answered, 'It is Papa.' She did not show any surprise, or any distress like mine, or any pleasure. Heavy steps clumped along the passage towards us, and finally the door was thrown open and a man put his head round the door. Rosamund did not look up at him. I was startled by the suspicion that though she was so calm a child she might have real trouble to bear. I did not consider the invasion of her home by demons to fall under the heading of real trouble, particularly now that it seemed to have been repelled. Real troubles were things like Cordelia being so cross and insisting on playing the violin when she could not, and Papa selling Aunt Clara's furniture when Mamma wanted to keep it.

I at once saw that Rosamund's Papa was real trouble. His head, so long as he kept it sticking round the door, was very nice. His face was long and fair, and his temples were delicately indented; his nostrils were thin as paper and his lips were pursed as if he were keeping a secret. If there had been a fourth real poet at the time of Byron and Shelley and Keats, he might have looked like that. But as soon as he saw who was in the kitchen and brought his body round the doorpost he changed. He canted his head on one side and surveyed us with a wide-eyed leer, while his mouth gaped open, the lips drawn close to his teeth and lifted at the corners, as if he would have said something impudent and amusing but was prevented by a flow of saliva.

He drawled, 'Well, well, who have we here?' and shook hands with Mamma, but stared at me without shaking hands when she told him which one of her three daughters I was. Children are used to rudeness from grown-ups, but this man was ruder than most. His Scottish accent was horrid, not like Mamma's or Constance's, but like the Edinburgh keelies you heard hawking at each other when you went down the Canongate to Holyrood. But Scottish people, if they were horrid, did do that. It was part of a determination to be funny though they could not think of anything really funny to say, and that was part of a determination to be better than other people though they were not. They were educated, nearly everybody is in Scotland, it is not like England, but to get the better of other educated people they pretended to be simpletons who were somehow much cleverer than educated people and were laughing at them all the time. I could hardly sit in my chair, I hated Cousin Jock so much. I did not like to think that he was related to Mamma and was married to Constance and was Rosamund's Papa. I also did not like to think that he was related to me. But of course it was worse for Rosamund. I saw that there were great advantages about our Papa, although of course there were disadvantages.

Constance let Cousin Jock get out something he wanted to say, which was not serious but not funny either, about being sorry that he had changed into carpet slippers in the lobby, but that anyway he was no ladies' man, and we must forgive him, though no doubt we were used to more refined ways in the ladida district of Lovegrove. Then she told him that the things were gone, there had been no sign of them for the last six hours, and she thought we had done it. At first he said he thought she was wrong, he was certain he had heard something go bump upstairs in one of the bedrooms as he came in; when Constance and Rosamund made him listen he had to admit that the house was quiet and he thanked us and said that he had always known that Mamma was a wonderful character. But I could see that really he was sorry the things had gone. He was on their side. You could tell that because the noises he made just coming into the house and changing his outdoor shoes were the same sort of noises that they would have made if they had been human and had not special advantages in being horrible.

After that it was only a question of how soon we could get home. We had to wait while he had tea. He chose himself an oatmeal scone and cut himself a slice of Scotch bun as if he were doing something sly and clever, and when he wanted more tea he passed his cup to Constance with the remark that he didna expect there was any mair tea for a puir man in this housefu' o' women. There was no possible reason why he should talk like that. Nobody else in the family talked like that. In fact very few Scottish people talked like that. I could not think of ever having heard anyone speak quite so broadly before except a disgusting man in kilts we had seen in a pantomime, who went round the stage on a scooter making skirling noises and smoothing his kilts down when they blew up as if he were ashamed, and was much the worst thing in the show. You could not think how Constance, who was so still and dignified, could have married Jock. You could not think how Rosamund, whom you could not imagine doing anything that people would want to laugh at, could be his daughter. You could see at once why my Papa and Mamma had married, they had the same eagle look about them, and my trouble was that people must always be surprised because I had so little in me, considering I was their daughter. Mamma was being very clever about Cousin Jock, pretending to be amused by his jokes, but not going over to his side. I was able to sit quiet because it occurred to me that he might die soon and leave Rosamund free, and then Constance and she could come and live near us.

When he had finished he pushed his cup and saucer right

into the middle of the table, wiped his mouth, slowly and much more than you would need to unless you were an animal and had eaten something on the floor, and said to Mamma, 'Now we've satisfied the inner man, may I ask if ye've kept up with your pianoforty playing?' Mamma said that, though of course she had had to give up practising now that she had all the children, she still played a little. 'Awa' into the next room,' he said, 'and ye'll have the preevilege of making music with your Cousin Jock, who's thrown awa' his immortal heritage and gone into the marts of trade.'

We all went into the drawing-room, which was in the front of the house, and I felt very sorry for Rosamund, because I felt sure that her father would not be able to play. The piano was an upright Broadwood, and though the candle brackets on it had been twisted till they hung upside down and the panels had been scratched, the keyboard and strings and hammers seemed to have suffered no damage. I found this out by running my hand over the treble keys, and Cousin Jock took my wrist and put my arm down by my side. It was a gentle movement yet extremely brutal. It told me that I had no rights, that I was a child, and children are slaves, and that I was a fool besides; I knew that I hated him and would hate him all my life. I also knew that he had wanted me to hate him, and had cleverly made it worse for me by seeing to it that I could never feel easy in hating him, because he had been so rude to me that I must always suspect my hatred of springing from hurt vanity.

I backed away from him into a corner and leaned against the wall, and Rosamund joined me. We could not sit down; there was not an undamaged chair in the room except the music-stool. Cousin Jock fumbled among the music in a Canterbury. None of it was torn. The things that had been driven out had evidently respected music. My mother stood watching him with an air of reserve quite unlike her. It would have been hard for a stranger to tell whether she liked him or not. With exaggerated uncouthness he poked a sheet of music at her, saying, 'Ye ken this weel. The auld arrangement of Mose-are's Flute Concerto in G major, or are ye so grand these days that ye maun call him Mozart?'

'I know it well,' Mamma answered, in quite an English accent. She often talked Scots to us at home, but she would not have it used as a silly joke. 'And I've never unlearned to call him Mozart, as you apparently have since we were both young.' She sat down at the piano and softly tried over the music, while he took his flute out of its case and put it together, with ugly movements, full of mean conceit in technique, which made the instrument seem as if it were something horrid from a chemist's shop, like the thing they used to give one an enema when one was ill. I looked down at the points of my boots and waited hungrily for the music to begin, so that I could enjoy despising him. But I was to have no such pleasure, only a new fear.

I had thought that Cousin Jock would play like Cordelia, and in a sense I was right. Both he and she removed all effort from music. It did not seem hard any more. But his playing was as good as hers was bad. It was in a sense as good as any playing I have ever heard before or since, on any instrument, indeed it was better, for reasons I was to spend all my latter life in learning to understand. I, or any other player, think how we should play a phrase, and take a vow that we shall play it in a certain way, but never succeed in keeping our vow. Our fingers are not clever enough to carry out the orders issued by our wills; also our wills themselves, when it comes to the point, flinch from even so much of perfection as they can conceive. But Cousin Jock played the music as he had heard it in his mind. His fingers had all the skill which could conceivably be demanded by any music written for the flute, and his will was not disconcerted by the idea of perfection. So the clean line of melody drew a delightful design on the silence, to fade and be replaced by another which was different yet belonged to the same order of delight as the first, and the listening mind at once clung on to the phrase it had first heard yet was refreshed by change.

But a long sigh shook the tall body of Rosamund, leaning against the wall beside me. Constance, who had seated herself on the side of an armchair that had its back torn out, was grave as an angel on a tomb. I thought this strange, for surely there could be no greater joy than seeing one of one's own family doing something really well. But as I listened it came to me that Cousin Jock was not playing really well at all. I think I understand now the dissatisfaction which was then only a strong but vague repulsion. When Mamma played well she was making clear something which the composer had found out and which nobody had known before him. It might even be that by the emphasis she placed on the different parts of his discovery she could add something to it of which nobody, not even the composer, had before been conscious. In her playing there was a gospel and an evangelist who preached it, and that implied a church which worshipped a God not yet fully revealed but in the course of revelation. But when Cousin Jock played he created about him a world in which all was known, and in which art was not a discovery but a decoration. All was then trivial, and there was no meaning in art or in life. His playing was perfect, yet it was a part of the same destruction that had defaced the room where we sat. I hated it and Rosamund put out her hand and stroked my shirt.

At the end Mamma rose and closed the piano and said, 'Well, Jock, you certainly play better than you did when you were a young man. Far better,' she added, with desperate justice.

'I'm no sae bad,' he said, putting his flute away. It had been obvious from the way she rose from the piano that she was not going to play for him again; and I think he had known that she would not. 'But I'm no one to pay compliments for the sake of paying compliments, and I'll no say the same of you. I would no say ye havena slipped a wheen.'

A tremor ran through Mamma's body. 'I have the four of them,' she said, 'and there is a great deal to do.'

'Ay, it's bound to tell,' said Cousin Jock; 'no use shutting the eyes on hard facts, it's bound to tell.'

My mother looked round the defaced room and its smashed furniture, as if she were thinking that she and it were wrecked alike. When her eyes fell on Rosamund they moved no further, and she said, smiling, 'Your girl is tall.'

'So she is,' agreed Constance placidly, her hands folded in front of her over her spreading skirts.

'Ay, a great maypole,' grumbled Cousin Jock, going on packing up his flute. But he could not hurt us any more when as we were all looking at Rosamund. Her shining golden curls, her solid white flesh that was full over her eyebrows, the deep cleft between her mouth and chin, her straight body, which even when she was at rest suggested the idea of leisurely movement, made us forget the horrid perfection of her father's flute playing and the cruelty of his attempt to hurt Mamma. She did not mind us all staring at her, and made it easy for us by smiling vaguely, as if she had gone away in her own thoughts. I noticed that Mamma was looking at her as I had never seen her look at anybody except us children, and it was strange; I was not angry, though usually I was very jealous of Mamma's affection.

'She must come over and play with the children,' said Mamma.

'How's your husband?' asked Cousin Jock. 'Will he keep this job?'

I hated the room with the smears on the walls, the twisted candlesticks on the piano, the stinted gaslight, and Cousin Jock. Papa and Mamma and my sisters and my brother and I, Constance and Rosamund, were all living in a more dangerous way than the children I knew at school and their fathers and mothers and teachers; and in this house somebody, and I supposed it was Cousin Jock, was trying to push us over the edge of the abyss to which we clung. I said violently, 'Can't Rosamund come back with us tonight?'

Rosamund slowly shook her head, smiling slightly.

'We'd love to take her,' said Mamma.

'Would you like to go?' asked Constance. 'Say if you would like it.'

Again Rosamund shook her head. Stammering she thanked Mamma and said that she would come for the whole day some time soon, but not that night.

After that Mamma and I went and got our hats and coats, and the others dressed too, to take us to the station. Cousin Jock said that we had come the wrong way, and he would send us off from another station. When we got out into the dark street we all halted and stood looking at the house and listening. There was no sound. Cousin Jock turned round and spoke rudely to a child who was bowling a hoop along the pavement, telling it to be quiet, though it was really not making much noise. He grumbled, 'Well, I expect that the morn will find them all the worse.'

'No,' said Constance, in her prim, hollow voice.

'What gars ye say that?' he asked crossly.

'I can feel that they have gone for good,' she answered with composure; 'there is a difference between feeling that a tooth has stopped aching and that it has been taken out.'

The three grown-ups moved ahead, and we children followed. 'Are you sure they've gone?' I asked Rosamund. She answered, stammering a little and looking on the ground, 'Oh yes; quite far away. Besides there was . . .' I knew we were both thinking of the stream of salt dripping from the kitchen mantelpiece and falling in a spray on the hearthstone. We walked through the darkness in silence for some minutes and then I said, 'I'll never tell.'

She murmured, 'It's better not,' still looking down.

We slackened our pace to be alone with our secrets, our sense of mystery and power, until the three in front turned round and called on us to hurry. As we obeyed Rosamund said, 'I never showed you the picture of my hare.'

I said, 'I'll see it another time.'

'I would have liked you to see him,' said Rosamund. 'I told you how lovely he was, but I don't believe I told you how really beautiful he is.'

'Oh, I know how you feel,' I said, 'one does get so fond of made-up animals. But I quite understand he's beautiful.'

The grown-ups called to us again, for they had reached the corner of a high street, where there were lighted shops and crowds, and they were always frightened of us children being in crowds, though actually nobody ever took any notice of us.

But grown-ups had all the power and we had to follow on our parents' heels more quickly than we liked past shops lit by naphtha flares, a form of street-lighting much more exciting than anything which has superseded it. Loose red and yellow flames burned on suspended plates, open to the wind, which sometimes blew them to a bunch of streaming ribbons and jerked all the shadows askew. 'I love these lights,' said Rosamund; 'do you like fireworks?'

'They are the loveliest things in the world,' I said.

'I once heard, or I read it somewhere in a book,' she went on dreamily, 'that sometimes people light bonfires on the top of mountains. I should like that too.'

'I've heard about that too, I can't think where,' I said, 'but it must be gorgeous. We'll probably see it sometime. We're lucky, don't you think? We know more than the other girls at school. We have mothers that are wonderful. I can see your mother is like mine, better than anyone else's. And we have a great advantage over the other girls at school, we have been through things they haven't. They don't have demons in the house, and so long as you can get rid of them it gives you a great advantage to know there are such things. I think we'll always be lucky. Don't you? Don't you?'

We came to a stop to watch some very fine flares outside a butcher's shop, where a big red-faced man in a blue smock was shouting out long things about meat, as if he were making a speech in a historical play by Shakespeare, 'attend me, lords, the proud insulting queen, with Clifford and the haughty Northumberland and of their feather many more proud birds, have wrought the easy melting kind like wax.' As we watched, my mind clung on to what it was saying, and I persisted, 'Don't you think we're lucky?' The lights and shadows wavered on her face without disturbing her look of being soft but immoveable. Then as I repeated my question again a spasm convulsed her face. I realised that she could not answer, that her inability was giving her acute physical pain. I stood in an agony of sympathy, and presently she said, 'I stammer. Didn't you know? I sometimes stammer. You must forgive me. It is just a way of being stupid.'

'Oh, no, it isn't,' I said. 'One of the cleverest girls at school with us in Edinburgh stammered. But I'm so sorry. I'm so sorry.'

We found ourselves waiting with our parents on the kerb till the traffic gave us a chance to cross. A string of tall scarlet trams loaded with light jerked past, making a nice rhythmic noise on the points. A coster and his family drove by in a cart drawn by two ash-coloured donkeys, he and his boys dressed in whitish corduroys sewn all over with pearl buttons, the women wearing huge hats trimmed with green and red and blue ostrich feathers, all made mysterious, like what you would think the people in the masque at the end of *The Tempest* would be, by the night and the cross-hatchings of light from the street-lamps. A hansom jingled by, with a man wearing a top-hat all askew and a lady swathed in a feather boa behind its wooden apron, and the grown-ups all exclaimed at the cost of taking such a vehicle down from the West End. At this talk of money I reflected on the financial position of Rosamund's family and my own, and felt a moment of terror. It seemed not nearly impossible enough that an unlucky happening would send me to the workhouse. But of course it would be all right when I was grown-up, I would be rich, I would be able to take hansoms anywhere. The traffic dwindled and we all ran across the cobbled road, and walked beside a patch of common, along a row of bright stalls where people were selling things to eat, and then we two lagged again.

'This coffee smells nearly like coffee at home, but not quite,' I said.

'Yes, it's a little like something burned in the garden,' said Rosamund.

We made these remarks with great distinctness, having no malice, just in front of the man who kept the coffee stall, and when he looked angrily at us we thought placidly and critically that he was one of the many grown-ups who were cross by nature, and strolled on to the next stall.

'Could you eat jellied eels?' I asked.

Hesitantly she answered, 'If I were dared.'

'Do they dare much at your school?' I asked. 'They do at ours, and I think it's so silly.'

'They dare all the time,' she said wearily, 'and such stupid little things.'

'They don't like us at our school,' I said, 'do they like you at yours?'

'No,' she answered.

We walked on in silence for a minute and I felt a desire to be honest about this. 'It's awful, I think they're horrid and silly, but I wish they liked me.'

'Oh yes,' she said, 'I don't think there's anything I should rather have than that they should like me,' and she spoke with such a quiet, candid admission of pain that I felt no longer lonely in my exclusion, and was certain that if she shared it it could not be a shame to me. Just when I got back my voice we passed a stall where they were selling roast chestnuts, and she said, 'That is the nicest smell of all.'

'When we have our hair washed,' I said, 'we all sit round the fire in our dressing-gowns and we roast chestnuts in a wire thing among the coals and eat them and drink milk.'

'Mamma and I do that, too,' she said. 'I think your Mamma and mine did it together when they were little.'

'And I'll tell you one thing,' I said, 'I like keeping a chestnut in my mouth and then taking a drink of milk. But Mamma says it's a horrid trick.'

'So does my Mamma,' said Rosamund.

'I can't think why,' I complained, 'people would have to look hard at you before they could see that you were doing it, so hard that they'd be in the wrong because they were being rude, and anyway there's nobody there but us.'

'And sucking chocolate, that's another thing,' said Rosamund. 'Mamma says you must eat it, not suck it, and surely nobody could see that without staring either.'

'Yet they let you cut your bread and butter into fingers and dip it in your egg,' I said, 'and I would have thought that if the other things were wrong that was too.'

'Yes,' said Rosamund, 'those are the things I really call queer.'

Now we had come to one of those South London stations which have taken to the air. The beautiful rubies and emeralds of the signals shone up in the dark sky, above the sloping slate roofs of the little dwelling houses, which in the night gleamed like water. The platforms and the waiting-rooms were a vague pavilion between these tilted slate ponds and the stars. We thought it so lovely that we stood stock still in a dream, and the grown-ups had to call us again. 'Don't you like the night far better than the day?' I asked Rosamund, as we ran up the steep wooden staircase. 'Yes,' she answered, 'it is more——' her mouth again became a struggling hole as her stammer seized her. She had not found her voice by the time the handsome train came in, spitting fire from its engine, and Mamma and I got into one of its golden compartments. But it did not matter that my conversation with Rosamund was not finished, for I would see her again and again, we would go through life together, she would never go over to the side of the enemy. I waved to her through the shut glass of the window with a fervour which I at once regretted, lest she should have thought me silly. But she took a step nearer the train when she waved to me, as if she mistrusted the hesitant motion of her hand, the blind softness of her smile, to tell me how little silly she thought me. The train puffed off, then stopped before it got out of the station, and backed, so that Mamma and I saw the three of them again, going along the platform to the exit. Cousin Jock was looking canny in his horrid Scots comedian way; what on earth was there for him to look canny about on a railway platform in the dark? But he was not putting on that expression very hard, because he did not know there was anybody looking at him very closely. You could pierce through it, and see how easily he did things, how easily he played the flute, with the ease of a snake gliding, casting its skin. Constance was stately beside him, taking no notice of him, though not looking cross with him; it was as if they had been told to walk side by side in a procession, and that was all she knew of him. Rosamund was a pace behind them, making no sign, yet eloquent, like a tree before its leaves have come out.

Mamma and I were alone in the carriage. Mamma took off her shoe to see what had been hurting her all day. We had to buy very cheap boots and shoes and they were always going wrong one way or another. 'There must be a nail coming through,' she muttered. 'Oh, it was good to have Constance back. We've had a grand day, have we not, my wee lamb.'

'Yes,' I said, 'and I do like Cousin Constance and Cousin Rosamund.'

'Rose and Rosamund we called you,' Mamma said, feeling inside the shoe; 'it was chance, we were far away from each other at the time.'

'But those horrible things,' I said, 'that were there when we first got there.'

'I doubt the heel of a hammer will take out that nail,' she mourned, 'if it doesn't I'll have to send it to the cobbler, and my other good pair is there already. Yes, they were horrible things.'

'I was frightened at first,' I said. Thinking of the day, I felt a little frightened.

'Yes, yes,' she said. Being very brave, she sometimes failed in tenderness to us when fear was our trouble.

I felt lost for a moment, then, remembering something I had read in a book, I said, 'Oughtn't we to have said the Lord's Prayer?'

She sighed. 'It's not so easy as all that. How should it be?'

and put her shoe on again, murmuring, 'Poor Constance, poor Constance.'

Our train slowed down at a station. Somebody got out of another carriage playing a mouth-organ, and as he went further away the sound became sad, and saddened the silence which followed. The guard's whistle sounded sad too. I thought of Constance and Rosamund going back to their dark and ravaged house with that fair, smooth, baldish man, and I could not stand it, I bounced on my seat with anger. I asked furiously, 'Why did Cousin Constance marry Cousin Jock?'

My mother repeated the question, and, with a thinness of voice which meant that she was very tired, gave me an answer to which I listened attentively, for I had noticed that when she spoke so she was not at all like a grown-up talking to a child, and was therefore telling the truth. 'I doubt if anybody else wanted her,' she said. There was no belittlement in her tone. She was making a statement of fact, and it perplexed me.

'But wasn't she nice-looking when she was young?' I asked. 'She looks as if she must have been.'

'Oh, yes, Constance was very handsome,' said Mamma, glowing generously, 'like a Roman woman, you could imagine her driving a chariot.'

'But then,' I asked, 'didn't lots of men want to marry her?' I was alarmed. Up till then I had thought it was all quite simple. If you were nice-looking men wanted to marry you, and if you were not you saw it for yourself in the mirror and decided to do something else.

'No,' said Mamma, 'the men were afraid of her.' She took the pinching shoe off again and picked away at the nail inside, her nose looking very thin and sharp. 'Indeed,' she added, 'they were afraid of me, too.'

I was appalled. I had known that many people were unfriendly to my mother when they first met her because she was so thin and wild-looking and badly dressed, and I had seen that it hurt her. She must have been far more hurt if they had disliked her when they had no cause, before she was ill and unhappy and poor. But at any rate she had married Papa and not Cousin Jock. 'Why,' I said, 'did Cousin Constance have to marry at all, if she couldn't get anybody better than Cousin Jock?'

'Why,' said my mother, her voice thin as a wisp of mist, 'how could she have got Rosamund if she hadn't married someone?' Her eyelids dropped, she fell into a doze. I looked out of the train at the dark rows of houses striped vertically with the lives of families, showing yellow through the windows, and was interested at my new knowledge of what a family was. It was as if Mamma, my Mamma, or Rosamund's Mamma, or anybody's Mamma, were in a place like the Zoo or Kew Gardens, and were waiting for her little girl and finally saw her standing outside the entrance, on the other side of the gate, and said to the attendant in charge of the gate, 'My little girl is outside, would you mind if I went outside and fetched her in?' She would have to be polite to the attendant who could let her through the gate, no matter what he might be like.

VI

WHEN we were very small, out in South Africa, Papa and Mamma had been walking with us in a garden on a cold afternoon just before Midsummer's Day, and Papa had told us to lay our hands on the trunk of a tree. He said that we would feel nothing but wood. But if we did it again, a week later, there would lie under our hands wood, and something more, for now was the time when the world was swinging over from winter to summer, and it was suspended between life and death. We wondered, but obediently laid our hands on the tree-trunk and were of the opinion that it felt dead, while Mamma exclaimed, telling us that her own Papa and Mamma had made her do the same thing, and she had thought it a rite peculiar to her family, and here was Papa practising it also. A week later we laid our hands on the tree-trunk again and were of the opinion that it felt alive, and cried out at the miracle, and Mamma said we would find it easier to understand if we went home to England, where it happened at Christmastime. So we had. We saw the week between Christmas and New Year as a time of suspense, when the world made up its mind whether to change from dying to living and thus fall in with Christ's promises, or to stand out and go its own way and spoil everything. In the night, in our bedroom, we had wondered whether there was anything to prevent the world deciding that it would not wake up and have a spring, and then everybody would get colder and colder, and the days would go on getting shorter and shorter, and in the end there would be only darkness. We asked Papa and Mamma about this, and Papa said, 'Well, it might happen, but not in your time.'

'But we don't want it to happen at all,' said Cordelia.

'Do not frighten the children,' said Mamma. 'Spring has always come, so we can take it that it will always come.'

'What an argument for a fellow-countrywoman of David Hume,' said Papa. 'Nobody has ever upset his contention that

114

there is no logical proof that because certain causes produce a certain effect on one occasion they are bound to produce it on another. We may yet see universal and eternal night.' He gave one of his grating laughs. 'But I do not think you children need worry about it.' Yet we worried because we obscurely felt that he felt a certain delight in contemplating a never-ending winter, chill and darkness not to be dispelled. It did not matter that Mamma told us then and often later that day and spring were bound to come, for we sometimes suspected that he had the greater power.

So we thought of ourselves during this week between Christmas and New Year as a besieged army waiting to be relieved. This time the period had been broken into by the visit Mamma and I had paid to Constance and Rosamund. To me it was as if we two had gone on a foray out into enemy country and brought home some of our lost forces. I did not tell any of the others about the poltergeist, though Mamma had not forbidden me to do so. Cordelia would have hated it, she would have got cross, and scolded me for telling a story that was not true. Mary would have been indifferent to the horrors of the supernatural assault in a way which would have galled me in my desire to win admiration for Rosamund. Richard Quin was of course too little to understand. But I told them all about how wonderful Rosamund was.

I must have talked about her incessantly, for I talked about her to myself when I could find no other listeners. I remember sitting on the hearthrug and looking at a spent fire of rosy coals and fine white ashes and repeating, 'Rosamund, Rosamund,' and forgetting to put on fresh coal; and I remember running round the lawn calling her name as loudly as if she were within earshot and could be made to come to me. Soon Cordelia began to make a fuss about this. She had been very consequential since Christmas Day and was always either practising or carrying about her violin, with an air which indicated that she was vainly looking for a place where she could practise in peace. She now enacted the part of an eldest sister distracted by the prattle of a young sister who would go on and on about something childish; and because the part delighted her she went on performing it long after I had ceased to speak of Rosamund to her, and kept my tale for Mary.

There I found an interested listener, for Mary was sure she would like Rosamund if I did, but could not understand for what reason either of us should, as she seemed to do nothing interesting.

'Are you sure she doesn't play any instrument?' she asked.

'Quite sure, she said she didn't,' I replied.

'Are you sure that she didn't simply say that she didn't play the piano?' she pressed. 'No? Well, I suppose it's all right. But she sounds just like one of the girls at school, nothing interesting at all. But I think we'll find out that she plays some instrument or other.'

Richard Quin too listened to all I had to say, because he liked the name of Rosamund as soon as he heard it, and liked it better when Mamma told him it meant Rose of the World. And Kate liked hearing about her, and said she was very glad of what she heard, for there were too few of us to keep ourselves company as we went through life.

When, on the morning of New Year's Day, as we were running about the garden, touching the trees and the shrubs, to feel the fresh life in them, Mamma flung open the French window and cried to us, 'See who has come.' We three girls were in the grove of chestnuts at the end of the garden, and hurried out to see Rosamund and her mother standing at the top of the iron steps. Constance looked a little odd, not only because she was even shabbier than Mamma, but because her carved quality, when it did not appear statuesque, and just now it did not partly because women then had to wear such silly hats, recalled Mrs. Noah. Rosamund was as fair as I had remembered her. She saw me, and smiled, but did not call. She was as golden as a cloud facing the summer sun. I was so overcome by the sight of her that I could not find my voice or move. Before I could go to her, Richard Quin, who had been among some syringa bushes nearer the house, ran towards her across the lawn, crying, 'Rosamund! Rosamund!' She came down the steps, and was on the path when he reached her and threw himself down before her, clasping her round the knees, looking up at her and laughing with joy. She bent over him, at a slower pace of delight, and they kissed and kissed. It was not as if they were meeting for the first time, but as if they had been long separated.

They spent the whole day with us, and it passed like an hour or so. We had barely time to show her our dolls' houses, and that not thoroughly. Even Cordelia liked her. She said in a patronising way, for of course she was older than Rosamund too, 'She is very well-behaved.' It was an inept tribute, because Rosamund possessed less behaviour than any other person I have ever known. She was simply there. Mary liked her, and asked her at once, 'I say, hasn't Rose got it wrong? You do play something, don't you?'

'No,' smiled Rosamund. 'I can do nothing at all.'

'Well, I'm sure you could, I'm sure you could play anything,' said Mary.

When we took her down to see Kate in the kitchen, Kate very soon asked her when her birthday was and wrote it down with ours in the Bible she kept on the dresser, and I felt that an important ratification of the relationship. And when Papa came back from the newspaper office for luncheon he looked at Rosamund with astonishment, the extent of which we did not guess till he returned home in the evening, and Mamma and I took the evening paper into the study.

'That child,' he said, 'is astonishing. She ought to make a great marriage.'

'Make a great marriage?' Mamma repeated in some astonishment. 'Why, my dear, how could she make a great marriage? I often wonder,' she said, with quiet desperation, 'how any of our girls are to marry.'

'But why not? They have not the tremendous air of this girl, but they are none of them ill-looking.'

'But we do not know any families into which they can marry,' said Mamma. 'We are not part of any world.'

My father was more taken aback than I have ever seen him. 'Well, when we have settled down here we will make more friends,' he said weakly; and then forced himself to say with sad honesty, 'though I know there are not many people in Lovegrove of the sort we would wish our daughters to marry. But there must be some solution. I must see.'

'Anyway we do not want to marry,' I said. 'Oh, you need not laugh! We have often talked it over.'

After that Rosamund came to us quite often, at weekends, and during the holidays. She knew we had to practise and did not think it was rude of us to keep to our usual hours at the piano as if she were not there. Either she was in the room, the ghost dogs in a circle round her, and played with Richard Quin so silently that we could not have told they were there, at curious games unknown to us, with circles and squares of coloured paper, or with his soldiers and the figures Papa carved for us, deployed in a new way; or they went into the garden, making so pleasant a picture that I remember it as much transposed from reality as if I had seen them on a tapestry, the walls annulled, the trees melting into distances as different from the actual neighbourhood as the landscape I had seen when, as I had perhaps dreamed, I went to the stables to find Mamma on the first night in this house. Soon Rosamund was as familiar with our made-up animals as we were. She recognised that they were such awful little dogs, such pampered, purse-proud, conventional little dogs, that they had to be called Ponto and Fido and Tray, and she brought us the book that had in it the portrait of her made-up hare, drawn by Dürer. Docile he sat, with his paws laid neat before him, resigned to what might be his portion here on earth; but his two tall ears, standing oddly erect considering that they were soft as velvet ribbon, and the nervous circle-sweep of feelers from his muzzle and his eyes showed that all the same he was resigned to nothing, he still feared. Yet the deep banks of fur ruffling his breast, his back, his haunches, showed him a natural fop, committed by his pelt to an effeminate timidity. This made us feel better about him. What he feared for was not his life but the unspotted condition of his lovely clothes. Gathered round him on the lawn, as well aware as if we really saw him sat there contented in our notice, his eyes shining like warm crystal, his tawny fur giving off a rainbow lustre, we jeered at him tenderly.

'He says he wants to travel,' said Rosamund.

'But he'd be frightened to travel in a railway carriage alone,' I said.

'Yes,' said Mary, 'he would insist on putting on his best clothes for travelling, because he would want everyone to see them, and then he'd get into a carriage and hide under the seat because he'd be afraid of everybody and he'd sit there seeing nothing and being terribly frightened, so he might just as well have stayed at home.'

'But, after all,' I said, anxious not to do the hare injustice, 'people do get murdered on the railway, like the poor man in the tunnel.'

'Yes, but he'd feel he was going to be murdered when he wasn't,' said Rosamund. She was not being unkind, she understood him, and knew that he did not mind being teased.

Together we met a lot more made-up animals, or rather discovered that a lot of real animals were made-up ones too. Once we went as far as Richmond Park and found a vast empire of rabbits who had odd political troubles, and a small and aristocratic community of deer, who were terrible snobs. Papa overheard us talking about them, and explained that the older deer were evidently trying to preserve the Hapsburg system of protocol, while the young ones wanted to introduce the easier German and English system. We instantly recognised that as true. Mamma took us several times to Kew, which was also a long way off, and we might have got tired had not her ingenuity in finding cross-country routes taken us through a landscape which we found grimly entertaining. We took a ten-minute ride in the train, and alighted in one of those strange suburban areas where the open country has been first invaded by public institutions, and other dwellings have never been built near their unkindliness. We walked down a poplar avenue, on our right a plain of harsh grass dotted with red-brick buildings which other people supposed to be an isolation hospital, a workhouse, and a sewage farm, but which we knew to be the tombs of ogres which had been found lying here after a rout of ogre forces in a battle. The long two-storied wings of the workhouse had been built round the taller ogres as they lay low on the field, and the tubbier bungalows and towers of the isolation hospital had been built round small squat ogres, who, though transfixed by the lances of the angels, had not fallen down, because they were broader than they were long. The question was whether, behind the brick, their eyes were open or shut, and whether the forces of light had been as thorough as they thought. 'Childe Roland to the Dark Tower came,' Mamma used to say as she led us down the gravel path under the poplar trees. On the left rose a hill, and over it spilled what might have been thought by adults to be the graves of an expanding cemetery. We knew, however, that a young doctor who had taken his degree in Baghdad at a university recently founded by Haroun-al-Raschid had settled in the district and now nobody even died, so that there had been a revolt of the tombstones in the yards of monumental masons, they had taken to the hills and were indulging in what, like all children, we believed to be called 'gorilla' warfare.

As we got to the end of the poplar avenue we always began to laugh till it hurt. At the end of the poplars was a dreadful little house built of red brick, not just red like the institutions but bluish-crimson, surrounded by a garden blazing with scarlet geraniums, blue lobelias, and yellow calceolarias, and on its pea-green gate was pinned a note: 'Wanted, a Lady Typewriter to take down letters from dictation in return for swimming-lessons.' The first time we had seen it Mamma had laughed so much that, when she wanted to tell us not to laugh in case the people in the house should see us from the windows and be hurt, she could not speak and had to slap us, as if she were a common mother. On all later occasions we started laughing as soon as we got out of the train, and it hurt like wanting to sneeze when we went along the path wondering whether the notice would still be there and holding back our laughter so that we could go politely past the house. It was really a very singular advertisement. There can have been no place within miles where swimming was possible, indoor or outdoor; it was exposed all the year round; the chances of any 'lady typewriter' passing by were remote, for the path was never used save by the nurses from the hospital and the labourers who worked on the sewage farm; and the advertiser never knew when he was beaten, for the notice was there year after year, and was replaced when the weather had faded it.

When we had passed it and got over our ecstasy we found ourselves at another station, secret in character, and took one of the three trains which ran in the day on a line built in the seventies under some apprehension concerning the future site of London industry. It has long been closed and grown over with grass; and even then we were often the only travellers on the train, which consisted of a single passenger coach at the front of some goods wagons. It took us past the camp of 'gorilla' tombstones of which we had seen the clambering outposts on the hill behind the poplars. Then we passed mean streets where there were nothing but rags on the lines in the back-yards, and then came neater villas, and we got out at a station, which was the most secret of all. It was beside an abandoned factory in a deserted garden, which we left by a wicket gate, and found ourselves in a street planted with big houses which had nothing to do with the factory, which were certainly inhabited by people who could never have wanted to travel to that odd place where there was an isolation hospital and a workhouse and a sewage farm.

This street was still and always dusty, unstirred by any wind, and we despised it and were angry when Cordelia once said she would like to live there. Mary and I got on each side of her and furiously asked why, and she said she was sure there was not a house on the road which had chairs covered with leather that was rubbing away into dust and stairs that had to be left bare because the stair-carpets were so worn they were not safe to use. We were astonished that she minded these things, because they could not be helped, and forgot to be cross with her any more in perplexity at her lack of logic.

In no time we were at Kew Green, and looking at the church that looks so like a comfortable four-poster bed that Mamma said that she expected the parson gave up and let the congregation bring pillows and quilts. Now we were within a stone's throw of the Gardens, but Mamma liked to walk slowly and look at the eighteenth-century houses. She loved the red of the brick, soft as red hawthorn blossom, the languishing flowers and leaves of the wistaria, which pretended to be so delicate they must surely fall, but were supported by gnarled tree-trunks thick as king-snakes, the gleaming window-panes which spoke of several perfectly trained housemaids. We used to run ahead to the gates and paw the ground like ponies till she came, and we were never disappointed in what we found inside the Gardens, although of course the very best time of all was Rosamund's very first visit. She was very nice about it when we told her we were going to take her there, but we could see she did not know what was waiting for her, she just thought it would be a garden like any other public gardens. But when she got in and saw the temple on the little hill, and the pagoda, and the lily with the great flat leaves in the tank in the greenhouse, she liked it so much that she could not speak. It was not that her stammer had come to her, it was that she could find no words. Richard took her about and showed her the place as if he were big and she were little. That same day it occurred to us that there was no reason why flowers should not be made up as well as animals, and after that there was for us a tree of fire down by the lake at the end of the broad grass walk, not far from the azaleas and magnolias, and not far from the rock garden there was a group of tall golden lilies, taller than a man, which in adult life I remembered so well that I had some trouble in believing the botanists who assured me that no such variety is known.

It irritated us that on our return from such expeditions Cordelia would not come down to the kitchen with the rest of us to tell Kate all about it, she rushed up to our room and picked up her violin and got in as much practising as she could before supper. She was practising longer and longer every day, and she did in fact improve her technique more than any of us had expected, though still this merely meant that her general musical inaptitude was more cruelly exposed. It may be thought that our household then, and myself several decades later, made much too much fuss because a little girl could not play the violin very well. But Cordelia was a dynamic person, any stone she threw into the water raised such enormous waves that we were drenched by them. She had left us in no doubt that when she played the violin other elements were involved. One of these elements was exposed one evening when her indifference to Rosamund became a dislike that never quite mended. Mr. Langham, the City financier, who had become involved with Papa in the abortive deal at Manchester, who was sometimes rich and sometimes poor, was a person of undistinguished appearance, lean and brisk and spritely in his dress, a specimen of the type, I now recognise with the help of the literature of the time, as a masher. We all gathered that Mamma disapproved of him, because he gave Papa the idea that he might some time make money on the Stock Exchange, and also because he was addicted to vulgar pleasures, and sometimes took Papa with him to call on ladies who lived on houseboats on the river near Maidenhead and spent the evening playing the banjo while their male guests smoked large cigars and drank champagne. This evening he had an appointment to come and play chess, and had telegraphed so late to say that he could not come that Papa already had the men out on the board. It occurred to me that he might care to play a game with Rosamund, though I did not suppose she was anything like as good as a grown-up would be, so I took her into his study. He was sitting there sunk in his disappointment, with blue hollows under his high cheekbones, his chin resting on his clasped hands, whicn were small and fine and stained with nicotine. 'The Wearing of the Green' was coming out of his closed lips in his flattened, groaning chant. When he saw Rosamund he greeted her with an unusual kindness, and they had a soft conversation, almost as empty of statement as the cooing of doves, but as amiable. Presently she stretched out her hand and held it level above the board. She stuttered, 'I p-p-play ch-ch-chess,' and Papa said kindly, 'Do you? Not one of my children has the brains to learn it. Sit down and let us have a game.'

She struck me as stupidly not afraid of playing with Papa, and the expression on her face was dreamy, she made no effort to pull herself together and become alert. She moved the pieces very slowly, and her hands, though they were white and well-shaped, seemed large and clumsy as she moved the chessmen. I was frightened lest Papa should get cross, and when he gave a sharp exclamation I felt wretched. But he told me, 'Rosamund knows what she is doing.'

She smiled faintly and said, 'It is a nice game.'

They went on playing, and Papa presently said to me, 'Do you know, I am finding it difficult to hold my own.'

I watched, though I found it hard to follow what was happening. But I could see that again and again he nearly got command over her, and she always escaped him by the exercise of her impeded and stumbling power.

At the end of the game he said, "You are a very clever little girl," and she answered, 'No, I am not. This is all I can do.'

'But that is a very great deal,' said Papa, 'you can play the most intricate game in the world, and if you can do that, then you can do a great many other things as well.'

Just then Mamma and Cordelia, who was carrying her violin, came in to tell us our supper was ready, and Papa said to them, 'Rosamund has just given me a sound beating. She plays chess very well indeed, very few grown-up people can play as well as she does.'

Cordelia lifted up her violin and hugged it to her breast as if it were a talisman which could save her from a grave danger. She looked astonished and bereft. I understood that she had wished to play the violin because Mamma and Mary and I played the piano, and now she would feel a still greater need to play it because Rosamund played chess. It was unfortunate that Mamma was caught off her guard and exclaimed, 'Oh no, Cordelia!'

It was shortly after this that Mamma told me that she had had a letter from Miss Beevor asking if she might call, and that she had asked her to tea the next day. 'You and Mary must be very good,' she said, 'for the poor woman must think us all savages after the way we treated her on Christmas Day, I had not the faintest idea who she was. You must leave the room as soon as I can tell you that you can go and play, she will want to talk about Cordelia.'

'Why do you let her talk to you about Cordelia?' I said. 'There's nothing to be said about Cordelia except that she can't play the violin and never will be able to. Why do you spoil Cordelia so?'

'You do not understand, dear,' said Mamma, vaguely, and went into reverie. 'On her first visit Miss Beevor wore sage-green, the second time violet purple, I wonder which she will wear this time. I wonder what the full range of what is called "art shades" includes.'

She spoke without irony but with an apprehension which was not justified. There was nothing new in Miss Beevor's appearance when she arrived. She wore the large purple beaver hat and a purple velveteen stole with the sage-green dress, but not the mosaic brooch showing the two doves drinking from a fountain. There could be traced in her costume a reflection that it was not Christmas, there was no need for festal attire, but that also it was probably wise to appear before such an eccentric woman as my mother with some slight advantage of the sort given by elegance. It could be seen from her bearing that she regarded herself as a shining and militant figure, prepared to do battle for the right, and she began the assault so soon that we never shared in the tea-party at all. For shortly after her arrival she announced that she had taught Cordelia a new piece called 'Humoreske' by Dvorak, staring into Mamma's eyes in the way that is said, though never on very good authority, to subdue dangerous animals, and casting a protective arm round Cordelia, who had crept to her side as seeking shelter. Mamma then gave us the signal to go, and we were glad to leave, because we were afraid we were going to giggle.

But later that evening I found Mamma sitting on the stairs, looking at the door of Papa's study and murmuring to herself, 'When she speaks of the child one hears the idiot voice of love itself.' I sat down beside her and asked her what the matter was, and she told me that at Miss Beevor's request she had given Cordelia permission to play at a concert to be given at a church hall in aid of a missionary society.

I was greatly shocked. 'Why did you do that, Mamma?'

She said in soft and wretched tones, 'If I did not let her play she would think that we were standing between her and success.' Suddenly hope shone about her like the noon. 'But people are very hard-hearted nowadays. It is a charity concert. Perhaps there will be nobody there.'

Her hope was to be disappointed. When she returned from the concert, she reported with affected gratification that the church hall had been packed, and it turned out later that the audience had been of a curiously active sort. So there was to follow a period when Mamma was driven to distraction by a double misery. As time went on there appeared in my father's study certain documents, the like of which I faintly remembered from our Edinburgh days. There were sheets of squared paper inscribed with jagged lines, which looked like the skylines of certain mountain plateaux to be seen in Spain and New Mexico. To this day I cannot look at such mountains without a feeling of horror, and I think of them as accumulations of copper instead of lime-stone, as they usually are; for those papers in my father's room were graphs showing the rise and fall of the copper market, and their presence meant that Papa was again gambling on the Stock Exchange. This was suicide. Mr. Morpurgo was paying him a good salary, much more substantial than would normally be drawn by the editor of a suburban newspaper, and he should have been able to give himself and his family all that they wanted and even save. But he had a need for gambling which I can under-stand only if I shut my eyes and see him as he used to pace the garden, vehemently arguing with an unseen adversary, pausing to retract his head like a cobra about to strike before he covered him with sneering laughter. I can understand it then. He so much disliked the situation which was produced by the logic of events that he wanted to appeal over the head of logic to chance, and this he did, without thought for us. So we slipped back into the poverty we had known during the last few months of our life in Edinburgh.

We got used to Kate coming and saying with a peculiar inflection in her voice that a man had come to see Papa. Then, if Papa was in, he went out by the back door and through the stables, without hurrying; Mamma used to turn her back so that she should not see him go. But whether he was in or out, Mamma had to deal with the dun. There was a sentence in our history books which we grimly enjoyed because we felt we had a special understanding of it. When we read, 'The garrison then sent out one of their number to parley with the attacking troops,' we knew exactly what it had been like, we had so often seen Mamma do it. Her task was particularly difficult, because sometimes they were not duns. Papa had performed a feat more extraordinary than we realised. His leaders in the little *Lovegrove Gazette* were collected in pamphlet form and were widely sold, and when he spoke in public he left an enduring impression of nobility and good sense on his audience. Hence more and more people wanted to enlist his support for causes in which they were interested, and though the more sensible among them wrote to him the others called at our house. Somebody had to see them, because they might be people who wanted to give Papa work for which he would be paid. Some of them were so mad that we were glad of their visits, they made Mamma laugh so much. She was happy for days after she had interviewed a man who said he would pay Papa a hundred pounds to write a book which would convert England to his belief that the way to cure a cold was to lie in the middle of a flower-bed and do deep-breathing exercises, and that all the public parks ought to be covered with flower-beds so that people with colds could lie down in them and be cured. But usually they were cranks who should have been watch-dogs, who dug their teeth into the attention of any persons whom they found breathing the same air, and would not let them go until they had been taken in charge by the intellectual police, as represented by some tedious and obscure economic theory.

I remember Mamma being closeted with one such crank for hours, so long that a second visitor arrived and would not be denied. He got his foot in the door, which we knew was a sign of danger. I went in to tell Mamma and found her sitting with glazed eyes while a man with a cleft white beard laboured for her salvation. When she heard what I said, she sprang to her feet and said to her tormenter with a surprised and delighted expression: 'Ah, at last, stupid though I am, I understand what you mean, you have explained it so well. But I assure you you need not trouble about converting my husband, what you have been saying is exactly what he believes. Goodbye, goodbye.' She showed him out and then went to interview the dun, who would not leave until she had emptied into his hands the contents of her purse, which she had hoped to spend on some such essential expenditure as the gas account.

When Papa returned that evening Mamma spent some time with him in his study. Later she sat with us children in the sitting-room, too tired to talk, too tired to read. Presently Papa came out with a visiting-card in his hand and said, 'My dear, this afternoon must have been quite terrible for you. I see it was Carlyon Maude who was here. I have heard him speak and lived to read his pamphlets, he is the greatest bore in the world. How did you get rid of him?'

'I forget now,' said Mamma. 'Oh, I know. I told him he need not trouble to convert you, you were of his way of thinking already.'

'What!' exclaimed Papa. 'You told him I agreed with him! My dear, you should not have done that!'

'Why not?' asked Mamma faintly.

'He is a bimetallist,' said Papa.

'Well, I had to get rid of him somehow,' said Mamma, blinking her eyes as if the light were too strong.

'Yes, but this is serious!' Papa protested. 'Now this wretched fellow will go about saying I am a bimetallist.'

Mamma said weakly, 'He may go about saying you are a bimetallist, but nobody will go about listening to him saying you are a bimetallist. It will remain a secret between him and his beard.' She shut her eyes altogether. 'I do not think I have done you much harm.'

Papa turned to go out of the room, then halted and said, 'Yes, you are right. Nobody listens to old Maude. And of course you have a lot on your mind just now. Don't think I don't realise that.'

'Oh, I know, dear,' said Mamma.

She continued to sit with her eyes closed after he had left the room. At length she said, 'It is funny to think that all that sort of thing matters as much to them as music does to us.'

'Yes, isn't it strange?' cried Cordelia, and at the sound of her voice Mamma opened her eyes to make sure that it was she who had spoken, and sighed deeply.

Cordelia had pleased the audience so much at that first concert given in aid of the missionary society that she had received a number of invitations to play on similar occasions, of which, it appeared, there were a vast number. All the rest of us, except Papa and Richard Quin, had been to hear her, and we had all been shocked. We were, indeed, really her victims. We were exposed to those inconveniences which must be suffered by any family which finds a public performer among its members. Often we had another timetable imposed on ours, Cordelia had to be taken to a concert or fetched from one. At this terrible time of financial anguish, her appearances involved some expenditure. Mamma had to buy her a concert dress, for which she paid by selling one of her last pieces of jewellery. It was painful to see the anxiety with which Cordelia chose that dress. Of necessity it had to be white, so that she could vary it with green and blue sashes and hair-ribbons, and this made the choice more difficult, as white stuff betrays its quality more candidly than coloured. When after long search Mamma found her a passable dress in the children's department of Lovegrove Bon Marche, Cordelia put it on and went to a cheval glass and looked at herself and grew pale pointing a finger, as if indicating a wound, at the line where the pleats were joined to the smooth yoke with a certain clumsiness. In her face was all the misery of a hunted animal; and indeed she had reached the stage through which many artists pass, when they feel themselves lone beasts persecuted by the herd and take such fierce defensive measures that presently the herd itself feels like a lone beast persecuted by a monster.

But she was not an artist. She knew a certain anxiety before all her performances. When she was getting ready for a concert she would examine her dress to see if Kate had ironed it properly, for it seemed to her that we were all waiting to fail her. But once she had got to the hall she lost all anxiety, she had no cause to worry, because she gave no performance. She was so confident that she was able to mimic that horrible malady, which has destroyed so many real musicians, stage-fright. She crept on the stage with wide eyes and parted lips, as if she had not known till she got to the hall that there was any question of giving a public performance. Then a faint smile would pass over those parted lips, her timid stare would soften, she would raise her bow and turn to the piano for her note as if she were putting herself in charge of her dear old Nanny, the spirit of music. Had the spirit of music appeared before her, it would have spanked her for there was nothing, absolutely nothing, in her performance except the desire to please. She would deform any sound or any group of sounds if she thought she could thereby please her audience's ear and so bribe it to give her its attention and see how pretty she looked as she played her violin. And she was not presenting herself as the pretty little girl she really was, she was affecting to be mindless and will-less as grown-ups like pretty little girls to be.

After Cordelia had been giving such performances for a year or so Miss Beevor paid another call on my mother. She had been to our home on several occasions, often enough for us to notice that the sage-green outfit had passed into decay and been replaced by similar garments of peacock blue. But this was a solemn call, previously announced by letter. It fell on a bad day, for Mamma had found that a sum of money on which she had relied to pay our school-fees, which she had believed to be safely in my father's banking account, was not available; and when she had suggested that now was the time to draw on certain miserable payments which Papa still drew from his family estate, it turned out that they also were mysteriously out of reach. I remember a mysterious ejaculation of Mamma's, 'Garnishee, that sounds like a man who has been crowned with parsley, but I am beginning to talk like Ophelia,' which remained incomprehensible to me until, many years later, I turned the pages of a dictionary and read the words: 'Garnishee, one in whose hands money belonging to a debtor or defendant is attached at the suit of credit or plaintiff.' So oppressive was the financial pre-occupation of my parents that once Papa broke a silence which had fallen on the dinner-table by saying to Mamma, very patiently as if he were trying to break her of extravagance, 'But you cannot stretch money, you know, my dear,' at which Mamma stared, afterwards bursting into laughter.

Kate was out the day Miss Beevor came to tea, so I let her in. She had gone back to her violet purple outfit, and this time she wore the mosaic brooch of the doves drinking at a fountain. Doubtless this was still her festal attire, and she had assumed it because she wished to use every possible means of asserting authority over my mother, but I could have told her that her intention was going to fail. Mamma had not liked that brooch when she first saw it, and she was now so much more tired than she had been when she saw it before that this time she not only made a grimace, she uttered a faint cry. I could not think that the visit was going to pass off smoothly. But I was not prepared for the speed with which it went wrong. Miss Beevor had brought, as usual, her white leather handbag tooled with the word, 'Bayreuth', and after the first conventional greetings had been exchanged she took from it a number of letters which she proceeded to read aloud. My mother at first listened without paying too much attention, from time to time saying, 'Yes, yes,' in a high, impatient voice. From her face I knew that had she been asked what Miss Beevor was doing, she would have replied that the poor thing was relaying the praises bestowed by her friends, as uninstructed as herself, on the deplorable performance given by Cordelia as the result of her unsolicited intervention. I am bound to say that Mamma's expression passed a final verdict on Miss Beevor which might have been left to the Judgment Day and other hands.

Suddenly Mamma's face was convulsed by comprehension, and she exclaimed, 'No! You are not really asking me to allow Cordelia to accept professional engagements?'

'Yes, yes,' cried Miss Beevor, archly shaking her long forefinger, 'that is just what I am asking you. All these people would be willing to pay our dear little Cordelia fees which may seem small, but would be a beginning.' She could start next week, it appeared, at a ballad concert which was to be given by a promising young tenor of the district, who had been let down by his violinist, and was most anxious that Cordelia should play the 'Meditation' from Thaïs and Gounod's 'Ave Maria' and a little thing, Miss Beevor could not remember the name at the minute, but it went la-la-la-*la*-la, between the vocal numbers; and then she paused, while my mother brought down her eyes from the ceiling.

In a flat tone which told Miss Beevor nothing, she said, 'I suppose he will sing Isidore de Lara's "Garden of Sleep."

Poor Miss Beevor said, 'I hope so, he sings it very nicely.'

My mother cried out in a tone which could not be misunderstood, 'I am sure he does. Miss Beevor, I cannot have this. Cordelia should not play at this sort of concert. She should not play at any concert. She cannot play the violin.' She checked herself. Cordelia could not hear her, but she could not bear to say the words which she thought, did Cordelia hear them, would break her heart. 'She cannot play the violin well enough yet to make a public performance anything but a farce. Of course she may improve, oh, yes, we hope she will improve,' she went on, in a tone which would have been recognised by the most complete stranger as proceeding from the extremity of despair. 'And what we must do is to raise her standards. If she is to be carted about to concerts and banquets where people who know nothing about music clap their hands because she is a beautiful little girl, she will never learn. She will wear herself out with the excitement, instead of working quietly and developing her technique, and, what is more important still, her taste. Surely you have noticed,' asked my mother piteously, 'that she has no taste?'

'But I am teaching her all the time,' said Miss Beevor sturdily.

My mother looked like Medusa, but Miss Beevor knew enough to have already lowered her eyes to the carpet. 'I am teaching her all the time,' she repeated. She was not without dignity. 'As for the excitement, I think the child can stand it. She is a wonderful child. I do not think you appreciate what a privileged mother you are, what a wonderful child you have brought into the world. There are some people,' she said, clasping her hands, 'who are different from all other people. They are born to shine, to go on platforms and give the audiences who come to see them a new life, they pour out refreshment and they are never tired. Cordelia is one of those people. You are her mother, and I know it is difficult for people to understand it sometimes when their own family has produced an exceptional person — oh, let's not beat about the bush, she's a genius, little Cordelia is a genius and you are standing in her way. I don't know why you do it, but that's all you do, you stand in her way. Let me have her, let me do what I can for her, I promise you I will make her famous and happy and, oh, yes, rich, very rich. She will have everything, if only you let me handle her.'

She was crying, and my mother was looking at her in sympathetic horror. 'The trouble is, you have let yourself get too fond of Cordelia,' she said.

'Of course I love the child,' sobbed Miss Beevor in her handkerchief, 'who would not, except you?'

'Oh, I love her,' said my mother grimly.

'You don't, you don't,' cried Miss Beevor, 'you show you don't in everything you do.'

'Sit down,' said my mother, 'I don't know why we both stood up just now. Let's sit down.'

'You are awful to her,' wept Miss Beevor, settling down on the sofa, 'you won't admit she's a born violinist, and you stand in her way all you can, and you can give her nothing, everybody knows you may have the bailiffs in at any moment, and you seem to care only for the other children, who are nothing, you even let this one stay in the room while I discuss Cordelia——'

Mamma put her hand to her head and explained that she was very tired and had forgotten that I was there, and told me to go away. I was determined not to leave her for long, for there had been something ghastly about her appearance ever since Miss Beevor had arrived.

I said, 'Yes, I will go and get tea.'

Miss Beevor blew her nose and said into her handkerchief, 'I do not want any tea.'

I said, 'That is not really to the point. Mamma looks as if she would be better for some tea, and of course we always have it about this time.'

Mamma groaned, 'Hush, dear,' and told me to go away at once.

I went up to our bedroom and found Mary, who was copying out some harmony lessons from a book we had got out of the public library, and asked her to come and help me to get tea. The kitchen was full of white glass cloths and tray towels hanging on the line to dry, and we moved under these dejected flags in a state of apprehension which was not despair, because we both believed that whatever happened we would be all right.

Certainly we would be all right. But it might be some time before we could get things settled.

'It is too awful that Miss Beevor should come to bother Mamma today of all days,' I said, 'when she has had bother enough about money.'

'I wonder,' said Mary, 'how bad the bother is. I am not putting out the best china, why should we, if she wears that brooch and those colours she cannot care how things look. Our school fees don't matter much. Some of those Irish relatives would pay them, they are always afraid that we will not be able to earn our livings when we grow up, they always enquire about us very nervously in that Christmas letter. But I do sometimes worry in case Cousin Ralph gets tired of the way we don't pay the rent. And I like this house, I should not like to leave it.'

'And where could we go if we had to leave it?' I pondered. 'I think you have to give landlords references.'

'We will have to go somewhere far away and pretend that we have just come from South Africa,' said Mary, 'I do not see how anybody could tell that was not true, and you and I and Richard Quin could tell everybody that we do so miss seeing a lot of black people.'

'That would be what Mamma calls falling lower and lower,' I said.

'Of course it would,' said Mary, 'I am only trying to be funny. But really I believe that whatever happens we will get through it without anything worse than people not seeing when we are funny.'

'You are burning the toast,' I said.

'You are letting the kettle boil over,' she answered, 'we are two silly sisters,' and we kissed each other and laughed.

When we carried in the two tea trays we saw that we need not have troubled to make enough toast for Miss Beevor and bring an extra cup. She would be going any moment now. As we went in Mamma, who was sitting beside her on the sofa, reared up like a striking cobra and said savagely, 'You evidently do not understand the true nature of *tempo rubato*.'

Miss Beevor rose to her feet, crying in a high, tremulous voice, 'I will leave this house this very instant.' But the letters offering Cordelia engagements had been lying in her lap, and as she rose they flew about the floor. She went down on her knees to pick them up, but she was confused by tears and rage, and we had to kneel down beside her and help.

Over our heads Mamma's voice sounded remorseful, pitiful, piteous, and yet constrained to uphold the truth as she knew it. 'I did not mean to be rude, but hardly anybody nowadays understands what *tempo rubato* really is, I did not myself fully grasp it till I was over twenty and had played in public many times, and one day my brother Ian said to me . . .'

We picked up all the letters, and the white kid handbag with the word 'Bayreuth,' and we took Miss Beevor out into the hall, found her umbrella in the stand, put it up for her in the porch, and stood watching her while she went unsteadily down the path through a fine rain. We had always been told by Mamma that it was terrible to shut the door on departing visitors till they had got outside the gate; it was like saying you had not liked them coming. We felt that we had a special duty not to shut the door prematurely in this case.

'I wish Rosamund were here,' said Mary, when she had shut the door.

'Where is Richard Quin?' I asked.

'He is in the stables, playing his flageolet to the horses. He says they like it.'

'I will go and fetch him,' I said, 'he will know what to do with Mamma.'

When we went into the sitting-room we found Mamma crying. 'I didn't mean to be rude,' she kept on saying, 'but I was rude, I hurt the poor creature's feelings. Oh, it is a dreadful thing never to know the effect you are making on people, and you are all like me in that.' We put our arms round her neck and kissed her and told her that nobody but horrible old Miss Beevor would have thought that she was rude, though about that we had thoughts we would not have shared with her. We could not ourselves understand anybody who, when told they had misunderstood the true nature of *tempo rubato*, felt any emotion except intellectual curiosity; but we had to admit that when Mamma was rejecting anybody on musical grounds her aspect was pretty murderous. But in any case she was, if not absolutely in the right, righter than anybody else. I poured her out a cup of tea and Mary buttered her some toast, and I hurried through the french windows out into the garden to fetch Richard Quin. The late spring rain was bringing a lovely scent out of the earth, and in the chestnut trees the furled candles were little and grey and downy. Mamma had said she would take us to Hampton Court to see the avenue in Bushey Park when the candles were all out. People said it was going to be a wet summer, but that would not matter, we would put up umbrellas and look at the candle-lit trees through the rain, Mamma was much more sensible than most grown-ups, she could enjoy things although it was not fine.

Before I passed through the blue-grey door in the wall I could hear the piping of Richard Quin's flageolet. He was playing, 'Believe me, if these endearing young charms', at least he was playing half of it, that was all he had got. I was sorry to hear that he had come to that tiresome time which happens when one is little. He had got past the stage of being contented with the things that are easy and natural because one was really born able to do them, and learning them was only a matter of teaching one's fingers what they knew they ought to do, and he had come to the stage when one realises how difficult playing is going to be, but one cannot go back and not be musical, that is how one hears things and there is no help for it. I could tell that he was feeling like that, partly because he sounded as if he were pushing against each note, in a fit of obstinacy, and partly because Mary and Richard Quin and I were not really separate beings. I passed through the yard, which was a little tidier than when we came, but not much, for we were all so terribly busy, and I found him just inside the stable door, close by Sultan's loose-box and facing Pompey and Caesar and Cream and Sugar. He was looking very little, his baby fingers solemnly busy on the stops, a frown of concentration on his baby brow. In this faded and dusty place his fairness was of another world. He was right in thinking the horses liked his music.

The horses had become made-up animals. I could nearly hear them stirring lightly on their hooves and munching their fodder in quiet content. Richard Quin finished the phrase he was playing, turned to me and nodded, then went from stall to stall, saying goodbye to the horses and patting them with that tactful touch necessary for caressing made-up animals, one has to touch them enough to show one is fond of them but one must not press so hard that it has to be admitted all round that they are insubstantial. When he was rubbing his head against Sugar's neck and Sugar whinnied he turned his eyes to me and laughed, as if to say this, seeing what is not to be seen and hearing sounds not uttered in this world, was a lovely game like finding the dyed eggs that Papa and Mamma always hid in the garden on Easter Day. I told him that Mamma was unhappy, and we wanted him to make her forget what was bothering her. He took my hand and we went back through the garden, putting our tongues out to taste the rain.

In the sitting-room Mamma was saying, 'So you see, Mary dear, even you did not realise what *tempo rubato* is and what it is not, and though I don't want you to think that your playing is anything more than elementary as yet, you probably know as much about the fine points of playing as Miss Beevor, so there was no harm in telling her what *tempo rubato* really means, though you must respect her, you must all respect her, she is doing her best, see what she has done for Cordelia.' Tears were running down each side of her long, thin nose.

Richard Quin carefully laid down his flageolet in a place where he thought it would not be touched, and then ran to Mamma and hugged her knees and kissed her, boisterously, as if he felt compelled to do it by love, but not so much that it was difficult for her to go on holding her teacup. 'I want a treat,' he said, nuzzling into her.

'What does my bad lamb want?' she asked, looking down at him in adoration. Of course she loved him more than the rest of us, anybody who ever saw him would know it had to be so.

'I want not to sit up during tea and behave properly,' he begged. 'I want to drink milk on the floor and have the sisters read *The City of Brass* to me.'

'But you can learn to read,' Mamma chided him, 'all your sisters were reading long books at your age.'

'Yes,' he answered with a shout of laughter great for his little body, 'they learned to read, so I needn't, it was kind of them.'

'But we shall have to work harder and harder at our playing, and then we won't have time to read to you,' said Mary, and I said, 'Besides, it's faster, you like things to go fast, you could read things to yourself far quicker than we can read them aloud.'

But as we spoke Mary was getting the *Arabian Nights* out of
the bookcase and was finding the place, while I filled his mug
with milk and buttered him some toast and put the mug and the
plate on the tray he used when he ate sitting on the floor. It
was a small eighteenth-century tray we had bought him one
Christmas from a rag-and-bone shop, and it was painted with a
Turkish scene of mosques and palaces and willow-hung canals.
It was so pretty that he let us keep it in the sitting-room, leaning
against the wall on the top of the bookcase. With the made-up
dogs, Ponto and Fido and Tray, lying in a semi-circle round
him, he ate and drank earnestly, for he was always very hungry,
pausing sometimes to trace the minarets of the mosques and the
domes of the palaces with the end of a crust. People who did not
know him would have thought that he was not listening, but if
one left out anything he cried out at once. If one skipped any of
the marvels on which the moonlight was shining when the travellers
came on the City of Brass, he would put it in, and to tease him
we would sometimes leave out some of the languages in which the
old sheikh spoke to the motionless sentinels when they did not
answer Arabic greetings. 'Greek you said, and the language of
Hind, and Hebrew and Persian and Ethiopian, but you have not
said Sudanese,' he would shrill. 'It spoils it all if you do not
say Sudanese.'

And he would get restless, sentences before we came to the
bit about the travellers finding the beautiful princess sleeping on
the bed spread with silken carpets on the ivory dais supported
by golden pillars, with two statues of slaves, one black and one
white, standing at the head of the bed. Then when we actually
got to the sentence which tells how one of the travellers climbed
on the dais and tried to kiss the sleeping princess, he would
whisper loudly and urgently, 'Leave out, leave out.' For he
could not bear it when the two statues moved and pierced the
traveller's head and heart with their pikes. He hated all violence.
So Mary left that bit out and we went on to the best part, where
the travellers went down to the sea shore and found the black
fishermen mending their nets. Mamma liked that bit very much,
particularly when the eldest fisherman was asked to explain the
mystery of the City of Brass and he answered, 'The people of the
City of Brass have been enchanted since the beginning of time
and will remain as they are until the Judgment Day.' She told

us that it was a very good thing to say about almost anybody. She also liked the bit about the copper jars in which the jinns who rebelled against King Solomon were imprisoned, and how they were sealed with his seal (Papa drew it for us) and thrown into the depths of the boiling sea, and how the fishermen used to unseal them because they wanted them to cook fish in, and told the travellers it was all right if one slapped the jar with one's hand before unsealing them and made the jinns inside confess that there was but one Allah and Mohammed was his prophet. When Kate made jellies for us we always used to slap the mould and force the jelly to acknowledge Allah and Mohammed before we turned it out.

We were just getting to this bit when Cordelia came in and banged the door and threw her satchel down on the sofa and stood and looked at Mamma and stamped.

She said, 'I have seen Miss Beevor and she has told me what you have done. Why do you hate me so? Why are you so cruel to me?'

Mamma said, 'Go and take off your good dress and we will talk of this quietly.' She put down her cup because her hand was trembling.

Cordelia screamed, 'How can I talk quietly about this? You are ruining my life.'

Mamma said, 'You mean because I have told Miss Beevor that you must not take professional engagements? That is not ruining your life. It is making sure that it will not be ruined. There is nothing worse for a musician, any sort of musician, than to perform in public too soon. It fixes a player at the stage he or she is at the time of their first appearance, and it is very hard to struggle on to the next stage.'

Mary and I looked at each other in bewilderment. Mamma got terribly angry with us when we made mistakes and the whole of Cordelia's playing was a mistake. But she was speaking to her quite gently about this horrible proposal. This was another instance of Mamma's curious tenderness towards her, which we could not understand.

Cordelia screamed again, 'It would not hurt my playing. Miss Beevor says she would go on teaching me all the time. It is not fair. You are only doing this because you cannot bear me to have more than the others.'

From the floor Richard cried, his light eyes on fire with anger, 'Go on with the story. The mermaids come next.'

Mamma said, 'But why do you want to play at these concerts? Wait, and if you are good enough you will play to audiences who really know what good music is, it will help you to have them listening to you. But these are second-rate affairs, it is impossible to think why you want to appear at them.'

Cordelia was still screaming when she answered, 'Why do I want to play at these concerts? Because I want the money.'

'But they will pay you very little,' said Mamma.

'Have we so much money that I can afford to refuse any?' asked Cordelia bitterly. She spoke so like a grown-up that we stared at her; she had the bitterness of grown-ups, the sort of shrewdness which never gets them anywhere. 'Mamma,' she said more gently but desperately, 'what is to happen to us all? We haven't any money. We children know that, we know there isn't the money to pay the gas and the school-fees, and even if you get the money from somewhere this time there will come a time when you won't.' Her face became a blue-white triangle, because of her intense fear. 'How can it possibly happen that the time won't come when Papa gambles everything away on the Stock Exchange and we won't have anywhere to go, anything to eat?'

Mamma stood up, then dropped back into her chair, her eyes staring stupidly, her jaw dropping. Mary and I drew nearer to her, to protect her, to dissociate ourselves from Cordelia. We were very much shocked. Of course we talked about our parents' affairs among ourselves; a child has a right to wonder what is going to become of it. But for children to speak of their parents' affairs in front of them was like going into the bathroom and finding either of them having a bath. We could not stop Cordelia with our angry looks, she went on, 'It isn't only the rent and the school fees, even as it is. We have horrible clothes, my boots are worn out, and I should not have been expected to wear them anyway, they are cheap and clumsy. Everybody laughs at us at school because we are so badly dressed. Mary and Rose do not notice it, there is only me to worry about us.'

'We do notice it,' I said, 'but we do not care.'

139

Cordelia waved at me impatiently. Her face was getting whiter and whiter. I thought she might faint as some of the girls at school did at prayers, and despised her. In our family we did not faint. 'We have nothing, nothing,' she said, 'and now that I have a chance to make something you will not let me take it because you love the others best. I want to make money and save it so that I can get a scholarship at the Royal Academy of Music or the Guildhall and have something to live on——' I do not think she had heard our mother's cry, she paused only because her desire for fame was like a winnowing fan in her throat — 'then I will make some money and study at Prague and then I will really make a lot of money and if I hurry up before the others get too old I will be able to help them. If I don't,' she cried, 'who will? Mary and Rose,' she said, after a pause, staring sadly at us, 'must do something to earn their living, they must teach or go into the Post Office, I will be able to pay for their training, and Richard Quin, something must, it must, be done for him.' With a tragic gesture of her whole arm she pointed at him as she sat on the floor by his tray. 'It's worse for him, because he's a boy. He must go to school, a proper school, he's so dreadfully spoiled, you know you say yourself what a pity it is that Papa was too delicate to stay at Harrow like Uncle Barry and that's why Uncle Barry has been a success and Papa hasn't. Richard Quin must go to a public school,' she said, looking at him with her upper lip curled in worried distaste, 'or he will be worse than Papa.'

Richard Quin brought his spoon down on his plate with a bang, and cried happily, trying to echo a phrase that my mother often used in argumentative crises, 'Change a subject. Change a subject. Silly Cordelia, change a subject.'

'See how he speaks to me,' said Cordelia hotly, 'and I am the eldest.' Suddenly she began to scream again. 'Oh, Mamma,' she shrieked, 'we are being so badly brought up.'

Mamma moved her lips, but we could not hear any words.

'I do not mean to be rude, Mamma,' said Cordelia, her voice dropping suddenly to a murmur, 'it is not your fault, it is Papa's——' again Mamma's lips moved, but she was still inaudible — 'but we are being so very badly brought up. Everybody at school,' she said, shivering, 'thinks Mary and Rose so odd.'

'Change a subject, change a subject,' advised Richard Quin robustly from the floor.

'We must be more like other people,' she went on frantically, 'we must fit in better, and you will not let me do anything to help, and if we only had ordinary clothes it would be better. If I made anything, anything at all, it would be something. Oh, let me earn what I can,' she wept, 'I am so miserable, and I am the only one that can do anything for us.'

She could speak no longer, and we all watched her in silence. We had to respect her tears because she had been painfully wounded by her destiny. But it was also true that she had inflicted wounds which would never completely heal on everybody in that room, except Richard, who was, for a particular reason of which neither she nor any of the rest of us was aware, proof against such injury. Mary slipped her left hand into my right. We had known the people at school did not like us, and we had wished it was not so; I had spoken of that very misery to Rosamund. But we had thought that some of the dislike felt against us was to our credit. Because of Papa and Mamma we knew the meaning of long words and were forward in our French and tried to speak it with a proper accent, and recognised the pictures the art mistress put up on the walls; so of course the people who were good at gymnastics and hockey thought we were silly, and many teachers are irredeemably cross by nature. Some of our unpopularity was our own fault, we knew that. We were often awkward and bumped up against things, and we often came out of our thoughts and found that something was expected of us and had no idea what, and then everybody laughed. And of course it is funny when everybody has sat down and only two people are left standing up, though perhaps they laughed rather a long time over it, for it is funny but not very funny. But now Cordelia had suggested to us that if people did not like us it was a sentence passed on our serious faults, and we were not merely absent-minded, there was a real flaw, a censurable unpleasantness, in our behaviour.

We did not quite believe her. We knew that she had always been silly and always would be. She was showing that by talking such nonsense about money. She would never be able to help us very much about that, and there would be no need, because we would earn all we needed as soon as we were grown-up. But we could not quite disbelieve her, for we knew that she was far nearer to the people at school than we were, and perhaps it is true that numbers count, it is not quite natural that two people should be right and hundreds of people wrong. So it happened that from this hour Mary and I had less power than before to make friends. Till that day we had supposed that the coldness strangers showed us could be broken down if we were nice to them, but for ever after we were impeded in our dealings with any but our familiars by the suspicion that the more they saw of us the more they were bound to dislike us.

I thought, 'Really Cordelia should not have done this to us,' and returned the pressure of Mary's hand. But we forgot our pain when Mamma rose to her feet. She seemed to have grown even thinner during the last few moments and her eyes were protruding. We wished she did not look so ugly when she was distressed, we knew that Cordelia would be feeling as horrid about it as if she were a stranger. But mercifully Mamma's voice was always much more beautiful when she was distressed. It became a thin, silver thread, rather high, spinning from behind her high forehead. The sound was quite lovely when she turned her face towards Cordelia and said, her eyes looking blank as if she did not see her, 'I will put on my bonnet and go and make my peace with Miss Beevor and she can accept all the professional engagements for you that you like.'

Cordelia cried, 'Oh, Mamma, thank you, thank you.' She glowed at having scored a point. But we were not sure. We knew that Mamma had been so hurt that she was astonished at her own pain, yet she looked also as if she were inflicting pain. When she went to the door her fingers came down on the handle as if she were reluctantly going out to perform some agonising mystery. She seemed very tired.

After she had gone Cordelia sighed with satisfaction and began to take off her gloves. Mary said, 'Come, Richard Quin, pick up your cup and plate.'

'It is not his bed-time,' said Cordelia.

'We are going down to sit in the kitchen till Mamma comes back,' said Mary.

After a moment's silence Cordelia said with an air of thrift, 'It will mean burning two gases.'

'I will give Mamma the half-crown Mr. Langham gave me last

142

time he was here,' said Mary, 'that will pay for a great deal of gas.'

'The book, *The Brass City*,' said Richard Quin, 'you did not get to the mermaids, you must read me the bit about the mermaids, I will have mermaids, lots and lots of mermaids, when I am grown-up.'

We three went down the steep stairs to the kitchen and I stood on the chair and lit the gas. It was more poetic than electric light, and I am sorry that so many children of today never see it. Over the gas-jet, inside the inverted glass bell, was a thing called an incandescent mantle, which, when you delicately turned on the tap in the gas-bracket and held a lit match over it, glimmered with a pale unsteady whiteness, like a little man risen from the dead whose cerements partook of the light of his immortality. There was also a faint pop as if a spirit was bursting its material bonds. Then you turned the tap full on and the shrouded man shone with the steady light of the angels, and you did not notice him any more, eternity had set in. Kate had left the kitchen looking very nice, she always did. The fire in the range was out because it was early summer and we did most of our cooking on a gas-stove, but she had blackleaded it so that it gave out brightness from its high lights. It was a huge range, but coal was so cheap in these days that we could afford to use it though we were so very poor. On the clean straw-coloured wooden table there were some folded sheets which Kate had been ironing before she went out, the strong business-like smell of the iron still rising from them. On the dresser there were the plates of our dinner service, which was a Mason Ironstone set, with three red and orange and gold Chinamen against a primrose background with little bits of deep blue scattered over it. On the top of the dresser were the polished copper moulds in which the blancmanges and jellies were made, we sometimes used them as castles in a game on the kitchen table. By gaslight it could not be seen that we had not had enough money to have the place properly done up since we moved into it, and coal ranges made kitchens very dirty. Mary sat down at the table and rested the *Arabian Nights* on the folded sheets, and turned over the leaves to find *The City of Brass*, while Richard Quin took a piece of kitchen paper out of a dresser drawer and a pencil out of his pocket. He enjoyed drawing while he was being read to; he always liked to do two things at once. I got some of our stockings out of Kate's work basket and sat in the creaky wicker armchair on the rag hearthrug and mended them. We all wished very much that this had not happened when both Rosamund and Kate were out. We would not have told either of them exactly what was wrong, but they would have understood, and the time would have passed more quickly while we were waiting for our Mamma to come back.

VII

THERE then began a period when, for the first time, I would have described myself as unhappy at home. I thought Mamma ought not to have allowed Miss Beevor to bring out Cordelia as a schoolgirl prodigy, partly because I was really a musician, and disliked my sister getting up on a platform and making a fool of herself, and partly because Cordelia had expressed contempt for Mary and me and I wanted her punished by frustration. But when I tackled Mamma I got an answer which seemed to me weak indeed.

'You see,' she said, 'supposing that you had a young musical genius of the magnitude of Mozart, and you had a wise and courageous teacher willing to give his life to save this genius from a cruel and unappreciative family . . .' she paused, letting her mouth fall open, and looking, I could not help thinking, rather foolish.

'Yes?' I said impatiently.

'Well, they would feel just like Cordelia and Miss Beevor.'

'But we know that Cordelia isn't a genius and Miss Beevor's awful.'

'Yes, but they do not know that. They feel just like Mozart and a guardian angel.'

'Well, tell them, tell them!'

'But they will not believe me. Why should they? And you know, it would be a bad thing if people always believed other people who said they were not geniuses. Many geniuses have been told at some stage or other that they were no good at all. Really, nature is very foolish. I do not see that there is much need for all of us to be able to distinguish in a second between a lion and a tiger, or a giraffe and a zebra, but there you are, it requires no knowledge of zoology to tell the difference at a glance. But only a good musician with a lot of time can tell the difference between a bad and a good musician.'

'Well, you're a good musician and you've had lots of time,' I persisted, 'and you know that Cordelia can't play for toffee. You ought to stop her. Really you should.'

'How can I dam up all that force?' sighed Mamma.

I thought she ought to try. Mary had once said to me that the adjectives which really suited grown-ups were 'lily-livered' and 'chicken-hearted'. They were incapable of taking decisive action when it was needed. For the first time it occurred to me that Mamma was infected with this vice. When Mamma found out about Aunt Clara's furniture having gone she should not have come to Lovegrove, she should have gone to some strange place without leaving an address, and gone with us to work in a factory, surely the four of us could have made enough to live on, and Papa would have been broken-hearted, and he would have got the police to trace us, and then he would have begged Mamma to bring us to Lovegrove, and she should have consented only on condition he promised never to gamble on the Stock Exchange again. But here we all were, with Mamma worrying all summer lest the gas were cut off, all winter lest the coal-merchant stopped supplies. And here was Cordelia who surely ought to have been whipped till she promised never to play the violin again. Whipping was, of course, wrong. It was a gross abuse of the physical advantage that grown-ups so unfairly enjoyed over children. But surely this was the one exception in which it would have been permissible.

I grew the more angry with Mamma because I detected that she had relaxed her attitude of hostility to Miss Beevor, whom I saw simply as the architect of our family disgrace, was beginning to regard her with compassion and even with amusement. She was always receiving little notes signed 'Beatrice Beevor' which announced triumphantly such news as that the Beckenham Freemasons had been so delighted with our little wonder-child's performance that the day after they had written to engage her for next year's banquet. Once, after Cordelia had appeared with dazzling success between Liza Lehmann's 'In a Persian Garden' and a selection from Amy Woodforde-Finden's 'Indian Love Lyrics', she enquired whether the usual note had come; and on hearing that it had not, she said, with deliberate nonchalance, 'I can't understand it, Aunt Bay-ah-tree-chay was most eager you should hear all about the reception I got.'

Mamma's eyebrows lifted at the news that Miss Beevor had joined our family, but a wanton light flamed up in her eye. 'Bay-ah-tree-chay?' she enquired.

'It is the Italian form of Beatrice,' Cordelia informed her.

'Yes, I know,' said Mamma. 'But why should Miss Beevor be called by an Italian name? I never met a woman more soundly English.'

'Of course she's English,' said Cordelia, pettishly. 'This is just a name that people call her if they know her awfully well. It seems that there's a very beautiful picture of Dante and some of his friends meeting Beatrice and some of her friends walking by the Arno, and just staring at each other because they don't know each other, and of course they didn't ever meet, which makes it all the more wonderful, and when Miss Beevor was young lots of people thought she looked just like Beatrice in the picture, so they started calling her Bay-ah-tree-chay.'

A series of expressions passed over my mother's face, the sum of which was, I recognised, pleasure. I thought this ridiculous. I knew the picture and Miss Beevor could not be telling the truth, she could never have looked anything like the Beatrice in it. I was shocked because my mother did not point this out, and on later occasions asked Cordelia for details of Miss Beevor's life with the shamefaced air of one seeking pleasure recognised as disgraceful. Beyond all doubt Mamma was not taking Miss Beevor seriously.

I had of course some happiness at this time. I derived it less than ever before or ever after from my sister Mary, who had grown silent and serious, and kept on writing fugues. It was my companionship with Richard Quin and Rosamund which irradiated my days with light. I never needed to feel jealous of their love for each other, as for the first moment of their meeting I feared I would, for when they were together without me they spent the time making our imagined world so solid that when I joined them it was a shelter and a joy about me. They would be sitting on the lawn, both fair, both visibly children of light, Rosamund so golden, Richard fair over dark, and Richard Quin would call to me, 'I say, you know Rosamund's hare?'

'Yes, why?'

'Well, you know it never will tell us its real name. We've found out why.'

'What is its reason? It'll be something silly. I never knew a cissier hare.'

'It is a silly reason. It told Rosamund it hoped that so long as we didn't know its name we would call it the Mysterious Stranger. It hasn't the least idea we call it Flopears.'

'Really, how ridiculous it is! It thinks it's romantic and like Lord Byron, and it's just old Flopears.'

But sometimes, like all made-up animals, that hare got out of hand and did more than we meant.

'What's it doing now?' 'Crouching down and rolling its eyes and waving its ears as if it wanted to show us something?'

'I can't think. And what's that coming out of the grass all round it?'

'Wheat, isn't it? It's trying to tell us that it once lived in a cornfield.'

'Yes, that's a poppy over there, behind its great tail. And there's some cornflowers.'

'So pretty. But Flopears looks frightened.'

But I knew suddenly what he was trying to tell us. I remembered our days on the Pentland Hills and knew that he had been killed, as so many of his kind are killed, at harvest time. He had been nibbling among the wheat when the cutter had started working round the edges of the field, and he had run to the middle because it was furthest from the sound, and thought himself safe. Then as the cutter went round the field in a closing spiral, the sound came nearer and nearer; and he and all the wild things which had gathered with him in the dwindling island of wheat must have been shaken by one pulse of fear. At last, when he could see the light through the stalks that had at first seemed solid as a wall, and when the cutter was a riot in his twitching ears, he left his island and ran for it across the raw stubble, and somebody lifted a gun and there was a bang, and he died, stretched out in a straight line because he had been running so fast. I got out my handkerchief and wiped my lips. I wished the hare had not brought this up in front of Richard Quin.

Rosamund said, 'Oh, I know why he's showing us the cornfield. As a matter of fact, it's one I know. It's by the seaside where Papa's cousin has that house. It's right beside the shore, and the sea is flat and blue and the cornfield is flat and yellow, and they both look like different kinds of water.'

'I know,' said Richard Quin, 'the fishermen are always making mistakes. They take out their boats to sail on the cornfield instead of the water.'

'And that's how they catch goldfish.'

'Yes, but they caught old Flopears too. They kept on hauling him up in a lobster-pot, and he kept on saying, "Sir! Sir! I would have you know——" and they kept on putting him back before he had time to tell them what he wanted them to know. That's why he wants to tell us about it now.'

'He says he could have sent them to the Tower. It's absurd.'

Very silly, of course, and I was really too old for that sort of thing, but it was a refuge from my teasing doubts about Mamma's wisdom, and my resentment against Cordelia; and I felt stripped and deprived when Rosamund was taken from us. But an old aunt who lived in Scotland got very ill, and so Constance went North and took Rosamund with her and sent her for a term to a Scotch school. Without her I was quite unable to deal with what circumstances turned into my formidable emotions. I know that Massenet and Gounod are really much better composers than is generally allowed today, and that Massenet's *Si tu veux, mignonne*, and Gounod's *Venise* would be conceded by everybody but the worst snobs to be lyric masterpieces, and that the two laid foundations on which Debussy and Fauré built much better; but when my sister Cordelia played arrangements of the less inspired works of these not infallible composers I suffered such agony as a Bishop would feel if a brother of his habitually got drunk and staggered down the aisle during Matins. I was wounded in my worldly and my more spiritual self. I hated a member of my family to be such a fool, and I felt that music was being profaned. Moreover Papa's finances were not improving and Mamma had had to tell us that we could not afford to go away to the seaside that year; and ever since Cordelia had been explaining to us that some day we would understand how hard she had worked and not had the pleasures the rest of us enjoyed, so that some day Mamma need not worry about money and we could all have happier lives. But since she had become a professional Mamma had had to buy her a second concert dress, and both had frequently to be cleaned; and Mary and I calculated that this ate so much into the profits that, by the time Cordelia had put by enough to pay for her musical education, and got on to providing us with a happier life, we should all be unable to worry about money, because we should be dead of old age.

It unfortunately happened that just at this time one of the relatives who had till now refused to have anything to do with us rescinded that decision. This was my Uncle Barry's widow, Aunt Theodora. A study of the memoirs of the period I am describing will show that the most admired women were large and unfeminine and severe, like women policemen, with passionate faces suggesting that they might presently be discharged from the force as a result of emotional complications. My Aunt Theodora was the wreck of such a woman, with pouches under her eyes and folds hanging from her jowls, and this disordered contour was due not to the destruction of her muscles by age but to the stamp left by an expression indicating outraged common sense. She saw the whole world as abandoned to improvident courses, and suspected it of allowing itself this irresponsibility because it counted on her to support it in the end. One of the most curious features of the age of plenty which ended with the First World War was the terror which rich people felt about their continued possession of their wealth. So when she came to see us it was very terrible. Most adults are rude to children, and many rich people are rude to the poor. We were children, we were poor, so we were victims of a double assault; and though we were bigger than we were we were still small, and she was very big. On entering our sitting-room she would say to Mamma, 'Well, you're still here, I see,' as if it surprised her that we had not been swept away into some abyss, which, however, might yet receive us. Her conversation consisted of comments on our circumstances too bluff and too indelicate to be called sympathetic, though if they were not that they could have no purpose, and when she could think of no more she used to turn her pouches and her jowls on us children, and enquire whether we realised we must earn our livings as soon as possible, adding, 'and there'll have to be no nonsense about it either.' This phrase was surely as destitute of meaning as the baying of a dog; and indeed we felt as if we were strayed alpine travellers, sunk in the snow, who found our faces snuffed by a huge St. Bernard, come not to bring us brandy but to take away any we might have.

One day during the holidays it happened that Mamma had gone out shopping with Richard Quin, Cordelia was in our bedroom making a sickly mess of the Berceuse from Goddard's 'Jocelyn', I was playing my arpeggios in the sitting-room and Mary was on the sofa doing her harmony lesson, and Papa was in his study working on his leader. There was a rat-tat on the door, and we knew at once that it was a telegram, for the telegraph boys who then dashed about England on red bicycles had a fine sense of the dramatic and had a bravura touch on the door-knocker. Kate was in the dining-room, so she took the telegram straight into the study, and then we heard Papa rush out into the hall and tear his coat and hat off the stand so that it fell over, and bang the front door behind him.

'He can't have lost any more money on the Stock Exchange,' said Mary, 'there can't be any left to lose.'

'Perhaps it is only politics,' I said.

Then Kate came in and said with a certain meaning, 'It's my day out. I could take you over to Wimbledon to have tea with my mother, if you wanted to go.'

We really did not have the time, Mamma was working with both of us on special pieces. But Kate repeated, her eyes dark like prunes, 'I did promise my Mum I would be taking you all out one of these days.'

So we said we would, knowing there was something up, and just then Mamma came back, and Kate said to her, 'I have just told Miss Mary and Miss Rose that my mother would be glad to have all of them, Miss Cordelia and Mr. Richard Quin too, for tea this afternoon. And, oh, Ma'am, a telegram came when you were out, and I took it to the master and he went straight out. But I think he said it was for you really, and it's on his desk now.'

Mamma said that of course she would be very pleased for us to go, and it was very kind of Kate and her mother, and went off to the study, later she came back and said that Aunt Theodora was coming to tea, but she had promised Kate she might take us out, so that must stand.

Absolutely no deception had been practised by anybody. By a refinement of honesty, Kate's manner had informed Mamma that there was another interpretation of the events she had recited, if she cared to enquire into it, though it was to be hoped she would not do so, as nothing would be gained. So there was not too much discussion of the situation before we three girls and

Richard Quin and Kate started off for Wimbledon. It was a pleasant bus-ride, though there was a horrid moment when an old lady on the top of the bus, delighted by Richard Quin's appearance, gave him a bright yellow cake out of a paper bag, the sort of cake that Mamma thought would kill us at once, and we all held our breaths until Richard Quin thanked her with a smile in which candid rapture came to its full tide, saying, 'Thank you, I am not hungry now, I will keep it for my tea, when I will really enjoy it'; and when she had got off the bus he handed the cake to Kate and made impudent use of a formula she often applied regarding unfavoured foods: 'You will oblige me by finding a poor child who would be glad of this.' And of course we had a nice time at Kate's mother's cottage, it was a special place.

She was tall and sailorly like her daughter and her home looked as if it were beside the sea. She lived in one of four cottages, some centuries old, on a cobbled causeway which was all that survived of some village street long since erased to make room for the gardens of two Italianate Victorian villas, the walls of which now towered above the little cottages. There was a great deal of holystoning, and a strong smell of tar; and the nets Kate's father had taken to sea now hung on the raspberry canes and the blackcurrant bushes. There was a ship's figurehead out in the garden, a lady carrying a lamb. It had come off the *Merciful Flora*, the ship Kate's father and grandfather had sailed in till she broke up off Sark in 1888. Inside the house were ships in bottles, and carved ivories of monkeys and elephants, and a kingfisher-feather head-dress, and a straw-coloured shawl with birds and flowers and ladies with little black pages holding high coloured parasols over them; and all these things Kate's mother told us we could handle as we liked, giving us a smile as prim and slow as Kate's, as she told us that if we should break anything it would not matter, there would be always another of her family to bring something to take its place. So we never broke anything. This visit was particularly enjoyable because the *Merciful Flora* needed repainting, and we were able to help by scraping all the old paint off her with sandpaper, so that when Kate's brother came next week he could put the paint straight on. We worked away and quite forgot how worried about money Papa and Mamma were; and I forgot all about Cordelia's playing, because she was really very nice when she was doing something she really could do, in circumstances which made her forget her need to prove her superiority.

But we went home quite early. Kate's mother always gave us a lovely tea, and she did this time too, though she had not expected us. She had some lardy cake in the house, and she made us some West Country splits, and she said she expected us to finish a whole new pot of her raspberry jam, which she did not cook, she heated the fruit and she heated the sugar and beat them up together for half an hour, so that it tasted like fresh raspberries. At tea Kate's mother told us with the comfortable steady sombreness of her daughter that a great trouble had fallen on England, but that nobody seemed to give it a thought. Mary said in an interrogative tone, 'And sorrow darkens hamlet and hall,' which is what Lord Tennyson said happened when the Duke of Wellington died. Kate's mother said, 'Yes, indeed, for it's just as bad for those in private service.' We had thought she was talking of some national calamity such as Papa prophesied in his leader, but she was speaking as a washerwoman. It seemed that her life, the lives of all who practised her craft, had been made twice as difficult because gentlemen had adopted the heathen custom of wearing pyjamas. She could not understand why they had got this silly notion of wearing coats and trousers in bed when nightshirts were so much easier to iron, and she never hung a pair of the horrid things on the line without saying to herself, 'Ah, since I come of a seafaring family I know what nasty savage parts you come from.' But she was not very unhappy about it, and soon she was telling us we could make lardy cake at home. We must go to the baker and buy a lump of his dough, and take it home and roll it out, and then fold it up as if it were a length of cloth we were going to send as a present through the post, and put in between each layer some lard and brown sugar and spices and currants and raisins, and bake it in our own oven, and remember to shake sugar over it just as we took it out. 'Gentlemen always like it,' she said, looking at Richard Quin as if he were a specimen of some wild but valuable variety of animal on which she was lecturing, 'you will find in every family that the mistress tries to have nothing low served up in the front of the house, but what pleases the master better than anything is to get hold of a good lardy cake or a piece of dripping toast.' Oh, wanton Papas, letting

153

Eastern gods into this green and pleasant land by wearing night-clothes hard to iron, and getting their hands greasy with coarse fare forbidden by refined Mammas. . . .

We could not have had a more pleasant afternoon. When we got home we ran straight into the sitting-room without taking off our hats and coats to tell Mamma how exceptionally lovely it had all been. She was looking very tired, and she sighed, 'Oh, I wish I had been with you!' And indeed she would have liked it. She would have enjoyed sand-papering the *Merciful Flora*, it was a job that was half a game like making-up an animal, she could have lost herself in it as she did in toy-making. 'But though, of course, I was glad that your Aunt Theodora came, but she stayed a little long.'

Cordelia said, 'Do you mean that Aunt Theodora called this afternoon?'

'Did you not know?' said Mamma, sleepily, passing her hands over her head. 'I would have had to keep you in to see her if I had not already promised Kate you could go with her.'

'I never knew!' exclaimed Cordelia. 'I never knew!'

I realised that she had been upstairs while Kate and Mary and I had made the few delicate arrangements necessary for our escape. 'Cordelia,' I said in astonishment, 'you wouldn't rather have stayed in and seen Aunt Theodora?'

'Of course I would!' said Cordelia. Each of us was astonished by the other.

'But why?' I asked.

Cordelia was on the point of tears. 'I could have told her about all the engagements I've got!' she wailed.

'But why?' I asked again.

'She would have been sure to be pleased,' she snivelled.

'But who wants to please that horrible old beast?' I raged.

'I cannot think why your Papa and I gave you the name of Rose,' said Mamma. 'From the first we should have seen it was quite unsuitable. Please be silent.'

'Mamma,' I said, trying to be reasonable, 'we have to have Aunt Theodora in the house, though I don't want any of us to please her. Not to please her. It would be like wanting us to please Nero, or what's the man who did all the murders, Charles Peace. None of us but Cordelia would want to please her.

Cordelia is . . .' I paused, choked by the intensity with which I wanted to murder her.

Now I recall my emotions at that moment, children seem to me a remarkable race. They want so much to murder so many people, and they so rarely murder anybody at all.

'Cordelia is such rubbish,' I concluded.

'Listen, Mamma,' exclaimed Cordelia, 'you see how it is, I am the eldest, but none of them treats me with the slightest respect. All the other girls at school who have younger sisters make them obey them and fetch things for them, and that is how it should be.'

'But perhaps,' suggested Mary, 'those other girls do not revolt their younger sisters by playing the violin and scooping all the high notes.'

'Aren't you glad, Mamma,' asked Richard Quin, 'that after having three little girls you had a little boy?'

'My lamb, you put it very well,' said Mamma. 'Will you run down now and ask Kate to give you your supper, and you, Cordelia, go up to the bedroom, and you, Mary, go up to my room, and you, Rose, go into the dining-room, and I will come in and talk to each of you separately before I tell Papa about this.'

I walked up and down the dining-room while I waited for her. None of us had been at all impressed by her threat to tell Papa about us. He was interested in nothing about us except our looks and our capacity to absorb ideas. If he explained to us why all parties engaged in the recent South African War had been wrong, and our comments were intelligent, then he burned with love for us, and if they were stupid, he shook his head like a horse rebelling against the bit and went away to be alone. The trouble was that to all intents and purposes there was no man in the house. I decided to supply the need.

'Why are you giving an imitation of Henry the Eighth?' enquired Mamma when I began. But I persisted, 'Mamma, why are you so weak with Cordelia? It makes life impossible for all of us. And it will ruin her character. I can't understand it. You seem to be doing everything wrong.' Suddenly panic seized me, and I was no longer the family solicitor, but a little schoolgirl. 'If you do silly things, what is to happen to us all? Why do you let that awful Miss Beevor make a fool of Cordelia?'

'I have told you,' said Mamma. 'Sit down, my dear. There are the raisins I bought this morning on that dessert plate. Bring it here and we will wickedly eat all the fat ones and complain at supper that they were not worth buying. I have told you why I cannot come between Miss Beevor and Cordelia, between Cordelia and her violin.'

'About them thinking they're like Mozart and some wonderful teacher?'

'Mozart and César Thomson,' she grimly suggested.

'Well! That's mad, and so it ought to be stopped,' I persisted.

'But I told you,' she said wearily, 'nobody can prove them wrong. It is no use trying to tell these two that Cordelia cannot play. They will not believe it, they will think that we are trying to cheat Cordelia out of her just glory.'

'But the nonsense would end if you kept Miss Beevor out of the house,' I droned on.

'We cannot keep Miss Beevor and Cordelia apart now,' sighed Mamma, 'people meet, and there's an end to it. Have another raisin. If you roll the little withered ones between your fingers they taste sweet and rich like the big fat ones.'

'Can we never keep people out of the house if we want to?' I grumbled.

'Not so many come,' said Mamma. 'Oh, I hope you have many friends, go to lots of parties, when you are grown up.'

'There is Miss Beevor,' I stormed, 'and there is Aunt Theodora. We should keep them out. They are so bad for Cordelia's character.'

'I should not worry about that, dear,' said Mamma.

'I must worry about it,' I said solemnly. 'Look what Cordelia said tonight. You know, Mamma, we had such a lovely time with Kate's mother. Sam is going to repaint the *Merciful Flora* his next leave, so we got all the old paint off with sandpaper. And she baked splits for us and gave us a whole pot of raspberry jam and said we must finish it. But I am worried, it had a lovely flavour, and I know that Kate's mother puts brandy in some of her jam, I hope this had none in it, or we shall not be able to claim the money Papa promised us.'

156

'What money was that, dear?' Mamma asked in surprise.

'Why, he is going to pay us each a hundred pounds when we are twenty-one if we can say we have never drunk anything alcoholic. It really matters about Richard Quin, of course, but Papa says he has seen girls at hunt-balls who drank champagne as if they were gentlemen, and he hears that nowadays they even drink port at dinner, which is terrible, so he said we could each have the money like Richard Quin if we earned it.'

'You should be grateful,' said Mamma, 'for having a father so mindful of your welfare.'

'Oh, we are,' I said, 'we are.' It crossed my mind that she spoke as if she were laughing at something, and I looked hard at her, but her face was smooth. So I went on, 'Well, anyway, the jam was lovely, and Kate's mother told us about pyjamas being heathen, and how to make lardy cake, and was very nice. And yet Cordelia said she would rather have been here telling Aunt Theodora about her idiotic engagements. Mamma, she wanted Aunt Theodora to approve of her. You can't really want her to try to please Aunt Theodora. Look where trying to please Miss Beevor has got her, and Aunt Theodora is worse than Miss Beevor, she is just a cruel beast.'

'You must not say that, Rose,' said Mamma.

'But I must say it, because it's true.'

'You must not say it,' said Mamma, 'you must never say one word against Aunt Theodora. I do not know what would have happened to us two months ago if Aunt Theodora had not given me quite a large sum of money.'

I have recorded my opinion that children are a remarkable race, because they want so much to murder so many people and murder so few. But they have a bad criminal record. Though Mamma's face always lit up when she was given the smallest present, it darkened when she spoke of Aunt Theodora's generosity, and I knew quite well that the gift must have been made in some disagreeable fashion. I was right. My mother had been subjected to deep humiliation during the last few weeks. The gift had been proffered before it had been requested, with an air of rollicking bonhomie, and protestations that all the donor asked of the recipient was that the matter should never be mentioned between them. On their next meeting, memory of this lively prohibition had restrained Mamma until her emotions forced out of her a quick expression of gratitude, and at once it was intimated to her that this had come too late and was inadequate. There had followed visits from Aunt Theodora, during which there always came a period when she grew grave, fell silent, and sank in her chair, while her jowls and pouches drooped, and all of her was drawn downwards by her fear that she had wasted her bounty on an object impossible to arrest on its wilful progress towards doom. There were also summonses to Aunt Theodora's house at Esher. There my poor mother had to sit over long luncheons, while Aunt Theodora found herself too depressed to speak, though afterwards she rallied sufficiently to ask my mother in driving tones whether she was really fully conscious of her situation. There were also letters. Aunt Theodora had for some time past stopped using the black-edged writing-paper of her widowhood, but she now brought it out again, to be covered with empty and solemnly impudent exhortations.

But I did not think of my mother's martyred pride. I thought of my own conceit. I gasped, 'Mamma, we shouldn't have taken money from Aunt Theodora.'

'I had to do it,' she told me. She was speaking very softly. I suppose she could not bear to speak of it aloud. She went on nibbling raisins, innocently unaware that I was being disagreeable.

'But anything would have been better than that! Mamma, you had no right to do this to me! You should have told me! I am ashamed to think I have been living on Aunt Theodora's money!'

She stared at me in astonishment. Her head dropped forward, but she held it high again. 'You need not be troubled, dear,' she said. 'Aunt Theodora's money went straight out of the house. Nobody could accuse you of living on it now.'

'You could have done something else,' I raged. 'You could have let Mary and me leave school, of course Cordelia would not mind, but we would far rather have gone to work in shops or factories and brought the money home.'

After a pause she said mildly, 'But you and Mary must go on with your piano lessons.' It seems to me remarkable that she resisted the temptation to say, 'You little fool, as if we could be helped by anything that you could do.'

I almost shouted, 'You don't really care about us! Not really! Or you wouldn't have put us in the position of taking money from Aunt Theodora!'

She murmured, 'My head is aching.'

'We must pay back every penny,' I said.

'Yes, dear, some time, but we cannot do it now.'

'We must do it as soon as possible,' I nagged, 'we should be saving every penny.' I pointed at her plate. 'You should not have bought those raisins. We could have done without them.'

She looked down at the stalks and pips, the last few smallest fruit, which were the incriminating evidence of her little, little greed. She said, 'I am sorry, dear, but you really do not understand. And you must leave Cordelia alone,' and she rose and left me.

We came together in spite of my brutish stupidity, because we loved each other, and by mere physical contact with her I was forced into a field of good behaviour, where I was better than I was of nature at this period. For I passed into a detestable phase. I felt that I was ill-done-by because I distrusted both my parents. I had long known Papa was wonderful but no good as a Papa; he should not have sold Aunt Clara's furniture. But now it seemed to me that Mamma was no good either, because she would not stop Cordelia playing the violin and because she seemed to be managing our financial affairs unwisely. I felt sure, of course, that in the end we would be all right. Mary and I never doubted that we would be all right. But we would have to have a framework in which to be all right, and about that I was no longer certain. I remember going out into the garden that autumn, into a warm and sleepy afternoon, and bending down to pick up a golden chestnut-leaf that had fallen on a flower-bed, and finding that the earth underneath was very cold. I felt again the fear, of which we had once spoken with Papa and Mamma during the week between Christmas and New Year, and had often discussed since, only convinced it was scotched when the time came for us to look for dyed eggs among the bushes on Easter Day: the thought that there might yet come a winter which would never end, which would never change to spring. Papa had said that might happen, but not for a long time. Now this thought frightened me, I conceived for the first time that the world might stop totally, and my mind ran past that, it seemed to me that was what was called immortal, what survived of men and animals after they died might also be mortal. I was truly aware of death for the first time, and I saw what it was as clearly as if someone walking beside me had spread out a large-scale map of it and held it before me as I walked, showing me nothingness and nothingness and nothingness, so that I could not fail to see where we were going. It was true that Mamma believed that there would always be a spring, but she was little and thin, much smaller than Papa, and this seemed to me to bear a discouraging significance, particularly when I lay in my bed between sleeping and waking. Then too I would see my brother Richard Quin as I had often seen him practising his flageolet in the stables, tiny under the high rafters, tiny in the empty distances. It did not seem to me that Mamma and Richard Quin could make the whole world go on working if it wanted to stop. I felt certain that I would be destroyed by death, and I wanted as much of life as I could get while I was still alive. In my eyes the life in my home was being impaired by my parents' ineffectiveness. It would have been better, I thought then and often afterwards, if only Rosamund had not gone away.

But we would have her back again soon. Mamma said it was very unlikely that Aunt Jean would live till the end of the year. The hope of having Rosamund with us for Christmas was a great encouragement to myself, and to Mary, who was unhappy too, though I do not know to what degree, for her smooth oval face kept its secrets, she never needed to resolve with her mind to practise reserve, for it was one of her physical qualities. We abandoned ourselves to the pleasure of our Christmas preparations, which were now principally concerned with Richard Quin and with Rosamund. For we were getting too old to play with our dolls' houses, though actually we always kept them about; and ever since Richard Quin had been given his first fortress he had been creating a world of contending armies dominated by Alexander the Great and Wellington, who were united against Napoleon and Charlemagne; and it required a good deal of furnishing; and Rosamund lacked a great many possessions which we would have thought anybody related to us was bound to have. We had lots of pencil-boxes, all of them very nice, which Papa had painted with things like the battle-mented churches and castles and blue hills from the backgrounds of Flemish and Italian pictures. But she had only one pencil-box, and that had been bought in a shop, we were so sorry for her. When Mary and I made our presents for these two we felt we were doing really necessary work, and the time would have passed quite pleasantly if it had not been for a very disagreeable experience we had just at the end of the school term.

There was a geography mistress whom we rather liked, Miss Furness, one of the few teachers we could imagine our-selves choosing to go on knowing when we had grown up. She had a timid, wavering voice, and green eyes, with flecks of dark green on a light-green iris, like gooseberries, and sandy hair which curved across the front of her head in a high hollow crescent, the shape of a boat turned upside down. We used to imagine her walking across England and coming to the Severn or the Wye or the Ouse, and taking off this crescent and launching it the right way up and floating in it to the opposite shore, shading her green eyes and calling apologetically, 'Ahoy, there.' She obviously wanted to be nice, she flushed and had to force her voice when it came to saying, 'And now for those girls who failed,' and she taught her subject in a quite interesting, gasping way. Even physical geography, which tells so many things one does not want to know, such as why there is night and day, was interesting because she spoke of the stars with such wistful respect. So we were very pleased when she asked us to tea, particularly as she lived in a part of Lovegrove we liked very much, where a dozen early Victorian villas stood white and betowered and battlemented round a three-cornered scrap of village green, shaded by a row of tall old limes.

The house was as nice as we had expected. Miss Furness' grandfather had bought it from the builder and her father and mother had moved there when he had given up teaching epigraphy at Oxford. There was a feeling that the same people had always lived there, and that there had always been enough money, which we liked very much. Nothing was shabby. She showed us everything, moving and speaking as hesitantly as if she were not hostess but guest. She put a timid forefinger to the curtains, to the wallpapers, which alike were a rich-coloured paste of little flowers, and told us that they were the work of William Morris;

and she took us to the fireplaces, where huge fires glowed orange, and pointed down at the tiles, which showed windmills and castles and men in armour, and said they were made by the clever Mr. William de Morgan, who made tiles better than anybody had made them for hundreds of years. There was much furniture, so highly polished that its very solidity made it the more airy, there were such broad surfaces reflecting the warmed and ruddy light. The winter day which was blanched and cold was annulled; and we were happy, particularly when Miss Furness took us to see her mother, who now never left her room. She wore a huge silver chignon, through which ran some streaks as sandy as her daughter's hair. We had always known that the other girls were talking nonsense when they said that the curious hollow crescent across Miss Furness' head was a transformation. Mrs. Furness had had a relative who was one of the first English amateur photographers, and she showed us some portraits, very sharp and linear and refined, almost like drawings, except for the pale, milky blacks, of Lewis Carroll and some little girls at a tea-party he gave to celebrate the publication of *Alice in Wonderland*. What amused us so much that we could hardly keep our minds on the photographs was that Mrs. Furness had an asthmatic pug lying beside her which was exactly like the pug we had made up when we were younger and had first come to Lovegrove Place. Finally we had to tell her, in case she thought we were rude, and she and her daughter quite understood.

Then we went down to tea in the dining-room. It was a very good tea, with cherry cake that had cherries all the way through, and not just at the bottom. It was a pity that Mrs. Furness could not come down, we had liked her so much. There was a big clock on the chimney-piece, with a beautiful tick, almost like a purr, but this room was not as nice as the others, for it was hung with large photographs, framed in reddish oak, of stones bearing inscriptions in ancient languages, with notices in black letters underneath saying where they had been found. They introduced a look of schoolroom squalor. When we had finished Miss Furness did not rise, we just went on sitting at the table. We listened to the agreeable tick of the clock, and we looked round the room. Mary asked Miss Furness if the inscriptions had ever turned out to be interesting when they had been translated. Miss Furness looked embarrassed, and then smiled, and said with an air of daring, 'Do you know, never. Never to me. The most interesting are laws. But such dull laws.' Then she relapsed into silence again. We did not mind, this was such a very safe, well-cared-for house, we liked being there.

The pug waddled in, and we asked if we might give him the last piece of bread-and-butter. She did not answer, but cleared her throat and said that she was much too fond of us to want us to be anything but happy, and a little bird had whispered to her that we had not been very happy lately. Mary and I stiffened. But of course everybody in Lovegrove knew about Papa's debts, lots of little things had told us that; and anyway whatever Miss Furness was trying to say she meant to be kind, her face was flushed and her voice was forced as it was when she had to give out the list of girls who had failed in the examination. Both of us began to assure her that we did not really mind being poor, that Mamma and Papa were wonderful to us, and that as to money, in a few years we would be pianists, and it would be all right. We really quite liked the turn the conversation had taken, though it was unexpected. Obviously both Miss Furness and the old lady upstairs would find great difficulty in imagining the day-to-day hazards of life with our Papa, no dun had ever waited in this room among the highly polished furniture, listening to the purring tick of the clock on the mantelpiece. But we felt that both these women were on the side of what was good, they would admire our Mamma for being so brave and never giving up, and we saw them inviting her to the house, and making her free for an hour of its ease and safety. We even thought they might approve of us, for between school and our piano we worked hard.

But Miss Furness would not let us speak. She closed her eyes and pressed on with the delicate task her goodness had forced her to undertake. Wincing, as one who uncovers a wound, she said she had reason to sympathise with us in our troubles, for she had two sisters who in every way far outshone her. She knew therefore too well what it was to hear a sister win praise and admiration and to receive none oneself. But what a pity it would be to stop loving a sister only because she had gifts which made her specially worth loving! That would be a waste of what was most precious, most precious here on earth, that was, and one must not let anything go so wrong, even if to put it right one had to conquer one's foolish pride and be brave enough, brave like a soldier, to admit that when one's sister got praise which was withheld from oneself it was because she alone deserved it.

Very clearly Mary and I were not to receive any such benison of approval as we had for a moment imagined. It had been significant that when Miss Furness had begun to speak her voice and bearing had reminded me of the occasions when she read out the list of girls who had failed. Miss Beevor, I supposed, had been talking: and perhaps we had too honestly failed to respond when our teachers and schoolfellows talked of Cordelia's local triumphs. It also occurred to me for the first time that nobody at school knew that Mary and I were studying seriously to become professional pianists. We did not take piano lessons at school, and though Mamma had sent us in for the usual local examinations and we had always passed with honours, we had never thought this worth mentioning. I tried for a minute or two to think of some way to dispel Miss Furness' misinterpretation of the musical situation in our home. There was a Broadwood baby grand in the drawing-room, and I had thought of asking if Mary and I might go upstairs and play a duet. Mamma was quite pleased with the way we played some of Schubert's 'Marches Héroïques.' But it occurred to me that probably Miss Furness understood nothing of music. I realised that, nice as she was, understanding on quite a number of subjects was probably not what one should ask of her; it was not in the bond. Also I realised that a drama about me and my family had been composed by someone and had for some time been in the course of performance, and it would be no use for me to walk on the stage and protest that the truth had been perverted, for every member of the audience had had their minds made up for them by what they had already heard. If at this moment Mary and I offered to play the piano for Miss Furness it would be taken as a sign that obstinate envy still kicked against the pricks. I suffered both as a child and an adult, for I heard in my memory that abominable thing that my eldest sister made of the opening strains of Goddard's 'Berceuse'; and the craftsmanship that my mother had built hour after hour into my hands crisped my fingers in impersonal anger. I sat quite still, and so did Mary, while the blood mounted under her skin, which I had never seen before but white; and Miss Furness raised her freckled hand to finger a small seed-pearl cross suspended from her throat and begged us, her green eyes crystalline with tears, to remember that if we went to Jesus He would help us.

VIII

WHEN we got home we said that we had enjoyed the tea party with Miss Furness very much. Even to each other we did not speak of what had really happened, and enclosed ourselves in very diligent work at the piano. Shortly before, Mamma had pronounced Mozart's 'Gigue in G' too difficult for me (and indeed it is very tricky) but I set myself to master it and within a few days I had learned it so thoroughly that though I have rarely played it in my adult life, it is to this day at the end of my fingers, I sometimes come out of my sleep remembering it note by note. But I was working in a desert. I was hungry and thirsty. Nothing seemed to be right in my life, for I was still a disagreeable egotist, and I resented Miss Furness' assault on my pride without reflecting that Mamma must have a hundred wounds to my one. But all would be well when Rosamund came back; and though I thought I distrusted Mamma I believed that Rosamund would be with us before the end of the year because Mamma had said so.

And a few days before Christmas, there was a knock at the door, and Kate called for Mamma, and then Mamma cried out, and Constance's voice, precise and level, sleepy and yet vigilant, gave a placid answer. I jumped up from the piano and Mary threw down her harmony book and Cordelia clattered down the stairs, and there they were in the hall, Mamma embracing them, the two so tall and calm, so shyly smiling. Richard Quin pushed past us and flung his arms round Rosamund, pulling her height down to him, crying, 'I have just found out, the gas comes from the gas-works.'

'Oh,' she said, slowly, opening her eyes wide. 'Those round things?'

'Yes,' he said. 'They look like castles, I never guessed.'

We all went into the sitting-room and they gave us the presents people bring from Scotland, Edinburgh rock and short-bread, and hair-ribbon for us, in Mamma's tartan. Then Mamma said to Constance, 'Is Aunt Jean gone?' and Constance said,

'Yes, a week ago,' and Mamma threw back her head and made a sweeping gesture, as if she were following the path of a falling star. 'Was it hard?' she said.

'Yes,' said Constance. 'But with all she knew it was not like going blind-fold.'

'To be sure,' sighed Mamma, 'but even so. . . . And it must have been wearying for you.'

'The nights were very long sometimes,' said Constance. 'I do not know what I would have done without Rosamund.'

Mamma looked at Rosamund with more respect than adults usually feel for a schoolgirl, and said, 'Yes, Rosamund would be a great help.'

It had already struck me that Rosamund had changed. I did not altogether like the change, for it took her further away from me. She had never been quite like any other girl I had ever seen. I was to realise as an adult how unique her appearance was. It was the peculiarity of her mother and herself that if they had been suddenly deprived of colour they would have been exactly like statues. This was not because they were lifeless but because they had an intense life which was independent of physical motion. In Constance this was a little funny. She was so like what a Victorian sculptor would have wanted to create that it was as if she were on holiday from the façade of a Town Hall. But Rosamund was like a Greek statue. Surely she stammered because stone should not be asked to speak, and she had been given by sculpture another sort of eloquence. Even as a child I realised that by simply existing, by simply having the face and body that she had, she conveyed a meaning of a sort that I found in music. Now she had come back from Scotland she meant still more. There was a veil about her face, made by what she knew and I did not know. I was full of wonder, I put out my hand and touched her as if I could learn her secret through my skin.

'Can you not come and stay with us?' said Mamma fondly. 'You know I have to put you in an attic up beside Kate, but you have been comfortable up there before.' We did not need to join our pleading with hers, for Constance and Rosamund looked at each other and smiled shyly, and owned that on their return they had found that Jock was to be away in the West Country for three days, and that they had come over in hopes of being invited to stay, but in case it was not convenient they had left their bag at the station. Then there was great happiness, and it was arranged that after luncheon Rosamund and Richard Quin and I would go to the station and fetch the bag, and Richard Quin told Rosamund that if we were lucky we could get the cab with a driver who was very proud because his horse had a brother who had won the Derby. I thought this delightfully childish of him, but it occurred to me that when we had first come to Lovegrove I too had believed this story, which must have been invented by the owner of that particular cab-horse in a spirit of despairing irony. 'We change,' I thought, 'and Rosamund has changed.' But she had not gone from me. It is hard to express the totality of Rosamund's effect; but in her it was not only the eyes and the mouth, which are communicators by profession, but every physical attribute, the heavy golden ringlets on her shoulders, her fair skin, which stopped the light like the petal of a large flower, the firm line of her flesh where it fell from the wide cheekbone to her sweeping jaw, her stooping and diffident body, her meditative hands, which promised me eternal friendship.

There was a ring at the front door, Cordelia was called out, and came back as fussy as the worst kind of grown-up. 'That was Nancy Phillips leaving my algebra book; she took it home by mistake. She was rather upset because I had to tell her that I could not come to her party tomorrow. But I have this unexpected engagement at Richmond. I never,' she said consequentially to Rosamund and Constance, 'have any little pleasures now, it is all work.'

My mother's lip tightened and she made an irritable movement of the hand. Cordelia responded by an old-maidish jerk of the head. In effect Mamma had said, 'Then do not play at the concert, you know that I loathe you to take these ridiculous professional engagements,' and Cordelia had replied, 'What is to become of all of us if I do not go on with my career?' I was blind with hatred; I saw Miss Furness' freckled hand playing with the small seed-pearl cross.

Cordelia went on to say, 'Nancy was very disappointed at hearing that I was not coming to the party. You know Mary had to refuse because she promised to go to tea with Ida Oppenheimer. Well, it seems Nancy's Mamma gets cross if anybody doesn't come, she says it is not worth while giving parties except for a large number, it is all such a bother. So could Rosamund go?'

'What a strange thing for a woman to tell her daughter,' said Mamma. 'I would so much like to give proper parties for you, but perhaps there is some trouble in the family that is on her mind. Anyway, Rosamund, you would be doing Nancy a kindness if you go with Rose tomorrow.'

Rosamund said politely that she would like it very much, and went back to the drawings Richard Quin was showing her. These were quite good, especially the ones of the ghost of Napoleon laughing at the Duke of Wellington, when the mob broke his windows on the anniversary of Waterloo, because he wanted them not to have votes. It was funny, Richard Quin was old enough to have understood most of what Papa told us about the Duke of Wellington, but he was so excited about gasometers that he had drawn one in the window of the room in which Napoleon's ghost was appearing.

'It must have happened,' said Richard Quin. 'It is so natural for it to happen, Napoleon's ghost must have laughed like that, it must have happened, I wonder if anybody else knows about it.'

When Rosamund came to the last drawing she sat back and sighed, 'Oh, how I have missed you all.'

'Did you miss the horses?' asked Richard Quin. 'They have asked after you. Regularly. Let's go and see them now.'

We crossed the garden, which was metallic with winter. Our breaths were smoke before us, our heels rang on the iron-hard gravel path, on its water-logged side the thin ice crackled like glass as we took turns in breaking it, above it the bare branches were fine smithy work. Richard Quin stopped before he opened the door in the wall, and said, 'You hear them whinnying?'

Slowly Rosamund nodded, slowly smiling. 'It's nice to be remembered. But how do they know it's me?'

'How do they know things?' shrugged Richard Quin.

In the stable they went from stall to stall, palms spread under unseen muzzles, offering unseen sugar, they plaited unseen manes with their fingers, they slapped and stroked unseen smoothness, answered unheard neighing. I watched them from the doorway, remembering the first night we had spent at Lovegrove, when Mamma and I had stood in the empty stable and had heard stamping hooves, and at last had seen luminous shapes about us; or I had dreamed it so. Surely these two others were also seeing what cannot be seen? I could even persuade myself that I saw the images which their eyes recovered from space, and it surprised me that though Cream and Sugar were as I had imagined since I had received the hint of those luminous shapes, with long curled lovelocks tumbling down their high foreheads and shining, docile eyes, and two rounded shining mounds on their chests, they were not cream-coloured but pearly grey. Soon, however, I could watch no longer, I was so bitterly cold. I had made Richard Quin put on his greatcoat and had come out without my coat or my gloves. The tips of my fingers were blue and numb. I breathed on them, and then held them away from me in distaste, thinking, 'This is how my whole body will be when I am dead.' And there might come a time when there would be no living hand anywhere, no hand that could play music, and no music, nor even, so long the reach of death, any remembered music.

I called to them, really for help, though what I said was, 'We must go back to the house, it is too cold,' and it sounded cheerful enough.

'Yes,' said Richard Quin, 'it is too cold, and silly sister came out without a coat.'

We all ran out of the stable shivering and hissing through our teeth and slapping ourselves. Rosamund said, the words jolted out of her by her running, 'It is so cold, I did not bring my hare.'

'He is well off underground,' said Richard Quin. 'You should not disturb him. He is all right down in that brown passage, lying curled up on himself, his ears folding back on him like a fur rug, his whiskers fanned by his breath, in-out, in-out, in-out, the whole winter long, till the spring comes.'

'Oh, he does well anywhere,' said Rosamund.

When we got to the iron steps up to the drawing-room Richard Quin ran up, and I held Rosamund back.

'Did you see your Great-Aunt Jean die?' I asked. I wanted her to tell me that death was all right.

She answered, 'No, she died at noon, when I was at school.'

'But you saw her every day until she died,' I persevered. 'You must have seen her that very day.'

'Yes,' she said, 'I carried in her breakfast. She took her porridge the same as any other morning. Do you know they all call porridge "them" instead of "it" in Scotland. I thought it was only my Papa who did that.'

'Did it hurt her to die?' I wanted so much to hear that it had not.

She stammered, 'Yes, it hurt her.'

I looked up at the steel-grey winter sky. I prayed for her to speak the word that would break the metal prison round the earth. 'It must be terrible to die?' I said.

She did not say anything at all. Looking as if she saw a horrible event in the far distance, she shuddered. Then she turned to me and gave me the assurance I needed with her eyes, in which I saw fear fade and serenity return.

I asked in awe, 'Did you see her afterwards?'

'Yes,' she answered, hesitantly. 'Mamma did not want me to, but I had to go into the room when she was shopping, the kitten had got in through the window, I heard it mewing so I went to let it out. But that was nothing. She only lay there looking very white.'

'I don't mean that,' I said impatiently. 'Have you seen her, her, I mean her ghost?'

'Oh no!' breathed Rosamund, coming as near to disgust as I ever knew her. 'Aunt Jean was very sensible, why would she have a ghost?'

I could go no further. There was a vast pyramid, a vast temple, a vast church, built across the path I had proposed to follow into the mysterious woods. I was disappointed. Mamma and Constance, Rosamund and I, had surely driven one poltergeist out of the house in Knightlily Road because we four possessed supernatural powers, and I had hoped to have my fears about death dispelled by something beneficent but as obvious as the careering saucepans, the flying curtains, which the powers we had defeated had used to manifest themselves. Now, as an adult, I realise that I have never been subtle about anything but music.

But all the same my fears about death were dispelled, though I hardly knew how; and a few minutes later I met Mary in the passage and she said, 'I do not mind about Cordelia, now that Rosamund is here.' So the next day, when Rosamund and I started off for Nancy Phillips' party, we were both quite happy, except for a slight anxiety about Richard Quin, who had awakened with a touch of fever and been kept in bed. We felt conscience-stricken lest he had caught a chill in the stables, though he was always allowed to go where he willed out of doors provided he had his greatcoat on. Anyway, we supposed he would be all right the next day, we all got over things very quickly. I was pleased to go to this party because Nancy Phillips was older than I was, she was in Cordelia's class, and I did not really know her, so I had never been able to satisfy a long-standing curiosity about her. She was tall for her age and had a mass of smooth yellow hair, not golden like Rosamund's, the yellow of wild mustard, but she showed none of the confidence which is usually felt by tall schoolgirls with pretty and tidy hair. Against this bright yellow extravagance, her face was pale and reticent and even resistant, and she moved languidly. But at the same time the frills and tucks of her gaily coloured blouses, and her numerous brooches and bangles, which annoyed the teachers by their unsuitability for school, spoke of a frivolity she never manifested in any other way. I felt there was something mysterious about her, and I fully expected to find her living in peculiar circumstances, perhaps with a cruel and crazed stepmother in a richly furnished but cobwebbed mansion. It had, indeed, been quite a shock to me the day before to hear that she had spoken of her Mamma.

Her home did in fact strike me as strange. It was a large red-brick villa in an avenue of such houses, and no family could have lived there had they not been quite rich. But inside the house could not have been more horrid if the Phillipses had been very poor. In the hall and the little room where we took off our outdoor things, which would have been a study if our sort of family had lived there, were hung pictures which had thick gold frames as if they were real pictures, but were just jokes. Most of them showed men and women in the huge coats and peaked caps which were worn by motorists then, either having breakdowns or driving into ponds or hedges or telephone-poles; and others showed dogs and cats and monkeys driving motor-cars and wearing motoring costume. Not a single picture was pretty, they were the sort of thing which sometimes got into our house as calendars sent us by shops at Christmas, and if they came to

Mamma she used to say, 'Tchk! Tchk!' and tear them across, though her hands were hardly strong enough, and throw them in the waste-paper basket, and if it was Papa who found them he would talk angrily about how he was not bringing us up in the world to which we belonged.

We were received in the drawing-room by Nancy, who gave us a faint, sweet smile, and said to Rosamund, 'You're taller than me.' She herself did indeed look foolishly tall, in a white silk dress with a flounced skirt, embroidered with rosebuds. Then we were greeted by a grown-up who strangely said, 'This is Nancy's old Aunt Lily, we're ever so glad you kiddies have put on your best tatas and come through the wild and stormy to do us honour.' For a moment this grown-up gave the impression of being very pretty, for she had bright-golden hair, blue eyes and pink cheeks, and these were then considered the essential ingredients of prettiness. But almost at once this impression disappeared, her colouring recalled a doll left out in the rain, she had the dislocated profile of a camel. Still she meant to be nice. There were about fifteen of us, all from school, and we stood about in the awkwardness of a party that has not yet become a party, looking about us at the room, which was indeed strange. It was completely furnished in the Japanese style, which was then fashionable. The end of the room was taken up by a gilded extension of the chimney-piece, which rose in tiers to the ceiling, each shelf divided into several compartments, in each of which was a single curio, a Japanese cup and saucer, a vase, a carving in jade or rose quartz or ivory, and about the room were lacquered tables and flimsy chairs with cushions of oriental fabric. But on the walls, which were covered with straw wall-paper striped with fine gold thread, there hung, alongside Japanese prints and Canton enamel dishes, more of these pictures in heavy gold frames representing motor-cars in ditches and cats and dogs dressed in motoring clothes. Nancy passed amongst us, holding out a plate of very large pink and white fondants in fluted paper cases, and I asked her whether her father had lived long in Japan. She made it plain that she thought this rather a stupid question. 'No, why should he? Mamma got tired of the drawing-room as it was. It was buhl. All this came down from Maple's. There's nothing here has anything to do with Papa except those pictures of motor-cars.

We have a motor-car, you know. It's in the coach-house. You could see it if you liked.'

I had been wondering why, if Nancy had a Mamma, she was not at the party; and as Nancy turned away from me she said, 'Oh, Rose, here's Mamma,' and I held out my hand to a dark and handsome woman, very tall, who did not see it. She had not come to receive her daughter's guests, at whom she was looking with an intense though impersonal dislike, as if we were intruders crowding in on her when she desired to think of something else. She was wearing a kind of elaborate dressing gown of a sort then called a matinée, made of pleated purple silk, and she told us, with an insincere smile that hardly disturbed the heavy mask of her preoccupation, that she was so glad to see us all but she was very tired, she had been doing too much, and she had to put her feet up. She was sure Nancy and Aunt Lily would look after us better than she would. As she spoke her eyes were ranging over the room, and suddenly she made a predatory gesture, her loose sleeve falling back and displaying a bare beautiful arm which seemed much gentler than herself, and snatched from a table a book that had had a chocolate box laid down on top of it. 'Lily,' she said, and over by the chimney-piece her sister spun round as if she had heard a shot. 'Lily, I just found that new Elinor Glyn you and that girl said wasn't anywhere in this room. Now perhaps I can get my liedown,' said Mrs. Phillips, terribly, and left the room without giving any of us another glance.

I shook with rage so that Rosamund laid a calming hand on my arm. Almost all grown-ups were constantly rude to children, but of late they had been going too far. I felt again the anguish I had experienced when Miss Furness had launched her insult against Mary and me. But I knew she had meant to be kind, I could not remember her freckled and unaccomplished hand, feeling for the little seed-pearl cross, without knowing that she had poured out something like love on my sister and myself. Besides she had been misled by Cordelia and Miss Beevor. But though Mrs. Phillips was a woman of many possessions I instinctively knew that a small seed-pearl cross was not among them, and low as I placed the plane on which Miss Beevor and Cordelia were I knew that Mrs. Phillips lived somewhere lower still. It gave me no consolation to realise that she had not

174

singled me out as a victim of her insolence, that all her daughter's guests had been included in the scope of her offensiveness. This only showed that she had not bothered to discriminate. I was in a state of anger that I can hardly account for, save by remembering that Mamma had of late tried to dissuade me from my fierce efforts to master Mozart's "Gigue in G" by telling me that I was overworking, and supposing that I was more jarred by the humiliations of our poverty than I admitted. Certainly there ran through my head all that afternoon resentment against the awkward and ungracious wealth of this house.

At first we all sat, most of us on the floor, and played games. But that did not go well, perhaps because there was an unpleasant scene before we had really got going with Postman's Knock. The fire flagged, and Aunt Lily rang for more logs, and the bell was answered by a tall, pale, queenly parlourmaid, handsome in the manner of a Tennysonian princess, who made her coronet cap and its long starched streamers seem medieval wear. But on hearing what was required this Lily Maid became brutally incensed, saying such things ought to be thought of while the boy was still about. Later she came back and dumped down a basket of logs with the clownish emphasis of the horribly funny people in pantomimes. The interchange between this big, coarse, beautiful girl in her becoming black and white dress, and little, ugly Aunt Lily in her sky-blue taffeta blouse and her trailing skirt of flounces and ruches, had indeed the air of a theatrical scene, for it was played on the hearth-rug before the strange Oriental extension of the chimney-piece, the gilded shelves on which little lolling Buddhas, ivory monkeys and elephants, and lumps of brilliantly coloured stone, were perfectly irrelevant to the two contending women.

When the door had shut on silence Aunt Lily rushed to the piano and started playing 'The Bees' Wedding,' very quickly, so quickly that the bees could never have been sure whether they were married or not, dipping her head over the keys and nodding till her hairpins dropped out, to convey that she was not at all embarrassed and was able to lose herself in music. We passed from games to accomplishments, greatly to my pleasure. Then and now I can enjoy almost any performance in any sphere except my own; if any musician plays me I am precipitated back into my particular combat with the angels, but if anybody acts or recites or dances I am there on my knees, there is isolated for me another specimen of the hopeless and idiotic and divine desire of imperfect beings to achieve perfection. That afternoon I was irritated when a girl played Chopin's "Nocturne in F", and indeed, with some reason, for she had been taught a strange aberrant practice of giving the last note in every slurred phrase half its value; also the piano was slightly out of tune. On the other hand, I enjoyed the accompaniments and voluntaries which Aunt Lily zestfully proffered. She played so badly that her performance was not within the scope of criticism, nor could evoke any emotion except amusement. She made the instrument sound like a barrel-organ; her trills and runs had a Cockney accent; and when she had sounded a volley of chords it was her habit to wink at her audience and say, 'Hi Tiddley Pom Pom,' absently, as if obeying some recognised convention. And I certainly enjoyed it when a fat girl called Elsie Biglow recited 'Lasca', a poem we had learned in elocution class, about a man who had been in love with a girl on a ranch in South America, and one day the cattle stampeded, and she saved his life by shielding him with her body, and was killed. Papa liked this poem, and said that if Lasca really performed this feat she must have been a yard or two wide and made of some substance like corrugated iron, but all the same as a man he was glad to hear that such self-sacrifice was held up to young girls as exemplary conduct. But Elsie believed in 'Lasca' and for the moment I was glad to share her belief. Then somebody danced an Irish jig and somebody else danced a skirt dance. But after that the tide of talent ebbed.

In a half-hearted way somebody asked, 'Doesn't Rose play the piano?' All heads were turned towards me but I shook my head. They would never hear me play. I was afraid they were all so stupid about music that even after they had heard me they might still think Cordelia played better than I did, and would misunderstand our family tragedy. I knew I was conceding power to their opinion which my independence should have disputed; but it would have been hard for me, with this uneasiness in my mind, to play at that piano. Yet I was a little troubled by my failure to be sociable, and I turned to Rosamund and murmured, 'I really can't play here.'

'No, indeed,' she answered softly, 'you could not be expected to, as the piano is out of tune.'

This astonished me. The piano was only slightly out of tune, and I had thought Rosamund quite unmusical. I felt as if some-one understood to be stone-deaf had suddenly joined in a general conversation.

The hitch in the entertainment continued. I heard it suggested that some of the girls should play a scene from *As You Like It*, which their form had been doing that term. This distressed me. The world is against me on this point, but it has always seemed to me that the exiles in the Forest of Arden must have been rejected by their communities on conversational grounds. I looked about me, and was repelled again by the pictures of motoring accidents and animals in motoring clothes, crowding in on the Oriental dishes, with their bright flowers shining in everlasting summer against milky backgrounds, and the prints in which a deer or a fish or a dragon disengaged itself just sufficiently from the surface of the paper to indicate the existence of a totally graceful world. I was incensed for another reason by the straw wall-paper, so faintly striped by a designer who used gold without ostentation, without thought for its secondary value as a sign of wealth, simply for its beauty. Lately the rain had got into Mamma's room through a faulty gutter, and Mamma had had to have it redecorated with the plainest paper because it was the cheapest. I looked round the room and made certain what I would have guessed, that every girl there had a nicer party-dress than mine; and at the same time I heard a girl sitting in the row in front of us say to her neighbour, 'I went to a party the other day, over in Croydon, and there was a girl who did the most curious thought-reading trick. She put her hands on each side of your face and told you to think of a number, and then she told you what number you had thought of.'

Immediately I knew I could do this trick. It was as if it had been waiting for years that I should hear of it and perform it. I had, after all, certain advantages over my school-fellows, over Nancy's horrible Mamma, who had been so rude to us all, her idiotic Papa who hung up these ugly pictures among the lovely plates and prints and wall-paper that he had acquired by no better right than by being able to pay for them. I had even advantages over Miss Furness and her mother. For I belonged to a family which had magical powers, there was no doubt of that. Did not everybody who knew our household well say that Mamma had second sight? And had not Mamma and Constance, Rosamund and I, driven the evil spirits out of the house in Knightlily Road by our mere presence? And Rosamund knew something about death that made it not terrible. Of course I could undertake this small interference with the ordinary processes of life, and everybody in the room would have to admit that I was a superior being.

I said to Rosamund in an excited whisper, 'I am going to do a thought-reading trick.'

She whispered back, 'Oh, but the Mammas would not like it.' She was convulsed with a painful attack of stammering, but I had no mercy on her. Though it was largely my recognition that she knew more than other people which gave me confidence in the extraordinary character of my family, I at once told myself that she did not do nearly as well at school as I did and I need pay no attention to what she said.

I stood up and said, 'Please, I can do a trick,' and Aunt Lily said, 'There's a clever kiddy. Come out here and do it, I'm sure we'll all enjoy it.'

The tigerskin in front of the fireplace had been lifted so that the two girls could do their dances, and I stood myself in the cleared space. Aunt Lily asked, 'It isn't a rough trick, is it?' and looked up at the curios on the mantelpiece. Without using my thought-reading powers I knew that if I broke anything she would be terribly blamed, and I liked the people in this house even less.

'No,' I said. 'Let me put my hands on each side of your face. Now think of a number. Think of it hard.' Up it came, slowly and clumsily, like a wheel-barrow being trundled out of a dark stable, fifty-three. She squealed, 'But that's the very number I was thinking of,' and everybody in the room gasped as if they were watching fireworks.

I was afraid I would not be able to do it again, but of course I could. Elsie Biglow, the girl who had recited 'Lasca', was the first to come up and as soon as my hands pressed into her plump cheeks I knew that she would think of an even number, even before it floated before me like a perfectly symmetrical pear floating in a syrup. I was, of course, performing an action which presents hardly more mystery than the undoubted fact that a person standing some feet away from the keyboard of a piano and speaking clearly will cause certain notes to sound of their own accord, often quite loudly. The only difference in the thought-reading trick is that it is not a question of transmitting a wave to a detached object, but of receiving it. Countless children have discovered this way of amusing themselves, and if there was anything remarkable about my performance it was in the invariability of my success. I never gave a wrong number till after twenty minutes or so, when I suddenly felt very tired and would not go on. But I had won the distinction I had wanted. All the girls were looking at me as they did at the head of the school or the winner of the tennis championship.

I went back to Rosamund and said, 'You see, it was all right,' but she did not answer. She was heavy and pale, as if she had suddenly caught a cold. But then we went in to tea, which was very good. There were several cakes made in the new way which had just been introduced from America, in layers with butter cream between them; and there was something we had never seen before. Brandy-snaps filled with whipped cream. Then we went back to the drawing-room, ready to play whatever game was proposed, since it was not polite to go home immediately after tea. But the parlourmaid came in and said something to Aunt Lily, and she nodded and tiptoed over to us and she wanted me to go into the dining-room and speak to Nancy's Mamma for a minute. At this I felt frightened. I did not want to see that tall, rude, too dark woman again, and I turned to Rosamund, whom I had been despising a short time before, and said quite urgently, 'You will come too?' She nodded, and it interested me, and even a little disturbed me, to see that when Aunt Lily tried to intimate that she was not required, Rosamund assumed that blind look which I had almost believed to be beyond her control, the result of either some actual defect of sight or of absorption in her inner life; and she pressed forward at my side in the dining-room, completely a big stupid girl, who never sees when she is not wanted.

At the disordered table sat Mrs. Phillips, the light pouring down from the big brass chandelier on her raw-boned handsomeness, her purple gown. She said angrily, 'Look, Lil, all the cakes carried down the very first moment the kids are out of the room, and all the dirty china left. You bet they're having a grand guzzle in the kitchen, and we'll have a late washing-up, for all I said they could have the char in, and a scamped dinner again. I don't think we've ever had a set of girls I hated worse. But there's two children. When you came up to my room you only spoke of one.'

'It's this one that's Rose, the clever little kiddy,' said Aunt Lily. 'The other one's just with her, chums, you know.'

'This is my cousin Rosamund,' I said, and Rosamund said gravely, with an affectation of simplicity, 'How do you do?'

'How do you do,' said Mrs. Phillips irritably. 'Rose, this thought-reading you do, I suppose it's some sort of trick?'

I stared into her eyes and said coldly, 'How could it be a trick?'

She surprised me by cringing. 'Of course, of course. I didn't mean anything. But could you do it with me?'

I might have said, 'I am too tired.' But I was glad of an opportunity to show this stupid and repulsive grown-up that I had powers of a sort that evidently impressed her. I got up and walked over to her with a deliberation in which there was some showmanship, and put my hands on each side of her face, loathing my contact with her hot skin. She was not really so very dark, not nearly so dark as would put her outside the limits beyond which it is recognised that admiration must stop; yet I felt that if she were any darker she would have been as revolting as if she had been entirely covered with the stain of a birthmark. It was not comfortable, reading her mind. Had there been numbers more uneven than odd ones her choice would have lain among them. I did it for her twice, to establish my superiority, and I refused her a third test, for the pleasure of refusing her.

When I was back in my seat, she asked me if my cousin and I would like more cake. I said, thank you, no, we had had all we wanted at tea-time, and that it had been lovely, particularly the brandy-snaps filled with whipped cream. She looked round the table and saw that there were none left, and told Aunt Lily to run down to the kitchen and put some more on a plate, she knew there were lots, for that was the sweet for dinner. But I said, thank you, no, we had had as many as we wanted at tea-time. Then she asked, smiling, if we had not a corner for another chocolate or two. It was at once amusing and horrible to see a grown-up so anxious to please a schoolgirl. When I said, no, we really wanted nothing, Mrs. Phillips fell silent and for a moment drew a pattern on the tablecloth with her finger, while we looked round the room. They had all sorts of things we did not have at home, particularly on the sideboard, where there were two silver biscuit boxes and a cutglass and silver thing with whisky in it, which I knew was called a tantalus, because my mother never could see one in a shop-window without pausing and bursting into indignant cries, because it had a mechanical device by which nobody without a key could open it, so that the servants should not steal a drink, and it seemed to her to advertise brutally a condition of mistrust. It was also interesting for me to see what leather-covered chairs were like when they were not worn out and torn like ours.

'Well, you're a very clever little girl,' said Mrs. Phillips, in tones indicative of impatience and dislike, and I rose and put out my hand as if to bid her goodbye, pretending that I thought this all she wanted. She did not take it and abruptly asked me whether I could tell fortunes; and Aunt Lily leaned forward in her chair, the light from the chandelier shining very brightly on the bridge of her nose, and slowly rubbed her thin hands together as if she were very anxious to hear the answer.

I was astonished by the question. To begin with, I thought them too old to be interested in the future. Mrs. Phillips was Nancy's Mamma, and her sister was Nancy's aunt, and that was the status which had been awarded them by destiny. What else did they think would or could happen to them? Also I was aware that only someone fairly stupid could take the simple act I had performed as an earnest that I could knock down the walls between the present and the future. My contempt for the household increased; and so did my desire to torment and jeer at its mistress. I said, 'Well, as a matter of fact, I can.'

I heard Rosamund's sigh through Mrs. Phillips' harsh uplifted voice: 'Well, let's have a go at it now. We can slip upstairs to my bedroom.'

'No,' I said cruelly. 'I couldn't do it now.'

'Why not?' asked Mrs. Phillips.

'Oh, I couldn't possibly do it now,' I repeated, enjoying her incompletely concealed exasperation.

'Not if you have some chocolates?' said Mrs. Phillips.

'No, not if I had anything,' I said. I could have laughed aloud at her expression of defeated hunger.

She had been playing with a teaspoon. Her tense fingers sent it flying to the floor, and Rosamund and poor Aunt Lily grovelled for it. Mrs. Phillips and I were left facing each other across the table, the two principals in the business.

'Well,' she said, surrendering, 'when could you do it?'

After a long pause I said Mamma did not like us to do it. I should not have brought Mamma into this horrid business, and for a minute I saw Mamma as she looked when she was very angry, her thin white face shining like polished bone. But when Papa told us about the times when he used to go fishing in Ireland and we said it must have been cruel, he said, yes, he supposed it was, but there was something entrancing about playing a trout. I said, 'We will come tomorrow.' But instantly I made up my mind to do nothing of the sort. I was sickened by her greed and by her submission to my cruelty. Grown-ups ought to have their pride, and I saw that I was making Rosamund unhappy. She now looked more than ever as if she had started a cold and was blowing her nose a lot. But Mrs. Phillips' nostrils spread broadly because she thought she had conquered me. She said that I must come about three, and we would get over the fortune-telling first, and then we would have tea, and she would see that there were plenty of brandy-snaps. Then doubt came into her eyes. It occurred to her that I might possibly mean to disappoint her, and she said, 'Lily, run up and get that new box of chocolates from my room, it will be nice for them.' I nearly said we did not like chocolates, it would have teased her so, but I wanted them for Richard Quin. While Aunt Lily was upstairs and we three were alone, it was awkward, there was nothing we could find to say, Mrs. Phillips was so obviously thinking of something with such fixity. The box Aunt Lily brought back was bigger than any Rosamund and I had ever seen, and it was tied up with very pretty pink ribbon, enough for hair-ribbons for both of us. When I thanked Mrs. Phillips I spoke of the ribbon, and she said, looking at my dress in a calculating way, 'Oh, you like pretty things, do you?' She was ready to give me anything if I would tell her fortune.

She did not expect us to go back to the other children; we had assumed a special importance in her eyes. She took us straight to the room where we had left our outdoor things, and was watching me put on my walking shoes with an expression that was at once hostile and obsequious, when the front door was opened with a bump. Whoever came in made a great noise in the passage, rubbing his shoes on the mat, pulling off what was evidently a very heavy overcoat, and singing the first two lines of 'Old Simon the Cellarer' over and over again. We knew, of course, that it was Nancy's Papa. This was the hour when Papas came home: when such sounds, of a different quality, brought to my Mamma's face a look of apprehension, which vanished altogether before delight if he were friendly and began to tell her all his news, but which hardened into a grimace of dread if he were in a bad mood and sat down in the big chair without taking any notice of anybody and read the evening paper. It was the hour when Constance and Rosamund in their cold and bare home turned towards the hall the obstinate calm faces which announced that though Cousin Jock was their enemy, they would do nothing against him. Of course I hoped Nancy's Papa would come in, for it was always interesting to see other people's Papas, but Nancy's Mamma was plainly hoping that he would not. I knew she would not want him to hear about the fortune-telling, I had never seen a grown-up more furtive; and, indeed, when he made his appearance he proved to be the kind of person you do not want about when you are trying to do anything, whether it is allowed or not. Rosamund and I simply wanted to go home, and Mrs. Phillips wished for nothing else; but it became impossible for any of us three to take action to that end once Nancy's Papa came into the room.

He was not so bad, really. Of course, he was not at all handsome and wonderful like my Papa. Nobody, not a single person at that school or at the Schools of Music where Mary and I studied later, had a father like ours. But Mr. Phillips seemed to be completely happy, which was surprising, in this unhappy house. When he came in he said to his wife, 'Hello, how's my trouble and strife?' and put his arm round her waist and pulled her face over so that he could kiss her. She did not help him, she just let her face go the way he was pulling, the way you are told to go with the bicycle when you are learning to ride. But of course it was very bad manners of him to kiss his wife in front of us. Then he said, 'Who are these young ladies? Which is Claribel, which is Anna Matilda? Which is going to marry my son?' Of course we had to pretend to laugh. 'Oh, that won't do,' he said, 'one of you has got to marry my son, that's why I'm giving him a slap-up education, that's the only reason I've sent him to Brighton College, so that he can marry Claribel or Anna Matilda.' He went on and on like that, until Mrs. Phillips tugged at his sleeve and said that we wanted to get home. 'Home?' he said. 'Claribel and Anna Matilda want to get home, well, there's nothing simpler. I take them in the motor-car.'

At that Mrs. Phillips gave a low moan. 'They don't live far away,' she told her husband, 'and George won't like being taken from his tea.'

'Nonsense, you funny old trouble and strife,' he said, 'you don't understand Georgie-Porgie, old Georgie-Porgie'll do anything for me, adores me, he won't mind a bit giving up the last bite of toast. And Claribel and Anna Matilda will be as pleased as punch, going home in a motor-car, won't they? What'll the family say, seeing the two come home in a real live motor-car? Why, look at the two of them, the mere thought of it has set 'em grinning like a couple of cats with a saucer of cream, though they're much prettier, being young ladies.'

Here he was quite right. We were intoxicated past speech by the idea of going home, or going anywhere, in a motor-car. Some months before, Papa, in the course of a visit to a Scottish peer who admired his political writings, had been driven from and to the station in such a vehicle; but he did such things, he had crossed the Andes on a mule, and had rounded the Cape of Good Hope four times, and had lived for a whole summer just below Pike's Peak. We had never hoped to rival our father in that sphere. We knew that motor-cars were the way people would travel in the future, but that brought us no nearer them, for as they grew more common we became more poor, and they were fabulously expensive. We knew that, for Mamma had read out of the paper that one cost £1,020 and she said it seemed shameful when there was no opera in England outside London and little enough inside it.

It would be quite extraordinary if we had got up that morning thinking everything was going to be just the same as usual and were to come home that evening in a motor-car. Of course we told Mr. Phillips that it was very kind of him, but he need not trouble, all the same we kept our eyes on his face to see if he were going to believe us, and happily he did not. Then it all became awkward, for he went away to get George, and we were left with Mrs. Phillips, who looked very cross and dark. She no longer tried to placate me and we sat there saying nothing, and feeling ashamed of not being embarrassed, we were so excited. Then Mr. Phillips came in with George, and it certainly appeared as if he had been wrong about George adoring him so much that he would not mind being taken from his tea, for George looked very cross, as cross as Mrs. Phillips.

The two men had both put on huge coats and caps with deep peaks and earflaps, and Mr. Phillips made his wife go and fetch rugs and shawls to wrap round us, which made her look more hollow-eyed and grim than ever. She really was not nice at all, she was wanting something very fiercely and drily, it felt like a sore throat, and yet she could not make allowances for other people wanting anything, she thought it was tiresome of us not to have refused to let Mr. Phillips take us home. Aunt Lily was much nicer. She came out of the drawing-room to help the servants bring in the lemonade that you get at a party when it is time for you to go home, and found us in the hall, waiting till the motor-car stopped at the gate, because Mr. Phillips and George said they did not want us to get in till they had brought it out of the coach-house, because the fumes in there were always rather horrid. When Mrs. Phillips saw her, she said, 'Here, you take over,' and told us that she was so sorry but she had not had her full rest, she must go upstairs and get what she could before dinner. We watched her go slowly up the stairs, looking at the carpet as if her fortune was written there. But Aunt Lily was very pleasant, and when Mr. Phillips opened the front door and asked where the two lovely ladies were who were going to Gretna Green with him and George, she shook hands with us, and bent down to whisper in my ear that she hoped that I would spare five minutes for old Auntie Lil when the fortunes were being told. I wished I had not started the whole business. As she whispered the bit of her that was most visible to me was her high net collar, held up by transparent pieces of whalebone and edged round the top with narrow lace, and the wild version she had made of this very usual fashion showed a vein of fantasy in her which no fortune-teller could satisfy.

Of course it was interesting to drive in a motor-car. The miracle of not being pulled by anything, of the nothingness in front of the driver, was more staggering than can now be believed, partly because it would seem impossible that people so long accustomed to trains should have been so startled by the motor-car. But a locomotive closely resembles an animal in its ardour and its breathy moodiness, and anyway it was there, in front of the carriage you sat in, pulling a weight, according to a principle grasped not only by the mind but also by the muscles. But to sit in anything which moved along by some impulse within itself, which seemed to have nothing to do with the lever and the fulcrum, was an experience which neither the brain nor the arms nor the legs could understand. Rosamund and I sat in a bewildered ecstasy which continued unabated for some time, surviving several discouragements. For there was no wind-screen and we were blown about as if we stood on an Atlantic headland. There was also a pestilential atmosphere, far worse than now seems credible on the mechanical facts. I cannot think why the interior of this motor-car, winnowed by the gale of its passage, should have been as murky and evil-smelling as a tunnel in the old Underground. Though Rosamund and I were very happy we felt very sick, partly because of the fumes, and partly because of our violent and irregular progress. The car went ahead quickly and passionately for a hundred or two hundred yards at a time, then halted with a spine-jerking crash, and either started again or ran backwards for some yards and stopped in a paroxysm of asthma, till George, crying to Mr. Phillips, 'Don't you touch nothing,' got us going again.

Three times we stopped dead. The first found us in Love-grove High Street, and we were immediately surrounded by a crowd of youths, who put their heads inside the car and in-sincerely pretended that we were in a position to sell them roasted chestnuts. 'I should hate to be King Edward,' said Rosamund.

'Why do you think of King Edward now?' I asked.

'Well, people stare at him all the time through the windows of his carriage,' said Rosamund.

'But they don't ask him to sell roast chestnuts,' I said; 'think of asking the King to sell you roast chestnuts.'

'Yes, asking the King to sell you roast chestnuts,' gasped Rosamund, and we laughed and laughed, rocking on our seats, so that the youths outside tapped on the glass and begged us to tell them the joke, and Mr. Phillips, who had kept his seat in front while George got down and struck something with a hammer, turned round and asked us what the good one was. We said it was nothing, but he made us tell him, and he said it was good, dashed good. Asking the King to sell one roast chestnuts, he hadn't heard anything funnier for years. Then he swivelled round on his seat and enquired, 'I say, Claribel and Anna Matilda, do you like picnics?' We said that we did, and he trumpeted, 'That's splendid, we'll have a picnic some day, my wife and poor old Lil and Nancy don't like picnics.' George came back at that moment, and Mr. Phillips said to him, 'George, these two young ladies like picnics, they must come down to Blackwater.' He turned to us, and said, 'I've got a little place down at Blackwater, and a little boat on the Crouch, we could all be as jolly as sandboys.' George said, 'Sand is right. We was stuck on the sands three hours the last Saturday we went down, out in the estuary, owing to those taking the tiller that shouldn't.' He jerked us on through the sea of mocking faces, and the suffocating smell began again.

Then at the corner of a crescent about ten minutes from our home, we began to reverse, working up to a considerable speed, emitting puffs of smoke. George had some trouble in coming to a stop, and got out with the hammer, saying, 'I want no help.' He never once called Mr. Phillips 'sir.' We sat still and tried to look calm, and we debated in whispers whether it would be rude to ask Mr. Phillips whether the car was actually on fire. We were just going to do so when he turned round and said to us, 'Funny chap, George, he must have his joke, often says things he doesn't mean. He loves it down at Blackwater as much as I do. And we weren't three hours out in the estuary. Barely two. And we had sandwiches with us. You'd love it, you really must come down as soon as it gets warmer. Where are we now? December? Pity, pity.'

At this point the smoke that was puffing out of the front of the car changed its rhythm, and he transferred his interest to it, leaning forward and calling questions to George, who did not answer. This left us still uncertain whether the car was on fire or not, and though we were not really frightened, we were feeling in the darkness for the door handle so that we could jump if the worst came to the worst, when George leaped back into the driver's seat, just in time to take the wheel before we rushed off on the longest continuous run of the journey. For more than five minutes we proceeded in the same direction, without reversing once, and at such a pace that people on the pavements stopped dead to look at us with expressions of alarm that Rosamund and I commented on as indicating cowardice and lack of enterprise but which we feared meant prophetic good sense. Then the car, after bumping the kerb, stopped with a suddenness which jolted us both off our seats, and began to emit smoke not in puffs but in a continuous stifling cloud.

George got out and, by the light coming from a lamp-post with which he had nearly collided, we saw that he looked very cross. Mr. Phillips turned round and asked, 'Does your Papa play snooker?' I explained that Rosamund and I had different Papas, but if snooker was a game neither of our Papas played it, for they did not play games. Mr. Phillips sighed, 'That's the worst of Lovegrove, there's nobody here wants to do anything, there's no life about the place,' and sat and stared in front of him in silence for a time, but presently turned back again to say, 'But yachting's not a game. Your fathers and mothers might like to come along to Blackwater. Probably they'd enjoy it as much as anything they'd done in their lives. It would put a bit of life in them. Just what they need. People mope, you know, they go about with faces as long as a fiddle, while if they'd get out and have some fun and fresh air they'd feel as right as rain.' He was silent again, and then turned to us and said sadly, 'Look at me, I'm always happy as a king.'

Some seconds later George reappeared at the side of the car and stood scowling at Mr. Phillips, who did not seem to notice him.

I said, 'I think Mr. George wants to speak to you,' and Mr. Phillips said, 'Oh, does he? Does he? Oh, there you are, George. Well, how are things going, George?'

George, after holding him with his eye as if he were an

animal that had to be tamed, asked, 'You been touching this engine?'

Mr. Phillips wriggled on his seat and said, 'What do you mean?'

George, maintaining the hypnotic stare, said, 'Wednesday, when I had my day off, you been touching this engine?'

'No, no,' said Mr. Phillips, 'Wednesday? Wednesday? I had dinner early and went straight off to the Conservative Club, they had a bit of a sing-song.'

There was a pause, during which George continued to stare at what was called, by an irony that struck me even then, his master.

'Never went into the coach-house at all that evening,' said Mr. Phillips jauntily.

After a further rude pause, George took his face away, and the sound of hammering started again.

Mr. Phillips did not turn round in his seat to speak to us for quite a long time. For a space we were amused by a man and woman who halted as they were walking by and stationed themselves under the lamp-post, regarding the car with a solemn expression, as if they were broad-minded and were determined to be friends of progress at any cost, come the smoke as thick and evil-smelling as it might. But they wearied of progress when it remained stationary for so long, and even Mr. Phillips, though plainly less liable to consciousness of tedium than his fellow-creatures, got out of the door and walked up and down outside. The yellow front of a little shop ahead of us suddenly darkened. It must be getting late, perhaps Mamma and Constance would be getting anxious, we were indeed ourselves quite looking forward to having supper and showing the others the huge box of chocolates and going to bed. We were now not more than three minutes from home, we were in the main street from which Lovegrove Place turned off. But was it as rude to get out of a motor-car because it had broken down as it would be to walk out of a party because the servants were late in bringing the tea? We did not know what the etiquette was, but Rosamund said, 'You know, they will be anxious.' So I pulled down the window and timidly called Mr. Phillips by his name.

He was within a foot of me, and for the moment had come to a halt. But he did not hear me. I said again, 'Mr. Phillips,' but he still made no reply. It was true that he was far below me, for in those days the passengers in a car were as high above the pavement as the speakers on a platform usually are above their audience. So I leaned out of the window and called down to him, 'Mr. Phillips, we are quite close to our home, we think our Mammas will be getting anxious, would you mind if we got out and walked home?' In the light shed by the street-lamp I could see his vein-streaked cheeks, his round ginger eye-brows, his prominent and aggrieved eyes, his tightly twirled and stiffly-waxed ginger moustache, the stag's-head pin in his tie. By the same light he might have seen me had he raised his eyes from the ground. But he neither heard nor saw me. He was contemplating some fact which had turned him to stone. We felt afraid, being still children, at finding ourselves in a strange machine which showed all the signs we had been taught to interpret as warnings of fire, at an hour when we were always at home having supper and thinking of bed, in the charge of a man who, though round and jolly, had thoughts that made him blind and deaf.

We sat and swung our legs and told each other that it would be all right. Then Mr. Phillips turned about and got in beside us, saying, 'It's all right, George always finds what's wrong. Splendid fellow, George, you mustn't mind what he says. But about our having some fun. The circus, now, that would be all right, wouldn't it? I mean, it's not a game, is it? Your fathers wouldn't object to that, would they? That's what we'll do, make up a big party and go to the circus, you can't have fun unless there's lots of you, with your minds made up to have a good time. All be jolly together, that's the ticket.' Then we sped forward, and with a great lurch at the corner, we found ourselves in Lovegrove Place, and we were again intoxicated with pride in our adventure and the nonchalance with which we had embarked on it, and were glad because the motor-car at that point developed a new and peculiar noise, like a kettledrum being played very slowly. Everybody would come running out to see what was happening, and they would be astonished when they discovered that it was us.

But nobody came out, and we did not even get in at once, though Mr. Phillips banged the knocker down on the door very hard indeed, so hard that he murmured apologetically, as if he were repeating something he had been told when he was a child, 'Mustn't alarm the ladies, mustn't alarm the ladies,' and then brought down the knocker very softly indeed, as if he were trying to strike an average. We saw the light in the hall go on. We were at that time so poor that we did not light the gas in the hall except when people knocked. Mamma opened the door, looking very tired, and she did not seem very interested in the motor-car; and though she thanked him for bringing us home, it was only as much as she would have done if he had brought us back in a cab, or had walked with us. Her face was as I had seen it when I had imagined her in Mrs. Phillips' drawing-room, it was gleaming white like polished bone. But it was possibly not anger which had made it so, and presently, after Mr. Phillips had finished telling her what a couple of charming young ladies he had found us, and that he wouldn't have had different passengers, no, not even the Princess of Wales and the Duchess of York, she said that she was sorry she could not ask him in, but Papa was out, and she was very anxious because her little boy had had a violent attack of a sort which had afflicted him several times this autumn.

This evoked response from Mr. Phillips so boisterous that she put up her hands to shield her temples. 'Your little boy ill?' he cried. 'Splendid, splendid, it couldn't be better.'

She echoed in amazement, 'It couldn't be better?'

'Yes, ma'am, it couldn't be better,' he repeated joyously, seizing her hand and shaking it as if he were congratulating her; 'your little boy's ill, I'm here, I've got my motor-car, I can go and fetch the doctor, he'll be here in no time, you won't believe how fast George can take us along, excellent fellow, George, if we tell him it's for a sick kiddy he'll skim along like the wind.'

'Thank you, thank you,' said my poor mother, 'but the doctor has seen him already.'

'Oh, the doctor's seen him,' said Mr. Phillips sadly. 'Seen him, has he? Well, then, I suppose I'd better be saying good night.' But he was daunted only for a second. '*When* did he see him?' he asked.

'We sent for him about four, and he came almost at once,' said Mamma, wearily.

'At four o'clock? Why, that's a long time ago, you have to be careful with a sick kiddy, if a kiddy's really sick a good doctor sees him every hour. Come, come, now, four o'clock, that's not good enough, it's time he saw him again,' said Mr. Phillips, with mounting happiness. 'I'll go and get him, high time he saw the little chap again, where does he live?'

'But we do not want the doctor to come again,' said Mamma, her tired voice getting very Scotch, 'he has left me powders for my son to take, I know all that we have to do.'

'Well, it wouldn't do any harm,' pressed Mr. Phillips, though without much hope. Long experience had evidently left him well acquainted with the signs of defeat. 'Are you quite sure you wouldn't like to see him again before you tuck the little fellow up for the night, just in case?' Firmly discouraged by my mother, he had said his goodbyes, and was going down the steps when another thought struck him, and he spun round and ran up to the door, crying, 'I say! What about medicines? I'm a demon at getting chemists to open after hours. I get 'em out like a boy getting a winkle out of its shell with a pin. What d'you need for the little man?'

'Nothing, nothing,' pleaded my mother, wringing her hands. I do not know how long this scene would have gone on had not Kate come up from the basement with the soup-tureen, which she took into the dining-room, and then returned to stand beside Mamma at the open door. She listened for a minute and then said to Mr. Phillips, with the same simple grimness that George employed when speaking to him, 'Quiet is what we want. We got to keep the little boy quiet.'

Immediately he was subdued. Nervously he agreed, 'Yes, quiet, that's the great thing for a sick kiddy. Well, I'll send George along in the morning, see what we can do, nothing more pathetic than a sick kiddy, I always say.'

We watched him hasten down the garden path to the motor-car, which was now making a hissing noise and was surrounded by sparks, and Kate closed the door. We all instantly forgot him. Kate and Mamma did not speak or move, they stood silent and still, sorrowful and perplexed. In those days, because of the flickering light given by gas-mantles, houses seemed shaken by a pulse, and the trembling hall and staircase seemed to be sharing in Richard Quin's fever. I hugged the great box of chocolates I was carrying as if it were he, and Rosamund stammered, 'Is he very ill?' Mamma replied hesitantly, 'Well, we cannot understand what is the matter with him,' and ran her forefinger back and forward over her closed lips. When we went up to say goodnight to him we could see that he was very ill. His hair was not fair over dark any longer, it had become altogether dark, and when he put his hand outside the coverlet, as he rolled over to see who had come in, his knuckles were blue and shining with sweat. You would not have thought him a pretty little boy any more, he was like a monkey. Rosamund laid her head down on the pillow beside him, and he moved so that his head rested on her hair, and they clasped hands. I bent over him and said softly, 'Nancy Phillips' Papa brought us home in their motor-car.'

'You are lucky!' he said, 'but you are older, I suppose it was sure to happen to you first.' The motor-car suddenly screamed and then slowly roared off into the darkness. 'A good djinn would be quieter,' he said and closed his eyes.

Mamma, at the foot of the bed, said, 'What an enormous box of chocolates! Where on earth did you get that?'

'Mrs. Phillips gave it to us,' I said, perhaps too artlessly.

'But why? Did all the children get presents like that?'

'No,' I said. 'She took a fancy to us. I will tell you about it afterwards.'

But Richard Quin asked for a drink, and all our affairs were forgotten. I went downstairs and found Mary lying on her tummy on the hearthrug copying out some Liszt fingering of a Beethoven sonata from an old edition someone had lent her, waving her legs in the air the way one did in those days when one was working really hard, and she said she would go on till she had finished. In the dining-room Cordelia was sitting alone at the table, for Papa was out, speaking at a public meeting held to demand the repeal of the excessive death duties introduced by Sir William Vernon Harcourt some years before, which were eating away the solid fortunes which should be the foundation stones of the nation; I think it probable that no human being alive at that moment was engaged in a more disinterested activity. Cordelia explained that it might be all right for Mary and Rosamund and me to go without supper until all hours, but she was utterly exhausted. The strain of public appearances was more than we could imagine.

In the early morning I awoke, and wondered what hour it was. There was no clock in my room, for our family found it impossible to keep any timepiece going. Papa had a big gold hunter and Mamma a little French watch which dangled from an

193

enamelled bow pinned to her blouse, but these were often so wildly out of order that even my parents noticed that they were fast or slow, and sent them to the watchmaker's. So we grew as clever at detecting signs of the progress of the hours as if we were peasants in some backward land. 'It is dark,' I thought, 'yes, but at this season it might be dark till eight.' But it was not eight, for there was as yet no traffic passing along the main road at the end of our street. Such traffic was then more reverberant than it is today. The highways were paved with cobblestones on which the horses' hooves made a great clattering, and the cobblestones were set in a bed of concrete which offered the surface of a drum. If the waggons coming up from Kent and Surrey were not yet on their way then it must be before half-past five. I must get some more sleep or I would not be able to do my practice well the next day, so I closed my eyes; and as I sank to sleep it came to me that I had forgotten some disagreeable thing that it was foolish and light-minded not to remember.

The blankness behind my eyelids was hollowed by two rooms, rooms in our house, but also pale luminous caves in a black cliff, caves rough-hewn out of stone, and hewn no more than need be, for they were low over the sleepers' heads. Richard Quin lay on his side with his folded hands beneath his cheek, bright pupa in a vague case. All night long his room was patterned with leaves and branches. While the lamp was alight in the street below, the shadows of a sycamore danced across his walls; after the lamp was put out in the early morning by the man with a tall rod, the gnarled arms of the wistaria round the window showed a black trellis against the softer light. Richard Quin would never have his curtains drawn, for mere light and darkness, mere night and day, apart from any happening, gave him pleasure. Rosamund slept just then in a bed put up for her in Kate's room. Like everything belonging to Kate or to any member of her family, her attic had a marine appearance, and it might have been that the night beneath her windows was the sea. Kate was no more than a roll of sheets and blankets, neat as a sailor taking his rest in his hammock. But Rosamund I could see, I could see all of her. She was sitting up in bed, her head upon her raised knees, her arms clasping her shins. The shining fall of her clean and curled hair hid her face, but I could not doubt but that she was sad. Her attitude formed a symbol of dejection. If I had drawn it and shown it to savages from the most distant lands, they would have known that this was someone who was sad. I wondered how I could have forgotten, even in my sleep, that Richard Quin was ill; but at least, I thought in my drowsing confusion, I had not forgotten Rosamund's misfortune, for I had never recognised it. But they were both crowned with light, light was all about them, it seemed to me as I sank deeper and deeper into the fulIness of sleep, and dreamed some music, curiously orchestrated, that this was perhaps the same as misfortune.

IX

WHEN I opened my eyes the next morning Mary had already risen and gone down to breakfast and to work, and the first thing I saw was Cordelia, still in bed, though usually she got up when she woke. She was lying flat on her back and reading a bound score which she was holding open in the air above her, her elbows digging into the mattress under the weight. She was really astonishingly pretty. Her red-gold curls were so bright and so soft, her skin was fairy-tale white, and there were parts of her face, such as her short and deeply cleft upper-lip, and the little triangular flat bit under the tip of her nose, which were specially lovely and somehow tenderly amusing; and she was free from the troubled quality of our family, she looked just like other people. The sight of her gave me the same sort of pleasure as the gayest songs of Schubert. But a shadow of crossness ran over her eyes and mouth. She knew herself perceived, so she was staking out an excessive claim.

Of course she must be reading the score just to show off. None of us at that time could read scores for pleasure, simply because we could afford to go to very few orchestral concerts, and were not familiar enough with the instruments to conjure them up to the mind's ear, although Mamma was bringing us on as well as she could, making us listen properly to every band we heard and taking us to the gallery when the Carl Rosa Opera Company came to the local theatre; and also Mamma had not had time to teach us how the different parts were written. I sat up and stretched over towards Cordelia to see what the score was. It was Mendelssohn's 'Violin Concerto'. That we had heard; all of us except Papa and Richard Quin had gone up to London to hear Joachim play it. It is so beautiful that I have always wished I could steal it and get a miracle worked to turn it into a piano concerto. But of course God Himself could not do that. The essence of a violin concerto lies in the conversation the violin carries on with the orchestra, in something much nearer the orchestra's own voice than a piano. When the violin solos it brings its cadenzas out of the chords played by the orchestra and returns them to it, it is as if a part had spoken for the whole but had never been detached from it; whereas the piano part in a piano concerto is a detached comment, it is almost as separate as consciousness is from the rest of our minds. Lying there, I heard Joachim's performance over again. Of course the concerto deserved to be played at a height to which practice could never take one, the height on which Mamma lived.

'You're not thinking of learning this?' I asked Cordelia.

She acted being called back from a long distance. 'Learning this?' she repeated absently. 'Oh, yes, yes. I shall start studying it soon. I shall have to play it at some not very distant date, you see.'

I recognised 'at some not very distant date' as Beevor English. Once again I thought that Mamma ought to stop all this. Irritably I jumped out of bed and went to the window to glare at the world. It had come back to me that Richard Quin was ill. I looked out on a garden that was doubly desolate, because nobody tended it and because it was December, and saw my father walking on the lawn. When it is said of people that they keep irregular hours it is usually meant that they stay up late and rise late in the morning, but that after all is a kind of regularity. My father kept such truly irregular hours that he was likely now and then to go to bed and rise earlier than his children. He had probably been up and about for a long time, for his thoughts were in full torrential flood, he was vehemently talking to himself, or rather arguing with an unseen adversary. Middle age, which was making Mamma frail and birdlike and even disguised her power, was making him look foreign, excessive, fevered. His skin had grown darker and was a pale tobaccoish brown, which might have been the work of tropical sunlight; and he was now so thin that his cheeks were hollow, and the fine line of his unusually high cheekbones was painfully accentuated. His eyes, of course, always burned.

Though it was cold he wore no overcoat, for he extended his contemptuous indifference to himself and his own sensations. The shapelessness of his old suit showed that, if his gambling prevented me and my sisters from having enough clothes, it kept him ill-clad too. But his grace counteracted his shabbiness. He walked as if he had no weight, as if no limitation affected him, as if he had only to command a thing for it to be. And that, I realised, was true in the world where people argued. He was always right. Had his adversary been real instead of airy he would have been wholly defeated. But what was the use of all this argument? As my father reached the end of the lawn nearest the house he threw back his head and stared up at me with unseeing eyes filled by a terrible vision. Surely he looked forward into time and saw it utterly desert. I watched him as he paced back to the further end of the garden and halted, the chestnut grove bare and black behind him, to look downwards and speak scornfully and grind a heel on the wet grass. He might have been dispatching a small groundless hope.

His despair reminded me that I was very cold. I went downstairs to the basement and filled a can with hot water from a kettle on the range and mounted the stairs again to the bathroom and washed. Only by exercising much forethought and always having full kettles on the range were we able to keep clean at this time. There was something wrong with the cistern, and as we were also behindhand with the rent we could hardly ask Cousin Ralph to repair it for us. I dressed and had breakfast, which was always the same in winter: porridge made of coarse oatmeal, which Mamma had sent specially from Scotland, smothered in milk and an unusual abundance of golden syrup, because Papa was a follower of Herbert Spencer and that philosopher held, against the opinion of his age, that it was good for children to eat sweet things. I remember holding the syrup spoon over my plate and shutting my eyes and saying, 'If it has stopped dropping by the time I open my eyes Richard Quin will be all right.' I went up to see him as soon as I had finished eating, and found Papa on the landing. We knocked at the attic door and Mamma opened it, staring as she did when she was very worried. Papa went and stood at the head of the bed and I stood at the foot, and Mamma was between us, holding a medicine bottle close to her, as if it were a charm. There was no doubt but that Richard Quin was very ill. He looked as if he were drowning under a wave of pain which had swept him off his feet, as if soon there would be a flood of pain between us and him through which he would not be able to speak loud enough for us to hear. But he turned his head first to Papa and then to me and smiled, a smile of such complete acceptance that it felt as if we had been drowning and he were in safety and had saved us. But he was not strong enough to smile so for long, he relaxed and was borne away from us on the tide.

Mamma said, 'If only we knew what is the matter with him?'

Papa muttered, 'It is nothing infectious?'

'The doctor says there are no symptoms of anything infectious, it is not scarlet fever or measles,' she answered, 'and the others are all right. No, it is something strange.'

Papa looked down very tenderly on Richard Quin, whom he loved best of all us children, which was only right, our brother was by far the best amongst us, and he was silent. Evidently he was setting his mind to rove through the hazards of his own childhood, for he asked presently, 'Have you been eating any poisonous berries in the garden?'

'There aren't any,' I told him.

'No,' sighed Papa, after a moment's reflection, 'of course. Those berries do not grow here. They were at home, they were in Ireland. Down by the boathouse. The other Richard Quin and I made ourselves very ill once eating them, and so, I think, did Barry. But it was over there. Not here. Why are you laughing, Richard Quin? You impudent boy, why are you laughing at your Papa?'

Gasping, Richard Quin answered, 'Funny Papa, who reads so many books and writes so many articles that he does not know that it is winter, and all the berries are shrivelled up.' As the words left his lips, he went to sleep.

We watched him sadly, till my mother left the room and beckoned to us from the open door. I went downstairs, and Papa and Mamma stayed on the landing. I turned to ask if Mamma wanted me to do anything for her, and saw that she had drawn near to him and had laid her hand on his sleeve, and that he had lowered his mustachioed mouth to her cheek. They seemed shy with each other. I found that Mary had stopped practising and was in her room getting on with her Christmas presents, so I went down to the piano and had got through the routine of all the major and minor scales and arpeggios with which we began each day, when Mamma came in to ask me to go with Rosamund and do the morning's shopping, as Papa had been sent for to go to the office and Constance was going to call in to ask the doctor to come again. She told me to buy herrings for our mid-day dinner, from which I now deduce that to add to her troubles

she must have had no money in the house, for we had had herrings for dinner on the previous day, and on the day before that
again. In those days they cost a penny each, and sometimes
less. I do not wish to exaggerate our poverty, it is true that
Mamma knew Papa's monthly cheque would be sure to be
coming and of this he always gave her enough to meet our day-to-
day expenses. But any extra outlay emptied her pockets, and
so Richard Quin's illness meant that she told me to buy herrings
again, and two cabbages and two loaves; and she did not add, as
she often did when there was a shilling or two to spare, now that
we were older and were sensible, 'And if you see anything . . .'
The missing words were, 'that is at once worth buying and
so cheap that we can buy it, for goodness' sake bring it
home.'

But Rosamund and I were not troubled about our family's
finances as we went to the shops. We were both sick with fear
lest Richard Quin should die. This was nearly half a century ago,
and we were much more familiar with the idea of children dying
than two little schoolgirls would be today. Though infant
mortality in our class had fallen so far by then that the death of a
schoolfellow was a rare and shocking event, and I can remember
only three such deaths in all my years at school, older people
often talked before us of brothers and sisters, and of uncles and
aunts, who had never reached maturity. We therefore knew that
we were not exempt from fatality because we were young, that a
grave might be dug not for a grown-up but for one of our kind.
We lived, as children do, much by omens, and we were depressed
when the fishmonger's cat shook each of its forepaws and turned
away as soon as it saw us, though it usually was very civil, and
went out to the front of the shop, and sat down with its back to us.
But as Rosamund pointed out, it was one of those stout, purse-
proud cats often found in butchers' and fishmongers' shops, who,
though they get lots of food given them, never see a live bird, and
keep mice down by their mere presence, are not nearly as kind to
human beings as ordinary cats who hunt and are cruel to birds
and mice. We might have known that this was how that particular cat would behave to people in trouble, and we had some
luck in the shop, for we got some whiting at the price of herrings,
and we always liked having those, because they were served with
their tails in their mouths. But we grew depressed again as we

went back along the road, and noticed what had escaped us in our outward journey, that by some failure in routine never remarked before or after, the man with the long rod had not come on his round at dawn, and the gas-jet in each lamp was still alight. This gave the whole street a look of joyless waste, like Papa's study when we came downstairs to breakfast and found that he had forgotten to turn the gas out when he went to bed.

When Kate opened the door she said she was glad about the whiting, because Mamma would like to give Papa a change though of course Papa would not notice, and as we heard Mamma's voice coming from the dining-room we went in to tell her the small cheering news. But as soon as I got into the room I came to a halt and my jaw dropped. Mamma and Constance were sitting one on each side of the dining-room, looking with an air of clinical curiosity at someone whose existence I had entirely forgotten during the night: Aunt Lily, who was sitting in the armchair by the fireplace, smiling as if bravely suppressing a desire to be sick, with a white cardboard box on her knees. Its wrapping of brown paper had already been removed and had slipped to the floor at her feet.

'Come in, children,' said Mamma, in accents hollow in bewilderment. 'A friend of yours has called to see you.' A convulsive expression with which I was familiar passed over her face. She found Aunt Lily's dress and ornament, which was girlish and frivolous, as repugnant as Miss Beevor's attempts at the romantic, perhaps more so, for Aunt Lily offered more targets. If Miss Beevor wore a mosaic brooch representing doves drinking from a fountain, Aunt Lily wore a necklace of enamel violets to enliven her tight-waisted coat and skirt, hat-pins with heads of enamel cupids to secure her large fawn beaver hat, and several jingling charm bracelets. I prepared a defence for use afterwards on the ground that if Cordelia had a Miss Beevor there was no reason why I should not have an Aunt Lily.

'Miss Moon tells me,' said Mamma, 'that there is some idea of your going round to Nancy Phillips' house again this afternoon.' She spoke wearily. Obviously this visit had taken her from Richard Quin's bedside, and she could hardly keep her patience. 'But I think she must be mistaken, it is so very soon, she cannot really be wanting visitors the day after a big party.'

'I did say I would go,' I mumbled, 'but I forgot.'

'Say you are sorry then,' said Mamma, 'for it was rude of you to forget so kind an invitation. But there is another thing.' The expression in her eye reminded me of a picture I had seen of a hind caught in a thicket. She looked so when the conditions of our life trapped her in hideousness, when she could not send a cheque to Cousin Ralph on the right date, when she had to see a dun. 'Mrs. Phillips has sent you and Rosamund both presents.'

I could see what had happened. Mrs. Phillips had been awake for a long time when they brought in her breakfast, and she had told them to fetch Aunt Lily at once; and when Aunt Lily had hurried in, blinking and yawning in her dressing-gown and curlers, she had told her to go out and get some presents for those horrible children and take them over to their house and be sure, sure, to get them to come along that afternoon.

'But really,' Mamma went on, very close to tears, 'I cannot let you accept them. They are much too good.'

'Oh, come now,' chattered Aunt Lily, 'they're just some little things we thought your clever kiddies would like.'

'They are far too good,' persisted Mamma, and this time Aunt Lily, persisting on her side, said, 'What's the good of Mr. Phillips being fortunate in the City if we can't do a thing like this when we want to?'

Mamma quivered and was still. 'These things are most beautiful,' she said. She did her best, but no member of her family would not have known that Mrs. Phillips' offerings struck her as the extreme of hideousness, ostentation, and grossly wasteful expenditure. She said, 'But, you see, we are not at all fortunate and we could not return your generosity in any form. I cannot let Mrs. Phillips give my daughter and my cousin's child these valuable presents, when we could not give a present of any sort to Nancy. It would be——'

But Aunt Lily cut into Mamma's wail, wailing herself. Her charms and bangles, her large beaver hat, were for a second agitated by fear. 'My sister will be ever so upset if I have to take those presents back.'

My mother melted. 'I will explain it to your sister myself, if you wish it, Miss Moon,' she said. Her great eyes blazed at me, enquiring: 'Why have you involved me with this vulgar and silly woman, to whom I cannot even be merciless, because she is so pitiful, who presses these idiot gifts on us and will not let me go back to Richard Quin's bedside?' Aloud she followed the same train of thought more temperately. 'But, dear me, how has all this come about? How did you pick out these two girls at that large party?' A ray of understanding showed its light. 'Oh, did Rose play the piano?'

'Oh no!' said Aunt Lily, with the promptitude of one who, with the best will in the world, cannot help telling the truth. 'It was more than that. Anyone can play the piano. I can myself. All by ear, I can't read a note of music. I wouldn't have thought so much of that. I've always been able to vamp ever since I was a kiddy, myself,' she added, suddenly smiling at Rosamund and me, to revive the supposition of a sudden and strong mutual attraction between us.

'It was more than that!' repeated Mamma in bewilderment. 'You wouldn't have thought so much of that! Well, what was it that you thought so much of?'

I had a great awe and admiration for Mamma's detective powers. I owned up. 'I did a thought-reading trick.'

'Oh, Rose!' groaned Mamma.

'It was not much,' I said. 'I put my hands on each side of a girl's face, and I made her guess the number and say it just to herself, and then I told her what the number was.'

I had never had an unkindly look from Constance before, but she was now staring at me very coldly; and Mamma was sealed in her anger, motionless.

Aunt Lily broke the silence, saying, 'Well, I'm sorry if I've spoken out of turn. And I'm sorry if I've got poor little Rose into trouble. But thought-reading. I don't see nothing wrong in that. I mean, I don't see anything wrong in that.'

The humility of that self-correction broke the ice of my mother's anger. She explained gently, 'Yes, there is no harm in thought-reading as a trick. But——'

'But it's not a trick,' interrupted Aunt Lily. In her embarrassment she had been looking down on her black open-work stockings and her high-heeled shoes, wriggling her feet as if she wanted to get the effect from different angles. Now she raised her head and said with a certain shrewdness and obstinacy, 'But it wasn't a trick. I watched her. It wasn't as if the two kiddies had done it together and had a code, like the people on the music-halls. She did it all herself, your daughter did. She's got a gift, the gift, some people call it.'

My mother shuddered as at an unbearable vulgarity. 'The trouble is that people who do such things go on to other things. To fortune-telling. To table-turning. To spirit-rapping.' 'Well, what's the harm in that?' said Aunt Lily. 'Fortune-telling I mean. The rest I don't care about. I don't want to have anything to do with spirits. But fortune-telling. If you don't know what's going to happen, and it might all come out one way, and then you'd be very happy all your life long, and the other hand it would come so that you'd never have anything to live for. Well, what's the harm in finding out which way it's going to work out?'

Hope overlaid with brightness the other bright colours of her face. Mamma and Constance looked on her with a sort of tender horror, and Mamma said softly, 'But it is wrong.'

'Oh, I grant you it may be wrong,' said Aunt Lily, 'but you don't really mean you think it's so wrong that you shouldn't do it? Don't you ever read tea-leaves?' Mamma and Constance shook their heads. 'Well, you are funny. It does no harm. That and the cards, how can there be any harm? If ever there was anything that was just a bit of fun, surely it's that?'

'If it is just a bit of fun,' asked Mamma, 'then why are you so eager for it?'

At that Aunt Lily looked as if she were going to cry, and I turned my back on the room and looked out on to the road. I had heard Constance pronounce with her peculiar large primness, 'It is wrong. The Roman Catholics forbid any of their people to practise it and I think they are right,' and Mamma declare fierily, 'If there is a wall between the present and the future it is not for us to pull it down,' when a hansom cab came jingling along the road. Mrs. Phillips got out. She had not been able to wait any longer. I wondered whether her arrival would make things worse or better. It would at any rate precipitate them, for she looked up at the driver on his perch behind the roof and spoke to him but did not hand him up his fare. Hansom cabs were so expensive by our family standards that I was unable to imagine anybody sane keeping one waiting for long, so I assumed that she and her sister would soon be gone.

That meant I would have to face my mother's naked anger. All the same I did not want Mrs. Phillips to stay long.

After she had spoken to the driver she stood still on the pavement under the lamp-post opposite our gate, where the still unextinguished light was sallow and owlish, and stared hungrily at our house. I wanted to lean out of the window and call to her that it was our house, she should not stare at it so. The cab-driver gazed down on her with complacence and approval, twirling his moustache. Hansom drivers took themselves seriously as at once servants and arbiters of elegance. They were always smartly dressed, this one had a button-hole though it was December, and they liked to have smart fares. In those days all tall women were admired, and Mrs. Phillips was very tall, and she was certainly elegant. She wore a wine-coloured beaver hat rising in a crest of darker plumes and a wine-coloured coat and skirt. The skirt touched the ground and was immensely flared; it was a triangle with the apex at her sternly corseted waist. A dark fur stole fell from her shoulders to her knees and her arms were buried to the elbow in a muff of the same fur. The inner darkness in the colours of her dress and fur, the swarthiness of her skin, made her part of the disgrace of winter; not its cold, not its rain, but the rutted grease on the roadway, the discoloration left by the wet night on the pavement. The regard she was concentrating on our house was also drab. She wanted something here but her face shone as little as if she wanted nothing. Mamma, paying homage to a diamond in a jewellers' window, gave out light like the jewel itself. Rosamund, wanting us all to go together to the seaside, was like a beach under noon. But Mrs. Phillips' craving was tedious.

'Mrs. Phillips is here,' I said to Aunt Lily, and she made a frightened noise and jumped up, saying, 'Let me open the door, it'll save the girl, and I'll explain.'

She ran from the room before we could forestall her and Mamma whispered to Constance, 'Oh, the poor thing!' and Constance whispered back. 'Yes, indeed, to hope, at that age, with that appearance!' Wheeling about, Mamma hissed at me, 'You put yourself into a position where you would have had to lie to that poor creature,' and Constance added in the same tone, 'That, or break her heart.' Their whispers had enormous force and seemed more impersonal than the kind of rebuke

I had ever received before. It was like being rebuked by the winds.

My first thought, when I saw how Mamma and Constance received Mrs. Phillips, was that they recognised her as somebody whom they already knew. So definite was their rejection of her that it seemed as if it must be fully informed and documented. But she had never seen them before. She showed it first by the half-amused knitting of her brows as she took in the odd Punch-and-Judy vehemence of my emaciated Mamma, the overhanging, sculptural quality of Constance, their shabby clothes, the poverty-stricken room; and then she too obviously thought that, Heaven help her if she failed to get her way, since this was all she was up against. Meanwhile Mamma and Constance paled and flinched, each stretched an arm to push her own child behind her. In an instant they recovered themselves, far too quickly for Mrs. Phillips, who was not one of those people whom Papa described as able to turn round in their own length, to be quite sure of what she had seen. But Mamma kept her hand on my arm as she said, 'I am sorry to receive you in the dining-room, Mrs. Phillips, but this is a small house and we are a large family, and I know that as these are the holidays what should be my drawing-room will be strewn with toys and books and music.'

Mrs. Phillips replied that she knew what it was, that when her Nancy and Cecil were at home the place looked like a pigsty, and settled in the armchair where Aunt Lily had been sitting. She turned her large picturesque face towards Rosamund and me, gave us a shallow smile, and told Mamma that she hoped her sister was wrong in thinking they weren't going to be able to borrow the kiddies for the afternoon. I heard Mamma sigh deeply. Winter her frailty could bear well enough, but not this extreme desolation, this universal lack. I felt very glad that hansoms were so expensive, that even Mrs. Phillips would not be able to keep one waiting for ever.

Mamma said, 'I must tell you that I am angry at the children for doing that thought-reading trick. You see, we are Scottish, and we take these things more seriously than the English,' and while she went on with her explanation Mrs. Phillips appeared to lose all interest. She was wearing only one glove, and she began examining the other, stretching and smoothing it She could not bear it, that a shabby little woman like my mother should stand between her and what she had arranged to have. But she ceased to feel that resentment or anything else, for she suddenly went from us, passing into the cavern of her preoccupation. She stood up suddenly, and spared us just enough of her attention as was necessary to say, 'Well, well, we must be going, and some time the kiddies must come along and have tea with Nancy, and we won't have any tricks, I promise you. Come on, Lily.' She needed to be out of this little room so full of people, she wanted to be alone, or with Lily, whom she could disregard, so that she could think of what she wanted. Mamma rose eager to say goodbye, but as their hands went out to meet a look of duty came into her eyes, and she sat down again, as if she must refuse to let this pair go until she had settled something with them. Gazing up at Mrs. Phillips, who was taking no notice of her, and was putting on her other glove with absorbed interest, she said, in a voice so tense that it cracked, 'You won't go on with — with the idea?'

Mrs. Phillips answered drowsily, 'Go on with the idea? With what idea? The thought-reading?' She laughed gently as if it were an absurd notion that she would pursue with assiduity anything connected with us. 'No, I won't think of it again. We're not a spooky family.'

'Tea-leaves and cards we do try sometimes,' interjected Aunt Lily stoutly, both for the sake of honesty and to show Mamma that she would not be browbeaten.

'Yes, just for fun,' admitted Mrs. Phillips, 'but I don't suppose we think of it twice in a year, and I wouldn't have thought of it now if it hadn't been for your dear clever little girlies. Little, say I. I do believe the fair one's as big as that great maypole my Nancy. Well, goodbye for now.'

Mamma opened her mouth, but she was defeated by the tall woman's indifference, which was nearly that of an inanimate object. It seemed as foolish to talk to her as it would have been to talk to a stove. At that moment Kate came in with the hot plates for luncheon, and Constance swooped down to pick up the cardboard box, which was lying on the hearthrug, and handed it to Aunt Lily, who said with a wry smile, 'Well, if that's not allowed, it's not allowed.'

It was not until the front door had closed that Mamma

and Constance spoke. I had expected them to turn on me at once, but first they exchanged broken expressions of horror. 'Why, she is half consumed!' exclaimed Mamma in loathing, and then nervously, as if she feared the answer, she asked, 'But what exactly, what exactly is it that she has in mind to do?'

'She means, I suppose, to go away and leave them,' said Constance grimly.

'Only that?' pondered Mamma. 'Well, one cannot warn people. And I have seen her husband. But still.' Her thoughts returned slowly to the visible world and me, and there came the cry which wrung me though I had been waiting for it. 'How could you, Rose, how could you!'

But before I could give an answer, which would have been angry, for it was not in my nature to meet rage with anything but rage, Rosamund had spoken. She had sat down at the table, and looking blind and stolid and more childish than usual, was drawing on the table-cloth with her fork. 'You see, it was a horrible party. We did not tell you, because you were worried about Richard Quin. But it was a horrid party, and a horrid house. You have seen how horrid Nancy's Mamma is. Yesterday she was very rude to all of us. She came down into the drawing-room in a sort of dressing-gown, to look for a book she wanted to read while she was lying down, and she did not say how do you do to any of us. And then when we started playing games a servant came in and was rude to Nancy's aunt, and you have seen, she is quite nice, she was not doing any harm, she only asked for some logs. She nearly cried.'

'Stop drawing on the table-cloth with that fork,' said Constance. 'It ruins the linen.'

Rosamund obeyed with a readiness that established her as a good, submissive child. 'Then Rose got into one of her states,' she said. I heard the announcement with surprise. Had I got into a state at the party? I had felt very cross, but I did not think that I had got into a state. Indeed I was unaware that I ever got into 'states,' yet the expression had evoked sounds of recognition from both Mamma and Constance. 'Then,' continued Rosamund, 'the party got horrider than ever. We had been playing games but that all stopped, somehow, when the servant was so rude. People did not seem to want to go on. Then they all began to do things, some girls danced and others

208

recited, and they wanted Rose to play the piano. But it was the last straw, the piano was terribly out of tune.'

'Oh, poor Rose!' cried Mamma.

'So Rose said she could not, but of course everybody was doing what they could, so it was a little awkward, and then somebody suggested this trick, and it just happened that Rose was the one who could do it. And she didn't do it long. And then there was tea, and after it was finished we went into the drawing-room, and we would have done what the others were doing, but Nancy's Mamma sent for Rose, and she started this about fortune-telling. You don't like her, do you?' she asked, turning a penetrating glance first on Constance, then on Mamma. 'Well, she is nicer to grown-ups than she is to children. And Rose never meant to go this afternoon, but Miss Moon was with you when we came back from shopping. So you see that Rose is not to blame at all.' She went back to the childish trick of drawing on the tablecloth with a fork, and again obeyed when she was checked.

This explanation satisfied Constance and Mamma, who then and for ever after regarded me as Mrs. Phillips' victim, but it did not entirely satisfy me, though it had saved me from terrible disgrace. As soon as Rosamund and I were alone after luncheon I said, 'But, Rosamund, it didn't happen quite like that at the party,' and she raised her eyebrows in bewilderment and answered, 'Yes, it did.'

'No, Rosamund, no,' I said, for my conscience was pricking me. 'I was naughtier than that. I did suggest doing the trick, and I did enjoy it when Mrs. Phillips wanted me so terribly to tell her fortune that she nearly went mad offering to give us things.'

'I did not say anything that did not happen,' she protested, stammering very badly.

'I think I had better tell Mamma I really was naughty,' I said.

'But, Rose, if you do that, then my Mamma and your Mamma will think that I was not telling the truth,' she said plaintively.

Perhaps she was as stupid as we sometimes thought her. Indeed the importance of the incident seemed to have passed her by, she evidently did not realise that we had been within a hair's breadth of one of those terrible clashes between Mamma and myself which had happened once or twice, when we had become fountains of rage and pain. Quite placidly she settled down to do some mending for Mamma, although I was not at ease and had serious qualms that evening when Mamma asked me to come into Papa's study and talk to her.

'It is a mercy he is out,' she said. 'I wanted to talk to you alone, and this is such a little house, and there are so many of us, it is hard to find a place for a private conversation. But if we had a bigger house no doubt we should not be so close together.' She sat down at Papa's desk and looked proudly round the room and its bookshelves. 'So many books, and your Papa has read them all. You should be very proud of him. It is a pity we do not live in some country where clever men are honoured.'

She had grown much younger since morning. 'Is Richard Quin much better?' I asked.

'Yes, the doctor is astonished, he is so much improved. But it was because I was so anxious about him that I was cross with you this morning when Mrs. Phillips came. Rose, I do not know how to say it to you, but do not ever do any thought-reading or anything like that again.'

'I promise, Mamma.'

'Oh, it is not to please me. It is because it is really dangerous. You see, you are allowed to read the newspapers now. I hope you will not attach too much importance to them. They give you a picture of a common-place world that does not exist. You must always believe that life is as extraordinary as music says it is.'

'Yes, Mamma.'

'It is always wrong to have anything to do with the supernatural. When the dead come back, or the future is no longer a mystery, then there is doubt and filth. There should not be if the world were what it were represented in the newspapers, but it is not. We are for some reason meant to live within limits, as music lives within a certain range of sound, and within a structure of rhythm. But you know all that. Well, if we do not live within limits, it all goes wrong.'

'Yes, Mamma.'

'So you see, you did a thought-reading trick at a party and then that brought Mrs. Phillips to this house.'

'Yes, Mamma.'

'I am sure of that, I know it,' said Mamma. 'And, my dear, you ought to know it too. I would not have taken you to

Knightlily Road if I had known about the poltergeist there, but you saw it, and having seen it, do not forget it. It was a hideous thing in itself, and it carried doubt with it. A lot of people came down from a learned society and investigated it, and some of them actually said Rosamund was playing tricks.'

'That was a shame,' I said, 'I saw things happen she could not have done.'

'Oh no, she did not do it,' said Mamma. 'She is good, like Richard Quin, good, as other people are not. But it got about the neighbourhood. And other people said that the mischief was done by someone who had the key of the house and crept in and laid traps.' She paused, and I knew that it was Cousin Jock who had been accused. 'But there were things happened that not even the most inventive malice could have contrived by natural means.' She paused again; and I thought it possible she was considering whether Cousin Jock could have contrived them by unnatural means. 'Oh, Rose,' she said, speaking with some emotion. 'if you played enough thought-reading tricks, if you dabbled long enough with the unseen, you might end up a medium, promising fathers and mothers to raise lost children from the grave in a dark room, and sometimes keeping faith with them but sometimes cheating them, and always disturbing the dead and keeping them from their duty. It could happen to any of us, if we let it.'

'Yes, Mamma, I will never do it again,' I said.

'I know you won't. But, Rose, life is so mysterious, and one knows so little about it. I was cross with you today because I thought if there was wickedness about, it might be why Richard Quin was so ill.' She looked at me with the simplicity of a child opening its heart to another. 'Do you think that was very foolish?'

'No,' I said. 'He is so good, wickedness must hate him.'

'I think so too. That is why I was frightened.' She sighed and looked about her at the shelves again. 'So many books and none of them really to the point. To this point, I mean. Your Papa never keeps a book he does not think well of. Now to supper.' She suddenly cast her arms about me. 'Oh, Rose, I hate being angry with you, you are the nearest to me of all you children.'

I asked in wonder, 'Am I really, Mamma?'

'Yes, Mary is so far away, and Cordelia——'

'Oh, her,' I said. 'No, I thought you loved Richard Quin best.'

'He is not mine, he belongs to Papa,' she explained. 'Why, they are exactly alike.'

I was puzzled, for I could see no resemblance between my dark, glowering Papa and Richard Quin, who was bright as silver. Sometimes it seemed to me that she knew things about Papa that we did not, though I did not see how that could be.

X

WE HAD a specially magnificent Christmas that year, though we were specially poor. For some reason that was left unstated Constance and Rosamund stayed with us all through the holidays: and they helped Mamma to make our dresses, which were the best we ever had; and Rosamund was beautiful to dress up. Richard was in good health by Christmas Day, and Papa had made for him an Arabian Nights Palace with looking-glass fountains in arcaded court-yards, and domes painted strange colours, very pale, very bright. When we saw it none of us could speak, and Mamma put her hand on his arm and said to us, 'No other father could do this for his children.' Several times, I remember, she came and sat on the floor with us when we were playing with it, and exclaimed every now and then, 'How does he think of such things? How does the idea come into his head?' Very soon I forgot the existence of Mrs. Phillips and Aunt Lily. But one morning all four of us, Cordelia and Mary and Rosamund and I, went into the best confectioner's at Lovegrove, to buy some meringues for Richard Quin's birthday tea; and because the assistant said there would be a batch of pink meringues coming up in a minute, we waited and watched the shop behind us reflected in the mirrored wall behind the counter. There was something called 'the confectioners' licence' which played its part in suburban society; and the place was a cave of well-being, crammed with tables at which well-dressed women, with cairns of parcels piled up on chairs beside them, leaned towards each other, their always large busts overhanging plates of tiny sandwiches and small glasses of port and sherry and madeira, and exchanged gossip that mounted to the low ceiling and was transformed to the twittering of birds in an aviary.

'Isn't that the aunt who comes to school and takes Nancy Phillips home when her nose bleeds?' asked Mary.

'Yes, and that is Nancy's Mamma,' said Cordelia. 'She looks very fast.'

I found them in the mirror. They were not chattering. Aunt Lily had an elbow on the table and cupped her chin in one hand, while her other hand twiddled the stem of a wine-glass, and she coquetted with nothingness. Mrs. Phillips was pushing her empty glass back and forwards on the tablecloth, rucking up the linen. As I looked up her fingers closed tightly round the stem and she sat back in her chair, as if she had made an unalterable resolution. Her swarthiness still recalled people far darker than herself, sweeps and miners. She wore a beige beaver hat even larger than the huge invitation to the wind she had worn at our house, and a bird with a greenish iridescent breast stretched black wings across its width; and that the edifice did not waver was proof of her brooding stillness. Suddenly her hands jerked at the fur on her shoulders, a tie made of a dozen or so small brown pelts, and threw it over the back of the chair beside her. Then she was still again.

'Could you put aside what we want of the meringues?' I asked the shop assistant. 'We could go away and come back.' But she told me they would be coming up at any moment.

Mary, her eyes in the mirror, said, 'Mrs. Phillips' furs,' and stopped.

'What about them?' said Cordelia. 'They are sure not to be in good taste.'

'It is not that,' said Mary. 'They look downspent.'

'Downspent?' said Cordelia. 'There isn't such a word.' Mary said nothing, and Cordelia got irritated. 'What do you mean?'

'I mean downspent,' said Mary.

'I tell you there's no such word,' fussed Cordelia. 'We'll look for it in Papa's big dictionary when we get home, but we won't find it, there's no such word.'

'There ought to be,' said Rosamund.

As we stared in the mirror, the fur tie slid down the back of the chair and fell on the seat, with the despair of a delicate beast revolted by a gross owner. Mrs. Phillips was one of those people who are natural emblems. One thought absurd things about her which could not be true, which were confused with recollections of disturbing dreams till then forgotten. Her fur cannot have had any opinion about her. Yet we felt a vague unease as we stood beside the piles of cakes and wrangled as to whether one should make up new words, whether it must be taken that there was enough language to fit everything that happened.

About a week later, Rosamund and Mary and I were playing with Richard Quin on the sitting-room floor after tea. It was sad in a way, for it was the last night Rosamund was to be with us, she had to go home because her school started again two days later. Mamma and Constance were sitting by the fire, Constance doing some last services in the way of mending, Mamma comparing the fingering in two editions of a Beethoven sonata that had been bothering both Mary and me. We had the Arabian Nights Palace out on the floor, and we were happily quarrelling about the exact details of a story Papa had told us to fit a particular courtyard when Cordelia came in. She had been playing at a concert and she was still in her outdoor clothes. Standing in the doorway, pulling off her gloves, she said, 'Do you know what I heard at my concert? Nancy Phillips' father is dead. He died last night.'

All of us children were silent, except Richard Quin, who went on telling the story, but in a whisper. I saw and heard Mr. Phillips do and say all he had so blusterously done and said during our brief acquaintance, and I marvelled that it now appeared quite different. For the first time I witnessed the miracle which is worked on the dead, which puts them in the right, though they were in the wrong. I thought I would go and sit at Mamma's feet in front of the fire for a little, but when I got up I saw that she had let our music books slide to the floor, that Constance had dropped her mending in her lap, and they were looking at each other without speaking.

I said, 'I want a drink of water.' Rosamund followed me out of the room and we went downstairs to the kitchen. Kate was sitting at the table with the *Daily Mail* spread out in front of her, reading the serial. We took cups from the dresser and filled them at the sink. When one is a child, water tastes better out of a cup than out of a glass, it is the other way round when one is grown-up.

I said to Kate, 'Nancy Phillips' Papa has died.' I knew she would remember him, because she had seen him on the door-step when he wanted to fetch the doctor for Richard Quin; but indeed she would have known all about him in any case, we told her all about the girls at school and she remembered them all.

'Oh, the poor man,' she said. 'But soon he will be at rest, and he will miss all the hard things that are to come.'

Rosamund and I finished drinking our cups of water, and Kate folded up the *Daily Mail*. The January evening looked in, yellowed by light fog, at the basement windows. Somewhere along the street, where the small houses were, a barrel organ was playing.

'Would you like a penny,' asked Kate, feeling in her full skirts for her pocket, 'to take out to the organ-grinder?'

I shook my head at her over the rim of my cup. 'It's kind of you,' I said, 'but I would rather not, unless you think the organ-grinder may need the penny specially.'

'No,' she said, 'you can give it to him some other time.'

We rinsed out our cups, and did not know what to do next.

'We're having stovies for supper tonight,' said Kate; 'if you two could cut up the potatoes I should be glad. You can do it in front of the fire.' And we spent the rest of the evening doing that and other tasks she made for us. Mary who had not known Mr. Phillips, could play with Richard Quin, we could not.

I was puzzled by the many signs which showed me that my mother and Constance were gravely distressed by the news about Mr. Phillips. Mamma had seen him for only a few minutes, and Constance had not seen him at all; and both of them knew more about death than other people. Yet when we came back from school the next day and sat down to dinner, and Cordelia reported that Nancy had not come back, and that the teachers had said they did not expect her until after the funeral, Mamma's face was convulsed as by pain. But I myself, thinking of Mrs. Phillips, felt an aching in the front of my head, and saw against the dark wall which backs the mind's eye a disturbing image of her as a court-card in a pack printed in earthy colours; her tight waist was in the centre of the card, her shoulders above were as broad as the hem of the spreading skirt below, her hungry face was here or there, above or below, her hunger pressing its claim everywhere.

When we came back from school that afternoon I ran upstairs, as we were always made to do, to take off my good clothes and change into an old dress and pinafore apron and wash my hands; and then I hurried down to get in my scales and arpeggios before tea. As I came round the turn in the stairs and looked down on the gaslit hall, I saw Mamma come out of the sitting-room, she must have heard Papa's key in the front door, for he was just coming in. She greeted him with the timid, lifting cockcrow in her voice that meant he had been cross last time he saw her, and that she wanted to give him a chance to be nice again; but he did not greet her back, though he did not look fierce. He said to her in a troubled voice, 'The father of that girl whom the children know, the man who died the other day, was his name Phillips?'

'Yes,' said Mamma, shuddering.

'Did he live at The Laurels, St. Clement's Avenue?'

'Yes, yes,' said Mamma.

Papa held out an evening newspaper to her. 'There has been an exhumation order. There will be an inquest.'

Under our feet an unknown male voice said, 'And his missus has gone. She's skipped.'

I ran downstairs into the hall, and we three peered down through the open door of the steps leading to the basement. Kate and the laundryman looked up at us, their tilted faces drowned in shadow. He said again, 'His missus has gone. She's skipped.'

Mamma said to Papa, 'Go, go at once. The child will be there, and that poor aunt. Bring them back if they want to come. You know how terrible people are.'

'Yes, yes,' he said, 'but I will go upstairs and put on some decent clothes, the police will be there.' He had a better over-coat than the old one he was wearing, Mamma had made him buy it, we had all helped to choose the stuff from patterns, he looked so well in good clothes that it was always an excitement when he bought anything.

He was down again very soon, and Mamma said, 'Thank you, my dear. Mind you, in justice, he was a most irritating man. But, of course, that is no reason.' The front door closed, she called down the basement stairs, 'Is the laundryman still there? I just wanted to thank you for telling us. You have done us a great service. Kate, give Mary and Cordelia their tea, tell them that Nancy and her Aunt Lily may he coming here, and

217

they must be nice to them, because . . .' She halted in perplexity. 'Tell them it is because . . . because people are saying things against Nancy's Mamma, and she has got frightened and has run away.'

'Well, that is no lie,' said Kate.

'While you are seeing to tea Rose and I will make up the two beds in my room, and when you are ready come up and help me put up the camp bed for me in Richard Quin's room. I cannot manage it alone.'

'There is no hurry, Ma'am,' said Kate. 'They will not want to go to bed at once. We have the whole evening to see to them.'

'And what shall I give them for supper?' Mamma mourned. 'God knows I have to buy from day to day, and I have gone on so long I have forgotten how other people live, they will expect all sorts of things that are not in the house. They will be used to late dinner, with soup, and some cream or jelly or tart after the main course, and fruit, it will be terrible.'

'Why should you care?' I asked stoutly.

'I care because it will all be so strange for the child,' she said. 'Losing her father and the police coming and then having to move out into a strange poor house.'

'But all that will not strike home till tomorrow,' said Kate, 'tonight they will hardly know where they are, and poached eggs and tea are the things for that.'

But Mamma had gone upstairs to the linen cupboard, where she fumbled in the poor light, muttering, 'My sheets were good once, but they are all so old, I think there is only one pair which is not patched.' When we had made up the two beds in Mamma's room, and Kate had neatly thrown and mastered the camp bed in Richard Quin's attic, we went down and found Mary and Cordelia still having their tea in the dining-room, sitting side by side and studying the evening paper, which they had spread out on the table between them.

They lifted solemn faces, and Cordelia asked, 'Does this mean they think Nancy's Mamma killed her Papa?'

We understood quite a lot about murders, chiefly because there were some famous cases in the bound volumes of *Temple Bar* in Papa's study. We knew the whole story of Constance Kent, who killed her little stepbrother, and confessed to it years afterwards when she was in a sisterhood at Brighton; it was hard

not to think of her wearing a nun's draperies when she carried
the little boy from his cot down the corridor to the outhouse,
although of course she was only sixteen then. Sometimes, too,
during the holidays, we used to take a bus to another part of
South London, in order to have a walk on a less familiar common, and then we passed a villa with an Italianate tower where
Mr. Bravo and his dashing golden-haired wife and the neat and
silent widow who was her companion had composed an uneasy
household until he died of poisoning.

Mamma answered, 'Yes. But you know you are supposed not
to read at table unless it is something by Papa that has just come
in.'

Mary and Cordelia stopped looking at the paper, but it went
on lying there. Mamma gave me my tea and poured out her
own, but did not drink.

'Oh, poor, poor Nancy,' said Cordelia.

'We will not be able to do enough for her,' said Mamma.

'She will mind, she has not the least idea that people are
unlucky,' said Mary.

'But why is she coming to us?' asked Cordelia. 'I always
think of other people as having lots of relatives and friends
help them.'

'No, many families are as alone in the world as we are,' said
Mamma. 'The least thing starts it.' After a minute she added,
'and this is not a little thing.'

We sat in silence, then Mamma said that I had better get on
with as much of my practice as I could before they came. In the
sitting-room Richard Quin was playing on the hearthrug with a
courtyard of his new palace, Mamma told him that he might go
on in the meantime but must leave when Papa came back with
some friends, and she sat down by the fire and listened to my
scales and arpeggios. Presently she said, 'Rose, you have not
begun to learn how to play. You start playing legato, and then
when your mind wanders from what you are doing your legato
stops being a legato at all, it is as rough as a bath-towel. But when
you tell your hand to play legato it should go on doing so till you
tell it to stop, no matter if you are thinking of the moon.' Later
I tried the third number of Beethoven's Sonata in D major
(op. 10), and when I got to the twenty-second bar of the first
movement, she cried, 'Rose, you are a musical half-wit. You

have forgotten what I told you, you must supply the high F sharp there though it is not written. Beethoven did not write it because it was not in the compass of the piano as he knew it, but he heard it, he heard it inside his head, and you cannot have understood one note of what you have been playing if you do not know that that is what he heard.' Later, when I got to the second subject, she cried, 'You are playing like an idiot. You are playing that appoggiatura not as a short one, thank God you are not such an imbecile as that, but you are not playing it as a long one either. It must have the strict value of a quaver, otherwise the half-bar does not repeat the pattern of the four descending notes.' Later on she moaned, when I got to the bounding octaves, 'Do you mean to say you cannot understand that though the weak beats are doubled by the left hand they must be kept weak, and the strong beats must be kept strong, although the whole thing is piano. I might as well have been teaching a chimpanzee.' I was disquieted by what seemed to be the unnatural mildness of these comments. Had Mamma been her usual self I would surely have heard that Beethoven would not have recognised what I had made of his work, that I had committed faults which nobody would commit if they had one drop of music in them, and that she blamed herself for having ever encouraged me to play. But she recovered her usual vigour when Papa brought in Aunt Lily and Nancy.

Any tragic scene in those days necessarily appeared grotesque, because of the clothes worn by the women. Aunt Lily looked like a wet bird, like one of those hens in the back gardens you see out of a railway-train as it approaches a London junction. The rims of her eyes were red, so were her nostrils, and the bridge of her nose shone bare like a beak. Under her winter coat she wore a pongee silk blouse with a high collar, and one of the transparent bone supports had worked loose and stuck out at an angle, so that it seemed as if someone had been trying to dispatch her in the method appropriate to a hen, by wringing her neck. Today she would have the right to look like that, plain and distraught and like a hen, but she was compelled by the mode of the day to make herself absurd as a clown by wearing a hat the size of a tea-tray, which dipped and jerked and swayed as often as she did, which was perpetually. She had adjusted her hat-pins carelessly in her distress, so every now and then her hat wobbled, and her hands flew up and tugged at it with a gesture which she herself felt to be clumsy and helpless, and tried to correct to elegance by shooting out her little fingers and crisping them. She could not stop talking, although it was evident that Papa, standing beside her almost as grimly as a policeman, wished she would. She asked Mamma if she could really want them to stay with her, had she thought that it would mean that the house would be watched, there would be coppers everywhere, poking and prying, and there was even one walking up the alley at the end of the garden, though that wasn't to be wondered at, with poor Queenie and all, but they would come here too. My father told her firmly that he had settled all that with the police, but she did not listen, she went on twisting and turning as the endless coil of words spun from her mouth, while Nancy waited at her side, her eyes half closed, as if she had gone to sleep as she stood.

As Aunt Lily talked on and on, it could be believed that she was Mrs. Phillips' sister, though till now there had seemed no likeness between them. It was not that she had become sombre and massive and threatening, she was still albinoish and insipid and flimsy and anxious only to please, though rightly despairing of success. But there was a reckless strength in her contemplation of her sister's reckless flight, she did not ask us to be sorry for her and Nancy, she spread her wings and soared over the field of their ruin, and her wild voice told us truly what she saw. The servants had all gone yesterday evening, they had never liked Queenie, Queenie was too hard on them, and when she took one of her mad fits to work herself and show them what was what she did it all too well, they knew she had had to work herself when she was young and thought nothing of her. It was the polishing that gave Queenie and herself away, for she admitted that she was the same, polish, polish, polish, as soon as she saw any brass, she couldn't stop herself, it gets a habit when you have to keep a bar nice, and those girls guessed it, sooner or later you found they all knew, they almost said so to your face. It was a curious thing, even though it was the other side of England people still seemed to find out anything. When the trouble had broken, the sluts had only stayed till evening to suit themselves, to pack up, and she would have liked to have searched their boxes, she was sure they were going out heavier than they came in, but she had not the spirit.

It had broken her heart, she said, and her voice shrilled, and Papa drew closer to her and, his fingers tremulous with reluctance, laid his hand on her sleeve, but he could not stop her. It had broken her heart, she continued, that Queenie had gone in the night without saying a word to her, so that she could not warn her. They didn't know yet how she had gone, there was a wheelbarrow up against the garden wall by the summer house, but there was the copper in the alley on the other side of the wall. She must have crept like a cat all the length of the alley along the top of that wall, fine big woman though she was, then dropped down into the garden of the corner house and out of the front gate when nobody was looking. Queenie had never had any fear, Aunt Lily had often told her that it would be better if she had. The warning Aunt Lily had wanted to give her was not to go back to Southampton. That is where they had both come from, and she would go back there. Ever since Queenie had heard that Mr. Mason had taken a position in Ostend, the very same day he heard that Harry was dead, she had not been herself, and then after the inspector with a beard had come and asked all those questions she had been just like a dumb animal, she couldn't speak and she couldn't understand speech, she just looked, and she would act like an animal, she would go back to where she came from. But of course the inspector with the beard knew where they both came from, he had not said so, but he knew anything. Mamma, who had tried to speak a dozen times but had been unheard, slipped her right hand in my right hand and her left hand on Nancy's left hand, and laid Nancy's hand on mine, and with a circular, ritual gesture bade us leave the room.

In the passage, I said, 'I say, can't grown-ups talk?'

Nancy giggled and said, 'Papa says about Aunt Lily that he wishes he could put a handkerchief over the cage.' Then she remembered that her father was dead, and she cried.

When I had wiped her eyes I took her into the dining-room. The tea had been cleared away and Mary and Cordelia were doing their homework. They said, 'Hello, Nancy,' and I went and got my homework. When I got back they were telling her about something funny that had happened at school during prayers, and I got my arithmetic and algebra done. Then Nancy heard Mary and Cordelia their French and German verbs, but she sometimes lifted her eyes from the page and looked about the room with a certain desolation. She put her hand down on the seat of the chair she was sitting on, and picked off one of the curly pieces which were peeling off the worn surface of the leather. Her eyes travelled over our faces, too, very doubtfully. You could see that she had heard the other girls talking about us at school, saying that we were odd, and very poor. Her unease at the place which she had to come for refuge had struck her sooner than Kate had foretold, perhaps because her mind was so poorly furnished that immediate impressions could move in and extend themselves. She was really very much disturbed by our household. We had so little in common with her that Cordelia struck Mary and me as very clever when she thought of telling her that we all wished so much that we had hair like hers, it was so long and so thick and so fair and so tidy. Nancy's response showed us that this was the sort of remark which she thought sensible people should exchange. She smiled, straightened her hair-bow, and said that her hair must be looking dreadful, she always had it washed the day before she went back to school, but this time there had been no chance of doing that, because of her Papa.

As her voice faded away, Mary said, 'Let's wash our hair. It's about time we did ours.'

I said, 'What a good idea. I'll go and ask Kate if there are any chestnuts in the house,' and Nancy exclaimed, 'What, do you wash your hair with chestnuts?' We all burst out laughing, explaining at once that we were laughing not at her but at me, for talking about chestnuts, before we had told her that in winter hair-washing was a sort of party in our family. Mary had, indeed, been proposing to comfort the afflicted stranger in our midst by admitting her to one of our chief private joys. On these occasions we all went to the bathroom with kettles of hot water and gave each other shampoos, then came down to the sitting-room while Richard, who was allowed to stay up late on these occasions, helped the drying process by pummelling our heads with hot bath-towels, which he enjoyed doing because, he said, it was his only chance to be cruel back to his cruel elder sisters; and at the same time we roasted chestnuts among the coals and ate them very hot with milk that had been put outside the window to get very cold.

All this we explained to Nancy, who said that of late her Mamma had been taking her to the big hairdresser's in the High Street opposite the Bon Marché, to save trouble. She said it with some pride. But there was nothing to do but go on with it now we had started it, so I went down to the kitchen and found that Kate had quite a lot of chestnuts, and would put them on to boil, and told Richard Quin that there was going to be a hairwashing, and came upstairs again, and found Papa standing at the front door talking to a policeman. I went into the sitting-room to ask Mamma if later on we could come in and dry our hair, and found her and Aunt Lily sitting in silence by the fire. Mamma looked very tired. Aunt Lily had just taken off her hat, the huge disc lay on top of the piano, its brim projecting over the instrument in front and behind; and she was leaning forward over the fire, her hands searching for combs and slides and hairpins lost in the disordered edifice of her yellow hair. As I came in she looked up and said, with her old jauntiness, 'Ah, here's the clever little kiddy,' and flashed one of her familiar smiles that reflected the light on her prominent teeth which shone too today, from the bridge of her reddened nose, and from the tears on her cheeks. Before I could ask Mamma what I wanted, she said, 'Who was it at the door?'

I answered that it was a policeman and Aunt Lily said, 'Perhaps he has news. But,' she sighed, 'perhaps he hasn't. I suppose it will be police, police, police, for ever and ever, amen, coming round about every little thing.' She put her hands round her knees, which showed boney through her skirt, and stared at the fire as if the news were there. I had a feeling that she often spoke falsely, like a popular song, she might have been singing 'The Honeysuckle and the Bee,' but sometimes she spoke as my father and mother did, sincerely, of what she really thought and felt.

Papa came back. He said, 'Miss Moon, a policeman has brought a message from the family solicitor which he sent down to the Laurels through the police office.' Even the Phillipses had not a telephone, so different was that world from this. It appeared that the solicitor had got in touch with a brother of Mr. Phillips, who lived in Nottingham, and he was coming down tomorrow and would go to the boarding-school on the South Coast where Nancy's brother was, and would bring him up to London, and then he would settle various business arising out of the recent unfortunate events, and the next day or the day after would take Nancy back to Nottingham. It was strange to hear this news about the movements of people we did not know, who lived in places we had never visited. It was as if towns marked on the map had begun to cry out and bleed.

'I'm glad,' said Aunt Lily, 'it will get them away from London. I don't think they sell newspapers as much in the street in those provincial sort of places, do they? It's a horrid sound, those boys calling out the news, up and down the street. And it's a lovely big house they have, they've pots of money, the kids will have everything. But what they'll hear about their mother I don't like to think, for all Harry's people were against Queenie from the start, I never could think why.' The tears that had been stationary on her cheeks began to roll again. 'It's good news,' she said, 'but I did think it might be something about Queenie.'

Mamma told me to go and give the news to Nancy, but not say a policeman had brought them. I wondered at the obtuseness of all grown-ups, even Mamma. Nancy had simply accepted the fact that she had entered a passage in time when policemen brought communications which decided her life. She had already left the dining-room and gone upstairs to take off her blouse and skirt and put on her dressing-gown in preparation for the hair-washing ceremony, and I found her sitting on her bed and looking round Mamma's room as she had looked round the dining-room. It must indeed have seemed a desolate apartment to poor Nancy, as it would have to most people, for it was almost bare except for remnants of obsolete fame, preserved in a form which few would have recognised, in tarnished laurel wreaths inscribed with such names as Dresden and Düsseldorf and Wien, and signed photographs and prints of conductors holding their batons.

I said to her, 'Cheer up, Nancy, you won't have to be here long. Your uncle in Nottingham is going to fetch Cecil from his school tomorrow, and then only a day or two after that he will take you both home with him.'

She said, 'Oh. My uncle. Nottingham? That will be Uncle Mat.' Her eyes wandered round the room and settled on the signed print over Mamma's bed.

'Brahms,' I said. 'He gave it to Mamma of his own accord. She did not even know he was at her concert. So of course she did not even ask for it, he brought it to her hotel the next morning.'

'Oh,' said Nancy politely, 'who was he?' Before I could answer she said, 'I don't know Uncle Mat very well. I can't even remember whether he is married to Aunt Nettie or Aunt Ada.'

'Does it make a difference?' I asked.

'It does, rather,' said Nancy wearily, and her eyes grew wet again.

I ran downstairs and asked Aunt Lily which it was. She said, 'Not Aunt Nettie — she's the sly one, I know well what poor Nancy was thinking about — it's all right — it's Uncle Mat and Aunt Ada, and they're both ever so jolly, quite different from Nettie.' She looked round at Papa and Mamma with a little laugh, as if she knew that she could count on their understanding and sympathy in her references to the amusing guerilla warfare of family life. They were obliging enough to return the smile, but I knew them to be depressed. When I got upstairs again Nancy was standing in the doorway, and she did not seem as pleased as I had thought she would be at hearing that Uncle Mat was married to Aunt Ada and not to Aunt Nettie, she just stood there. Presently she said, choking, 'I can't wash my hair.'

'Don't be silly,' I said, 'be a good girl, it is fun.'

She muttered, 'I keep on crying . . . I'd better stay by myself and people won't see.'

I could hear Cordelia and Mary getting the lather ready in the bathroom. I called to them, and when they came, I said, 'Look here, Nancy doesn't want to wash her hair with us because we'll see her crying. Tell her it's all right.'

'We will not think any worse of you if you cry,' Cordelia assured her, 'we always cry when we are upset.'

'Yes,' said Mary, 'and we have none of us had nearly as much to upset us as you have. It would really be very odd if you had lost your Papa and did not cry a lot.'

'Yes, it would be sharper than the serpent's tooth,' I said, 'go on and cry as much as you like, and you can do it all right while you're washing your hair.'

'Just pretend we are not here,' said Cordelia.

But Nancy looked with some alarm at the three girls, not very well known to her and generally reputed to be rather odd, who were crowding in on her, dressed in shabby dressing-gowns, and inciting her to cry. 'Well, it's not the right thing to do, is it?'

she said, vaguely; and indeed she and we were thinking of quite different things. To us, a girl whose father had just died and whose mother was suspected of murdering him had passed into the world of Shakespearean tragedy, and we wanted to help her to exercise the functions she would find it necessary to discharge now that she had suffered this abrupt translation from the ordinary. We had imagined that unless she were allowed to walk up and down a room, shedding tremendous tears and uttering cries which would purge her heart of its grief, there would be just such a hole in the universe as would have been left had Lady Macbeth been deprived of her sleep-walking scene. But Nancy saw the situation in quite another light. She did not know much, but among the things she had learned was the disgracefulness of crying. It had perhaps been brought home to her that she had made Aunt Lily's hard lot harder than it need be by untimely bawling. So she looked at us with puzzled disapproval, and we drifted away.

But the hair-washing worked out not so badly. When we went down to the sitting-room only Aunt Lily was there. Mamma had gone to see about supper, and Papa came in with three glasses and one of the bottles the margarine manufacturer had given him. He asked Aunt Lily if she would like some sherry, and then looked at the label, and in that soft, polite, withdrawn voice which meant he was speaking about something of no interest to him, said that he was afraid that it was port. But Aunt Lily said that that was all the better, for she understood that port was a temperance drink. Papa hesitated for a minute before replying, 'Well, there is no advantage in regarding port as a temperance drink unless one is a teetotaller,' and filled the glass.

Papa had meant nothing more than he said, he was simply considering the manifestly false proposition that port was a temperance drink and wondering whether it served any useful purpose in spite of its falsity, or deserved to be pulled up and destroyed like any other intellectual weed. But Aunt Lily was unused to remarks which had not a directly personal application, and was greatly puzzled by his answer. She threw a sharp glance at him, which she might better have directed at us children who were settling down before the fire, for my sisters and I (as we were to find out when we first mentioned the matter to each other, many years later) were all thinking of the time when we had seen her drinking sherry in the confectioner's shop without any visible distaste for its alcoholic nature. We were recalling that memory without malice, indeed it was the foundation of our lasting affection for her, because it suggested to us that she was not really a grown-up, and, like a child, was always having to protect herself against criticism that asked more of her than she could give. We liked her too because she came to the conclusion that Papa was nice, she withdrew her eyes from him, said mildly, 'Ah, I can see you are a great tease,' and comfortably took up her glass of port.

Then the grown-ups went away and we took over the hearth; and Richard Quin, who had always, from the time he was very small, had a quick, pliant social gift, saw to it that things went better with Nancy. He rubbed our heads as he always did, really hurting us just a little, just so much that we should ask him to stop urgently enough to make it really exciting; but he did not hurt Nancy at all, and he told her that she had nicer hair than any of us sisters. Just then he was passing through a stage when he loved nonsense more than anything, he was always reciting that funny silly thing by Samuel Foote, which begins, 'So she went into the garden to cut a cabbage leaf, to make an apple pie, and at the same time a great she-bear, coming up the street, pops its head into the shop and says, "What, no soap?"' So we told him how Nancy had thought we washed our hair with chestnuts, and he was delighted, he rolled laughing on the floor, crying out that he was going to wash his hair with a rolling-pin, with the Houses of Parliament, with a bus-horse, with the Crown Jewels. Suddenly Nancy said shyly, 'I am going to wash my hair with a railway ticket.' She had, as we found out later, hardly ever made up things. She had never made up an animal in all her life, which seemed to us quite dreadful. Now she was too old for Richard Quin's games, but she liked helping him play them, and he did not seem to puzzle her as we did. Also she liked roasting the chestnuts, she had never done it before. We had a special chestnut-roaster, I have not seen one in the shops for years, it was like a dust-pan made of wire netting, with a very long handle.

We were quieter after Richard Quin went up to bed; and suddenly we saw that Nancy had gone to sleep with her head on the seat of the armchair. We knew the grown-ups would come back some time, so we just waited. Then Aunt Lily put her head round the door (which was an action she performed quite literally; it was no mere phrase, she really stood outside and twisted her neck round the edge of the door) and said, 'There's something I'd love you kiddies to do for me,' and when we interrupted her and pointed to Nancy, she went on, 'Well, the poor chickabiddy has had a long day. But first can you just help me, and get me a teeny-weeny bit of note-paper? Your Papa's gone into the den and your Mamma's with the sweet little boy, and I just want to have some paper by me so that I can get on with a letter when I've a moment.' We found her some in Mamma's desk, and she seemed strangely pleased, as if now she would pursue some delightful occupation that would wipe out the darkness round her. 'And your Papa will have a stamp, I'll be bound,' she said, 'gentlemen always have stamps.' Then she woke Nancy, saying, 'Well, the sandman's been visiting you all right,' and took her upstairs, and soon was down again, and sat herself at the table in front of the paper.

'Now, I've got something all you kiddies would like to see,' she said, diving into the deep pocket in the side of her skirt just below her waistband, and taking out a short, stubby cardboard box. We gathered round her, marvelling at her brightness, which our prophetic blood knew to be pitiful, while she showed us the first fountain pen we had ever seen. 'Harry was given one by an American gentleman he does business with, and he was so taken with it that he gave us each one at Christmas. Queenie and Nancy, and me too, he was always very fair,' she said, woe touching her voice again, and she held out the unusual object so that we could admire it. She suggested that she might get one to give Papa for a Christmas present; but though we were fascinated, we dissuaded her, for we really could not imagine him writing with anything but a quill pen, an ordinary swan or goose quill for the rough draft, and for his fair copy the crow quill used by draughtsmen. But she was glad when we left her and she could get down to the delicious task of writing her letter, which she was still pursuing, though it did not seem to be a long one, at our bedtime twenty minutes later. She did not hear us when we first said good night, but looked up absently, joy shining curiously from her tear-raddled face. She called us back to ask when the last post went, which, as a journalist's children, we were able to tell her with perfect accuracy, and she seemed disappointed when we told her that it had already gone.

The next morning Mamma had to give us a note for our form-mistresses, excusing us for not having finished all our homework. Cordelia and Mary had not touched their arithmetic and mathe-matics, and I had not touched my French translation, and we had just looked at our history when we were going to bed, because we had been looking after Nancy. Our homework, I realise now, presented a difficult moral problem to Mamma at any time. Because she was Scottish she believed that there was nothing more important in a child's life than its lessons, but as a musician she knew that there was nothing more important to us than our music. This meant that our homework was perfunctory but never wholly neglected; and Mamma really suffered in writing that note. This was the first and trifling sample of the disorganisation brought upon our lives by our involvement in one of the most notorious murder cases of the Edwardian era.

I cannot list all the inconveniences suffered by my father and mother. It is to be remembered that my father was not a young man, for he had married late. He now did not spare himself at all in the service of the Phillips family. By dint of staying up nearly all night to write his leaders for the paper, he made him-self free to escort Aunt Lily up to the City on the various errands which, with prudence and tenderness, he had persuaded her to undertake. While we were sitting by the fire in our dressing-gowns on that first evening, we had heard Papa say to her, 'You must go to a good solicitor,' and when she answered, 'Oh, that's all right, Harry's solicitor is a very good man,' gently persist, 'No, you cannot have that solicitor, you must have one of your own'; and when she had answered again, 'Well, I don't see why, but if you say so, I'll do it, but I wouldn't bother just for myself, time for that when Queenie turns up,' he had said, lowering his voice, 'No, you must have a solicitor to help you at the inquest. If you tell him everything, everything, he will be ready to help your sister too.' The next day he went up to London with Aunt Lily and saw a member of the anti-socialist organisation for which he spoke, who was a partner in a famous firm of solicitors, and he managed to induce him to accept her as his client, though he owed this man a considerable sum of money and had angered him by forgetting to appear at a public meeting he had arranged.

There was no stopping Papa when he was engaged in a crusade for a victory which would bring him no benefit. There were other visits to London, which, I supposed, were made at her request. On all these expeditions Papa was Aunt Lily's patient escort; and always he gnawed his fingers when he was waiting in the hall for her to come downstairs in the festal array which she assumed in the hope of showing a proper sense of the social elevation of both Papa and his friends.

This festal array had been to some degree restrained by the efforts of Mamma. When she was helping Aunt Lily to unpack she had mentioned to her that, though she saw that she had some very nice scent, she must ask her not to use it during her visit, as Papa had an abnormal dislike of it, it really made him quite ill to smell it. 'What,' Aunt Lily had wistfully enquired, 'even some nice violet essence from Paris? It's good, you know.' 'Not even that,' Mamma answered firmly, adding, 'It is the same thing, you know, as Lord Roberts and his hatred for cats. They cannot help it.' She had also prevented Aunt Lily from going back to The Laurels to fetch her best hat, on the plea that since envy was a prevalent human trait, a certain moderation should be observed at this moment, if only in order to influence public opinion in Queenie's favour. It is possible that the hat would really have been quite a nice one, and the scents as good as Grasse could make; for though the Phillipses had, as we were to find out, rewarded Aunt Lily for her many services by nothing more than meagre pocket-money, Queenie had quite often bought handsomely for her sister at the shops to which she herself gave her custom.

But the elegancies Aunt Lily thus acquired lost their character when set in conjunction with her nodding and winking bony plainness; and they would indeed have been hard put to it to assert their rightness against the wrongness of the minor touches which she added to her appearance with indefatigable industry and with taste that was never better than infamous. Her necklace of enamel violets had two fellows, one of pansies and one of marguerites. She had a remarkable collection of hatpins and prized highest a set of four, each with one of Sir Joshua Reynolds' cherubs on its head. With a white veil spotted with black lozenges, she wore black glacé kid gloves with white buttons and strappings, and openwork stockings, sometimes

231

embroidered with violets. When she wanted to make a particularly good impression she added a mauve feather boa. As she descended the staircase my father would raise his eyes and take in the special features of the day's toilette, and would force himself to nod slowly and make a vague courtly gesture, as if in approbation. Then he would open the front door without his usual haste, hold it while she fluttered out, and slowly set out on his long day of public appearance in her company.

But Papa and Mamma were further tormented by Aunt Lily's garrulity. She talked all the time. Every evening, in Papa's study, they gave her a couple of glasses of port, sometimes, I think, even more, though to their fierce abstinence this must have seemed like procuration. I went in once and heard her say, 'Anybody but Queenie could have got on with Harry, but of course he never looked at me,' and I am sure, from my recollection of their faces, that she had been uttering a string of confidences which they would have liked to annul by magic, not because these were disgraceful, but because they were more innocent and honest than is safe in this world. But more often Aunt Lily talked not well enough. In her world silence was suspect. With us it was taken for granted that a person who did not speak was thinking, or needed to rest, or, quite simply, had nothing to say at the moment; but to her such a person must either be sad (in which case they were described as 'moping') or nourishing some resentment. In both cases it was the duty of the well-intentioned to distract the affected person by a flow of cheerful conversation, and Aunt Lily was above all dutiful.

Our household found itself peculiarly vulnerable to this diagnosis and to the cure. We were all of us given to spells of silence, particularly Mary and Papa; and none of us (and here again this particularly applied to Mary and Papa) agreed with Aunt Lily's theory that the use of certain facetious phrases was enough to stamp an occasion with gaiety, however unrelated they were, provided it was unremitting and accompanied by laughter. The second evening she was with us, as it got near Richard Quin's bedtime, she said brightly that she thought she knew who was ready for a trip to Bedfordshire, a joke which we had heard from Kate years before, when we were all small enough to think it very funny; and she felt it necessary every evening to meet that moment with some synonymous phrase which she considered equally entertaining. In the same way she felt it necessary to say, 'When father lays the carpet on the stairs,' if she happened to see Papa performing any small task such as putting in a new incandescent gasmantle, and 'Alice, Where Art Thou,' if Mamma called for any of us and we did not hear. We liked her all the more for this, because it meant that she was trying hard to be nice, but it made us very tired.

But my father and mother suffered most acutely from the contact of their fullness with the emptiness of those they were befriending. Nancy's Uncle Mat was not able to fetch her as soon as she had hoped, though he had taken away her brother, and she remained in our house for some time. It was obviously not the place for her to be. Aunt Lily derived many benefits from staying with us, Nancy none. She could not go to school, and she would not go out for fear of being recognised; and the fear was justified, for everybody in the district had known her handsome and splendidly dressed mother and her expansive father with his snorting motor-car, and the boy and girl, both pale with yellow hair, who silently accompanied them. But there was nowhere to send the girl. Mr. Phillips had had a partner who had sent a message that his wife would be pleased to take the girl, but she did not come herself nor write to Mamma, and this seemed cold and ill-mannered, and Mamma did not like to follow it up. Mr. Phillips' solicitor spoke of other friends who might be of service, and who were sometimes said to have expressed a kindly concern for the two children. But they too neither called nor wrote. In time it dawned on Papa and Mamma that probably these people were unused to the idea of calling on strangers, and while they would certainly be able to write, they would be at a loss to compose a delicate letter dealing with unusual circumstances.

For Mamma was very conscious that she was bringing her children up in a social vacuum, and she dreaded lest this horrid catastrophe should put Nancy off from a world ready to accept her. So she questioned the girl often, to find out which of her parents' friends had lingered in her memory as likely to be affectionate. But they had left only physical impressions on the girl's mind. She could describe them only by reference to the houses they lived in, to their carriages, to the clothes the women wore, the number and sex of their children, the sort of children's parties they gave, and the presents they had sent at Christmas. She could not remember anything they had said, or anything they had done, which had a personal significance. They had often met, but not to practise the art of conversation. 'Mrs. Robinson? Oh, she was a very big woman. Mamma said she wore too bright colours for anybody so stout,' said Nancy. 'What did she talk about?' pressed Mamma. 'Oh, about going to the Derby, and she used to go to the piano and sing all the songs that Connie Ediss sings at the Gaiety.'

There spread before Papa and Mamma a terrible nullity of which they had not known before. Nancy sat all day about the house, exercising what was evidently a practised ability for doing nothing. She did not want to read the newspapers, or any books. She had never read the *Alices* or the *Jungle Books* or *Treasure Island* or *Jackanapes* or *The Secret Garden*. Mamma was aware that there were many people who read what she called trashy books, but it was news to her that there were people who read nothing at all. She was more sympathetic when Nancy owned that she could not play the violin or the piano and had no voice and did not care for music, for since the development of Cordelia's ambition she had seen a new virtue in the acceptance of such limitations. But it alarmed her again when she told Nancy that she was sure none of us would mind if she used our paint-boxes, and Nancy looked surprised and said that she did not take art at school. She took pleasure in helping Mamma with some of the housework, but was plainly unused to the task, and a little embarrassed by it, while she grew obviously apprehensive when Mamma suggested that she should go down to the kitchen and see if there was anything she could do for Kate. She had been trained, like many of our school-fellows, to think that helping servants with their work and feeling love for servants was a risky thing to do, that it was likely to cost her some obscure distinction she might otherwise retain.

The only occupation she had which she seemed to think legitimate was what she called her 'work': a linen nightdress case stamped on one side with a trivial design of trailing flowers, which she was outlining in the simplest possible embroidery stitch. It must have been important to her, or she would not have packed it among her clothes the night she left the Laurels. But it was a poor defence from fear and grief. She often tired of it, and Mamma would find her quite motionless in the arm-chair by the sitting-room fire, idle and unprotected, her blue-grey eyes, which were gentle and limpid but nothing more, fixed on the window and the wintry world outside. My mother's heart was wrung, but she could do very little to comfort the girl, who was as effectively separated from her by her lack of interests as she would have been by deafness, or ignorance of all but some exotic language.

'What did they do all day, sitting in that house?' I heard Mamma asking Papa one evening at this time, horror in her voice, as if she spoke of naked savages, pent in their darkened huts while filth and tropical disease and fear of jungle gods consumed them.

'God knows, God knows,' he answered. 'This is the new barbarism.'

'What is so terrible,' my mother continued, 'is that the girl is quite nice.'

That was indeed the terrible thing. Though Nancy came from a world where life was reduced to nothingness, she was herself not nothing. We had thought that of her at first, but we saw that we were wrong. That she should have had a great love for her aunt was natural enough; in the shadow of her sombre mother she had played with another child who sometimes turned into a protective grown-up. But very soon she came to love Mamma and follow her about the house, very soon she came to see that there was something grand and strange about Papa, and to look about her at his books with proper reverence when she went into his study, and in spite of herself she became fond of Kate. Though we had felt so awkward with her when she came, she liked us too. She could not have enough of Richard Quin, she was enraptured because he was such a pretty little boy, she thought it a shame we did not have a Little Lord Fauntleroy suit for him to wear, and awed because he knew so much that she did not. All this liking she expressed by actions which were of little moment, which were hardly actions at all, but which showed sweetness. They did not amount to very much; one might say she had performed the moral equivalent of laying a few lavender-sachets among the sheets in the linen-cupboard. But it was enough to make her one of our family.

So we were sorry when Uncle Mat came to take her away. There was nothing good about that. He came on a Saturday morning, when we children were all in, indeed everybody was in, except Aunt Lily, who had gone up to see some shops in the West End and tell them not to carry out the orders they were fulfilling for her and her sister, if there were still time. Richard Quin and I watched him out of the dining-room window as he was getting out of the cab, and we could tell at once that it would not do. He was big and stout like Mr. Phillips and should have been jolly like him; and his sad expression looked all wrong on him, it was like a serious person wearing a paper hat. He stopped still and looked up at the house before he opened the gate, as if he thought someone inside was going to take advantage of him, and he was organising his forces so that he should give as good as he got. We opened the door, because we knew that Kate was in the middle of her week-end baking, and he asked if he could see Papa, reading his name very slowly off a piece of paper he took out of his pocket, doubtfully, as if he suspected Papa was probably really called something quite different.

Mary was practising in the sitting-room, but we took him in there, and Richard went and pulled her hair, that recognised social signal among the young, so that she stopped and realised who had come. I asked Uncle Mat to sit down, which he did exactly in the fashion of an actor in a play Kate had taken us to in the local theatre some time before. The actor had walked round in a circle on his way to his chair, staring at the tops of the walls as if looking at the pictures, but fixing his eyes on a level far above that which pictures are normally hung, and continuing to do so while he slowly sat down. This is a universal convention among bad actors, and I find it interesting that Uncle Mat should have followed it when he wished to emphasise how strange he found it that he should have to visit our house. Then we fetched Papa out of his study, and ran upstairs and told Mamma, who lifted her hand as if she were a conductor collecting his orchestra, and said, 'What must we do?' She answered herself by saying that while she was getting tea and biscuits for the visitor, we must find Nancy, and send her down to her uncle, and get on with her packing if we could do it without her.

I found Nancy in the bathroom with Cordelia, they were gossiping over a tedious chore we children always had to do, they were washing all the hair-brushes and clothes-brushes in the house. It was horrid to give her the message, it seemed so natural that she should be in the bathroom, we did not mind her seeing how old the brushes were, she no longer asked us why all our brushes were not silver-backed; as I came in she had been looking at a clothes-brush and wondering how much longer it would last just as if she were one of us by birth.

Struck still, she said, 'Aunt Lily is out, I won't be able to say good-bye to her,' and turned blue-white.

'But your Uncle Mat will ask her to come and see you in Nottingham,' I said.

She said, 'He won't,' not with the howling despair we used sometimes to purge our fears, but with a shrewd hopelessness that was far grimmer. She laid the worn clothes-brush back in the suds, and set about drying her hands, but gave up, shaking her head. If one is unhappy and one's hands are really wet it is a bother to dry them. Cordelia took the towel away from her and did it for her. Nancy said, 'I don't want to leave here.'

Cordelia said, 'Oh, Nancy, we don't want you to go. We wish you could stay. But you must have noticed that we are very poor. If you stayed here you would find yourself missing a lot of things you had at home.'

'Yes, it's really awfully like a picnic,' I said, 'such fun, but one has to go home.'

'This is not a picnic,' said Nancy. 'It is something I want to last for ever.'

'Live with your uncle,' said Mary, 'and come back here quite often, we will always want you.'

'Come back in summer specially,' said Richard Quin, who was suddenly there, 'we go to Kew, and we do have picnics then, and tea in shops, with ices. I will always take you about with me. You have lots of things my silly sisters have not got.'

'I don't think I'll be able to get back,' said Nancy.

'Oh, we will always know each other,' I said, and, of course, I was right.

Mamma called, and we dispersed, our family nodding confidently, Nancy as still as stone. Mary and I went downstairs to scrabble for Nancy's shoes in the dark cupboard under the stairs, and presently Mary stopped, and said, 'Can you believe that

237

Nancy is right and her Uncle Mat won't ask even Aunt Lily to come and see her?'

'I think it's probably true,' I said, 'Nancy isn't silly, you know.'

'But that is awful,' said Mary. 'Nancy loves Aunt Lily. She is rude to her sometimes, but she loves her.'

'I know,' I said, and confessed, choking, 'I am horrible, I am so sorry Nancy is going, but I did think too that when she was gone it would be easier about our practising.'

'I am horrible too, I thought of that,' said Mary, 'but we are like that, and we cannot help it.' All the same we both settled down among the boots and shoes and wept, until we heard Nancy coming down the staircase above our heads, her feet lagging from step to step. Mary sobbed, 'Well, anyway Papa and Mamma have had a little time to work on the beastly old man before he sees her,' and we got on with our hunt, drawing comfort from what now strikes me as one of the oddest paradoxes in our parents' being. They were incapable of getting on terms with their fellow creatures on the plane where most of us find that easy. My mother could not dress herself to go out of her house tidily enough to avoid attracting hostile stares, she could not speak to strangers except with such naïveté that they thought her a simpleton, or with such subtlety that they thought her mad. She was never much more negotiable than William Blake. My father was unable to abandon to the slightest degree his addiction to unpunctuality, swarthy and muttering scorn, and insolvency, no matter how earnestly his admirers (and there were always new ones to replace those he alienated) begged it as a favour. Yet when people had passed a certain threshold in the lives of either Papa or Mamma, which they did easily enough by attaining a high pitch of desolation, both were able to exercise on behalf of these desolates a celestial form of cunning nearly irresistible. They were as tricky as a couple of winged foxes. They never had a conversation in the interests of those they were protecting which did not sensibly alter the situation in the way they wished, while those with whom they conversed remained quite unconscious of any propulsive force in their surroundings.

Uncle Mat, as we were to learn years later, set them a severe test. It had to be pointed out to him that when Nancy came down he had better stop saying over and over again, 'Saw Harry only a month ago. As well as you and me. And a healthy man.

Never been ill in his life. It's no use telling me they won't find something. Saw him only a month ago . . .' He had, so to speak, to be taught the facts of life in Nancy's special case; to be induced to realise that the girl was the child not only of his brother's wife, who was believed to have murdered his brother, but of his brother, who was believed to have been murdered; and that therefore she must be treated tenderly. I cannot think how Papa and Mamma succeeded in doing this, but certainly when we all gathered on the doorstep to wave Nancy goodbye Uncle Mat was bending on her a gaze that was more kindly than we could ever have hoped. I remember that gaze as proceeding from an eye embedded in crimson jelly like a bull's; but that is perhaps because of Papa's answer when we asked whether Uncle Mat had said anything about taking Aunt Lily up to Nottingham. He replied, 'No. It would have been as foolish as to ask a bull to be kind to a horse.' He turned about and walked towards his study, but turned again to say, 'Man is a political animal. But seeing what the animal is, what may politics become?' His door closed on us.

XI

WHEN Aunt Lily came in at tea-time she did not notice
Mamma's disturbed face, she was so eager to know if
there was a letter for her. This was always the first
thing she asked when she came down in the morning, and when
she returned to the house after even the briefest absence. We
had told her the times of the posts quite often, but she did not
seem to take them in. This afternoon some letters had come for
her but not, it appeared, the one she wanted. She was very tired,
and this time she could not bear it that the letter had not come.
Her face crumpled, and as soon as she heard that Nancy had
been taken away she wept without shame, and it could be seen
that she was lamenting both her griefs at once, the letter which
had not come, the lost girl. But she was inordinately pleased
because Nancy had left her the completed nightdress-case, her
'work,' as a present. Aunt Lily sat down and drank several cups
of tea with the nightdress-case spread out on the arm of her
chair, breaking off every now and then to say, 'It's the thought
that I appreciate, she's such a thoughtful kiddy,' and, again,
'All she had, and she left it as a keepsake for her poor old auntie,'
and, yet again, 'Well, like my own I always felt towards her, and
like my own she feels towards me.' It did not escape us that there
was a certain falsity, a greasy and posing self-consciousness,
about these expressions. We had very often been sharply warned
against sentimentality, and though we might have been able to
define it only vaguely as the way one should not play Bach, we
recognised it. But there was never any doubt that here the false
merely overlaid the true. We had got accustomed to the idea that
Aunt Lily had formed the vulgarest image of herself as having a
heart of gold, and often wrote herself atrocious lines to be said in
that character, and delivered them like the worst of actresses,
yet had in fact a heart of gold. It is not unlikely that she owed
this pollution of her pure self to her origins, for there had never
been a population so doomed to excessive relish of themselves
and their own emotions as the Southern English who dropped

their h's in the late nineteenth and early twentieth centuries. The music-hall comedians and the funny papers never left them alone for a moment. But we had pierced her affectations and knew she mourned Nancy as poignantly as our austere Mamma would mourn for us, were we taken from her.

Aunt Lily told us what luck she had had in the day's business. They had been very nice at Jay's, saying that the musquash cape had indeed been started but in the circumstances (she repeated that they used that word) they would put it in stock and say no more about it; and Peter Robinson's has been as good about two garments of the sort Mrs. Phillips had worn when she appeared in her drawing-room, two matinées. But there had been two tea-gowns (I do not know how these differed from matinées) ordered from a shop in Bond Street, which was unfortunately not disposed to be nice about them at all, although Queenie had spent a small fortune there. '"Well," I said, "I'm only telling you, you can go on with the order if you like, but you won't get your money, and don't say I didn't tell you you'd have to whistle for it, for I'm telling you straight."' Mamma made the appropriate sounds, though her eyes were bright as stars because she was not there, she had withdrawn to some musical paradise for refreshment. 'Mind you,' said Aunt Lily, confidently, taking Mamma's starry gaze as proof of complete communion, 'I should have known, you can always tell, there's not a creature in the place that hasn't a French name, this manageress person calls herself Madame Victoire, they're all Stephanies and Yvettes and Lisettes, and not one of them's ever been nearer France than the Elephant and Castle. You can't tell me. And it's all false. So really you oughtn't to be surprised when they're low and tricky, That,' she said, taking a sip from the glass of sherry Papa had poured out for her when he came to help Mamma tell her the sad news, 'that is what my Ma used to say. And whatever you could say about my Ma, you couldn't say she didn't know her way about.' She shook her head and gazed into the distance, and then asked, very childishly, very pitifully, 'What was it I was telling you my Ma used to say?' And none of us found it quite easy to answer.

Richard Quin, who was lying on the hearth-rug reading a newspaper, called out, 'Mamma, what is a pork-pie hat?' and Aunt Lily clutched at this straw, saying, 'Fancy a sharp little

241

boy like you not knowing what a pork-pie hat is, well I never. Can somebody give me a newspaper and a pair of scissors?' She cut it out with some cleverness and put it on her head and made a funny face, and we all laughed, and she went on to say, 'And if there's those who don't know what a pork-pie hat is, there's lots more that don't know what a pork-pie is. It's a very rare thing, let me tell you, a good pork-pie, and I can say so, for I'm one of the few people who can make one, though I say it myself.'

Richard stood up, advanced on her crying, 'A magic?'

'Well, cooking is,' she answered.

'Make me a magic pork-pie, make me a magic pork-pie with spell and onions,' he bade her, laughing.

'Well, I will, but there's a whole lot of things you have to get in,' she warned him; 'there's conger eel, for one thing.'

'Conger eel,' exclaimed Mamma, coming out of her musical remoteness, as she was willing to do if just cause were shown.

'Conger eel, conger eel, conger eel,' cried Richard Quin, in triplicate.

'Yes, indeed, conger eel,' said Aunt Lily, gravely, as if she did not want us to make a joke of something serious, 'veal and ham pie you can have without conger eel, that's quite natural, but you can't have a real pork-pie without a nice bit of conger eel in it.'

Richard Quin clasped her knees and laid his head in her lap, chuckling, 'This is lovely like the *Arabian Nights*,' while Mamma, gazing into the upper air at vast interlacing forms, like supple drainpipes, murmured, 'Conger eels, conger eels,' and the name, by reiteration, became something else, even more extraordinary.

'You are a funny crowd,' said Aunt Lily, delighted at the sensation she was creating, 'everybody who can make a good pork-pie knows that, though as I say there's few enough of us who can. I never would have learned the trick, if it hadn't been that old Uncle Joe Salter who did the cold table for the Admiral Benbow down at the Old Harbour took a fancy to me and showed me.'

Richard Quin seized on this superb supply of raw material for nonsense. 'Admiral Benbow, he had a cold table, a very — cold — table — a table dripping with stalactites,' he chanted in ecstasy, shuddering and turning up an imaginary coat collar, 'down by the harbour, the very old harbour the one they don't use any more, it's far too old and far too deep, and there's the thing with two

242

heads that eats the anchors, so nobody goes there now except Uncle Joe Salter, and Uncle Joe Salt, and Uncle Joe Saltest — Aunt Lily, Aunt Lily, do, do go on.'

'Hark at the child,' said Aunt Lily, 'goodness, I do wish old Uncle Joe Salter was alive to hear that, Uncle Joe Salt and Uncle Joe Saltest, he'd have died of laughing. But now, since you're all so interested in pork-pies, I wonder if I could make one tonight. Do you know if the girl's got a good stock-pot going?'

Kate had indeed. And Mamma did what was almost unthinkable, she gave us permission to go out after dark, and presently Richard Quin and I were scurrying through the night beside Aunt Lily, who walked with excessive speed and frequently burst into excessive laughter, and threaded her way through alleys we had never noticed before, into little black shops where Aunt Lily demanded the ingredients necessary to a real pork-pie with an air of adept cunning and troglodytish shop-keepers sold them to her with an equally zestful air of complicity. She paused to tell us that whereas there were a great many good butchers, ordinary butchers, a good *pork* butcher was as rare as an archbishop. After that she shot with an air of having dodged a barrier into an establishment where she found some good lean fillets of pork and some lard, which, we gathered from her unctuous explanation, was white as the new snow because it came from the farm belonging to the father-in-law of the plump gentleman in a blue overall behind the marble counter. This increased Richard Quin's sense of the magic inherent in a pork-pie, and thereafter a pork-butcher wizard and his father-in-law, a djinn who lived in a haystack and wore a smock, constantly appeared in our games and stories. In a shop crusted like a bottle of port an old grocer with whitening eyes sold us what Aunt Lily certified as by far the best black pepper-corns to be bought in the whole of London. There was a conspiracy of silence over the impossibility of obtaining conger eel. We pretended we had done all in order. Then we came back into the commonplace high street and hurried contemptuously by the people who were going to buy the usual things in the shops everyone knew about, and got back to the kitchen just about the right time to take off the bones that had been simmering on the range for gravy since morning.

At length Aunt Lily came to, as it were, her cadenza. She had to build the pastry she had made with the lard into a tower, we called the others down to look, and Kate stood behind us, her hands on her hips, nodding in professional sympathy. It was really very clever, because not only did Aunt Lily have to build the pastry into a tower, she had to fill it with pieces of meat and hard-boiled egg, and pour in some gravy, and put on a pastry hat just to fit, and as you have to make that sort of pastry by boiling the lard with some water and mixing it into the flour it was quite warm and soft, so that the whole thing might have fallen down if she had not been quick and careful. There was an easy way of making it by moulding the pastry on a jar, but Aunt Lily said that that was a mug's game, and one had one's pride; and she smiled proudly as she watched her hands perform the remembered trick. 'Nancy never saw me do this,' she sighed. 'Queenie would never let the children eat anything vulgar. Harry liked it, when he went out in his boat, but I could never get into the kitchen, with those blessed maids always hanging about.' She gave Kate a quick smile. 'Not like you.'

'I know what you mean,' said Kate. 'That's why I am a general. I know what girls are like when there's more than one kept.'

They nodded in understanding. We all felt safe in the warm cave of our kitchen.

'Haven't any reason, now I come to think of it, to think Ada isn't a good woman,' meditated Aunt Lily, her fingers still busy. 'She's from the North. They say North Country people are very homely.'

So we got through that sad evening; and we ate the pork-pie the following day at luncheon and we thought it wonderful, though Aunt Lily suffered over it as artists do when they have to make compromises for the sake of their friends, for Kate had reminded her that, like most children at that time, we were allowed no condiments, and she had been obliged to leave out the unique peppercorns. But she owned it was as good as could be expected, considering that omission. It was the last satisfaction she was to have for a long time, for a day or two later a policeman came to tell her that her sister had been found and was alive.

Queenie was at liberty so long because a bank of fog had fallen on the South Coast about the time of her disappearance, and hung over it for an unusual number of days. Not till it lifted did a policeman, standing in the early morning at the end of an esplanade of a seaside resort somewhere near Southampton, look down on the line of shacks and bathing-huts which ran along the sandy beach away from the town, and notice that from one chimney there was rising a column of smoke. It was still only February. The policeman went down and looked at the shack, which was one of those places which would now be called a café, which had then, oddly enough, no name, and was vaguely referred to as 'a refreshments' or 'a minerals.' But it was the same thing. In summer you could be served there with tea or gingerbeer and buy oranges and bananas and chocolates; and there was always a mosaic of orangepeel and banana-skins and silver paper from the chocolates trodden into the sand about the threshold. The windows of this shack were boarded up, and when the policeman knocked there was no answer. He went back and sent a message to the station; and when he and the sergeant and another policeman broke in they found Queenie lying in the bar on a mattress set on the bare floor, among piles of chairs stacked on tables. Somebody had brought her bedding, and had every day fetched food and fuel to her. The owner of the place proved that it was not he, and it was never discovered who it was.

After Aunt Lily had heard the news she spoke nothing that was not brave and false and jarring, save once, in the course of a long monologue over her evening sherry, when she said, wandering into honest sadness, 'Bread and corned beef and coal and milk, and the risk of prison. I know who that would be. Mind you, I'd never say. But fancy him caring for her after all these years. Particularly when she treated him the way she did. But there, some people can steal a horse, and others aren't allowed to look over the gate.' She could not be jealous of her sister Queenie, whom she loved so dearly, but for an instant, she who was vowed to mildness could not help wondering why the tigress should be set above the lamb.

There began the worst part of my parents' ordeal. Papa had to take Aunt Lily to Holloway Jail, to the local police court, where a preliminary charge relating to the purchase of poison was brought against her sister, to the inquest, to the local police court again when another and graver charge was preferred, again and again to her solicitors, and in the end to the Old Bailey; and he gave her hours of instruction, the purpose of which was to prepare her for her appearance in the witness-box, and to control the pious enthusiasm with which she was contemplating perjury as the new cross she must bear for Queenie. Meanwhile Mamma had to censor her costume every morning and get her off in time, and then be ready to receive her at the end of the long day, to force her upstairs to take off the cruel clothes of the day, the huge hat, the boned dresses, the corsets, and suggest she tell her story, since she must tell it, in bed, in one of those flannel nightdresses Mamma lent her because Queenie had not let her wear anything but lawn at the Laurels, in case the servants thought her common. Moreover, my parents were perpetually tormented by compunction lest by obeying their moral sense and befriending an unfortunate family, they had exposed their children to experiences unsuitable for their years. Perhaps to be mistaken is a constant human condition; for I cannot imagine parents in that situation who would not feel a like sense of guilt; but I am sure that their self-reproach was quite unjustified. It would perhaps have been different if we had not read Shakespeare from our earliest years, but as it was, though we felt horror and pity, we also felt that this was the last act, and, thank goodness, we were minor characters. Besides, we always thought that everything in the end was going to be all right.

Really, it worked out far better than could have been supposed. One evening I was sent up to Aunt Lily's room after supper with a fresh hot-water bottle, and she detained me by saying, 'Rose, I'd like to tell you something. I feel you'll understand, you're such an old-fashioned kiddy.' This, in her language, meant that I was old beyond my years. 'It's something you might like to remember when you're grown up and got kiddies of your own. Your Papa is doing much more for me than he knows. The coppers wouldn't be half so nice to me if he wasn't there. They're only nice because he's a gentleman. You can't tell me that coppers are like that all the time. Oh, they're nice, on and off. But I once worked in a place that backed on a police station and I lived in, and you could hear everything.

Why, they used their belts in the cells if anybody made trouble, particularly on Saturday nights. Mind you, you couldn't blame them, most of the people they had to do with were under the influence, and there isn't anything more tiresome than people who are under the influence. But, take it from me, I wouldn't be getting yes Madam, this way, Madam, and if you please, Madam, and never a push, and me on the wrong side this time, if it wasn't for your dear Papa. But I don't think he has the slightest idea. I don't think either your Papa or Mamma have the slightest idea about half the things that go on in this wicked world.'

I do not suppose that most parents, even in these days, would actually hope that their little schoolgirl daughters should be told, by one who knows, how policemen belt drunks in their cells on Saturday nights; but I went from the room exalted by a vision. I saw a vast prison such as I had seen in a volume of drawings by Piranesi, and in its innumerable cells innumerable Dogberries were beating innumerable Borachios or, better still, Launcelot Gobbos, an action which I thought quite pardonable; I had often wondered how it came about that Shakespeare had as much gift for drawing comic characters as my sister Cordelia had for playing the violin. Through the black galleries which pierced this penal mass passed my father and mother, crowned with haloes, robed in light, on their way to succour more worthy prisoners than these, whom I had not time to invent, opening dungeon doors with a touch, annulling fetters with a glance, because they were innocent. I was, in fact, inspired to reach the heights of filial piety.

There were a few occasions when Aunt Lily was weak and pitiful; but they were not so trying as those on which she felt herself strong and gloried in her strength. Then her addiction to linguistic fantasy became more than we could bear. Nothing was called by its own name. Money was the ready, to lack it was to be hearts-of-oak, potatoes were murphies, a slice of pork was a cut from the jolly old city of York, when she put anything in her pocket it went into her sky-rocket. Like Japanese poetry her conversation required to be carefully translated into the same language in which it was composed. But it differed from Japanese poetry in being far from brief. Each day she set her listeners a task equal to the translation of a long novel, which they could not refuse, because her darting glances sought for signs of inattention, which she modestly misread as signs of cold disapproval. She was always offering to leave us, and once she did. A letter came for her which was not the one she awaited, but which nevertheless gave her great pleasure, for it was from a friend she had known long ago, asking, just as if they had met last week, if there was anything she could do for her. 'Why, it's years and years and years since we met, we were just girls,' said Aunt Lily, quite absurdly, for she was not old, she was in her early thirties. 'We both worked together in the same place, it was a nice place, I never would have left it, but they weren't fair to Queenie, and she showed spirit, and they turned nasty, and we had to leave. But I've always been sorry, this girl and me were thick as thieves, always giggling together, and everybody made jokes about us, because she was Milly, and I was Lily. Milly and Lily, you see. Oh,' she said ecstatically, 'there's nothing like a friend.' She felt about for a tag about friendship, but was not quite successful. 'They say a man's best friend is his dog,' was all she could do, 'but who wouldn't rather just have a friend?' Now Milly was married to a man who had a nice little pub of his own down on the river and she begged Lily to come and stay with her; and so Lily did, announcing she had gone for four days. There began a delicious period, when we all hardly spoke, and practised for hours, and felt as if we were on holiday.

But Aunt Lily was back in three days, not failing to mention a bad penny, though Milly had been as kind as kind, because her dreadful business was not done, and she could not bear to think that a policeman might come to the door and speak of some new trap that had opened before Queenie, and she would not be there to save her sister, supported by the celestial cunning of both Papa and Mamma, and relying by day on Papa's spectral aristocracy, the ghost of privilege, and by night on Mamma's fierce tenderness. My parents made a little festivity of her return and reassumed their burden. But it would be untruthful to represent this as simply self-sacrifice on their part. I spoke in that sense to Mamma, saying, 'How good you are,' and she answered, impatiently, 'Nonsense, Aunt Lily is such an honest creature that, with all the tiresomeness, it is refreshing to be with her. Oh, it is more than that. I deeply respect her. She is so honest.'

'So honest?' I said. 'But doesn't Papa have to tell her all the time she mustn't commit perjury to save her sister?'

'Yes, indeed,' said Mamma. 'And to everybody she meets she says that she can't believe how the police could be silly enough to think that Queenie would lift a finger against Harry, as there never was a cross word between them during the whole of their married life, and she ought to know, seeing she lived with them from the honeymoon. But I hope you think no worse of her for that. It is very difficult, my dear, you must try to understand. It is always disgraceful for you to tell a lie, but if other people tell lies there is often a very good reason for it, and you must just note that they are lying and pass on.'

'But how can that be?' I asked. 'Why isn't it disgraceful for them to tell lies, if it is disgraceful for me to tell lies?'

'Well, it is disgraceful for them to tell lies, they should tell themselves that and not do it, but all the same if they do tell lies you should not think it disgraceful, for you would probably be wrong.'

'But that is nonsense, Mamma,' I protested, 'either it is disgraceful or it is not!'

'No, no,' said Mamma, 'you are thinking of it as if it were arithmetic. And do not raise your voice. You shriek too often. Of course dear Aunt Lily is not particular about the truth, and we wish she was more so. But whatever she says to strangers she never pretends to Papa and to me that her sister is not guilty. That must be a great sacrifice for her to make.'

'Why does she do that?' I asked. 'Is it because she feels she cannot lie to people who have taken her in to live with them?'

Mamma hesitated. 'No. I think she might not feel that. I only concede that I am not sure she would feel that because she feels something far better. She wants there to be one place in the world where she can admit what Queenie is and yet say she loves her.'

'But what good does that do to you and Papa?' I said. I was not so stupid that I had no glimmering of the answer, but I was very curious about any emotion or opinion that my father and mother held in common.

'Why, it means she loves Queenie quite honestly,' said Mamma. 'There is no element of delusion about it. And that is a good thing to think of. Besides,' she said, 'Aunt Lily is very brave. She never expresses any anxiety about her future, but she has nothing. They gave her no salary at The Laurels, only a little pocket-money, which I suppose was natural enough, since they expected to give her a home for the rest of her life. But now she has only a few pounds in the Savings Bank and that jewellery. It must be terrible, to have nothing, absolutely nothing behind one.'

She spoke with a solemnity which puzzled me. I had rather thought that was our own situation and that we had got used to it.

I must admit that as Queenie's trial drew nearer, we were subject to experiences which bore hard on our youth. We began to be very conscious of Queenie herself. We saw her stolid and still as a chessman taken off the board, a black queen, compressed in a cell too small for the violent feeling which was like a huge cube encasing her. It seemed certain she was to be taken by a smaller space than her cell. We had heard Papa say to Mamma, when he had brought Aunt Lily home from the first hearing of the worse charge at the police court, that there could be no acquittal, because the story George the chauffeur had to tell left not a loop-hole open. The distress this opinion caused us was not on Queenie's account, for she seemed to us simply a chessman, a black queen encased in an evil mist itself encased in a small cell, something strayed out of those disagreeable tales by the brothers Grimm which when we were small we had twice ejected from our nursery, with cries that we were being given corrupt literature unsuitable for children, because Aunt Theodora had twice given them to us as Christmas presents. Our feeling of Queenie's unreality had been increased since we learned, I do not know exactly how, for we were not reading the newspapers, that the cause of the Phillips tragedy was Queenie's desire to run away from her husband with Mr. Mason, a clerk in the firm of house-agents which handled all Cousin Ralph's property in the district, including our house. It seemed to us odd that anybody should be shocked because Queenie had intended to desert her family; we could not imagine anything that would have been nicer for Nancy. But we were astonished by the selection of Mr. Mason, whom we knew quite well, as Mamma often took us with her when, each time glowing with triumph, and long after quarter-day, she went to pay the rent.

He was a tall and slender young man with the fresh complexion of a child and a small moustache, whom we called the Gilly-flower, and we could not understand it at all. Mary reminded us that some medieval queens and ladies who lived in castles seemed to have got very fond of their pages, who always sounded just like girls. But Queenie did not fit into the age of chivalry, and we saw her rather as a witch of the kind that longs for straw-berries in winter-time, or the central feather from the tail of the mother starling in the third nest in the eaves of the porch of the Grand Vizier's palace, and like a witch, we supposed, she would break into flames and disappear. Also in the back of our minds, as if we had read it in a newspaper which had not yet appeared, we knew that the worst was not going to happen to Queenie. It was going, we thought, to be all right. But we could not be sure, and in any case something would happen to Queenie, and Aunt Lily would grieve, and we grieved for her.

Mamma wanted to send us to Kate's mother during the trial, but we would not go. We told her that Richard Quin would be better out of the way, but that we must stay, because we could help her. We thought that when Queenie had been sentenced Aunt Lily would be brought back from the court very ill, and that there would be a lot of running about to the doctor and the chemist, and maybe Mamma would have to sit up with Aunt Lily at night, and would have to be allowed to sleep by day. Also we were too young to have any fear of spectacular events. In the end we bribed Mamma to let us stay by pointing out that these were the Easter holidays, and to go to Kate's mother would be to leave our pianos at a time when we could play all day. This weakness on the part of my mother did us no harm at all. For though we let ourselves in for an unpleasant time, since Aunt Lily did not wait for her sister to be sentenced to pass into hysterical frenzy, we learned that courage has no power to convert its surroundings into a field of fantasy. It had appeared to us that till then, if we said boldly that we would perform a dis-agreeable feat, a listening Providence would reward us by seeing that the feat became agreeable. Now we knew better.

It had been evident, the very first time Papa brought Aunt Lily back from the Old Bailey, that the trial was not taking the course he had expected. He was as silent as if he were reading, or watching something develop which had not yet disclosed its true nature. And before they started out on the third morning he told Mamma that he thought the trial would end the following morning, and added, 'Do you know, I think this business is not going to finish as we thought it would.'

Mamma gaped, 'But she is guilty?'

'Yes, but there is something that can be done. That ought to be done,' he added, his face looking as resolute as a cat's.

That afternoon Mamma was giving me my lesson, when we heard a noise in the hall. I stopped playing and Mamma stood up, singing the phrase which I had failed to finish. We found the front door held open by Kate, and a cab at the gate, and Papa lifting Aunt Lily out of it. He carried her along the path and up the steps, looking himself so thin and fevered that the cabby walked alongside them, ready to catch her in case poor Papa dropped her. Once in the hall, Papa handed her like a bundle of clothes to tall Kate, while he fumbled in his pockets for money to give the cabby. With habitual anguish I thought he might find none, but he had enough. Kate gently lowered Aunt Lily to the ground; we all knew that Aunt Lily could perfectly well have walked, and was obeying some self-made convention which ordained it improper for a woman who had just heard her sister sentenced to death at the Old Bailey to have perfect control over her limbs. But there was such real grief on her face that we let her have her way, and stood back while she wailed, with sugary falsity, 'My darling Queenie! My angel Queenie!' Immediately she passed to more sincere exclamations, and I learned for the first time that it is impossible to predict accurately an event of any magnitude. I had thought she would utter classical lamentations, almost wordless wails of pure grief, over the approaching doom of her sister. But sharper cries, of an argumentative sort, issued from her lips.

'They're going to hang Queenie. And it isn't fair. That horrible old man got them to find her guilty. And I tell you it isn't fair. He went on nohow.'

'Come and sit down, my dear,' said Mamma.

'Lemme tell you,' said Aunt Lily, 'he wasn't a Judge. I don't know how he had the nerve to call himself a Judge. I know what a Judge ought to be, he sits up there big and calm and says what's what to the highest in the land, not altogether of course, but more or less. This dirty old man took sides from the first, oh, I kept my mind open at first, because your dear husband has always been telling me how fair it all would be, but all the time that old man's been falling off the Bench, to shut up witnesses who could say a word for Queenie. He should have been down in the court with that heartless beast what was prosecuting her. And then this summing-up, he went for her like a wild cat. But nothing so decent.'

'Come, dear,' said Mamma.

'No, I will have my say,' said Aunt Lily. 'Nothing so decent. Oh, the old brute. I know his sort. He'll get caught yet. In Hyde Park, I shouldn't wonder.' She was passing the hall-table as she spoke, and she looked down on the letters. 'No letter for me?' she asked. 'Of course there isn't. Why should I ask? There would have been one long ago if there was to be one at all. But you'd think that when a person had pretended to be a friend, just a friend I grant you, but a friend, they'd write now. But not a line, and it all fits in. Pretending to be a friend, and this old man pretending to be a Judge when what he was you saw as soon as he looked at poor Queenie. My feet hurt, they've swelled up like balloons, I wore my oldest shoes, but it hasn't made no difference.'

'Go upstairs to bed, my dear,' said Mamma.

'I don't want to go to bed, not laying down straight and waiting for the dark, oh, poor Queenie,' said Aunt Lily, 'but it's that beast of a Judge, let me go and sit down by the fire and have a cup of tea.'

Shaking her clenched fists, she passed into the sitting-room, and Papa said in an undertone to Mamma, 'What she is saying is quite sensible. So sensible that I think we will be able to get her sister reprieved.'

'Bless you, you are so good,' said Mamma. 'Rose, get your father a nice tea and give it to him in his study,' and went to listen to Aunt Lily.

Papa was passing his hand backwards and forwards over his head, and really looked quite old. I said to him, 'What would you like for tea, Papa?'

'Some anchovy toast,' he said. 'And ask Kate to make the tea strong. Stronger than your Mamma likes it. We have it very strong in Ireland. And did any new books come for me this morning after I left?'

'Three,' I said. 'One is the French one you have been angry about because it did not come. Mamma put them on your desk.'

Down in the kitchen Kate grumbled at what I told her. When there was trouble in the house she always grew fierce against the servants who had looked after Papa and Mamma when they were little. All this week she had been scolding a long-dead Scotch nurse who had spoiled Mamma's appetite by making her eat fat and serving it up to her at meal after meal till she ate it, though it had turned bad. Now she said, 'Your Papa wants his tea black, the way it takes an hour to stew, and what he really wants is somebody who will wet it for him that way that likes to please him but doesn't care about his inside. I suppose there are plenty of that flattering and cruel sort in Ireland. And anchovy paste, it is far too sharp to be good for such a thin gentleman, but he has been allowed it since he was a child, more's the pity.'

I took the tray up to him, and found him reading the French book that had come that morning, bending over the pages like an animal at a pool. He surveyed me with an eye which was not indifferent, for he considered it imperative to impress the truth on me, but which perhaps did not inform him with certainty who I actually was. I might have been the audience whom he had addressed the previous night or was to address the next night, and I also might have been any one of my two sisters instead of myself. But with absolute certainty he said, 'The French make the single tax more logical and more elegant, but it is still the single tax, it will not impose itself, it is not of the order of conceptions which impose themselves. You will see, multiple taxation will be one of the chief instruments by which humanity gladly imposes on itself the slavery of the state.'

He retreated into the savage peace which he found in the contemplation of doom. I left him and went into the sitting-room and found Aunt Lily in the full spate of a description of the Judge, and Mamma said, 'Oh, not before Rose, please.' Then there was a knock at the door, and Kate came in, and was hardly in before she was pushed aside by a man. Mamma asked him what he wanted, but he did not answer, he stood silent with his eyes on the top of Aunt Lily's head, which was all he could see of her, as she sat huddled in her armchair. She did not turn round to see who it was, because she had picked up her empty cup and was scrutinising the tea-leaves at the bottom of the cup. She evidently remembered Mamma's emphatic disapproval of this method of divination and had seized her opportunity while Mamma's attention was distracted.

'What do you want?' Mamma asked the man again.

He was turning a peaked cap round and round in his hands, and he jerked it towards Aunt Lily.

'It is Mr. Phillips' chauffeur,' I told Mamma.

Aunt Lily put down the cup and said, starting to turn her head and then giving up from sheer weariness, 'Oh, it's you, George.'

'I come,' he said, 'to say I hope you don't blame me for telling the truth.'

'No, George, I don't blame you,' she answered, 'you were on your oath, and you weren't a relative, you had to tell the truth.'

She fell to weeping silently, breaking off once to say, 'Mind you, I think there was something unlucky about that house, there wasn't any reason why we shouldn't all have been happy there.'

George stood still, turning his cap round and round, and at length he said, 'I wish to God I had been nicer to the little bastard when he was alive. It was his motor-car. Why didn't I let him do what he wanted with it?' looked round the room, saw the french window, opened it, and walked down the iron steps into the garden. He lay down on the lawn and stretched himself out with his face pressed against the grass. It must have been damp for him, spring had set some green leaves on the soot-black branches of the trees and bushes, but it had not dried the earth. Mamma washed out her cup with hot water, filled it with tea, hesitated, said, 'There is no way of finding out if he takes sugar,' put two lumps on the saucer, said, 'Open the french window, dear,' and went out into the garden and put down the cup and saucer within George's reach on the lawn. Then she came back and persuaded Aunt Lily to go to bed, and told me to go on with my practising. I had played for about half an hour when George knocked on the french window and handed in the empty cup and said thank you and went away by the path round the house.

Mary came in and said it was her turn for practice now, though I think she was at least five minutes too early, if not ten. But she was tired as we all were, and I did not care to take it up with her. I went into Papa's study, though I knew he wanted to go on reading, because I wanted to be more sure that we were right in thinking that Mrs. Phillips would not be hanged. He began at once to tell me, because he never concurred in the insulting pretence that the young must watch things happen without being told the explanation: a pretence which imposes on them a peculiar suffering, as of the carted animal, which few adults could support. But I noticed he was keeping his finger in his book, which did not look comfortable, so I said, 'Where is your bookmark?' He had a favourite one that had come from Mamma's home, of a type that was popular in early Victorian days, a spatula of ivory cut in the shape of the sole of a ballet-shoe, so thin that it could be used both as a paper-knife and a bookmark. 'Somebody has taken it, it has gone, and I must keep my place, the air in the court was so bad that I am stupid,' he said, miserably. We can always find lost things for other people, because we are free of the discontent with life that makes them push out of their own sight the possessions it has left them with. I saw the bookmark hardly hidden by the papers on his desk. So Papa was able to lay down his book and set himself to explaining why it was very unlikely that the sentence on Mrs. Phillips would be carried out.

It was the Judge, he said, and laughed suddenly. I must have noticed, he went on, that Mrs. Phillips differed in many respects from that admirable woman, her sister. It happened that the Judge who tried her had been an unusual sort of person for a Judge. Mr. Justice Ludost was cleverer than most Judges, having a mind that might be called great. His writings on political history and theory were on an eighteenth-century level.

'An eighteenth-century level?' I asked. 'But Mr. Herbert Spencer is alive today, and I thought you considered him as good as anybody.'

'No, no,' said Papa regretfully. 'Poor Mr. Spencer cannot write at all. He has intimated his ideas to us, and we can see that they are of the first order of importance, but he has unfortunately never been able to express them. So they do not live.' He stared before him at the dark disorder of his study, then went on to explain that the Judge's conduct of the trial had been curiously incompetent. It was as if there was more in him than could be contained by the procedure of the court. He was, well, not like other people.

'Like somebody in Shakespeare?' I suggested. It was our way of describing people who, while not musicians, showed in their speech and actions that they had inside them the mass of things that are in music. Papa agreed, and said, in dragging tones, as if speaking of a secret he was reluctant to share, that the Judge was a very evil man. But, he added, speaking now more like an outsider who was trying to be fair, that the Judge did not like being evil, and indeed had probably performed only a few of the evil deeds he had imagined. His intellect was incorruptible; and a baser side of him was against corruption too, for he greatly loved power and wealth and feared lest he should strip himself of all his honour by falling into detectable offences. When he saw Mrs. Phillips in the dock the evil in him recognised her for what she was, the same stuff as himself, while his intellect detested her as a pollution and his worldliness feared her as impoverishment. But she was so strongly what she was that the evil in him grew strong at the sight of her, and his detestation and his fear grew at the same rate of strength, and there was confusion in him, and he raved. 'Like King Lear?' I breathed, full of the shocked sorrow that children feel for grown-ups who throw away their authority.

Papa considered the question seriously. The old man's harrying of the counsel for the defence, the sneer with which he had listened to her statement from the dock, though it had its dignity, the rambling savagery of his summing-up, the gusto with which he had sentenced her to death: all this, Papa thought, amounted to something, yes, if I thought of King Lear, I would realise the prodigious excess of the old man's disorder. He doubted if an English law-court had been the scene of such scandalous abandonment of passion for a hundred years. He set his head back against his tall chair, shut his eyes, and laughed silently. Now, he told me, I could see what humanity was worth. It could form the conception of justice, but could not trust its flesh to provide Judges. Whatever it started was likely to end in old men raving. There was ruin everywhere and we should see more of it. He fell again into silent laughter and shut his eyes. Mary was playing over and over again ten bars out of a Mozart sonata. She was trying to get it clear enough, though

257

really she had got it very clear. Papa opened his eyes and said, 'What is that? It is really very pretty. She is playing the same thing over and over again, is she not?'

I laughed at him. 'Clever Papa! Clever Papa! Is she playing the same thing over and over again?'

'I know what Lear felt, I have an impudent daughter who mocks me,' he answered, smiling, and playing with my long hair. He continued, 'But I have not told you why I have some hope for Miss Moon. God moves in a mysterious way, His wonders to perform. This detestable old man, who has let the immortal part of him be rotted by his mortality, will serve a purpose. His attack on Queenie's witnesses, his attack on her in his summing-up, his last attack on her when he sentenced her, when he had got the jury to give him his verdict and then savaged his kill, yes, indeed, the beast painted himself in bright colours on a banner and carried it about himself, between his brutish paws, for all men to see. There was something heraldic about it. All that, I think, should make it possible to get the woman reprieved.'

'Who will see to that?' I asked.

'Who?' answered Papa. 'Oh, I will do it if I have the strength. But I am very tired. Still, I will probably feel better when I have rested.' His eyes dropped back to the refreshment he so oddly found in the single tax. I left him and called Mary out of the sitting-room to tell her that it was all right, ran upstairs to give the news to Cordelia, and went down to the basement and gave it to Kate. All alike nodded with relief, completely convinced of the power of my beggared father to intervene in the affairs of state.

XII

For the next three days, except for an afternoon when Aunt Lily had to be taken to Holloway Jail to see her sister, Papa followed a routine which we had often seen him adopt before. He rose late; through the day a shadow grew blacker round his jaw for lack of shaving, and he shuffled about the house in carpet slippers, or paced the garden, talking to himself or droning 'The Wearing of the Green'; in the late afternoon he went to his study and worked there through the evening, through the night, into the morning. At such times a stranger would have thought him a seedy eccentric, whose life had been a failure and whose substance was now failing, and might have pitied Mamma, and even his children for having to live with him. But it was then that he was most like Mamma in vigorous purpose; for it always meant that he was writing something less ephemeral than his usual journalism, a pamphlet or an essay to be included in a book. We felt a special reverence for him then, though we were always sensible that he was not lucky. No creation was painless, Mamma had told us. The composers also wrestled with angels by night and by day, but surely they had kindlier adversaries, who, when they succumbed, embraced and were reconciled. Surely they were not left as hollow-eyed, as hollow-cheeked, as dusty with fatigue, and subject to the horrible obligation of beginning the conflict all over again tomorrow. Could Papa not write stories or plays or poems, *something* as unargumentative as music?

The days passed. Mamma tended Aunt Lily, who developed, as suffering people do, a minor ailment, and wheezed with not very grave bronchitis. There was an outcry in the press about her sister; it was not then such a serious matter to criticise a Judge as it is today, and there were protests against the sentence which brought a lot of letters to Papa, asking him to write or speak on her behalf, which Cordelia and I answered, signing them P. Golightly, secretary, saying that Papa was attending to the matter in another way. Some people called, though nobody was admitted save Mr. Langham, who through the years went on fetching and carrying for Papa. Many of them took their exclusion badly, specially a deputation from a society of working-class anti-socialist revolutionaries, side-whiskered men who wore string round the knees of their corduroy trousers and carried on a tall pole announcing that they were the Sons of Freedom, and asked to see Papa, because the older ones among them had fought for the Tichborne Claimant and they were not going to see justice defeated twice. When we told them that Papa was not in they got very angry and said that it was not true. That was of course correct, but we felt no sense of guilt, for they would have said it anyway. They went off with the banner bobbing angrily, and the one with the fiercest whiskers reciting, 'Just for a handful of silver he left us.' We gave out to the messengers of the *Lovegrove Gazette* the leaders he was supposed to have just written, though they had been prepared beforehand in a gamble on what the news would be. We all grew nervous. 'How's your Papa getting on?' Aunt Lily would ask. 'Queenie's only got a fortnight to turn round in.' This was true.

But in the early afternoon of the fourth day Papa came into the sitting-room, looking very thin and tired, and carrying two rolls of manuscript in his hand. Would Cordelia take them to the printer? He already had his orders. He must strike two thousand of the one, two thousand of the other. Cordelia rose to do the errand, very smug, and I was left with my jealousy. Papa had got into the way of giving Cordelia his manuscripts to take to the office or to the printer when Mary and I were still little and she was the only one who was sensible. It was a practice which, as our history books said, had 'crept in.' But then Papa said that he hardly liked to trouble Mamma, but the business did not finish with the pamphlets, there was much to be done, he had to go up to the House of Commons, and see a man who had influence with Brackenbird, the Home Secretary, who was indeed a relative of his. He knew Mamma had to stay with poor Aunt Lily, but he would be glad if either Mary or Rose could come with him, so that if he felt faint someone could fetch a cab. 'Mary has not done her practice,' said Mamma, 'it must be Rose. Rose, go up and put on your coat, your best coat. And, Piers, my dear, you must take a cup of soup before you go. Oh, if we only had a carriage.'

The soup was what he needed. He was much restored, and he slept in the train, his coat-collar turned up round his lean face. He was cheerful enough when we walked across Westminster Bridge and called on me to admire the fretted majesty of the Houses of Parliament, dark against a spring sky of mackerel clouds floating on pale bright space. A fresh wind dappled the river and blew in our faces with a force I would have thought more than his fatigue would have liked. But he strode on happily, his eyes set on the great Gothic mass. 'That is the terrace,' he said, 'you have heard of people having tea on the terrace? Well, there it is.'

Surely this was what he really liked. 'Papa,' I said, 'would you have liked to be a Member of Parliament?'

'More than anything in the world,' he said.

Rage against the world silenced me for a step or two. If Papa wished to be a Member of Parliament, why should people not have let him be one? 'You would be a wonderful Prime Minister,' I said.

'Well, I am so far from being Prime Minister that if I say I would have made a good one it is not immodest,' said Papa, 'for if my claim has anything in it, then I am very guilty in not having come nearer to the post.'

'But could you not still become at least a Member of Parliament?' I asked.

'No,' said Papa. 'Almost anybody can become a Member of Parliament. The rabble is pouring in. But I could not become a Member of Parliament. I have no Party. Only a handful of men in all England believe what I believe. Many people read me, and seem to think well of my writings. But almost nobody credits a word I say. It is a very curious feeling, my dear. I exist and I do not exist. Sometimes I think I know as well as any man that ever lived what it is to be a ghost before death. I hope nothing like this happens to you, my dear. But your Mamma has made a musician of you, and I suppose things go more easily in that world, you either play well or you do not.'

We were off the bridge now, and turning round by Palace Yard. 'That is where we would go in if I were a Member,' he said, and sighed. 'But it is the Strangers' Entrance for us.'

Papa showed the attendant at the door his press ticket and added that he had come to see a Member of the House of Commons, Mr. Oswald Pennington. The name was familiar to me, as many names were familiar to me in my childhood. He had been a great friend of my father's for some months, then we heard no more of him, and if Mamma mentioned him Papa laughed contemptuously. No figure was continuously present in my father's life except, strangely enough, poor Mr. Langham, who would not have been expected to stay the course. We went up the stairs, and then Papa said, 'Stop, you must see this,' and I looked down for the first time on Westminster Hall. We had entered a Victorian building and had come on Shakespeare. The stone chamber was splendid like blank verse, the golden angels who held up the roof matched the poetry of earth with heavenly hymns, great embodiments of the passions had gone out a minute before, trailing their gold and crimson cloaks on the staircase that leads up the wall and into the end of the play. 'We must hurry, we have business to do,' said Papa. 'But you are right, there is nothing more beautiful in all the world, not in Paris, not in Rome. And nearly all that is worth calling political science came to being in that hall.'

We hurried along a corridor where there were many statues representing statesmen and many frescoes representing historical events, all in the spirit of a school play, while my father grumbled comments on the past sounding like curses and based on quite another conception of history than this innocent painting and sculpture. He suggested that in the hall we had seen fools and brutes, forced to this meeting by mutual treacheries; sometimes one snake had its head in the other's mouth, and sometimes change about; under the pressure of reality each time they met they discovered some truth relating to the fundamental problem of politics, which was, he hoped I knew, what the state might ask of the individual, what the individual might ask of the state. The approximation to the truth thus attained was beautiful but how unbeautiful the instrument of its discovery! Give them the chance, he grumbled, their foul hands would destroy the fair things they had made, half by accident. Even then I realised that a corridor decorated by sculptors and mural painters who adhered to my father's conception of history would have been a most uncomfortable place.

We sat in the round central lobby for quite a long time after my father sent his name in to Mr. Pennington. It was like sitting in the midst of a tureen full of gravy soup. I was growing up at the end of an age which, partly by necessity and partly by choice, was very brown. In the towns chimneys poured out smoke from open fires and kitchen ranges, and light itself was permanently stained; and town-dwellers, who then so largely set the way of thinking, romanticised the obscurity to which they were accustomed. Such sights as a narrow shaft of light struggling through a heavily mullioned window to lay a thread of sunlight over a broad dark passage aroused none of the impatience we would feel today but rather a sense that here was something as acceptable as a succession of major chords or a properly scanned line of verse. The House of Commons was a supreme effort of brownness. I can remember looking at one such needle-broad shaft of sunlight that afternoon, struggling through an interior brown in itself, what with brown wood, brown paint, and brown upholstery, and made more brown because the struggling rays of defeated natural light were supplemented by the dark yellow syrup of gas-light. Through the opacity there passed before us and the other suppliants who waited in the seat round the circular hall, a number of men whom I remember as being far more corpulent than the mass of men today; and the older ones wore beards which seemed to be corpulent too. My father noted that a number of the younger men were cleanshaven and said that when he first came to the House of Commons there was not a single man with a bare face on either side of the House. Some of these passers-by nodded to my father, a few stopped to greet him. Most of these, he told me, were Members of Parliament for Ulster constituencies. 'Poor men, they will probably be betrayed,' he said, 'they are loyal to the British Empire, but this is Judas' holiday.' His head began to nod.

A man halted in front of us and looked down on my father and saw that he slept. His lips parted, he raised his eyebrows cynically, he swung his weight to his back foot. I knew he was saying to himself, 'I never wanted to see this man, and since I have this unlooked-for opportunity to get away I might as well take it.' That would have been a cruel thing to do to my father, and to the schoolgirl who sat beside him. Yet Mr. Pennington did not look cruel. Abundant brown hair fell back from his forehead, a deep wave forcing itself forward in spite of brilliantine, and a fine moustache covered his handsomely curved upper lip; he had a clean bright skin; and his clothes were beautiful. He made the

263

pleasant impression of a well-bred well-trained dog in good condition, wearing a handsome collar. A thought simple enough to have passed through a dog's head made him wish to leave us to our troubles. Still, he did not give way to it. Something in my father's sleeping face surprised him and aroused his curiosity, and he continued to look down on him.

I tugged at Papa's coat, and he was on his feet at once, like a swordsman who feared ambush and went to sleep with his rapier in his hand. He greeted Mr. Pennington politely, introduced me and explained that he had brought me to this unsuitable place because he felt too ill to come alone, and then said: 'I have not come to you for the reason you might fear.'

'Oh, that,' said Mr. Pennington. He gave me a sideways glance, and then assumed a very amiable expression. It was evidently his theory that if he said something disagreeable to Papa and looked bluff and hearty when he said it, the meaning of his words would escape me. 'It would be discourteous,' he said in a roistering way, 'to say that it would have been quite useless if you had. Yet I am glad to see you after all this time. Upon my word, it is an extraordinary thing, I am almost as glad as I was during the first weeks of our acquaintance. A lot of people would think that impossible, after all that happened.'

My father seemed to be sadly remembering that in more favourable circumstances he might have let himself answer angrily. Then he looked disconcerted, as if he had been arguing with a friend over an arithmetical problem and had worked it out for himself and found that he was wrong. 'You are of course quite right,' he said. 'But I have nothing. Believe me, I have nothing.' Mr. Pennington nodded humorously, as if that were so well known it hardly needed to be repeated. But light was now shining on my father's face. He was possessed by the cause which had brought him here.

He said: 'I have come to see you about the Phillips case. I have some interest in it. Mrs. Phillips' girl is at school with this daughter of mine. When the woman went away my wife took in the Phillips girl and Mrs. Phillips' sister, an excellent woman. The girl has now gone to a relative but the sister we still have with us.'

'Have you indeed?' said Mr. Pennington, dropping his affectation. 'That's very kind of you. That's very kind of you indeed. I say, what extraordinary things happen to you, old man!'

'One does not read of murderers' relatives sleeping in the street, though murders commonly destroy homes as well as lives,' said my father. 'Somebody takes them in. So many people do what you call extraordinary things that you must be wrong in calling them extraordinary. You should remember that. But the point is this. You have seen that there is an outcry in the press against the way Queenie Phillips was tried, and a demand that she should be reprieved?'

'Yes, indeed,' said Mr. Pennington.

'I thought it would have come under your notice,' said Papa, 'since you are a nephew of Mr. Brackenbird, and he is so conscientious a Home Secretary, and you have been seeing so much of him lately. Of late I have been reading the Court Circular in *The Times* as attentively as if I were a General's widow living in Bath.'

'Well, anyway,' said Mr. Pennington, who seemed displeased with the turn the conversation had taken. 'There can't be much hope of a reprieve. The woman was as guilty as Lucrezia Borgia.'

'Guiltier than that,' said Papa impatiently. I knew he would have liked to stop and explain that to class Lucrezia Borgia as a murderess was a vulgar error, unsupported by serious historians. But he continued: 'I would ask you to consider that there are two separate strands in this agitation for Mrs. Phillips' reprieve. Everything framed by the popular mind is impure. There are a number of imbeciles who believe that Mrs. Phillips did not poison her husband, that the nurse mixed up the medicines, and that the servants entered into a conspiracy to give false evidence against a mistress whom they detested. Of course, that is nonsense. But not entirely nonsense. The popular mind cannot even get its nonsense pure. For the servants did in fact detest Mrs. Phillips, and did in fact give perjured evidence against her till my blood ran cold, wondering what black outcrop of Hell had produced the wretches. But there is another strand to the agitation. A number of people claim that Mrs. Phillips should be reprieved because she did not have a fair trial. That claim is justified. I sat in court with the woman's sister from the moment she was brought into the dock till the moment she went down to the cells under sentence of death. She did not get a fair trial. Mr. Justice Ludost conducted the trial like a lunatic, because he is a lunatic. He interrupted the counsel for the defence times without number. He intervened to bully her witnesses. He interjected remarks designed to create a prejudice against her on issues not before the court. His summing-up presented her to the jury as a person to whom they did not need to do justice; and, even worse, he instructed the jury on matters of fact as well as matters of law. And this he did because he is as much a raving lunatic as any man in Bedlam today.'

'Oh, old Ludost!' sighed Mr. Pennington. 'Such a brilliant man!'

'Why, how did you know that?' asked Papa.

'I've been told,' said Mr. Pennington, with great simplicity. 'And, of course, the news about him not being himself is getting round. We've had that in my own constituency. He's been round the Northern Circuit just lately, you know. My uncle was worried about that when it happened. He's getting old, of course.'

'Age did not account for what happened at the Phillips trial,' said Papa. 'Let me tell you what I heard and saw.'

'Oh, you needn't trouble,' said Mr. Pennington. 'I read it all in the papers.'

'What you read in the papers was not written by me,' said Papa. 'I may have something to tell you which my inferiors could not. Wait here, Rose.'

He and Mr. Pennington walked to the centre of the great round lobby, and they stood for perhaps a quarter of an hour, while my father had his hand on the other's arm, and to my surprise, looked very calm as he told his story. When he talked to himself in the garden, his gestures were often wild and, if he paused to repeat a phrase, laughing with satisfaction, it seemed certain that it had satisfied him by its violence. But now the words were coming from him in a moderate flow, evidently adapted to Mr. Pennington's more placid disposition; for Mr. Pennington, being the taller of the two, had bent his head down to hear better, and turned it sideways, so that I was able to watch his expression. Though he sometimes looked saddened by what my father said, he never looked incredulous, or as people often did when any member of our family told them something, as if

266

we were taking it too hard. Papa had evidently found the right note for his audience. I sat in the middle of the huge tureen of gravy soup, and looked through its brown depths at my father as he saved Mrs. Phillips' life, and thereby spared Aunt Lily and Nancy the shocking grief they feared, and I was lifted up by pride. I looked at the passers-by, who sometimes stared at me, surprised to see a schoolgirl sitting alone in a place where, at that time, there were few women. I gave them pitying glances, because they were not the children of my father.

At last they strolled back to the bench, Mr. Pennington saying gravely, 'So that is how it was.'

'Yes,' said Papa, and suddenly he became more like his violent self, though he talked quietly through his teeth. 'And it is the unanswerable argument for the establishment of a Court of Appeal. I cannot think why your uncle is so obstinately opposed to it. The conception of a judiciary independent of the executive is one of the main foundations of our liberties. But the flesh and blood figure of a judge who has free rein for his will stinks to heaven, because human flesh and blood stink and the human will stinks. We have the faculty of secreting political wisdom and voiding it in the form of systems exquisite in their logic and their pertinence to our needs. But we remain illogical and impertinent, so all our systems are realised in gross imperfection, since we have to operate them. So we build up the common law of England and we place the judge on his bench at the correct point of the constitution, but there comes a day when time and, I suspect, a stroke of misfortune converts a judge into a senile and enraged Pan, his goat-leg visible under his robe, his horns piercing his full-bottomed wig. It is ridiculous to make judges independent of all control. If we exempt a judge from political control we can still set a judge to catch a judge. Not one judge alone to correct another judge. Then you will have stinking flesh and blood and will rolling in the dust with stinking flesh and blood and will. You must have three judges acting together, so that each can think of the system, which he will do chiefly to abash the other, but which will nevertheless compel them to the proper service of the law. But you must know all about the scheme, your uncle has been so busy in blinding his eyes to these undoubted truths.'

'I say, what a chap you are!' protested Mr. Pennington.

'You run on so. Nobody else thinks of this proposed Court of Appeal as you do. Even the strongest supporters of the scheme among the people I know in the House don't think of it as you do. They simply think that a poor chap may come up before a judge that's too old, or before a jury of fatheads, or has a lawyer that's no good, and then in that case it's only fair he should have another chance. And my uncle doesn't agree with them. He says that one way of helping people is to keep them from committing crimes in the first place, and that one way of doing that is to make them respect the law, and that if you admit that judges can do wrong you weaken the respect for a very important part of the law. That's how he sees it, and you've got to be practical, you know. That's your weakness, isn't it, old chap? You can't say you're practical, can you? I mean to say!'

'You will be surprised to see how practical I am,' said my father. 'Now listen. About a year ago you were with your uncle in the Stranger's Dining-Room, giving a party for some Frenchman, when I was dining with Cresson. We greeted one another. Afterwards I saw out of the corner of my eye that he asked you who I was, and you told him. What did you tell him about me?'

'What did I say about you?' stammered Mr. Pennington, with a sideways glance at me.

'What did you say about me?'

'Why, that you are the most brilliant controversial writer of your time, and that you edited a small suburban newspaper, but the national newspapers quoted your leaders, and I reminded him that it was you who had written the Turner pamphlet. Well, of course, he didn't like that.'

'I am sure he didn't. I thought myself that if I got Turner out of Calcutta Jail it would have been enough. All that compensation was not necessary. The man was a scoundrel. I refused to receive him on his return to England. But the public demanded it. And in principle they were right. He had been the victim of completely unconstitutional practices. But go on. What else did you tell him?'

'I said,' sighed Mr. Pennington, 'that you were incorruptible.'

'I think you probably put it some other way. Tell me your exact words.'

'A year ago,' pleaded Mr. Pennington, 'how can I remember? Oh, well, I said you were incorruptible, that if you took

268

a bribe you would be too intellectually honest to give value
for it.'

'Why, that's almost an epigram, Pennington,' said Papa.
'You're coming on nicely. But I could not be better pleased
that you etched my portrait on the tablet of your uncle's mind;
and I am even gratified to imagine that you employed fiercer
acids than you own. But now listen, I have written a pamphlet
on the trial of Queenie Phillips. I have described it exactly
as I have described it to you, but I write a good deal better
than I speak. The pamphlet is as good as anything Swift wrote.
It will not be the talk of London, but it will be the talk of Fleet
Street, which is a better thing. I have not said that Queenie
Phillips is innocent, because she is not. But I have related
how her servants perjured themselves in their evidence against
her so that my young daughter here would have known they lied;
and I have related how the judge nearly fell off the bench in his
slavering desire to whip them on from perjury to perjury. I
have related how, from day to day, the old satyr raved against
what has destroyed him, and that if Queenie Phillips is hanged
she will be the victim of a judicial murder, for what happened
in the Central Criminal Court when she stood in the dock was
not a trial.'

'But, I say, you'll stand trial yourself if you publish that!'
exclaimed Mr. Pennington.

'Yes, indeed,' said my father. 'I will be sent to prison.'

I have never known such ecstasy. My father was all we thought
him. A thousand candles were lit in my head, the blood rushed
hot and icy through my veins, and my eyes were full of tears.
But as my vision cleared, I saw that Mr. Pennington was not
gazing at my father, awed by his courage, as I had thought he
must, but was looking at me; and there was pity in his face.
Smiling, I wondered why. Then it occurred to me that I
had no idea what would happen to Mamma and the rest of us
if Papa went to prison. Certainly Papa would not be able to
go on editing the *Lovegrove Gazette* in a cell; and though Mamma
had often said that she could not understand why Mr. Morpurgo
continued to employ Papa in spite of his frequent derelictions
of duty, and had said he must either admire Papa very much
or care not at all what happened to the *Lovegrove Gazette*, he
would surely rebel at paying a salary to an editor who was so

completely prevented from even appearing to perform his functions. Neither Mary nor I was anything like ready to be concert pianists, and we had learned in the last year or so that our confidence in our powers to support ourselves and our family in comfort by going into factories or shops was unfounded. I looked through Mr. Pennington's kind face into bleakness, and had to force myself to hold my head high, and say, 'Mamma and my sisters and my brother will be very proud if Papa goes to prison.'

Well, that was true. Papa must be doing the right thing, if it averted horror from Aunt Lily and Nancy. And as for the principle involved, of course it was right to go to prison for the sake of a cause. That I felt so strongly that my feeling was localised, I could touch it, somewhere near the breast-bone; and this was one of the rare cases where grownups did not contradict one's instincts but actually confirmed them. Our history books were full of people like John Bunyan, who had, as the historians put it in their particular English, 'languished in dungeons' rather than renounce their beliefs. If Papa went to prison to save Queenie, and it meant that we were suddenly left with nothing to live on, well, this was the application of that principle to us. Any sufferings that came to us would be martyrdom of the same order as my father's, though less as we ourselves were less than him.

Still, it would have helped if Papa had seemed to hear what I had said. But he continued: 'When I go to prison, however, that will not be the end of this affair. For I have written a second pamphlet which will be published as soon as the jail doors close on me. In this I do not attack Mr. Justice Ludost as much as I attack your uncle the Home Secretary. It will be impossible to suppress this pamphlet. It is not contempt of court to attack a politician, and I have been scrupulously careful to avoid making any statement which could possibly be the basis for a prosecution under the libel laws. You may remember how impossible it was to prosecute me for any statement made in the Turner pamphlet. That was so partly because they were all true, partly because I exercised an ingenuity which really gave the pamphlet a parallel existence in the spheres of literature and the game of chess. It will, you realise, be generally known that I have been sent to prison for saying that Mr. Justice Ludost is mad and that his conduct of the trial of Queenie Phillips was shameful. My second pamphlet will reprint reports in Northern newspapers which give accounts of what happened at the trials of certain women criminals which took place before Mr. Justice Ludost on the Northern circuit during the last few weeks. They provide evidence that the man is mad. But I shall not say so. I shall simply say that certain persons present at these trials laid the facts revealed in these cuttings before the Home Secretary. Two of those trials took place in your constituency and several of your constituents wrote to you about them. You and he got those letters, for you acknowledged them.'

'Now how can you know that?' wondered Mr. Pennington.

'After the first morning of the trial I got to work,' said my father. 'I found out what had been his last circuit, and I sent Langham——'

'What, do you still hunt in couples?' asked Mr. Pennington, with intense distaste.

'The world will think he comes off far better in this business than you do,' said my father. 'He believes in liberty, and he takes my word for truth, and he went up North and at my direction found the historic truth in the places where it is warehoused by the bale and nobody ever looks for it, the offices of local newspapers. There were the reports you saw; and the men who had written to you and to your uncle had written to their local newspapers also, and could be traced, and were still angry. I have to own that several of them were your political opponents, and I would not stake my life on the purity of their resentment, but what they did serves my purpose.'

'But these Northern trials were nothing like as bad as what you say happened at the Old Bailey!' protested Mr. Pennington. 'And it's very awkward, my uncle found out there was nothing he could do. There's no way of removing a judge.'

'The Northern trials were nothing like so bad as the trial of Queenie Phillips,' my father agreed, 'and indeed your uncle is quite helpless. There is no way of removing a judge, nor should there ever be, lest barbarism comes back again, and politicians try to deprive the people of their liberties. But let us remind you that every sentence in the second pamphlet will have a force superior to argument. It will be written by a man in prison, and that is always a great thing with the mob.

271

I will write with the authority of a martyr; and I will have behind me the support of quite a number of reasonable citizens who prefer judges to be in their right mind, and of a huge army of idiots who believe Queenie Phillips to be innocent. For no better causes than these, people will believe every word I write and make a saint and hero of me, and will think your uncle a monster, and you another, though on a smaller scale. Say that Mr. Brackenbird will be a minotaur, Queenie Phillips having been by that time converted by popular legend into a virgin sacrifice, and you will be a gryphon. When Mr. Justice Ludost is certified as insane, as he certainly will be in a very short time, the popular image of you two will not be improved, and it will be very black indeed if in the meantime you have hanged Queenie. I have written this pamphlet as well as I have ever written anything in my life and the dirt will stick to you both till the day you die.'

'I could remind you,' said Mr. Pennington, 'that I once did you a kindness.'

'You would not balance a kindness, however considerable both you and I might think it, against a tribunal which would preserve the law from the corruption of the flesh,' my father said. 'Or,' he added as an afterthought, 'against the life of Queenie Phillips. For surely you understand what I'm telling you.'

'No, except that it's disagreeable.'

'I have been trying to convey to you that neither the first nor the second pamphlet will be published if Queenie Phillips is reprieved,' said my father, 'but that they will be issued later in one form or another unless your uncle withdraws his opposition to the establishment of a Court of Appeal. Now my daughter and I must go. The first pamphlet will be issued in three days' time. Ten thousand of each are in the printing.'

'This is blackmail,' said Mr. Pennington.

'I understand that blackmailers hear that superfluous remark constantly,' said my father, 'but I never hear of any but the least intelligent practitioners of the art begging their bread from door to door. I shall expect your uncle to reprieve Queenie Phillips.'

'My uncle is not a man you can threaten.'

'I do not hope that he will give in to my threats,' said my father. 'When he reads my pamphlet he will see that Mr.

Justice Ludost did in fact behave like a lunatic and that Queenie Phillips had nothing that could be called a trial, and he will not wish to defend what is morally indefensible. Then my threats will help the parts of him which are not on the same moral level to come to an agreement. But we must go.'

Mr. Pennington, however, seemed reluctant to part from us. 'I say,' he said. 'You pamphleteers. You really are an extraordinary race. You and Wilkes and Voltaire and Mirabeau——'

'And Milton,' suggested my father. 'As unpleasant a set of men as I can imagine.'

'But you believe all you say, don't you?' persisted the large, puzzled man. 'You mean you'd go to prison for the sake of all this, don't you? Oh, I believe you. When I came up and you were asleep, I looked at your face and really you . . .' He gave up. By a weak gesture he indicated that he had found my father more admirable then than when awake. 'And there's so much you don't seem to think of?' I guessed, from a wavering of his gesture, that he meant me. 'Can't you,' he demanded, 'just be a writer and not keep getting into all these fights? Our lot could find you work to do. You're a magnificent writer. I'll never forget that first article of yours I ever saw. Why, the other evening I read it again, and in spite of all that's happened I think it's wonderful, there's nobody like you . . .'

But my father had turned away, in what looked like an arrogant refusal to discuss that challenge he had laid down. His arrogance might have had another appointment elsewhere. But the truth was that he was too tired to go on talking. As he and I went along the corridor between the statues and the frescoes he complained that the floor rocked under his feet, and that it was not within the strength of any man to write as much as he had written within the last three days. Out in the street his strained eyes blinked at the full afternoon light and he said he felt too sick to start on the journey home. We turned our backs on the towers and spires and might of St. Stephen's, and tried to find some shelter in the mediocre London lying before us not likely to involve us in too great expense. At the corner of Victoria Street there was a teashop in a basement, which looked as if it might be dark; and there we found a table in a shaded alcove. Papa asked for specially strong tea and drank cup after cup, and sat back in his chair, and muttered, and forgot me.

I thought how oddly things worked out for the best. In an attempt at decorative fantasy somebody had twisted strands of purple and green cloth round an electric bulb, and it looked hideous; but it created a half-light in which Papa could rest his eyes and doze. I looked at him to satisfy myself that he was really sleeping and it struck me how fragile was this man who planned to go to prison. No candles were lit in my head this time, but I was again exalted by his bravery. And again I was chilled by his vast indifference to my fate. He had woven a cobweb of thoughts and feelings about his intention to run the risk of imprisonment, and not one of these thoughts and feelings related to me or to any of his family, I had a glorious father, I had no father at all. Moreover, I had understood enough of the conversation in the central lobby to realise that my father had on some occasion treated Mr. Pennington badly, and that his dealings with him during the present crisis were hardly too scrupulous. The force which had taken Aunt Clara's furniture out of our lives had often been at work elsewhere, and was active at the present moment. But it was now working to protect Aunt Lily and Nancy from a cruel grief. Papa was brave, he was cruel, he was dishonest, he was kind, he said he had ordered ten thousand copies of each pamphlet when he had ordered two thousand, he had this terrible cold way of mentioning Queenie as an afterthought. I might have added to the list of his paradoxical qualities that he was penniless and discredited and enormously powerful; for twenty-four hours later Mr. Brackenbird reprieved Queenie Phillips.

So it happened that one morning we all stood outside the gate, waving goodbye to Aunt Lily as she drove away in a dog-cart with Milly's husband, a retired bookmaker, a florid bloodhound of a man, who had already asked us to call him Uncle Len. Though we were sorry to see Aunt Lily go, our hearts were light. There had been lifted from our house a horror: if we had still to think of Queenie as a block of blackness compressed into a cell too small for it, we had not to think of anything worse. There was also lifted from us the heavy burden of good works too long continued: at last the piano was ours alone, we need not fear that Aunt Lily would seat herself at it, and to cheer us up, would play by ear (in her case a most treacherous organ) popular songs of the day with the loud

274

pedal down; we need not, if a stray dog ran into the garden or a thrush hopped on the window-sill, nerve ourselves till we heard, 'My daddy won't buy me a bow-wow,' or 'The little bird said twee-twee.' The relief was enormous, though we dearly loved Aunt Lily and were glad to see her go away in the charge of such a kind man. For he was very kind, though oddly realistic. We had heard him say, as he took sherry and a biscuit with Papa in the sitting-room while Aunt Lily did the last of her packing, that everybody had warned him against marrying Milly, and he had just told them to mind their own business, though he knew what they meant. But they had been wrong. She had gone as straight as a die ever since, he repeated twice. A better wife he couldn't have wished for, and if she said she wanted Lily behind the bar at the Dog and Duck, she had to have her. But he had to admit that Aunt Lily wasn't what he had hoped to see in his licensed premises, particularly after Ruby, who had been a good-looking girl.

'That face,' he said sadly, his jowls hanging the heavier; and he said it again when Mamma came down to see him and told him how impressed we had been by Aunt Lily's loyalty to her sister, and the depth of her unselfish grief. His air suggested that perhaps Mamma was making too much of troubles that would pass, whereas what he deplored was a permanent tragedy. But he meant well by Lily, he hoped to mitigate that tragedy. When she cried at leaving us as she got up into the dog-cart, he smacked her on the behind and told her to turn off the water-works, very tenderly.

When they had clattered out of sight Mamma, her arm in Papa's, sighed, 'Well, that is over,' and we all went back into the house, Kate, who was the last, shutting the door with a ceremonial bang. Cordelia ran upstairs and started her violin practice, the rest of us went into the sitting-room. Richard found his three balls that he used for juggling and went out into the garden. Mary hung about the piano, longing for Mamma to start her lesson. We would have expected Papa to go straight to his study, but he seemed to want to be with us. He went to the table where the sherry and biscuits were, and took a biscuit, and stood nibbling it at the french window. We each took a biscuit too, and went and ate them beside him.

He said to Mamma. 'Look, Clare, all the bushes are in leaf,

275

most of the trees. It is nearly summer. This thing began in mid-winter.'

She sighed, 'Yes, Piers, it has been very long for the poor creatures.'

'It has been very long for you,' he said.

'Long for all of us,' she told him, 'longest for you, with all the other things you have to do. Oh, what you did for them! And I have had no time to ask how you did it.'

'I hardly know myself,' he answered. 'But it is not what one does so much as the way time runs past one. You always take such pleasure in the spring, you have seen nothing of this one.'

'Well, we will make up for that, we must get some days at Kew and Richmond,' she said, 'and it will be lovely for the children if you could take them out on the river.'

'Yes, I must do that,' he said, and after we had nibbled in silence for a minute or two, he said, sadly, 'It is a pity we are so far from the river, none of the children can row properly. My brothers and I all learned on the lake when we were far younger than Richard Quin.'

'Oh, it will come, my dear, you are so good with them,' said Mamma. She nibbled on, staring out through the window and murmured, 'In justice, a most tiresome man. But still a terrible woman.' Something outside caught her attention, she choked on her crumb, she waved her biscuit at the garden to show she had seen something of great moment out there, and would give us news of it as soon as she could. 'The second lilac in that row of four is almost out, see, it has several flowers,' she proclaimed. 'It is always the first of the lilacs to bloom. Now, why should that be?' Her mouth fell open at the mystery. Then she went on, 'I always think that it looks so nice when the lilacs are out and Rosamund and Richard Quin play their games amongst them. Would you mind, my dear, if I had Constance and Rosamund to stay, now the room is free?'

'No, no,' said Papa eagerly.

XIII

THE LILACS were fully out when Constance and Rosamund came to stay with us. Richard Quin and I took the luggage up to their room and then went down and sat on the iron steps that led from the sitting-room into the garden, and waited for Rosamund. We supposed we would first go round the stables, and though we were now all too old to go on pretending with made-up animals, we thought we might recall the days when such play was possible by greeting Cream and Sugar, Caesar and Pompey. But when Rosamund came down there hung over her arm a billow of white taffeta, and she told us that she must finish making a petticoat. I exclaimed in distress, for it was the kind of female garment that my sisters and I bitterly resented and thought an insult to our native force. At that time schoolgirls were dressed sensibly enough and we were happy enough in blouses and skirts joined by petersham belts with silver buckles, but the adult costume of our sex waited for us round the next bend in the path, as a handicap and a humiliation, heavy, crippling, loaded with rows of buttons and hooks and eyes that were always coming off and had to be sewn on again, and boned in all sorts of places where bones break. I thought she had gone into slavery before she need.

'You're not going to wear that?' I asked furiously.

Laughing, she shook her head. It was astonishing how her golden simplicity dispelled Queenie's blackness. Then she stammered out that now she and her mother were sewing for a shop in Bond Street.

'But why? Your Papa has lots of money,' I raged.

'He does not like to spend it,' she smiled.

'But that is horrible,' I said. 'Our Papa cannot give us enough money because he keeps on gambling it away, in the hope of making a lot more. But if he ever won anything he would give it all except what he kept to go on gambling. But do you mean to say your Papa has it and doesn't gamble and doesn't give you any?'

Richard Quin said, 'Never mind. One Papa with another, it works out that we all have nothing, and we can break that into as many pieces as we like, you can do that with nothing, there will be a share for us all.'

'I will make my cakes of nothing, then everybody in the world can have a slice,' said Rosamund, beginning to sew.

'What does nothing taste like?'

She thought. 'Nice nothing or horrid nothing?'

'Both.'

'Nice nothing is like lemon sponge. Horrid nothing is like a very thin dusty biscuit, I can't think of its name.'

'It can't have a name if it is nothing.'

'But then you can't call it a biscuit.'

'I didn't call it a biscuit, you did. It is your bit of nothing. You are giving me nothing and expecting me to find names for it, it is not fair.' He took some strands of her golden hair and pulled it, she threw back her head and laughed at him.

They were not serious-minded. I said, 'But look here, about this money——'

'Oh, of course it is very silly,' said Rosamund, getting on with her sewing, 'but Mamma says we would be worse off if he were a really poor man, or if he were dead. And we are both very fond of sewing, you know.'

They were indeed as tranquil as could be, though their situation was, as I afterwards came to realise, as exasperating as ever wife and daughter suffered. Cousin Jock was so able that his firm not only paid him a considerable salary as chief accountant but had made him a director of one of its subsidiary companies; but he refused to move from Knightlily Road and he could have been said to live like a poor man, had he not spent large sums on spiritualism. He passed half his evenings playing the flute and the other half taking part in seances; and he even imported mediums from the Continent and supported them for weeks while societies investigated their claims. So little did he give to Constance and Rosamund that, even though they were with us only at holidays or at week-ends, they had to bring their sewing with them. But they explained in a good-tempered way that they needed to work continuously because they were so slow, and indeed by their industry they introduced an element of contented leisure into our household, they set an easier pace. They used to settle down on the lawn in two deep wicker chairs we had found in the house when we came, lay clean cloths on their laps, and bring out of bags the lengths of silk and batiste they had to prepare for women who were probably not richer than themselves but were not persecuted by their natural protectors; and very comfortably they would work for some hours. The scallops flowed round the hem of a petticoat under Constance's fingers, slowly, as the shadows of the grove behind them moved across the lawn; and Rosamund built stitches on the bosom of a nightdress till, as gradually as a bud changes to a flower, they made a monogram. In the afternoons we went for a walk, Richard Quin always at Rosamund's side, going the round of the loved exceptional places children always find in their environment, remembering at the right season to peer through the railings at the house which had so long been empty that the rose-trees had all gone back to briars and were now bushes standing higher than the shuttered ground-floor windows, covered with flat coppery flowers. We had some new pleasures too. Richard Quin was very good at arithmetic and mathematics, and he had a liking for numbers as things in themselves. As we went up a long dull street he would pause in delight when we came to a house with a number which was one of those prime numbers which are four times something plus one and can always be expressed as the sum of two squares. About these he felt as somebody fond of roses might feel in a garden full of them when he came on one rose that was larger and brighter and more fragrant than the others; and of course they were the same to us. He wrote out a table of these prime numbers, and we took it about with us. We had a rapturous moment when, in an endless horrid street with many shops, we found Number 281 before he noticed it.

During these walks Rosamund was perfectly happy. She exercised a great influence on my sisters and myself, we looked up to her as our superior, but she was most at home talking with our younger brother, and now he was growing older it was apparent that she was lingering on another plane. He spoke of the facts and ideas he learned at school and from his precocious reading of books and magazines, and she answered him on a nursery rhyme level. Yet even so what she said seemed to him more to the point than what we said. Still, no matter how much she was enjoying her walk with him she always and without complaint turned homeward in time for her to start work again at the proper hour. And by that work she governed me. I was having difficulties with my playing: my mother's teaching had brought me, perhaps prematurely, to a stage of technical advancement when the spirit flags and passes through a desert. The sight of Rosamund and her mother, their laps full of pale fine stuffs, their eyes lowered on their unhurried hands, always made me conscious that I was apt to get into 'states' and sent me back to my piano.

Rosamund's power to make us calm and industrious was not perfect in its exercise. It included Cordelia in its scope; she played the violin no better, and incessantly. But it left Richard Quin untouched. He was doing well, in a way. We had been apprehensive when he had to move to a school for bigger boys, because he was so good-looking and rather like a girl, and he liked doing things his own way. But he was far more of a success at his school than we were at ours. For one thing, he was good at games. He could do anything he liked with a ball. If he threw it or hit it with a bat or kicked it, it did something which nobody expected but himself, and laughing he took advantage of everybody's astonishment. He could run very quickly too. At his lessons he was good, arithmetic and mathematics were like another game to him, but he was naughty about his homework. He neglected it for his music, but that might not be sure, for he was not industrious about that either. He was more interested in playing a number of instruments than in playing any of them really well. Like Cordelia, he had absolute pitch, which neither Mamma nor Mary nor I, had, and he had a far better musical memory than any of us. He had a violin quite early, one of his teachers had given him one that was in the family. People were always giving him presents. The father of one of the boys gave him a flute, and he had always had a recorder. So with the piano that was four instruments to start with; but he would practise none of them properly. What he enjoyed most was playing the flute or the recorder in the stables or to Rosamund in the garden, making up variations on tunes, sometimes absurd ones, so that you had to laugh, and sometimes making up new tunes, which made Mamma very angry.

I remember her throwing up a bedroom window and leaning out to cry, 'What is the use of pouring out that stuff if you will not

sit down and learn about harmony and counterpoint?' Like all
artists, she feared improvisation, though of course you are not
really an artist unless you can improvise. 'It is like — it is
like——'

'Gargling?' suggested Richard Quin, looking up at her very
gravely.

'Yes, that is it, gargling,' she agreed, and banged down the
window when he laughed and waved his flute at her.

But it did not really matter. We knew he would be all right in
the end. Things went very well for us at this time, for so long as
a year, or perhaps even two. Papa enjoyed an unusual period of
success and prosperity, as an unlooked-for consequence of his
intervention in the Phillips case. About a fortnight later Mr.
Pennington drove down in his carriage to see him, and burst into
our house, the deep wave in his handsome brown hair quite
loose and uncontrolled, so excited was he. As soon as I took him
into the study he grasped both Papa's hands and cried, 'Really,
I have to apologise to you! I see now that you came to the
Commons that afternoon to do my uncle and me the greatest of
kindnesses! I quite misunderstood you! You came to give me a
warning and my uncle and I thought you were forcing our hands,
and didn't like you any better for it. But, upon my word, if you
hadn't told us what you did we should have been in a terrible
mess today!'

'Down, Rover, down,' said my father.

Mr. Pennington cast a puzzled glance about the floor.

'I thought my dog was in here,' explained my father. We
had no dog, nor ever had had one. 'What exactly has happened?'

'Ludost went mad this morning.'

'Now what does your uncle say about the establishment of a
Court of Appeal?' enquired my father.

But Mr. Pennington wanted to tell his story and would not be
denied. 'And in such a public place too, God knows what we
would have done if that poor woman had been hanged, this thing
can't be hushed up, but, if you'll excuse me, I don't think what I
have to say will much amuse young Miss Rose here, if it is Miss
Rose, isn't it?'

That was all I was to see of him that afternoon, but he was
to visit us on many other occasions. He insisted on regarding
my father as a benevolent oracle and came to consult him

whenever he was troubled by a political perplexity. My father liked his devotion, for he had now few disciples left, and he also liked the young man's health and handsomeness, and the candour with which he gaped when he heard something he had never known before. But Papa would have been better pleased if he had sometimes consulted him about some matter which he did not think that a Member of Parliament should understand fairly well before he offered himself for election.

Once, when I went to tell him that supper was ready, at the end of such a visit, Papa said to me, 'I understand that you and your sisters think very badly of *Lamb's Tales from Shakespeare*.'

'Of course we do,' I said. 'Who wants to read all that without the poetry?'

'Believe me,' he sighed, '*Lamb's Tales from Edmund Burke* is a far more lamentable production.'

'Did they do that? I never heard of it.'

'Oh, this abridgment of Burke's doctrines is not prepared by the Lambs, but for the use of a lamb.' He suddenly shot up into vigour. 'Come now, I should write that pamphlet he wants from me. There is an immense sheep population in this country. Why should they not know the conditions of the field they graze? It is only kind to tell them.'

He wrote several pamphlets on the elements of political theory and on contemporary problems at the instigation of Mr. Pennington, and they were much admired, and he made some money out of them. It very fortunately happened that at this time Mr. Langham brought Papa a scheme for making money out of hitherto unexploited minerals in Australia, which was so vague that Mr. Langham himself had to go out to Ballarat to find out the mere name and address of the waiting fortune; and this meant that though Papa and Mr. Langham lost their money, they lost it at a much slower rate than usual, and anyway it was nearly all what Papa made out of the pamphlets, and that left his salary untouched. Mamma said sometimes, stretching out her long, narrow, bony hands to touch the nearest wood, that she had never been so well satisfied. Papa was busy and happy, and there was no doubt at all now that we were going to be professional pianists. Mamma became apparently more and more anguished about our playing: Jeremiah spoke no less kindly about the tribes of Israel than she did concerning our powers of technique and interpretation. This distress was quite genuine, she knew we were very far from being fit to play Beethoven to Beethoven and Mozart to Mozart in the courts of heaven, which is the impossible aim that all pianists must hold before themselves, but what she thought of us by the standards of earth we gathered from certain lamentations which my father would quite suddenly utter as he went for walks with us or we sat with him in his study. He would express despair at the problem of how we were to make our return from the evening concerts that we were going to give, as we had no lady's maid to accompany us, and Mamma would not be strong enough to go out so often at night. As he grew older he spoke more and more as from the eighteenth-century enclave that Ireland had been in the nineteenth century, and to him the streets after dark had not yet been cleared of the Mohocks, and were full of open ditches exhaling miasma specially dangerous by night. But for the rest he too seemed content.

It also made for a more placid home that Mary and Richard Quin and I were much easier in our minds about Cordelia That dated from one summer afternoon, when we went with her and Miss Beevor to a Thames Valley suburb. She was going to play at a concert in the Town Hall, we went because we wanted an hour on the river, for though Papa was grieved by our bad rowing we could now handle a boat well enough to go out by ourselves, and somehow or other we had got hold of money enough to give us a dinghy for an hour and a tip for the man. Of course Cordelia's concert lasted much longer than an hour, and after we had returned the boat we went and sat in a square outside the Town Hall, which overlooked the river. It was very pretty. There were benches with old people and mothers with prams, and children bowling their hoops, and a balloon-seller, and sunlight pouring down on these people, and beds of flowers rising between them, dividing them by banks of blue delphiniums, crescents of rosy geraniums, lozenges of lilies. Running alongside the Town Hall, below a terrace, were beds full of pale pink peonies, at the stage when they are loose swirls held in by bands of curiously prim outer petals. We went to look at them, and saw that along the terrace were tubs of fuchsias, which were a flower dear to us for a family reason. Because the flowers look so like little ballet-dancers Mamma never could remember their name,

283

and she always called them 'Taglionis — Vestris — what do I mean?' We thought we would like a closer look at them, and we found a brick stair-case by the side of a toolshed, hidden away behind a hedge, which looked as if it would take us up, but it made a sharp turn and mounted to a locked doorway at some height in the Town Hall tower. Mary and I went down again, but Richard Quin called us back. There was an oeil-de-boeuf window beside the doorway and he was leaning on the ledge. 'I say, come and see Cordelia!' he said.

We looked down into the concert-hall. There was the audience, the backs of their heads towards us, all very still, not a bob or stir out of the flowery hats and brilliantined male scalps; and there on the platform at the end was our sister fiddling away, and keeping them so still. The sight of her was a revelation to us. Till that moment we really had not noticed what she was like, or, rather, what she had come to look like in the last year or so. If one sees people every day one never sees them at all. Now we were viewing her through a lens that made her appear as a stranger. To a degree to be comprehended only by the musical, our eldest sister was to all the rest of the family first and foremost a pervert who insisted on drawing deplorable sounds from the violin. But we were now seeing her in circumstances which presented quite another aspect of her. For the window was closed, it was not made to open. Not the faintest sound penetrated the thick glass and the heavy imperforate metal casing. What we saw had its disadvantageous musical significance. We could see her bowing horribly; but not a rasp reached us. We could see her faulty stance waver and knew her tone must do worse than waver, it must wobble; but we did not hear it. We could see a phrase slide to sheer grease, we could see her resort to a sledgehammer pizzicato; but for us the silence was unbroken. Hence we saw clearly enough that though Cordelia's violin-playing was a blot on the family name, Cordelia playing the violin was an occasion for pride and glory.

She was, of course, deliciously pretty. We had always known that, and I think we knew too, though we could not then have put it into words, that any sensible female would rather be pretty than beautiful. Cordelia had her tight-red-gold curls, her white skin, her large eyes, set just the right distance apart, her neatly incised features, so definitely drawn that as we looked down into the hall we could recognise, even at that distance, the amusing character of her face, its delicate stubbornness, its solemn, innocently contentious simplicity. Also she was exquisite in detail, her wrists and ankles were slender, and her throat was long, but there was a trick in her proportions which suggested that she was really as sturdy as a little pony; and this was a teasing, challenging contradiction. She was now, however, much more than just this pretty girl. When she came to the end of whatever it was that she was playing, she lowered her bow and curtseyed. At the beginning of her career she had affected a foolish surprise because the audience was clapping her, though obviously what would have surprised her would have been if they had booed. But now she was incapable of that or any other vulgarity, her body lacked the necessary resources. To this applauding audience she merely continued to present her loveliness, clouded with a tender smile. They would not forget her. They were flailing their hands together, which might have been made of cotton-wool as far as our ears were concerned, but must have been raising far more noise than one would have expected to hear in a suburban Town Hall at an afternoon concert.

Certainly Cordelia had not given these people music. But she had given them something, something, something which reminded me of the hour we had just spent on the Thames, watching the glassy river run past our plunging oars, the water netted like cracked glass, watching the network spread and break and broaden the green images of the trees on the banks, till we floated on the greenness of green, on the glassiness of glass. She reminded me of the pink peonies in the beds outside, and I was not wide of the mark. Then, and all through the years to come, Cordelia was to be one of those women whose flesh betrays nothing of the human trouble that is within, and who refreshes the eye like water, trees and flowers.

'I tell you what,' exclaimed Mary, 'we needn't worry about Cordelia. She'll get married.'

'Get married!' I repeated. 'Of course, she would, like a shot, if we were an ordinary family. But you know quite well none of us will ever get married. We don't know anybody we could marry.'

This conviction of my parents had increased with the years, and we were well acquainted with it. They had matched the circumstances of their youths with our situation, and felt

285

despair. When Papa was young he had seen that the young women of his family married as soon as young men of equally distinguished families looked round for handsome and agreeable and not destitute wives, and when their fathers could agree about settlements. Mamma, brought up in the less elegant but still lively and prosperous world of Edinburgh professional and musical society, regarded marriage as the result of shaking up a number of young men and women at such festivities as dances, musical evenings, picnics and parties given on such occasions as New Year's Eve, or Hallow-e'en, or Midsummer's Night, at which natural attractions would declare themselves with some slight financial bias. Papa, as I knew, was capable of forgetting the fact of our existence at moments when he should have been most careful to remember it, but from time to time suffered agonies because he realised that we were never going to be presented at court and that the Irish landowners who might have been our husbands could in all probability never hear of our existence; and Mamma often surveyed the social stagnation of Lovegrove and never at any time saw a Professor of Greek improvising iambic pentameters as he ladled out egg-nogg at midnight, or Hans von Bülow dropping in for supper. They had thought we had better realise the worst. We thought it not bad at all. How, Mary had impatiently asked me more than once, did they think that we could run a big house and look after a husband and children and travel all over the world giving concerts? But we took their word for it that the occasion was not going to arise.

'No, Rose,' said Richard Quin, 'Mary is right. Someone will come along and insist on marrying Cordelia.'

'If people fall in love at all,' said Mary, 'and novels and poetry seem to be about almost nothing else, far too much, really, and they can't have suddenly stopped doing it, some stranger will see Cordelia in the street, and arrange to get to know us, and will ask Papa's permission to marry her, and there we are, she will be happy, and there will be no more nonsense about playing the violin.'

We watched her give her encore. At the end she spread out her arms, as she curtseyed, and she made such a charming, symmetrical emblem of prettiness that I could imagine some absent-minded woman of the future calling some flower a Cordelia as my mother called a fuchsia a Taglioni.

'I tell you she's sure, absolutely sure to get married,' said Mary. 'I shouldn't be surprised if it happened quite soon. After all we are nearly old enough.'

'Yes, she is absolutely lovely,' said Richard Quin. At once he added, with his usual anxiety that nobody should be hurt, 'It isn't that you two aren't pretty too. You're just as pretty, really. But somehow it's more noticeable in her.'

'It would be grand, it would stop all this nonsense with Miss Beevor,' I said, 'and she would probably have a lovely big house, and she could give concerts, and we could play for her for nothing.'

At the end of the concert we sought her out in the artists' room, and we were so full of our new admiration and goodwill that we did not really mind finding her impersonating a genius exhausted by having given her all. She was sitting limp before the mirror, breathing languidly while Miss Beevor applied pads soaked in eau-de-Cologne to her temples, and she was playing for an unseen audience as well, by giving tiny indications that Miss Beevor was not being as neat-handed as she might have been, and that she herself was exhibiting the possession of moral as well as artistic gifts of a high order by not expressing impatience. Because she did not want to spoil her concert finery by wearing it on the bus and train she was about to change into a cotton dress, but instead of just changing from one to the other, she had brought a wrapper and was sitting in it, as if to give this least of all artists' rooms the glamour of a dressing-room in a theatre. When we came in she gave us a glazed look, intended to suggest that, lost in art, she had forgotten all earthly ties. This was succeeded by a smile of too celestial sweetness, with overtones of courage and gravity, of refusal to show panic before the appalling responsibilities which pressed so hard on one who might well have been left free like the nightingale or fire-fly. But who knows, did not this quiet acceptance of duty lift her far above those who were merely beautiful, merely brilliant, merely gifted? I have never known anybody whose secret thoughts had such carrying-power as Cordelia's. We did not care a bit. We now knew that if she could not play the violin she had another attribute that was rare and splendid; and we had always known that she was really all right. She did not always join in the same fights that we did, but when she did she was very good indeed. She had been splendidly rude to all the girls at school who were horrid about the Phillipses.

We said we had seen the concert from an unusual viewpoint, and Richard Quin said, 'Yes, through a window, high up. You looked lovely, and the people all thought so, the ladies in their flowery hats all knew they were none of them as lovely as you.' She was pleased; but her desire to provide another appealing scene for her imaginary audience made her assume the expression of one in the last stage of fatigue, who wanted nothing less than a noisy tribute from a boisterous young brother, but who would rather have died than let any trace of her suffering be detected. Our possession of our new discovery about her future kept us benevolent, but we left after a moment or two, pleading that we must get back to do our home-work and our practice, because Miss Beevor asked us with a certain archness whether we had liked the encore, and we guessed there was a salient point on which she expected we would have a comment. It had probably been some adaptation of a classical composition signally unsuited to the violin, the poor creature, as Mamma had once sighed, having a weakness for that kind of thing. We were in no hurry to explain that the window through which we viewed the concert had been closed, so we were soon on our way to a bus-stop.

'Oh, how I wish we were going back to practice and not to home-work,' sighed Mary. 'How I should like to work and work on Schumann's "Carnival".'

'I say, are you ready for that, yet?' I asked. 'I'm not. I have had a go at it, but I'm not there.'

'No, I can't really play it, not as Mamma does,' said Mary. 'But that's an absurd way of putting it, if we studied for a hundred years we should never play like her. But I can't play it even by our standards, but I think I would have got there by now if only I could give all my time to my work.'

'But what fun it will be when you are great concert pianists,' said Richard Quin, 'everybody liking you everywhere.'

'Yes,' I said, 'fancy having a full orchestra to play with.'

'Or the pick of the violinists to play all the sonatas for piano and violin.'

'It will be heaven.'

'That was our bus that went by and stopped lower down,' said Mary. 'How stupid of us, we are like something in that old beast La Fontaine, not getting our bus because we are talking of the time when we will be great. He was horrid, the way he

liked ants better than grasshoppers, and frogs that wanted to be
big, though surely that's harmless enough, and wretched dairy-
maids who break jugs of milk, he was always kicking what's
down.'

'Yes, he was awful,' said Richard Quin. 'We are just learning
Le Corbeau et le Fromage. He's positively pleased because a poor
wretched bird does itself out of a bit of cheese.'

'Ruskin was a beast too,' I said. '*Sesame and Lilies* has made
this term disgusting. It's all about how every woman ought to
behave like a queen. Why should she, when there are such lots
of exciting things to do?'

'Think of spoiling our minds with all this sort of rubbish
when we might be playing the piano,' said Mary.

Indeed, the family was getting on very well. Mary and I
were in the state of monomania proper to our destiny, and our
relations with Cordelia were much improved by our certainty,
which was as absolute as if we had read the news in *The Times*,
that Cordelia would shortly stop playing the violin and get
married, Mamma was quite pleased with us all, though Richard
Quin did not always make her wholly happy. I remember her
once passing her hand over her brow and saying apprehensively,
'He is like quicksilver.' But often he made her supremely
happy, more ecstatically happy than any of the rest of us could
do, particularly when he consented to show what he could do if
he worked at his music. The social restrictions of Lovegrove
never cramped Richard Quin, who would by mysterious means
discover the existence of interesting groups in the dreariest social
landscape, and though they were total strangers would establish
connection with them by means that never struck them as odd.
He unearthed some amateur musicians who practised chamber
music in their homes and though they were adults and he was
still a schoolboy, became their flautist. My mother went to
hear one of their practices and we jeered at her because she came
home and said, quite indignantly, 'I wish Mozart could have
heard Richard Quin play the flute.' It seemed that Mozart had
once complained (as others among the great have done) that
flautists are never in tune; and it seemed to her for one idiotic
maternal moment, as if he had shown gross carelessness in not
being prophetically aware of her son's perfect ear and astonishing, idle, gay technique. But the ground cracked under our

feet again. Papa at last set himself the task of writing a book: not just a pamphlet but a full-length book. At first he was very happy in this enterprise and wondered why he had left it so long. He re-read many old books and read many new ones, and talked them over with himself as he paced the garden; and on his desk a pile of manuscript grew higher through the weeks. But after a certain time it grew no higher, and though reading was a function he could no more abandon than breathing, he read much less than before. Then a change came over him which we recognised with alarm. He became self-confident and worldly in manner, he dressed with a perfunctory effort at care, he took to going out a great deal, and he brought home a number of strangers. It was quite clear to us that our father had once again fallen into despair at the state of the world, and had once again resolved to set aside the useless tool of the intellect and trust himself to blind chance, which he imagined was the presiding genius responsible for the successes of those who had another sort of intelligence than his.

Once again we foresaw distress for our mother, and privation for all of us, no holidays, no new clothes, no concerts, and we had not long to wait for that catastrophe. But it struck us in an even fiercer form than we had yet experienced. For about a week half a dozen angry men kept on driving up in cabs and going away and coming back still angry. Not for one moment do I think my father had done anything criminal or illegal. He had simply done something infuriating. But he had never before infuriated so many people at the same time. One night they all came together, and did not go till all of us children were in bed. At last the front door banged and we heard for hours, from the room below ours, Mamma's astonished voice asking questions, many questions, and when Papa had answered them with his sneering laugh, pressing for another answer. Then Papa's voice swept up and down the scale, an assurance that a fuss was being made about nothing. We knew he was not telling the truth, for when we lied it was in those very cadences. Suddenly it was daylight, and Mamma was standing at the door, telling us that we must hurry or we would be late for school, somehow everybody had overslept.

That crisis passed. Our crises always passed. Mary and I nodded wisely at each other and said, 'You see, in the end it turned out all right.' In those days, when the navy led a more leisured life, a certain number of naval officers read enormously when they were afloat and picked up some very strange notions; and as soon as they retired became evangelists for some religious or political movement of the more eccentric kind. An old Admiral who had formed an admiration for my father's writings on the high seas came to his rescue. We felt gratitude to the Admiral but were sadly aware that the rescue was incomplete. As usual, Papa instantly effaced from his mind the memory of his skirmish with ruin, he was unembarrassed, he felt the contempt for the world natural in one who, so far as he remembered, had never known failure. But the ruin he refused to acknowledge would not consent to leave him and was visible. It was his hands which distressed me. They were beautiful in shape, and had always been alive and busy, even when he was reading, for then they twisted and turned according to the course of his argument with the writer. One had only to look at them to see that he could carve and paint and chisel. But now they were immobile and dirty, not as if he had failed to wash them but as if some internal dinginess were working outward. He had always some dark hairs on the back of his hands, now they were longer and thicker and greyish. Now, too, his wrists were thin, they looked worn like the cuffs of his old suit, and his sleeves hung loose.

But more had altered than his body. Whenever I read the word 'estrangement' I think of my father's relations with us at this time. It is a word misused as a synonym for hostility; its pure meaning describes our situation. My father had no enmity towards any of us, but he had become a stranger. There was no warmth between us. He would still approve of us, tell us that we were walking well and had straight backs, and warn us that whatever looks we had would go for nothing if we stooped or poked our chins, he would bowl to Richard Quin in the garden and would note how his batting was coming on, but it was as if what he had found to praise in us was the only recommendation we had to his favour. We felt obliged to let ourselves suspect that he would have passed us by if we had been plain and clumsy. He still had some interest in Richard Quin and in Rosamund, but we were not jealous. We knew that among a crowd of adolescents who meant nothing to him, he could pick these out most easily, for Richard was his only son and good at games, and Rosamund was tall and fair, as he liked women to be. They were themselves aware that there was no stronger reason for his preference, and were careful not to confuse him by too warm a response.

But sometimes Rosamund was of special use for him. In the evening she and her mother always brought their sewing down to the sitting-room, and settled down on the sofa and worked on the lapfuls of delicate stuff, without making a sound while Mamma gave Mary and me our lessons. Sometimes, as one or other of us played, Mamma would suddenly say, 'Stop, dear.' However intent on the music she had seemed, she knew at once when Papa had come into the room. He would stand in the doorway, his quill pen a long pale feather in his hands and would say in a tired voice that he could not go on with his writing, and would be glad if Rosamund could play a game of chess with him. Constance would answer in her prim voice that it would be a pleasure for Rosamund, who would gather up the pale garments from her lap, roll them in a woollen cloth, lay them on the table, and, rising carefully, so that no pins fell on the carpet, follow him into the study. If I had finished all my lessons, I would go with them, though my father's study, like everything else about him, was no longer as pleasant as it had been. It had always been apparently disordered. When he was writing an article there were papers and open books spread out on his desk and the deep window-ledge and even on the floor. But when the article was finished the papers were gathered up and the books closed and put back in the shelves, and though their place was immediately taken by others, there was real order there, we would have known that anybody who thought Papa's study untidy was uneducated. But now the disorder of the room was real. The books and papers were never cleared up nor replaced by others. They lay one on the other, overlapping under dust, and in the shelves they were treated with a new and shocking disrespect. A Blue Book, something about South Africa, had been thrust into the case back upwards, the pages crushed down in a roll on the shelf. I watched it day by day and noted that though Papa sometimes took books from this same shelf, he never set this maltreated volume to rights.

When Rosamund had seated herself he would sweep clear his

desk, open the chess-board and take the pieces out of the dark lacquer box, faintly patterned with gold figures, which his own father had given him when he was a boy. I do not like the game; all such exercises of ingenuity make me feel as though the mind is being treated like a performing animal and forced to do tricks. But to watch these players was to consider a mystery peculiar to themselves. Usually my father's speech and movements were swift to the point of fierceness. But now he moved more slowly than slow Rosamund. There would be long periods when he sat staring at the chess-board in silence, so long that my thoughts would settle in a standing pool. I would not think or feel, I would be aware of the sound of the wind, of Cordelia playing the violin upstairs, or Mary playing the piano across the hall, and it would seem as if they were all the sounds I should ever hear, and they would become charged with significance. I would expect a revelation, until my father's stained and wasted hand shot forward from his frayed cuff and contentiously moved a piece. Then it would be Rosamund's turn for deliberation, but hers was of a different character from his. My father plainly thought out every move. When my sisters and I were little we had noticed that grown-ups' foreheads were often hot and dry, and were sure it had something to do with the way they worried. It seemed certain that my father's forehead must have been hotter and drier when he played chess.

But when it was time for Rosamund to make a move it was as if the game already existed, and she was waiting for her slow senses to tell her not what the next move should be, but what it unalterably was. She would stretch out her hand to the board, and her loose sleeve would fall back and show her milky wrists and fore-arms; she had very nice arms and a nice neck, she always looked well in her petticoat when she was dressing. She and her mother were like statues; we had often remarked it. Now she was like one of the Greek statues in the British Museum, she was like stone that dreamed. Her hand had a sleeping look as it travelled across the board and moved the piece that was foreordained to move.

Then, if the game were drawing near to the close, Papa would throw himself back in his chair with an exclamation of bewilderment, for she was always right. He never won now. He would try. I could see him consciously reviving his fires, commanding his mind to be acute and powerful, and prophetic about little things, as it had been before; but Rosamund, firm behind the veil of trance, would establish the fact of her game, and it would be other than the game he tried to enforce. Sooner or later he would scatter the pieces and close the board, saying that she had grown far too clever for him. He said it in many ways, all of them kind and well-mannered, but she nearly always answered in the same words: 'No, I am not clever.' Then they would together put the chessmen back in the box, and we would sit together for a little time longer, as if the game were still going on, Papa black and lean, Rosamund giving out light from her fairness.

I could not understand it at all What they had been playing was stranger than a game, for here was Papa thinking out each move, obviously often choosing between two or three alternatives and altering his mind at the last minute, yet here was Rosamund, not using her reason at all, simply knowing what moves succeeded each other in a game that existed somewhere in full completion, even before they had sat down to play it. How could there be one game which Papa made up as he went along, and another which existed before it began, and how could they both be the same game? I would ask myself that question, and various passages of music would come into my mind, until Papa would begin to mutter phrases and feel for his quill pen, though he dropped it as soon as he had found it, and Rosamund's hand would twitch as if she missed her needle. Papa would rise and thank her for having given him such a good game, and force himself to find some action which would assure me that I also meant something to him, running his hand through my hair and telling me that I was like some relative of whom I had never heard. When we returned to the sitting-room Mamma always asked, 'Did you have a nice game with Papa?' It was her habit now to question us whenever we had been with him, as if he lived a long way away from her, and she wished for news of him.

XIV

IN SPITE of everything, all our family, even Cordelia, who
plainly was the most discontented of us, remained conscious
of Papa's enormous worth, of the good fortune we enjoyed
in contrast to the predicament of poor Rosamund, who had to
call Cousin Jock Papa. We realised this very strongly when he
paid us a visit one summer night, just after supper, without
warning. I opened the door to him. In those distant days it
shamed a household not to have a servant on hand to open the
door to visitors, but, as a generation younger than mine was to
rediscover, the host gained an advantage if he did it himself.
After a visitor has rung the bell or dropped the knocker he falls
into a dream about what he is going to do or say when he is
admitted to the house; so if it be the host who opens the door to
him he will have a second before the visitor comes out of his
dream during which he can divine the purpose of the visit.
Through the light summer dusk I saw the curious fair beauty,
the slender Mercury look, of this objectionable elderly man, and
I had an impression that he had come to us because he had been
hurt and wanted help. Nothing seemed more unlikely, he was
of proven malignancy, and I then took it for granted that
malignant people do not need help. Very doubtfully I stared at
him. He had very strongly the air of belonging to the century
we had just left, even to the beginning of it. I had thought years
ago that he resembled an old portrait of a poet, and I could
imagine him an enigmatic and transient companion of the Lake
Poets, a promising young man who stayed a night with Words-
worth and made a nuisance of himself, wandered off uncivilly
the next morning, reappeared as getting on well with de Quincey,
and died in a garret, with lots of laudanum. I thought authors
foolish people who gave themselves airs, for they permitted
themselves to behave as foolishly as the most foolish musicians,
though their product was manifestly so much less important.
But then I noticed that he had his flute-case under his arm and
his gloved fingers were moving as if on the keys. He was a

musician. He was even a very fine musician. Since I had opened the door, I had been not only identifying him as a sensitive poet too sensitive to write any poetry, I had been childishly wondering if it would be any good shutting it again in his face and telling Mamma that it had been a drunk man, for I feared that he had come to take away Constance and Rosamund, who were on what had been promised as a long visit to us. Between my views of him, I did not ask him to come in. But in a second he assumed his chosen clownishness and pushed his way into the hall with the bow-legged stride of the Scottish comedian, the pointless leer.

'Weel,' he said, 'how are you all in this guid Scots home that's established itself among the heathen? One of you scrapin' on the fiddle till all hours, I hear, while the rest of you are going on pom-pom-tweedle-tweedle on the pianno-forty, as I've nae doot ye call it in your refined cirrcles. I just thocht I'd call in and tak awa' ma leddy wife and ma young duchess of a daughter, who have graced ower long your hospitable halls. Hey there!'

He had laid his flute-case on the hall chair, and I had laid his hat and coat on top of it. It was with a snarl that he snatched it up, and I snarled back at him. Then it occurred to me that he thought his flute-case might have been in an unsafe place under a coat which anybody might have picked up, and after all a musical instrument is a musical instrument, no matter whose it is, so I swallowed and said I was sorry, and prepared to take him into the sitting-room, but he pushed past me, with a movement that said he despised me, because I was not grown-up, and a female and a fool at that.

Mamma swung round on the piano-stool and said, 'Why, Jock! You should have told us that you were coming!' Constance said placidly, 'Where in the world have you come from?' Rosamund laid aside her needlework and went to kiss her father's cheek, not hurrying to get it over, but ready to turn away at once just as any of us might have kissed Papa when we did not know whether he wanted to talk or not. I felt angry with them for being nice to him.

'What way would ony mon need to explain the irresistible attractions that draw all and sundry to the fair toon of Lovegrove? Forebye,' he added, as if he were saying something very clever and satirical, 'I am playing first flute in the Croywood Choral

Society's performance of the *Messiah* next month. A repeat performance. We played it at Easter and thousands were turned away. Or so it was believed by the more simple-minded members. So we are giving it again, God help us, and I came down for a wee rehairsal and a crack with the secretary.'

'How does it happen that you belong to the Croywood Choral Society?' asked Mamma. Croywood was a borough some miles south of us, outside London, in Surrey.

'I do not, but there's not a mon living has played first flute in the *Messiah* more often and with a greater number of associations devoted to the art of song than your humble sairvant,' said Cousin Jock. 'And I'm tellin' ye all, there's something gey and wrong with that composition, ower mony gowks sing it, ower mony gowks listen to it. Give a lug to one that kens.'

Mamma asked, 'Have you had supper? Will you not have something to eat?'

Rosamund had pushed forward a chair for him, but he preferred the one from which Mary had risen on his entrance. Though she was standing in front of it, he waved her away loutishly and planted himself down in it. 'A humble glass of beer I wouldna' scorn, if anything so low and vulgar can be found in this genteel home. Ay,' he said, after a pause during which he breathed deeply and noisily, 'and a sawndwich. I think I desairve a sawndwich. For tee-hee, tee-hee,' he giggled, 'I've been at heavier work in Lovegrove than attending a rehairsal. Ay, I wasna idle this afternoon.'

Plainly he wanted Mamma to enquire what it was that he had been doing, but she would not let herself be drawn. He was playing an intolerable game. He was hoping that some of us might be embarrassed by having a relative who spoke with so coarse an accent, but hoping even more strongly that we might be acute enough to see through his affectation and know a fiercer embarrassment at having a relative who had visited us with an uncivil and a candid intention of embarrassing us. He had asked for beer with that same double intention. It was certain we would have none in the house, for it was considered a vulgar drink in those days; I do not think that my father ever tasted it in his life. If Cousin Jock lost on the roundabouts he would get it back on the swings; either we would be ashamed of a beer-drinking relative or of one who pretended to drink beer for malicious purposes. But each time he produced his twin-pointed barb we answered him as if he had put before us a simple and reasonable proposition.

Richard Quin said: 'Mamma, I will get Cousin Jock some beer. The old man at the second of the little houses down the road, he drinks beer, he always has a bottle or two, he likes me very much, he has seen me play cricket, he goes to all the cricket matches round here, he was a groundsman at the Oval for thirty years, he says I could be a great cricketer if I would work at it, he will give me some beer.' He ran out of the room.

'Games, games,' sighed Cousin Jock, 'that'll never boil the pot.' He repeated it with a worse accent. 'That'll niver bile th' pot.'

'What kind of sandwich would you like?' asked Mamma.

'Och, I canna expect a meal, coming at this hour, and me no invited.'

'A ham sandwich is what he prefers,' said Constance placidly. 'I think there was some ham left over at mid-day. Perhaps Rosamund might go down and cut a sandwich, if there is any stale bread. Remember your Papa likes pepper as well as mustard.'

'She'll need the reminder,' said Cousin Jock. 'She will have forgotten a' her puir feyther's foolish and unfashionable ways, being awbsent from his hairth so long.'

My mother said, 'Girls, if you want to go and finish your home-work, you can.'

'Am I to be treated like a leper?' asked Cousin Jock, suddenly in full whine. 'I suppose things have been said about me round here that are past a' believing. Ah, weel, that was a' that could be expected.'

I went down with Rosamund to the kitchen. On the stairs she said, 'I hope we will find some pepper. None of you take it, but perhaps Kate does.'

'Perhaps she does,' I said, 'she likes some horrid things, like pickles and vinegar. But listen, your Papa said when I opened the door to him that he had come to take you and your Mamma away with him. What are you going to do?'

'Well, if he wants us to go home with him, I suppose we will have to go,' said Rosamund. I tried to hold her back so that we would discuss this hateful crisis in the passage, but she hurried on into the kitchen and stammered, 'Kate, my Papa has come, and I have to make him a sandwich. No, I will make it for him, I know how to make it for him. But have you any pepper?' The gaslight streamed down on her and showed her as wonderful as I thought her, golden, elect, superior; but she was taking the threat of her degradation with what seemed to me stupid calm.

Kate put down the *Daily Mail* and told us: 'Of course we have pepper. It is up there in that small blue canister. We have to have it for Irish stew, it wouldn't be right to make Irish stew without pepper.'

'That's why none of us ever like Irish stew,' I said furiously, 'we like the onions and the way the mutton comes off the bone, but we hate the pepper, why can't you leave it out? And, Kate, it is too horrible, Rosamund's father wants her to go home! We must not let her go with him!'

'It would not be Irish stew if you left out the pepper,' said Kate, 'and if Miss Rosamund's Papa wants her to go home, she cannot stay.'

'It can't be right to put pepper in Irish stew if it makes it nasty,' I said, 'and why should Rosamund go home with her horrible Papa?'

'It is right,' said Kate.

'Oh, like the pepper,' I raged.

'Have you black and white pepper?' asked Rosamund.

'Yes, the white is in the little blue canister, as I said, the black is in a plain tin,' said Kate. 'But why do you want both?'

'Papa likes to grumble,' said Rosamund, in full tranquillity. 'I am going to make him two sandwiches, one with the ham thick and the other with the ham thin. He will bite into one, and complain of the way the ham is in that particular one, and then I will tell him to try the other one. And I am going to cut each in half, and in one I will put black pepper, and in the other white; and when he bites into one of those he will say that he likes the other kind of pepper, and again I will tell him to try the other one.'

These words shocked me. I was prepared to think it right that Rosamund should hate her father, but not that she should regard him with what seemed to me a hard and frivolous amusement. I tried to make her speak more honestly and more savagely, and I called, 'But he is a monster! He is a cruel monster! You cannot go back to him!'

'Oh, poor Papa, poor Papa,' said Rosamund, with a lazy smile, as she continued to cut the sandwiches.

'Miss Rose,' said Kate, 'you must not speak so about Miss Rosamund's Papa, or you will become plain Rose, and plain Kate will box your ears. Growing-up is going to do you no good at all with me. You are not built big, and you will never come up to my shoulder. I will not have these tempers in my kitchen, and I will not be taught how to make Irish stew, and I will not have you speaking so rudely about a visitor's Papa. Miss Rosamund, does all this mean that they would be better for a pot of tea upstairs?'

'I think they would,' said Rosamund.

As Kate busied herself with the kettle at the range, I stood in miserable silence beside Rosamund. But as she sprinkled the pepper from a knife on the ham, I noticed how the right side of her forefinger was roughened. by continual sewing, and I burst out in anger: 'How can you bear to go back to him when he is so disgustingly mean about money?'

Through her laughter, she slowly stammered, 'Oh, p-p-poor P-p-papa! Oh, p-p-poor Papa!' My love was laced with hatred. I even wished I could have found it in my heart to mock her by imitating her stammer.

'Now, Miss Rose, take up this tray and remember to honour thy father and mother that thy days shall be long in the land,' said Kate.

'He is not my father,' I sulked.

'Everything in the Bible includes visitors,' said Kate. 'You should know that, the way you have been brought up.'

I carried the tray upstairs, with Rosamund just behind me, stammering conciliatory remarks which I ignored because there was surely still amusement in her voice. In the sitting-room we found Mamma passing her handkerchief over her brows and saying gently: 'No, Jock, I have not heard of this Mrs. O'Shaughnessy, and I will not go near her.'

'Awa' wi' ye, for an unspiritual woman,' said Cousin Jock. 'There she sits, a wee hauf-mile fra' here, bang opposite Lovegrove Station, a bairn could na miss it, and she kindly offers to welcome you or ony ither buddy that has a mind to pairt with five shillings of the King's silver and for that she'll share with you a' the secrets of Etairnity. Think shame on yersel' for no taking advawntage of such a handsome offer.'

'I would have thought,' said my mother, 'that you of all people would have known why you should not encourage this poor woman in this horrible way of making a living.'

'A nice wee flat above a fishermonger's shop is where she bides,' pursued Cousin Jock. 'Verra commodious, though the smell of the fish rises strong as Agag in his armour, towards the end of the day, when all things should rest, but it seems ye canna bring home the necessity to a herring. And up in a nice wee room in this nice wee flat sits Mrs. O'Shaughnessy, a decent widdy woman in her blacks, trussed up like a chicken and bound hand and foot so that there canna be any conjuring tricks, and the curtains are drawn, and the sitting begins. My, but the curtains have surely been dyed. The smell of the dye jines with the smell of the fish, very eloquent to the nose. But yon curtains sairve their purposes. They're drawn close as if there was a corpse in the house, and they turn day into nicht, a black nicht of fish and dye and dust. And doon fall the walls between the quick and the dead.'

'It has been an exceptionally fine afternoon,' said Constance. 'It was a pity to spend it in this way.'

'Woman, you lack a' sense of the mysteries of time and space and our miserable being,' said Cousin Jock, piously rolling his eyes. 'What better way to spend a fine afternoon than to hear the comfortable doctrine of the Lord? For there was Mrs. O'Shaughnessy's Red Indian control roaring down a trumpet to tell us that death has no sting, the grave no victory, endeavouring to convey the same message as Corinthians First Fifteen Fifty-Five, but with a poorer command of language, no sae surprising in the offspring of a taciturn race. Ay, but there was better than doctrine. It did me guid to see how the mourning were comforted, even as it is promised in the best of Buiks. There was a decent body who was assured by her father, passed on thirty years before, that her guid man would recover from his galloping consumption in six 'months' time, ay, and very affecting, there was a puir soul whose face was stroked by the wee hand of the wean she lost last Christmas Day.'

'Yet I have heard you say yourself,' said Constance, 'that such hands may be made of inflated balloon tissue.'

'Why, Jock,' said Mamma coldly, 'you know that some day there will be a horrible scene in that wretched flat, someone will tear down the dyed curtains, the light will stream in, and those poor idiots, God pity them, will see that they have been cheated. Will they blame themselves for their idiocy in thinking that Eternity has taken lodgings over a fishmonger opposite Lovegrove Station? You know they will not. They will turn on this unhappy woman, exposed there with the slipped knots hanging round her wrists and ankles — what indignity! — and they will find yards of balloon tissue——'

'Nae doot inside her corsets, saving your presence,' giggled Cousin Jock, 'or inside the elastic of less mentionable garments. Oh, what a stromash, to shame the sacred ground on the verra frontiers of time and Etairnity!'

'You are not showing the goodwill I would hope you might to a creature much less fortunate than yourself,' Mamma remarked with distaste. 'You know that Mrs. O'Shaughnessy may be a fraud, and then you should have nothing to do with her unless you can help her to be honest. But if she has real powers, she must be a worse fraud still. For if there be such powers, then one of the few things we know about them is that they come and go and are not at the command of those who possess them. This woman must be very poor if she lives in that sordid station square; though that fishmonger is a very decent man. So if she tells a woman that for a fee of five shillings she will show her dead child at three o'clock on Wednesday afternoon, she will be tempted to keep her engagement. It is all on a very low level indeed, and, children, I hope none of you will ever have anything to do with it. It is so low that, see, I have done the woman an injustice. She might as well be moved by pity as by the thought of the five shillings.'

'Rosamund and I have had our poltergeist,' said Constance, 'and we want nothing more to do with the occult world.'

'Your poltergeist, Jock!' said my mother with sudden heat. 'I have read very strange things about poltergeists. I have heard that many are caused by fraud. Malicious people who want to alarm their families decide, it seems, to play a trick on them by contriving it so that it seems as if evil spirits had taken possession of the house. They fix up curtains so that they are bound to fall when nobody is by them. They pay mischievous boys to steal into the house and rattle fire-irons and break furniture. But these malicious people sometimes get more than they bargain for. Curtains they never fixed fall down when nobody is by them; the fire-irons follow when the mischievous boys are in their beds. The malicious people end by fearing they have helpers they never hired.'

There was silence in the room. Cousin Jock said, 'Aweel, aweel!' and then demanded, in an aggrieved tone, 'Ma sawndwich. Wis na there great talk about cuttin' me a sawndwich?'

'It is here, Papa,' said Rooamund.

'The ham's awfu' thick.'

'It is thin in the other one, Papa.'

'Thick or thin, I doot I can monage it with ma dentures,' grieved Cousin Jock, 'it's awfu' thing to have ill-fitting dentures. They roll about like a ship on the sea, and if I was to tell ye what I found under them at nicht——'

He might, we feared, have taken them out to exhibit their defects, had not Richard Quin at that very moment come back with a bottle of beer and a glass. He said, 'The old man had a spare bottle. But he was having supper, and he had a bottle, and he let me taste it, and it was beastly, why do you like it?'

As he filled the glass he looked very handsome, for his skin was flushed with hurry and his features clear-cut with scorn. Cousin Jock looked up at him, and let his own beauty come back to him. He ceased to leer, again he might have been a young poet when a great poetical age was young. He asked, 'You play the flute yourself, don't you, laddy?'

Richard Quin shocked us all by answering, 'Not a note.'

Cousin Jock opened his mouth as if he were going to protest that he had often been told otherwise. But he closed it again. He recognised that Richard Quin was playing his own game, he was being insolent and letting it be seen that he knew he was seen to be insolent. At last Cousin Jock said slowly, and with no comedian accent, 'No? Then I was wrong. But I play the flute. I will play it for you now.'

He rose, paused for an instant. He was taller than we thought, when he stretched up his long delicate hand and turned out the lights in the gas chandelier he looked very tall. While the last whiteness turned to rose in the incandescent mantles, he went out and got his flute from the hall. While he was gone we were all silent. Mamma's eyes went to the windows, which were still uncurtained though the darkness had fallen. There was a square of light on the lawn, which meant Papa was working in his study. Constance filled her chair with her usual monumental calm, but Rosamund went and sat at her feet, bending her head back so that her golden hair flowed on to her mother's lap; I had seen her do this before when she thought her mother sad, it was a remote form of caress. Cousin Jock came back into the room, quiet as a spectre, and took his stand at the fireplace. We could see nothing of him through the gloom but his fair hair and the whiteness of his shirt.

A note from a flute is like the call of a young owl through the summer night. It is extraordinary that the flute should make what seems like a simple natural sound and should be so subtle in its work, lingering on the ear and yet responding to the player's fingers and tongue and breath with a readiness which makes it one of the most agile of instruments. When I had heard Cousin Jock play before, I had thought he played too perfectly; it was as if he had sold his soul to the devil for power of performance and naturally enough performed without a soul. But now his powers dealt humbly and faithfully with the triple mystery of the music he had chosen, which was the famous flute solo from Gluck's opera, "Orpheus and Eurydice," with some variations which I think he had composed himself. That passage is sublime as pure sound; the mere relationship between the notes must cause delight. It is also a clear rendering of the climate of the legend, of the pure light of imagined classic Greece. It also states what is felt by all human beings when they have suffered a deep grief which is still, because they are not barbarians, within control, but is yet irreparable, even if its consequences should be afterwards annulled. Gluck described what filled my mother's heart when her eyes looked through the window into the dark garden and saw the square of light on the lawn. He described what Constance must have felt within her large marmoreal body as she was confronted with the grotesque disturber of her peace. That was another mystery, that the man who disturbed her peace should transmit Gluck's restoration of it.

304

When he came to an end we sat silent in the darkness. So I was not prepared for it when my mother burst out, in the full flood of impatience, 'Jock, nobody could play the flute like that with ill-fitting dentures. I do not believe you have false teeth at all.'

'So far as I know he has not,' said Constance.

'He would not have them, since he is so young for his age,' my mother angrily pursued. 'Jock, why must you play the clown? Mrs. O'Shaughnessy! That way of talking Scotch? When you can play the flute like that! Why must you try to spoil everything?'

He answered with no more accent than herself. 'Life is so terrible. There is nothing to do with it but break it down into nonsense.'

'Terrible?' asked Mamma in surprise.

'What's the good of music,' he asked, 'if there's all this cancer in the world?'

There came a voice out of the darkness, speaking so earnestly that it was shaken with tears: 'What's the harm in cancer, if there's all this music in the world?'

I knew that Mamma and Mary and Richard Quin would be as disconcerted as I was by this brave answer, for it was Cordelia who had given it, Cordelia who would never know what music was. It was as if Cousin Jock had not gone far enough, it was as if life were breaking itself down into nonsense. Mamma said, 'Light the gas, please, Richard Quin,' and we were all suddenly visible, blinking under the brightness, still pleased and startled by the beautiful music we had heard, and confused by the interchange that had followed it. Mamma looked tenderly at Cordelia and said, 'We must leave those poor souls who have cancer, please God we all are spared, to work out that argument.' Then she turned her eyes to Cousin Jock, who had gone back to his chair and was sitting with his face in his hands. 'Why, Jock!' she said. Of course she felt kindly to him now, nobody could dislike a man who played the flute like that, no matter what he was like. 'We all love you when you are reasonable. And from today you can ask my children for anything you want. None of them will forget your playing till the last day of their lives. Drink your beer, eat your sandwich.'

He answered into his hands, 'Oh, thank you, my dear, but

I want nothing. I never want anything now. I cannot bear this ugly world we live in.'

'Do you want us to come back with you?' asked Constance.

'I would be very grateful,' said Cousin Jock, humbly. 'I hoped you would. I have the brougham outside.'

'We have only to pack, dear,' said Constance, 'and we will not take long.'

'God bless you,' said Cousin Jock.

'Is there anything that you would like better than that ham sandwich?' asked Mamma. 'We could heat some soup. I have an idea you have not eaten all day. Oh, why did you not take up the flute professionally?'

'I will do the packing, Mamma,' said Rosamund. 'We did not bring many clothes. We have not many clothes to bring.'

I went up to help her. In the intoxication of listening to the Gluck music I had quite forgotten our disaccord in the kitchen. Now I was merely sorry that she was going away, but I no longer saw her as showing cowardly submission to a tyrannous and repulsive parent. Cousin Jock had established himself in my mind as the possessor of a unique talent, and if he showed strange and inconvenient preferences I was willing to admit that Rosamund might know something else about him which justified her in gratifying them. But this time it was she who seemed reluctant to go. Leisurely as she always was in her movements, she was now almost provoking in her refusal to hurry over her packing; and when we went into the bedroom I shared with my sisters, in order to see if one of her nightdresses had been put among ours, she sat down on my bed, and looked about her, and shuffled her feet on the ground as if she were practising a dance-step, and showed every sign of defiant loitering.

It was unlike her, she was always so dutiful. I was surprised too when she pointed her finger at each of the three copies of family portraits which hung over our beds: at the Gainsborough cat-woman crowned with a sugar-loaf of plumes and gauze; at the Lawrence calm woman, so like Mary, who though her tight Empire bodice was cut so low seemed fully clothed in her reserve; at our mischievous great grand-aunt, with her bright curls, her bright eyes, the bright jewels on her head and on her hands and arms, her bright gold cup. For it was with such sharp irony that my cousin said: 'What sensible Papas those ladies must have had.'

'Why, how can you tell that?' I asked.

'They could not have had all those lovely dresses and those jewels and feathers and cloaks, or looked so smooth and content, if their Papas had not stayed quiet and got on with what they had to do.'

This was a new idea to me, and I was shocked. Temperamentally I was born to acquiesce in patriarchy.

'But they have so much to think about,' I said, vaguely. 'Have they?' she asked. 'They leave themselves little time to think, they make such a fuss about everything. Oh, really,' she said, laughing, 'I get very tired of it all. It is like bulls. Why should a bull roar and stamp the ground and blow out of his nostrils and chase poor people that cross the field where he is, just because he is a bull? It can be no more difficult to be a bull than to be a cow.' She swung up her feet and lay flat on the bed, her gold curls spilling over my pillow, and laughed up at me. 'Silly Papas, silly Papas.'

'But Mamma says that men have quite different sorts of minds, not better but different, and can do work we cannot,' I said.

'Oh, I am not talking of their work,' said Rosamund, 'it is all the states they get into. Your Papa goes on and on about the world falling into ruin. But what would that mean but that a whole lot of people are going to live as he has made you and your Mamma live? And if my Papa is so sad because life is terrible, why does he do so little to make it less terrible for my Mamma and me? If he feels so horrified at the thought of people getting cancer, might it not occur to him that Mamma and I are just as likely to get cancer as anybody else and let us have a little gaiety?'

'Yes, they are awful, when you come to think of it,' I said. 'But they cannot help it. Nobody teaches bulls to bellow and stamp, it is their nature. But we must go. Mamma is calling us.'

She made no move to rise, and went on, 'And think how foolish they will look later on.'

'When? Why?' I asked, rather tartly. I felt this conversation to be impious.

'Well, the world must be getting worse, if they say so,' she explained. 'Both your Papa and my Papa are very clever. So life is not so hard as it is going to be when we are grown up. But our Papas are doing very well in the present. Someone always saves your Papa at the last moment, and my Papa makes lots of money. But as for you and me, and Cordelia and Mary and Richard Quin, all the trouble the Papas foresee will come down on us. It is we who will have to bear the hardships and do heroic things.' She broke into laughter that was malicious, but only gently so. 'Oh, the Papas will seem such fuss-and-botherers then.'

I felt dazed as I followed her downstairs. This was not such a surprising conversation for the period when feminism was spreading like a forest fire, even in households like ours, where the father vehemently disapproved, and the mother was too busy to consider it, and no propagandist literature entered the home. We were, after all, only a year or so below the age when we might have gone to the university, had we had that sort of a mind, and many girl undergraduates at that time might have discussed their fathers as disrespectfully, though not so artlessly. But I was as startled as I had been at Nancy Phillips' party when Rosamund, whom we all supposed tone-deaf, had turned to me and remarked that the piano was slightly out of tune. She never criticised anybody. Her comments were invariably bland. When we had raged against Cordelia's violin-playing she had always pointed out (what we afterwards had seen to be the real issue at stake) that she looked charming when she was playing the violin, that nearly everybody had ugly elbows but hers were beautiful. But now Rosamund had laid an axe at the roots of a tree which I did not care to identify; and I was displeased too because she mocked at what angered her. It was the way in our family to hate without humour, and now it seemed to me that was the only fair way of fighting. You did not hit people below the belt or take from them their seriousness. But I had to admit that this did not apply. She had not spoken as if she hated either my father or her father; she only laughed at them, lying on my bed among her spilled golden hair.

But it could not be said that she was wrong. The next few weeks were to prove abundantly that fathers behaved surely more strangely than was necessary. We were all unhappily aware that Papa's friendships passed through a cycle. A man would give my father over years unstinted admiration and would give or lend him money. (It could be believed only by those who have had a gambler in the family how poor we were in our childhood, and how large the sums acquired in the same period by my father, as earnings and gifts and loans that became gifts.) Then his unpunctuality and irrationality, and his instant and contemptuous rupture of any arrangement made for his benefit which required patience and some reciprocal effort, would become more than any admirer could bear without protest. My father never became aware of these protests; he was aware that people kept on making them, but then organ-grinders kept on grinding out popular tunes on their barrel-organs, and obviously he would not be expected to pay them any attention. But at the same time he would tire of his friend, for reasons that were genuine enough. No ordinary intelligence could long satisfy the demands he made from his intellectual companions. Then the friend, to save his pride, would announce that his patience was exhausted, and there would be a long quarrel late at night, ending with a banged door; and afterwards Mamma would reproach Papa for his unkindness and Papa would answer with his mocking laugh and go out to pace the garden.

Then years would pass, and my father would suffer some conspicuous misfortune. The friend would return, glad to have an excuse for finding his way back to the enjoyment of my father's charm. It salved his pride that he could appear in the guise of a Good Samaritan, and it was usually true that he was the kind of man who found a real pleasure in benevolence. My father's response was always a quite honest welcome. He was not interested in his friend as a Good Samaritan, because, though he had often been rescued, he had never noticed it. But he was eager to know what his friend had been thinking about of late. The man was certain to have a fairly good mind, or he would not have been admitted to my father's intimacy in the first place; and though my father had exhausted its contents at the time of the breach, it must by this time have accumulated fresh material. So there would follow long and enthralling conversations, which would break up only when the friend left our house in the early hours of the morning, full of an elation which would presently engender a desire to relieve my father's anxieties and give him a chance to do his work untroubled. Papa would at once spend the money on some speculation which, he would say, was bound to end all this dependence on his friends, which was always irksome, however good they were. The cycle then started all over again.

But now we were really alarmed. This time Papa was not turning against a friend who had given or lent him money, he was turning against the friend who, through the years, had helped him to lose it; and this, given my father's temperament, was quite unnatural. He had at last tired of Mr. Langham. This man had been a familiar of our household since we arrived in London, and we thought him one of the dullest people we had ever met, dull even for a man, and we thought men much the duller sex. He was tall and thin with a gliding walk, and he reminded us of an eel in his City uniform of morning coat and top hat, and the neatness of his rolled-up umbrella seemed to us very prissy; and when he put on sporting checks, for he was not insensible to the gaieties of life, he still looked dull inside the checks. He had a pale and undistinguished oval face, which was always harrowed by a sense of impending political doom, due to the advance of socialism, and by affectionate and lugubrious concern for my father. Nothing he said ever interested us, which I am now willing to concede was not his fault. He had taken a First in Natural Philosophy at Cambridge, and in between his disastrous attempts at making a fortune in the City he engaged in some mathematical studies of statistics which were of permanent value. But to us he was a dull old family retainer, and we did not like to see Papa turn him away.

But if Mr. Langham came when Papa was in, he was no longer welcomed. Papa was polite to him, even tender, but hardly spoke to him. Mamma would find the two men sitting silent in the study, drawing on their pipes, and would send in Richard Quin, to ask advice about something he was painting, or one of his lessons, so that there could be a basis for some sort of talk. This would smooth over that particular visit, for Richard Quin's tact was perfect, and every stranger presented him with a technical problem which he enjoyed solving. It was more difficult when Papa made appointments with Mr. Langham and forgot all about them. Then Richard Quin would do his best to follow up things that he had noticed interested Mr. Langham, they would talk about mathematics, and Cordelia would talk to him like a grown-up, and Mamma would give him whisky, which, such was her pity for him, she had bought out of her meagre housekeeping money just for the purpose of solacing him on these wounding occasions. At first he used to like sitting quietly and talking to us about Papa and how wonderful he was, and all about the wonderful times they had had together in the past, such as Papa's famous debate with the red-haired young Irish Socialist named George Bernard Shaw, which had begun at seven o'clock one evening in a small hall somewhere near the Gray's Inn Road, and when that closed had been carried on in various public places till the police interfered and they had to move on, and ended on the steps of St. Paul's at two in the morning. But presently Mr. Langham stayed not nearly so long. I think he dreaded the moment when we would hear the key in the front door, and Papa would come in and look at him with a dead eye, instead of plunging at once into a mournful denunciation of Municipal Trading and the growing contempt for State Rights in the United States, ask how he was, with a weary civility which spoke of iciness struggling to thaw itself. So the poor man would come at the exact appointed hour, hoping against hope that the miracle had happened and he was restored to favour, and he would go as soon as it became certain that he had again been scorned.

Mr. Langham tried to do that very thing as promptly as might be, one late afternoon, when he arrived and found that not only was Papa absent at the appointed hour, but that Mamma was out shopping. Kate brought up the whisky and biscuits, and he listened to Mary playing a Chopin Nocturne, and he told Richard Quin how he had seen Lord Hawke bowling at Hove a fortnight before; and then he sadly said he must go. But just then we heard the front door open, and Mr. Langham sank happily back into his chair, saying. 'Not so late after all, not for him, I don't know why I was so impatient.'

I went out into the hall and found it was Mamma, her arms full of parcels. When she saw me, she let them fall on the floor. I heard glass break, but she was so white that I did not trouble to see what it was. She said, 'Rose, Rose, you are sensible, I can tell you. Your Papa walked past me in the High Street and looked me full in the face, and did not speak a word, and went on.'

'Oh, Mamma, he was thinking of something in one of his articles,' I said. 'Think how absent-minded we all are, we always lose our gloves.'

'No, no,' insisted Mamma, gasping for breath, 'he saw me, he saw me.'

'Oh, Mrs. Aubrey, come and sit down,' said Mr. Langham. He had followed me out of the room. Very kindly he guided Mamma to a chair and I poured out a glass of water for her. He sat down beside her, without invitation, not that either of us minded that, so pathetic was his desire to keep a foothold in the house on any pretext, and said, 'If you've had any little difference with him, that's common enough between husband and wife, however fond they may be of each other, and it usually doesn't last long if there's good sense shown by one or other of the parties. If I could be of any help in clearing up any little misunderstanding. . . .'

My mother was astonished at the idea. 'No, there are no differences between my husband and myself.' She thought for some time, and then exclaimed, 'It would be terrible if my husband and I did not get on together,' and took a sip of water.

Staring down at the carpet and tapping it with his foot, Mr. Langham meditated for a while; and then asked, choking, 'Is he mad, do you think? To turn against you, you're the best of wives. To turn against me.'

'What is the good of talking about madness?' asked my mother. 'When people say someone is mad, they mean something strange is going on in him. It is no help if one does not know what it is that is going on. It just puts a name to it.'

Her distress was so great that Mr. Langham felt about for one of the approved phrases used to victims of catastrophe. 'Whether he is or not,' he said, piously, 'it is out of our hands.'

My mother was so uninterested in words that she never recognised a cliché. 'Well, that is exactly what one does not like,' she said, in some perplexity.

But Mr. Langham was enveloped in his own grief. 'There is nobody like him, nobody I ever met.'

Mamma gazed at him in sudden pity. With as much blame in her voice as I ever heard it carry when she was speaking of my father, she said, 'My husband has not been grateful enough to you. But he is not himself.'

'Oh, this is nothing new,' said Mr. Langham, bitterly 'He has treated everybody like this. But somehow I never thought that it would be my turn.'

'He has always had such special difficulties,' said Mamma. 'Oh, if I knew what to do!'

There was more than appeared in Mr. Langham's query about my father's sanity. There was a general feeling just then that his writings showed a sharp decline as a writer. Up to that time he had won respect to a degree that was remarkable for the editor, or rather leader-writer of a suburban newspaper. He now attracted an amount of ridicule almost as extraordinary for such a hidden target. One of the national newspapers christened him the 'Seer of Lovegrove,' and ran funny columns about him, illustrated with cartoons. The tradesmen in shops and the people at school looked at us quizzically, and the worst ones asked us how our father was. How far this public mockery of him had gone and what suspicions it had engendered was brought home to us one day in late summer, after kind Mr. Pennington, the M.P. with the deep wave in his brown hair, wrote Mamma a letter asking her to give him an appointment at some hour when my father was likely to be away from home. He reminded her that he had often proved the warmth of his friendship for my father, and that he would not make this request without good reason. She told him to come on any day at any hour that suited him. Papa was very often out at this period, and when he came in he sat in his study; and if Mamma received a visitor in the sitting-room he would never know. It was characteristic of Mamma that she happily wondered what new and flattering employment Mr. Pennington had found for Papa, and why he wished her to know of it first.

When Mr. Pennington arrived he was disconcerted to find me with Mamma. But she did not consider herself separate from her children, she would have said, 'Yes, I was quite alone,' of an occasion when all four of us were with her. Mr. Pennington looked at me very hard and said, 'Miss Rose will find this a dull affair,' but I looked stolid and would not go, for I was afraid since he stood so near the sources of power that my father might through him become involved again in some deed of heroism which would leave my mother and all of us without resources.

313

But there was nothing of that sort afoot. Mr. Pennington had a roll of typewritten papers in his hand, and he spread these out on his knee, and said, 'Mrs. Aubrey, do you not think that your husband should take a holiday?'

'I am sure he needs it,' said Mamma brightly, hoping that the old days had come back and Papa was going to be asked to some great house.

'Where could you take him?' asked Mr. Pennington.

'Oh, I see. That is difficult. Sometimes I take my girls and my boy to the seaside, but my husband never cares to come with us.'

'Has he not a family in Ireland?'

Mamma hesitated and looked tired. 'Yes. But all the relatives he was fond of are dead. He could not go there.'

'Can you think of somewhere else he could go? For a complete rest? A complete rest. Listen, Mrs. Aubrey. You know I have the friendliest feelings towards your husband. I have never forgotten, I never shall forget the afternoon when Miss Rose here' — he looked at me very kindly — 'and her father came up to the House of Commons and your husband gave me a warning which I nearly did not take, and it would have been the worst thing for my uncle and for me if we had not acted on it. I quite misunderstood him, I really did. Afterwards it was a revelation to me that a thing like that can ever happen to a man, and he could so utterly fail to get the hang of what was happening. It was a lesson to me, it really was. Well, it's because I am so grateful to your husband that I've come to see you today. I suppose you know our little group commissioned him to write a short pamphlet on the future. The Future of Europe and our Foreign Policy.'

We had noticed that some weeks before he had written steadily for some days, but he had not told us of this pamphlet. No doubt he had been paid for it and had already lost the money in advance.

'Well, I can't publish it. I really can't. Every line he has written till now has seemed to me wonderful, I think he'll be among the classics when he is dead. But, Mrs. Aubrey, I can't publish this. He needs a holiday. A long holiday.'

'I see what you are trying to convey,' said Mamma. 'But I find it very odd that anything written on such a cloudy theme as the future, when nobody can say if the author is right or wrong,

314

should provoke such strong feelings in you. What has my husband said that disturbs you so?'

'Mrs. Aubrey, I hope you will forgive me, and Miss Rose here, if I tell you that it's the most terrible stuff.'

'Do tell us what he says.'

'Well, it's hardly stuff to amuse the ladies.'

'Ladies are more accustomed to not being amused than gentlemen seem to realise,' said Mamma. 'Please tell us what is in the pamphlet.'

'Well, it starts all right. It says that it is dangerous to give the State powers beyond those necessary to maintain public services plainly outside the scope of individual effort, such as the army, the navy, the police force, and the postal system. So far so good. My friends and I agreed on that. Socialism's an awful thing,' he said, suddenly raising his head and looking at my mother like a big dog that thinks it has heard burglars. 'And then Mr. Aubrey goes into the theory of it all. I'm not good at that. But my uncle says it's all right. Your husband says it is far more difficult to punish the State than it is to punish individuals, and that there is no reason to suppose the State, if given as free rein as the individual, will be any less likely to deserve punishment. The only way to control the State is to leave so much power in the hands of individuals that the State is at the disadvantage in dealing with individuals unless it acts in conformity with their desires. It is impossible to exaggerate the calamities that would befall if this precaution were abandoned. Well, up to there, it's all right.'

'Yes, I think I could understand it if I wanted to,' said Mamma.

'But then, really, Mrs. Aubrey, your husband goes quite off the rails. He says that if we give too much power to the State we go back to barbarism. At present the State sends out its police force in pursuit of such men as Charles Peace, because the experience of ages has convinced the average man that robbery and murder are wrong. But when the State grows strong enough to snap its fingers at the average man, service in the State would appeal to the more audacious kind of criminal as an organisation which, if he and his kind capture it, will enable him to rob and kill without fear of Wormwood Scrubs and Dartmoor, and we will see police forces which consist of none but Charles Peaces, and do no work but hound down and drag to prison those people who will not abandon their poor

315

opinion of robbery and murder. Mrs. Aubrey, if there's one
thing we know it is that the world is getting better and better.
There's such a thing as the law of progress. Your husband
puts down in black and white the idea that we're not going
forward, we're going backward. He says that civilisation's
going to collapse. It's going to shrink instead of spreading.
He says that country after country is going to be taken over by
common criminals.'

'Well, perhaps that is true,' said Mamma.

'Oh, Mrs. Aubrey, you can't possibly agree with him. He
doesn't mean the United States or South America, or Australia,
which would make some sense, there is a lot of rag, tag and
bobtail there. He says this may happen in Europe. And he
goes on to say the most extraordinary things about the wars
we are going to have after the criminals have taken over. He
says there will have to be wars, because when these criminals
have wiped out all the resistance in their own countries they
will need some other excuse for killing, and they will get it
in war; and they will be pressed by economic need because
once they had stolen all the wealth honest men had stored up
in their countries, there would be nothing more being accumulated,
honest men would be reluctant to go on working just to lay
up loot for a criminal government, and they would be forced
to make war to get at the wealth of other countries. Really,
Mrs. Aubrey, did you ever hear anything so extraordinary in
your life? He talks as if these criminals would take over the
whole machinery of a country, the Parliament, the civil service,
the banks, the factories, everything. It's preposterous.'

'Well, the world is a preposterous place,' said Mamma. 'It
is very brave of us to teach history in schools, it is so discouraging.'

'But what your husband says couldn't possibly happen in
history. It really couldn't. Do you know that he says that the
Austrian Empire is going to crumble to pieces? Something about
the nationalist ideas of the nineteenth century. Well the
Austrian Empire's as sound as a bell. And he says the most
extraordinary things about the wars that are to come. He takes
aeroplanes seriously. He says they may wipe out cities. Oh,
he makes the most dreadful forecasts, they cannot come true,
and God forbid they ever should.'

'I do not know what strikes you as so strange about all this,' said Mamma. 'The fall of Constantinople must have been very disagreeable.'

'Yes, but that was a long time ago,' Mr. Pennington said.

'What difference does that make?' asked Mamma. 'Why should it distress you more that a great many people should die by violence in the future than that a great many people should have died by violence in the past? The suffering must be the same.'

'Oh, it is different,' Mr. Pennington almost moaned. 'Wouldn't you care less if your great-grandmother had been killed in war than if your great-grand-daughter were to be killed?'

'No, I should pray as much for the one as for the other,' said my mother in astonishment.

'Did you say pray for them? Oh, yes, I see. Well, I suppose it's stupid of me,' said Mr. Pennington, 'I'm wrong on this perhaps because it always seems worse for a young person to die than an old one.' We gazed at him in some surprise. He was not really so stupid as to suppose that when one's great-grandmother died she must necessarily be old, and that when one's great grand-child dies she must necessarily be young, but he had been shaken to his foundations by Papa's pamphlet, and he had been further disturbed by my mother's conversation. She had tried to answer him quite simply, on the plane of commonsense, in terms he would find acceptable; but wherever Richard Quin got his power to adapt himself to strangers, it was not from her. She felt about for a soothing remark, and sighed. 'Oh, Mr. Pennington, I am sure that if I knew anything about the Austrian Empire, I would agree with you over that.'

'Well, the Austrian Empire, that's a long story,' said Mr. Pennington thoughtfully. 'And, come to think of it,' he added after a second's reflection, 'I don't know it.' A silence fell, and he turned back to the typescript on his knee, and read bits of it to himself, shaking his head and sometimes groaning. 'It's terrible to see such things in black and white,' he muttered.

'But, Mr. Pennington,' Mamma said, 'you gave me to understand that you feared my husband was going out of his mind because you thought that this pamphlet he has written on the Future of Europe says that a lot of things are going to happen which you think will not happen. But it is quite evident that

317

this is not the situation at all. You must think that my husband's forecasts are probably going to come true, or you would not feel such distress as you read them. Had you not better admit that perhaps my husband is a prophet and a seer?'

'Why, you don't believe in clairvoyance and crystal gazing and all that sort of thing?' demanded Mr. Pennington.

'No, not the vulgar thing,' said Mamma, 'but there is such a thing as a wide, general foreknowledge. I am a musician, you know. We find that in the great composers. Much of Bach and Mozart and Beethoven is much more comprehensible than it was when it was written, or even than it was when I was young. We used to think Beethoven's later quartets quite baffling. That can only mean that he wrote in full knowledge of a musical universe which was still chaos while he lived.' Her voice died away. Her eye went to the clock under the water-colour of a Spanish cathedral which hung over the chimney-piece. 'Rose, go and tell Kate we will not wait till half past four for tea.'

'You may be right, Mrs. Aubrey,' said Mr. Pennington, 'but music is not about real things. There's the difference. You can't just lunge away as you like in a pamphlet called "The Future of Europe and Foreign Policy," you really can't.'

'If you can find Richard Quin,' Mamma begged me.

'And what he says about India!' Mr. Pennington was saying as I left the room. 'What he says about India!'

After he had gone my mother seemed very agitated and played Schumann's 'Carnival' right through, but even at the end still was forced to say: 'How tiresome it is to have at any point in one's life to consider the opinion of such a stupid man as poor Mr. Pennington. I suppose he buys the right of admission by reliability or some such sort of virtue, and we must not despise that. Oh, he is very nice!' she said with an attempt at justice. 'You did not appreciate it, Rose, but his manner to you was meant to be very kind. He tried to tell you that he thought you pretty, and that you need not feel shy about coming out next year, and being presented at court and going to balls. If you were that sort of girl it would have been charming. But how misplaced! And how misplaced his attempts to judge your father. Who has his own sort of reliability,' she added hotly, 'if it comes to that.'

I realised what she meant by that not so long afterwards. One afternoon I came home from school and found some familiar luggage in the hall, and called out, 'Where are you, Rosamund?' She ran downstairs and hung over the banisters, stammering. 'My Papa has started brooding on the sorrows of the world again, and has so greatly added to them, so far as we are concerned, that we have come to take refuge with you for a time.' She was shaken by mild laughter, and I could not make out whether she minded this calamity not at all or very much indeed. But it was so grave a calamity that my mother was at that moment asking my father if Constance and Rosamund could make their home with us, while Rosamund had her last year's education at the school we attended, before she went to nurse in a children's hospital: this meant no expense, for Constance had a small income and she and Rosamund would continue sewing for the shop in Bond Street. But it meant a crowded house, and already Papa seemed to grow tired if all of us were in the room with him at once. Still he said without hesitation that they could come, and that night he had supper with us all, though for some time we had been taking him a tray to his study in the evening, and he looked down the table and said to Mamma, 'I like it better now.'

'What do you like better now, my dear?' asked Mamma.

'Having more people at the table,' he said, 'at home, when I was a child, there were always so many of us.'

It was so pleasantly said, so casually, as if the thought had just passed through his mind, Constance and Rosamund were bound to believe him. He could still be kind. He could still be very kind. He always went with Aunt Lily when she visited Queenie in Aylesbury Prison, though it might have been hoped that he would not have to do so. She was now living very happily as barmaid at the Dog and Duck at Harpleford, an inn standing beside a flint church on a bend of the Thames above Reading; and her friend's husband, Len, the retired bookmaker, was better fitted to escort her to Aylesbury than most men. He was not an unimaginative man, but he economised his forces, and he had refused to become excited about the murder of Mr. Phillips. It was his opinion that there had been a lot of people in the house at the time, and so far as he could see anyone might have done it, and he thought it might have been left at that. He could have taken Aunt Lily to Aylesbury, and brought her back without a tremor of his bloodhound jowls, and he would gladly have done it, not because he sympathised with her passion for her sister, but because he still felt tenderly for her as one of the ugliest women he had ever seen, and thought it was a shame. But Aunt Lily was haunted by a fear that Aylesbury Prison, or indeed any other prison, was a stone version of a fly-catching orchid. She thought that she might enter it as a visitor and that the walls would close round her and she would become a prisoner, and that she dared not run the risk unless she was accompanied by a magician, that is to say, a real gentleman. Such a companion would also bring it home to the prison officials how exceptional it was that Queenie should have got herself into this fix.

So on these occasions Kate would brush my father's clothes and his Homburg hat and polish his shoes with special care, and he would dress as neatly as if he were going up to the House of Commons; and he would start off with Aunt Lily, who did not disgrace him, for she was soberly attired. This did not mean that her parakeet taste had been tamed, but that Mamma's benign cunning had made another such discovery as had served us well during the trial, when she represented that it would be a pity if Aunt Lily's beautiful clothes should arouse envious rage against her, and consequently against poor Queenie, in the breasts of women unable to afford them. Mamma now ascribed a similar envy to wardresses, not blaming them, but pointing out how depressing it must be for any true woman to wear uniform. So Aunt Lily consented to assume for these visits garments which seemed to her the next thing to sackcloth and ashes. 'Don't I look odd in this plain serge?' she used to ask, and Mamma used to answer, 'You must remember those poor women.' But if that worry were lifted from my father's shoulders others remained.

'What was it like, Papa?' I asked, when he brought Aunt Lily home in the twilight, and when Mamma had taken Aunt Lily off his hands. He had strayed into the sitting-room and found me about to take away the tea-tray, and had asked for a cup of tea, saying that it might not be hot but it would be as he liked it, very strong, strong as they had it in Ireland.

'The outward journey is always bad,' he said. 'If there is a really absorbing serial story in *Home Chat* it is all right, she reads it and is quiet. If not, she plays her trick, she invokes cheerfulness by the use of phrases which have old and exhausted associations with levity. As the train goes into a tunnel she will say, "Ah, where was Moses when the light went out?" and she repeats the remark until I take the point. But it is even worse when she thinks she must not ask me to descend to her intellectual level, and she rises to mine, by leaning far forward and asking some such question as "And what has Mr. Labouchere been doing lately?" and, good creature, she waits for an answer.'

He drank some tea, and I brought him a cushion for his back, and would have drawn the curtains, but he said he liked to see the darkness come down.

Later he said, 'But the homeward journey is better. There is a mechanism at work, which it is interesting to watch. We drive back in the cab to Aylesbury town, and I take her into a public-house which is used to such visitors, and gives us a little sitting-room where she can have tea and weep. Then she wipes her eyes and starts to spit out a hundred stupid and baseless suspicions of the prison authorities. I tell her she is talking nonsense, because one should protest against any lie, and they are treating her sister quite well. But she is dealing, you see, with a situation that well might wound her. The wretched Queenie is now feeling more vigorous and she is snarling with the pain such a woman must feel in prison, through the vast constriction of her forces in her small cell. She snarls like a dog at her poor faithful sister. Surely she would have been better hanged. But we saved her. I forget really why we saved her. Oh, yes, the Court of Appeal Bill, we have that now. But your mother says this woman was worth saving for herself, that she will come to something. I wonder why your mother says that? But she is sure to be right.

'We got into the train, and then the mechanism set to work and by the time we were puffing through Amersham Wood Aunt Lily had decided to regard her sister's snarling as a wholly admirable demonstration of integrity and courage. "They can't get her down, Mr. Aubrey," she said, and tapped me on my knee. I am getting very thin. By the time the train reached Chorley Wood, she was sure that the prison staff must share her opinion. "Mark my words," she said, "you'll find they respect her, they won't have many come in and keep their heads high

321

the way she's doing." When we got out at Baker Street she had developed a theory that her sister could not be behaving with such magnificent defiance had she not been innocent. During the journey across London she developed a pendant to that theory which supposes that the prison governor, finding that his own admiration for Queenie is shared by his entire staff, high and low, will send the Home Secretary a recommendation that she should be immediately released, which will reach him at the same moment as some irrefutable proof that somebody else had done away with poor Harry. Now her mind is steaming with plans for expediting and exploiting this happy state of affairs and when I opened the front door with my key she ran past me into the hall, calling for your Mamma, crying, "Oh, she was marvellous, that girl, I tell you, I was proud of her." Listen. You can hear her telling the story to your Mamma on the landing.' And indeed the Cockney voice was going on and on, like a child skipping. 'She is telling it honestly, too,' said my father, 'that gimcrack style is her way of admitting to your Mamma that she herself knows that not a word of what she says is true. Really it is wonderful to see how this simple mind has developed this device for protecting itself from despair. But more complicated minds do not enjoy such protection. Thought that is worth calling thought has no mercy on itself, that is the dreadful proof of its quality.'

He drank his tea and rose, and said humbly, 'Aunt Lily is an admirable woman, a most admirable woman,' and went to his study. Later I looked out of the uncurtained panes to see the lighted square his study window cast upon the lawn. But there was none. He was sitting in the dark.

XV

O NE SATURDAY morning, not long after the beginning of the Autumn term, we three girls were all dressing, and Mary and I were quarrelling with Cordelia, though not really badly, when Mamma came in with a sheet of writing paper in her hand.

She said, 'Your Papa has gone away and is not coming back.'

We stopped dressing and stared at her. We were all in our cambric camisoles and petticoats; Cordelia was brushing her hair in front of the mirror, Mary was brushing hers as she lay on her bed, I was putting on my black thread stockings. Mamma's eyes were staring and her mouth was open, she looked more shocked than she had done the evening Papa had passed her in the High Street without speaking to her. Mary and Cordelia threw down their brushes, we all went to her and kissed her. She quivered like an animal under an unwelcome caress, backed away from us, and repeated, 'Your Papa has gone away.'

None of us could think what to say. This was something new and worse than anything which had happened to us before. We could not advance in intelligence and worldly knowledge without becoming daily more conscious of how much less he was doing for us than other fathers did for their children. But to have lost him was terrible. He had apparently given us more than we knew, for now we felt bitterly cold.

Mamma said, 'I loved him so.'

Cordelia said with sudden hopefulness, 'Do you mean that he has died in the night?' It was not that she lacked love for Papa, she loved him so much that all her life long she looked specially lovely when she spoke of him. But now that she had to lose him she would have preferred that it should be by death, which happened to even the most respectable fathers, rather than by desertion.

'I said he had gone away,' answered Mamma, with a flash of irritation, 'if he had died I would have said so. I went downstairs just now and found this letter on the hall table.

323

He says he cannot stay with us any longer, and we must forgive
him, and he has taken away his clothes, and his bed has not
been slept in. He has gone away.'

I said, 'We must find out where he has gone and get him to
come back.'

'If he does not want to stay with us,' said Mary, 'it will be
no use finding him.'

'What shall I do?' asked Mamma, shivering. 'What shall
I do? Dress yourselves, dress yourselves, or we shall never get
breakfast.'

We made her sit down on a bed, and she sat in a heap, looking
furtively at the letter in her hand, plainly not wanting us to
ask her to let us read it. We were glad to get on with our dressing,
our loss continued to chill us, we felt as if it were the middle of
winter.

'Don't worry about money, Mamma,' said Mary, as she
pulled on her clothes, 'now we can really do what we always
wanted to do as children, leave/school and earn our livings, we
are old enough.'

'Yes, yes,' I said, 'and we will get back to our music somehow
later on.'

'If only this had happened a year or two later,' said Cordelia,
'I would have got somewhere, and we would all be all right.'

At this point Mamma cried out and at the same time raised
her head and looked quite wildly at the three copies of family
portraits which hung above our beds. I wondered if she, like
Rosamund, had been exasperated by the sight of those women
whose protective menfolk had made it possible for them to be
so smooth and beautiful and bejewelled. But it was not likely.
Mamma had never envied women who did not work, while
Rosamund would see nothing wrong in the enjoyment of
leisure. In the midst of my preoccupation I recognised this as
a sharp difference between two people whom I loved.

'Oh, as to money, as to money,' Mamma began, but just then
Constance came into the room. All three of us, we learned
afterwards, felt the same hope: 'Constance will tell us something which will prove that this is not true.' But she said to
Mamma, 'Kate tells me you are upset about something.'

Mamma, sitting amongst the tumbled bedclothes, said,
'He has gone away.' She lifted her head and suffered Constance

to kiss her, but while Constance's lips were still on her cheek, she said, 'Where will he go? He has tired out all his friends.'

I turned on Mary and said angrily, 'It is no use saying we should not go after him because he does not want to stay with us. That is being proud. He will have nowhere to go, nobody to look after him. He will have no money. Why, if he leaves us, he leaves everything. If he goes away from Lovegrove he will not be able to edit the paper any more, and he will not be able to write articles without his books, and I do not suppose he took them with him in the middle of the night. What has he taken from his study? I will run downstairs and look.'

'Even if all his books and papers are still there,' said Mamma, divining my thought, 'it is still no use hoping that he will come back. He has gone.'

It seemed to me that she was helping my father to desert us by accepting the fact that he had done so, and I stamped my foot. But at that moment Rosamund and Richard Quin came into the room, and again we hoped, 'They will tell us something which will prove that what Mamma says is not true.' It was, however, other news which made them both troubled and excited. Richard Quin said, 'Mamma do not be frightened, but there were burglars in the house last night.'

'I do not think so, dear,' said Mamma. 'I suppose you have found a door or window open, but it must have been Papa who left it like that when he went away. For he has gone away. But burglars would not come to this house. There is no silver or jewellery here, nor anything which is known to be valuable, and they would not think it worth their trouble.'

'No, Mamma, there really have been burglars. Come and see.'

'Richard Quin,' said Cordelia, irritably. She had been shaking her head and frowning at him ever since he came into the room. 'This, I suppose, is one of your silly jokes, but this is no time for joking.'

'It is half-past eight in the morning,' said Richard Quin, impatiently. 'I must always remember that at half-past eight in the morning I must not make jokes. Please do not tell me why. I realise perfectly that I will understand when I am older. But, the rest of you, there really have been burglars in the sitting-room. Haven't there, Rosamund?'

She nodded. She was looking from face to face, noting our signs of distress shrewdly as well as sympathetically, wondering, I imagine, whether some real misfortune had broken over us, or if we were wantonly attacking the calm which was her only luxury. Constance asked, 'Is anything missing?' and she answered, 'No, nothing seems to have gone. Or, at least nothing that they knew they had.'

Infantile dreams upheld us. Perhaps if the burglars had taken nothing, they were not burglars but kidnappers, and had made him write that letter to Mamma against his will, and the police and some detective like Sherlock Holmes would find him for us. Cordelia and Mary and I rushed downstairs and stopped at the sitting-room door.

'Look,' said Richard, behind us, 'over the chimney-piece.'

The picture which always hung there, the watercolour of a Spanish cathedral by an early Victorian painter, had been taken down and set up on a chair where it would come to no harm. The person who had put it there had then cut into the square of wall-paper which it had covered. He had known there was a cupboard behind it. Now the door of that cupboard swung out into the room, showing a neat cedar-wood interior, which was empty.

'This reminds me of something,' murmured Cordelia. 'Something that happened when we first came here from Scotland.'

'Yes, I have not thought of it for years,' said Mary.

'I almost thought it was a dream,' I said.

Impatiently Richard Quin asked, 'What are you all talking about?'

We did not answer him, we were in a daze, we were small again, and Papa was with us, instead of just having gone away he had just come back. Richard Quin pulled my hair to attract my attention, saying, 'Oh, you have all taken up being older than me as a profession. Tell me what you are remembering.'

Mary said, 'The first day we came to this house from Edinburgh, Mamma brought us, and we thought Papa was miles away, and when we opened the front door we heard a noise, and Mamma thought it was a burglar, but she ran straight in, and it was Papa scraping away at the wall-paper just where it comes down to the chimney-piece, and he said there was something hidden behind it. But he stopped when we came in, and we were all so glad to see him after the long journey, he picked me up and kissed me.'

'Well, he picked up all of us and kissed us,' I said. 'And he told us that this was the house where he had stayed with his Grand-Aunt Georgiana when he was a boy, and we were all very pleased, and we went out to the stables, and he told us all about Cream and Sugar, Caesar and Pompey, and Sultan. You were there, Richard Quin, it was the first time you heard him tell that story you often used to ask him for, about the time that Sultan bolted with the French tutor.'

'How maddening that I was so small I cannot remember that day,' said Richard Quin. Like all of us, he was gluttonous for every glimpse of him.

'It was quite unexpected Papa being here,' said Cordelia, 'because of course Mamma had the key, so he had had to climb in over the coach-house roof.'

'Over the coach-house roof? But he must have been quite old even then,' said Richard Quin.

'Well, it was years later that he climbed up the elm tree by the big gates to get your kite,' I said.

'He always had wonderful balance,' said Mary.

Richard Quin grew white. 'Why are you talking about him like this? And why are you all nearly crying? What has happened to Papa?'

None of us could bear to tell him.

'Nothing, nothing,' said Cordelia, wringing her hands.

'Oh,' he said, with a burst of angry laughter, 'is it something I am not old enough to learn?'

'None of us is old enough for this,' said Mary.

'Do you mean that he is dead?' he asked.

'No, no,' I said, 'but he has gone away, to live somewhere else, without us.'

'I do not mind anything so long as he is not dead,' said Richard Quin. He turned on Cordelia. 'You fool, not to tell me. For a minute I thought he was dead.' He covered his face with his hand, forced down his still cupped fingers, and smiled down at them. 'Papa is not dead,' he said exultantly. 'But he can't have gone away. Why should he go away? We cannot want him so much without him wanting us. Surely he cannot. How can he bear to leave us, when we loved him so much?' Now he was angry; and he pointed to the open cupboard with an accusing finger. 'Why did he never tell us that that was there? It would have been just the thing for some of those games we used to play, and we could have put presents in there at Christmas. We would have told him, if it had been we who found it.'

Mamma called down to us from the landing. 'Well, what is it?'

'Hush, hush,' we said to Richard Quin and he bit his knuckles.

Her voice came again, cracking with exhaustion. 'Children, has there really been someone in the house?'

Richard Quin went towards the door, calling up to her. 'Well, even my clever sisters admit I was right, and there has been some sort of adventure. Come down and see.' He strolled back to us, whispering lest she should come back and overhear, 'But really it is not so bad, so long as he is not dead.'

But I was troubled. I could remember Papa saying that the wall-paper over the chimney-piece covered a flat paper panel. Why had he said that it was a panel and not a cupboard? And I had heard him say that the panel had been painted, and was rather good. But that could never have been true. The wall-paper was torn away round the smashed lock, and it could be seen that the door of the cupboard was plain cedar-wood, like the lining of the interior. And from the doorway Mamma said, slowly and stupidly, 'Why did he say it was a painted panel and not a cupboard? He told me it would be silly to uncover it, the painting would have been spoiled by the wall-paper, and we would just have the expense of having it done over again. And why did he open it before he went?'

'Before he went,' repeated Richard Quin. 'Mamma, has Papa really gone away?'

'Yes,' she sighed, and went over to the chimney-piece.

'What do you think was inside it?' asked Mary, harshly.

'I don't know, dear,' Mamma answered languidly. Then her voice rose, as if in hope. 'All sorts of things may have been in there.' She put her hand inside the cupboard, and suddenly cried, 'Oh, look. Oh, look. She held up to us some lengths of string, some of them joined by knots caked with red sealing-wax, and her face was flooded with joy. We gathered round her to see if we could detect her reason for relief, and to our blank faces she explained. 'There were some packets in here, valuable packets. It must be so. People do not seal up packets with this sort of string unless there is something valuable inside. Oh, thank God, children, thank God, your father had something to take away with him, he has not gone out into the world penniless.'

We did not respond. She cried again, 'You must be thankful, dears. Your father will have something.'

'Yes, Mamma,' said Mary, 'but Papa might have thought of you and left something behind of what he found.'

'Yes, he might have thought of his children,' said Cordelia. 'I don't mean myself. I shall be all right in a year or two. But there are the others.'

'Oh, hush,' cried Mamma. 'You do not understand.'

'I don't care what was in the cupboard,' said Richard Quin. 'But I do think he might have told us it was there.'

I was remembering how I had felt in the lobby of the House of Commons when I had realised that Papa proposed to go to prison without sparing a thought for his family and how they were to live. I thought it would be heaven if I could shut my eyes and open them again and find myself standing beside him in that brown place, while I said fiercely, 'He should have thought of you, Mamma.'

'No,' she said, 'children, you do not understand. I will tell you afterwards, but I cannot now, this morning has been too much for me. As I was coming downstairs, I looked down on the hall-table, and I saw the letter lying there, and though he has often left notes out for me, asking me to call him or let him sleep, he has never put the sheet of paper in an envelope before, and I knew there must be something wrong. I knew exactly what was wrong. It is what it all meant, what has been happening for a long time, though none of us dared put a name to it. But do not worry about yourselves, children, you need only be sorry for your Papa. You will be all right, at least I think so, I do not know what the amount will be. I thought your Papa had gone out into the world empty-handed, and thank God, thank God, he has not.' But then she halted, her joy fell from her, she lamented, 'But what is the use of that? Whatever the value of what he took with him, he will gamble the money away in no time, he will be penniless, and now he will be all alone.'

'Mamma, it will be all right,' said Richard Quin. 'If Papa has money for just a little time, he will find somebody else like Mr. Langham, and they will go about together, and he will meet people, and you know how much people like him to begin with.'

'Yes,' said Mamma, 'and he likes them too. But they are so hard on him in the end. I cannot think why nobody trusts him.' We were silent, and her words evidently rang in her own ears as disputable. 'People distrust him before he has done anything untrustworthy,' she explained, but still she knew it was not right. 'Oh, if people would only consider the large things in him and not the small!' she raged. 'And you, I hope you will not think me too wicked when I tell you everything. You promise you will remember that I have always struggled to do what I could for you children?'

Puzzled, we assured her that of course we knew it well, and she puzzled us further by saying, 'That is the trouble.' But she went no further, for Constance said from the doorway, 'Had we not better all have breakfast?'

We all ate a lot because we felt as if we had been up for hours, and had done a great deal. Mamma took her cup of tea to the window and said, 'How queer, it is a lovely day. But windy, the leaves are falling fast.' She spun round suddenly and asked, 'Children, is it not about this time that the lapageria comes out at Kew?' We told her that it was, and she said, 'Rosamund, have you ever seen the lapageria in the Temperate House?' and when Rosamund said that she did not think she had, we all told her that she would have remembered it if she had, for it was one of the loveliest creepers in the world, and Mamma said we would spend the day at Kew.

It was no use starting too early, as the hothouses were not opened until one. But we started earlier than we meant, because somebody from the *Lovegrove Gazette* came to ask where Papa was, as he had not been to the office for the last three days; and as soon as Mamma had dealt with him another man came about some money Papa owed him. It was not a big debt, but Mamma had not heard of it before. Then she came into the sitting-room and listened to Mary practising, and said, more quietly than she had ever spoken before when we were playing badly, 'You are doing no good.' Then she took my French composition out of my hands and said, 'I have told you ten thousand times that the past participles of verbs conjugated with avoir take the gender of the object if it precedes them, and I know it is difficult to remember, because it is hard to see what can be the thought behind this foolish practice, but you have broken the rule six times in this exercise which is obviously written to test your knowledge of it, you are doing no good either.' She opened the french window and stood on the iron steps to hear whether Cordelia was practising out in the stables, and after listening a minute uttered one of her low moans. Cordelia's private thoughts, always so public, were never less private than when she was playing the violin. One could constantly hear her thinking, 'They must admire the feeling I put into this phrase that is just coming;' and now she was playing or rather trampling down the solo part of the Beethoven Violin Concerto with what both Mamma and myself recognised as an intention to show that after this first experience of tragedy her art was going to mature and deepen to a degree astonishing in one so young. Mamma said, 'Go and get the poor child to stop, and I will put on my hat and coat and we will start at once. I keep on thinking the front-door bell is going to sound again. I cannot talk to any more strangers about Papa.'

When my sisters and I had dressed we all waited for Mamma and Rosamund in the hall. It was as if we were going on a long journey and it seemed odd that there was no luggage. When Rosamund came downstairs, we all exclaimed, she looked so grown-up. She was wearing her new winter coat for the first time, and coats meant much to us just then, for though one was manifestly a school-girl till one's skirt touched the ground, a coat could steal such adult privileges as a waist. This coat was cut close to her bust and had a full skirt, and it was the same blue as distance. We nodded our heads in grave admiration. She had proved that our generation could do it too, we could become grown-ups. We had need of the assurance.

She and her mother had made the coat, but nobody could have told that it had not come from a shop. 'It seems almost a pity you should be a nurse,' said Cordelia. 'You and your mother should have a shop in Bond Street.'

Rosamund said, her grey-blue eyes cool with prudence, 'No, we thought of that, but it is impossible to have your own shop unless you have something which they call capital, though it seems to be just money.'

331

'It isn't just money,' I said. 'It is money you do not spend but put aside and use for buying land and machinery and paying people who work for you so that you make more things and get more money selling them, and you have to be jolly careful that the money comes in at more than a certain rate. Papa explained it to me once.'

I had spoken his name, he was among us once more.

When Mamma came downstairs we had to tidy her up for going out, she looked too distraught. She was wearing a jacket which was really a disgrace, but we did not make her take it off. She liked wearing it whenever she was assailed by misfortune, deriving confidence from the fact that it was made of sealskin. She had never noticed that it was worn down to the shiny underpelt, and we did not point this out to her, as she had no other garment which she could possibly have supposed to be impressive. We retied the veil of her hat, too, so that a big hole did not come just over her nose, while she was giving Kate directions as to what she was to do if Papa came back while we were out. At last the front door closed behind us. She paused at the gate to say, 'Kate is sensible, she would send for the doctor if he should be looking ill. Or should we tell her?' But we hurried her on. We knew and she knew that he would never come back. Otherwise we would none of us have left the house.

It was one of those autumn mornings which are devoid of melancholy, when the weather seems to be cleaning its house. A broom of wind sent the clouds above flying briskly and kept the fallen leaves scudding along the pavements, the trees looked as if they were being stripped to let the rains get at them better. On a neighbour's apple trees the fruit shone clear yellow-green, sharp as the taste would be. The people who walked towards us had faces overlaid with colour by the low red sun, and might have been bronzed holiday-makers. We would have been running and jumping among the scurrying leaves, had we been a year or two younger. Now we walked slowly, because we were older, because our mother had suddenly become much older, and was walking with short pattering steps, and taking in the air by shallow and distressed breaths. We felt distress at the prospect of having to trust her fragility on a crowded bus or train, but our fears were unfounded. When we reached the High Street, though there were many more people than usual travelling on trams and buses, and also in traps and waggons and carriages, they were all going in the opposite direction to the one we wanted to follow, they were all going northwards, to the heart of London, and we remembered that there was to be some sort of Royal procession that day. It cannot have been a major ceremony, for had it been so the spectators would have taken up their positions in the streets or in houses on the route nearer breakfast-time. But it was important enough to draw to itself so many Londoners that we travelled on a bus as empty as if it had been forbidden to take passengers and we were phantoms who could steal a ride because we were invisible, while there streamed past us a counter-traffic of vehicles crammed with people as happy as we were sad, often playing on little trumpets and mouth-organs and penny whistles. At the end of our ride we got into as empty a train, and we reached the peculiar station which stood in a suburban landscape bare save for a hospital and a workhouse and a sewage-farm, we saw that the opposite platform was thronged with a crowd ready to board the London-bound train, all carrying packets of sandwiches or field-glasses or Brownie cameras, tapping their feet in light, tolerable impatience, and turning their contented faces to catch the warmth of the tawny sun.

'They are like a choir,' said Mamma, and so they were. Perhaps because the men and women came from the staffs of the different institutions, the sexes had not mixed, and the men were massed on the left and the women to the right, according to the conventional rule of choral societies. Since Mamma presented so strange a figure, in her worn fur jacket, with her stricken face, all their eyes turned towards her, as if she were the conductor and they were waiting for the beat. 'How wonderful it would be,' she said, 'if they suddenly started singing, and what they sang happened by chance to be as good as "The Messiah" or "The Creation."' For a second or two, she floated on her fancy, and then turned away, murmuring, 'If extraordinary things must happen, what a pity it is not that sort of extraordinary thing that happens.'

As we set foot on the path beside the poplar trees which led to the other station, a fist of wind struck each tree in turn, the golden leaves sprayed across the path, out to the muddy fields, Mamma reeled as if she herself had been hit, and she clutched her worthless hat as if it had been precious. Cordelia and Rosamund closed in on her, and she leaned on them, and in the rear Mary and Richard Quin and I loitered to keep pace with her slowness, and noted a change. We had played, when we were younger, that the red-brick buildings on the landscape before us, the hospital and the workhouse and the sewage farm, were tombs built round ogres that had been slain in battle and were too vast to bury. It had delighted us to discover, or rather to decide, that the long barracks of the workhouse enclosed the corpses of tall ogres, the bungalows and towers of the hospital and the sewage farm had been built round the squat ogres which were broader than they were long. Why did it give us no delight today to think on that happy nonsense? When we got near the dreadful little bluish-crimson brick house at the end of the poplar walk we could see that the familiar notice was pinned on the garden gate, we spoke aloud the demand we knew it would proclaim: 'Wanted, a Lady Typewriter to take down letters from dictation in return for swimming lessons.' But these words, which always before had made us laugh until it hurt our middles, now seemed like any other dull public words, like 'Please keep off the grass' or 'This way to the Goods Yard.' Had it been necessary, then, before buildings could become a joke, that Papa should be at home and working in his study? It seemed so now. Mary fell behind, dragging her feet, as if we were not nearly grown-up, as if we were still small.

We saw the white graves flowing over the hill from the cemetery beyond. Richard Quin pointed to them and muttered, 'That is all that matters. Papa is not dead. Oh, Rose, I am so frightened of death.'

I asked, 'Why? It cannot be so bad.'

'What? Not so bad,' he demanded, 'to lie outside in the rain and cold?'

'One will not feel the rain and the cold,' I said.

'Well, at any rate live people will be warmer,' he said.

'But dying will be over in a moment,' I said. 'Oh, poor Richard Quin, I am so sorry you are frightened about that, it must be horrid.'

'You don't understand,' he said, 'I'm not frightened of it like that, if I had to die I could do it, I would not run away. But it's' — he laughed shyly — 'such an expensive business, such a trouble, so disagreeable.' Suddenly he shrugged his shoulders, looked ahead of him at Rosamund, and as if he knew she would understand what he meant better than I did, ran forward to her.

When we reached the other station, people were streaming out of it, flushed not only by the ruddy sunshine, but also with haste. They had to take their places in a line of brakes, and the drivers and conductors were crying out that they must hurry, the train had been late, and there was not a moment to spare. But we had all the day on our hands, it did not distress us when we mounted the train they had just left and it did not start for a long time. It did not matter when we got to Kew, it did not matter when we got home, Papa would not be there. We looked out at the encampment of white graves on the hill and no longer did it seem the army of crosses and broken pillars and obelisks that had routed the ogres lying encased in red brick on the plains behind; nor did we try to work out from the washing on the lines in the backyards the train passed (where it was always washing-day even on Saturday) which of the horrid little houses were inhabited by abnormally shaped families. 'Nonsense, children, that is not a garment, that is a mat,' Mamma would say, trying to restore us to reason, though only as part of the game. 'No, Mamma,' Richard Quin would assure her, 'in that house one of the elder children is completely oval and fond of pink.' Now no games were worth playing, none at all. When we got out at the station we had not a look to spare for the reflective rustic derrick by the deserted factory, we went out into the street of villas in silence, as if we were quite another family.

Mary and I lagged behind, but Cordelia left the rest and turned back to stand in our path. She pointed to the villas on each side of us, and said, 'You have always been angry with me for wanting to live in a street like this. But if we were the kind of family that lives here, Papa would not have gone away.'

The tears in her eyes did not move Mary. 'The kind of family that lives here? Didn't the Phillipses live in a house like these?'

It did no good. Cordelia drifted away from us, her eyes stricken, as if we had taken her last refuge away from her, she could not even fancy that somewhere else she would have been safe.

Kew Gardens was not what it had always been before. There was nothing there but grass and trees and plants and hothouses and museums, and gardeners sweeping up dead leaves, there

335

was no cause for ecstasy. Without joy we walked about for a time looking at the beds of Michaelmas daisies and outdoor chrysanthemums and late dahlias. You could see them a long way off, patches of brightness, beyond lawns of dark sullen winter grass, behind the meagre screen of shrubs that had more leaves lying on the wet earth round them than on their branches. We liked the flowers, but not much, for they were much less beautiful than before. All of them ran too much to a coarse reddish-purple, a maroon stained with magenta, which was miscalled wine-colour and the indoor chrysanthemums suffered from a prevalence of muddy bronze. Mamma sharply cried out her disapproval of the worst of them, as if their colour was what ailed the world. Then we turned aside to walk among the trees which were scarlet and gold and silver except where the pines and holm-oaks were dark. Then we found ourselves going down Syon Vista, the broad grass avenue which runs alongside the narrow winding lake, and looks down towards the Thames and, on the other bank, the Duke of Northumberland's battlemented palace, Syon House. Our father had walked here with us, six months before. Each of us drew apart from the rest, because of that memory, and we spread right across it. I kept my head up and my eyes open so that no gardener working among the groves on either side of the walk should look up and see that I was weeping.

Where was my father? He might be here. He might as well be in Kew Gardens as at any place that was not our home. Perhaps he was in the pagoda which we saw over the treetops to the south; on any one of its ten red balconies, under any of their blue roofs, he might be standing. Or he might be in one of the hothouses, immobile, perhaps, among the weightless, saw-toothed monotony of the great ferns. He might be across the river, sheltering within the arcades on the ground floor of Syon House. He might be in one of those twilit museums in the Gardens, where cross-sections of trees and plaster models of beetles swim in half-light behind the glass doors of the cupboards, under the glass lids of show-cases, which give back the weak light weakly, and create a dusk where one might take a man for a shadow, a shadow for a man. I shut my eyes and pretended that my father was in any of these places, that he would be in all of them, that there were several of him and I would find them all. I would find him wherever he was, and if he wanted to reject me, that would be all right, if it gave him pleasure. The only thing that mattered was that he should be there to do something to me, it was of no importance what it was. But surely he would not reject me, for it was I whom he had loved the best. I had to smile at myself, for of course each of us was thinking that, with the exception of Mamma, who would be thinking only of how she had loved him.

Cordelia crossed the avenue to say in grieved tones, 'Look at Richard Quin.'

Ahead of us was Mamma, her long black skirts trailing on the grass, her head wagging as she talked to Papa, and ahead of her were Rosamund and Richard Quin. He was running backwards, running lightly, though his face was grave and juggling with three balls. Sometimes he stopped and threw a ball slowly to Rosamund, who sent it back to him. It was always a great pleasure for her, to play ball with him. A clumsiness which was the muscular equivalent of her stammering overcame her when she tried to play games; she dropped any ball sent to her at a normal speed, however hard she tried. So Richard Quin used sometimes to abandon his brilliant skill, and bowl to her gently, from a flat hand that hardly closed, and it was strange when the ball came so slowly, so very slowly through the air, and she sent it so slowly back to him, it was agreeable to watch them, it was how one might see the stars move through space, if one were great enough to watch the whole universe.

Cordelia said, 'He should not have brought those balls. Not today.' She burst out wretchedly, 'Oh, if only he could have gone to a public school. He is getting no bringing up at all. He thinks of nothing but silly games, not just cricket, and playing all those instruments without working at any of them. It is not fair on any of us.'

Perhaps my father was in the pagoda: high up, in the small round room that each floor must be, with a spiral staircase he would never tread again, as a hole at his feet, as a convolution in the ceiling overhead; standing quite still, vowed to stay there until he died, not looking out of the window, not doing anything, the hollows under his high cheekbones growing darker and darker. If he were going to do anything so absurd as live without me, he might do something as absurd as that.

Cordelia was annoyed because I did not answer. 'All this,' she sighed, 'is going to be so terribly hard on me. In a year or two it would have been all right.' She walked away, looking down on the ground and shaking her head, her hands folded behind her back.

Now we had reached the lake, and Mamma and the others had halted on the verge, but I ran past them away from my pain, towards the end of the vista, into the face of the wind that was tearing the leaves from the chestnuts overhead. But Richard Quin ran faster and caught me up.

'Come back,' he said, 'Mamma heard a siren in the distance, so we think it must be one o'clock, though we are not quite sure as it is Saturday, and the hothouses should be open.' In our clockless, watchless household time was always deduced rather than told, often from premises less substantial than this. 'So now they are wondering what to do, whether to go out and eat our sandwiches on the seats by the big pond, or to see the lapageria at once, as we are near it.'

Mamma and the others stood with their backs to the brown lake, beside a willow which was slowly shedding on the grass and on the waters its narrow lemon-yellow leaves. One leaf, turning round and round in the air, fell on the shoulder of Mamma's dark jacket and stayed there, like the flash of a strange uniform. It was an opaque yellow, as if it were made of some thick and not still living material, like leather. She said feebly, 'What shall we do?' We had suffered another strange loss, like our games. Papa had never made plans for us as other fathers did, if there was anything to be done about school, or such holidays at the seaside as we ever had, Mamma had always to do that; and we children often had to choose for ourselves when most people would have thought us too young. We did not count this a hardship, because we enjoyed making up our minds. But now that Papa was gone, we could not make up our minds. Evidently just having him there had been a help.

Mamma said, 'You should eat now, you are growing so fast, it is important that you should have meals at regular times. But the lapageria is near.'

'Let us go and see the lapageria,' said Mary, 'you are tired, and it will mean less walking.' But it could be heard that she did not care.

338

'I would be walking up and down, wherever I was,' said Mamma, 'I will not be able to rest, do not think of me.'

'It is more sensible to go and see the lapageria and walk less,' Cordelia said.

'But you children always like to eat your sandwiches by the pond,' she said.

'Yes, but chiefly so as not to give anything to the black swans,' said Richard Quin. We had settled that the bad-tempered black Australian swans on the pond housed the souls of people who were horrible to Mamma when they came to ask for money, or who were rude to children, and we took pleasure in never giving them any of our bread and keeping it all for the nicer birds. 'And don't let's bother about them today, they might feel pleased today because we are all so wretched.'

Yet nobody moved, we could not make up our minds.

Rosamund said, 'Please, I would so much like to see the lapageria now.'

'Why, of course, I had forgotten,' said Mamma, 'we came here because Rosamund had never seen it.'

It grows across a corner of the Temperate House where the roof is low, and you can really see it. The leaves are nothing much, like the leaves of a clematis, which is good, because you need only look at the flowers. They are rose-pink and might be made of wax. They are not very big, about as long as one's little finger. The buds are folded into oblongs like neatly packed parcels to hold small Christmas presents, and when they open they are like bells; and there are not too many of them, they hang far apart on the stems, so that you can enjoy each one of them, but not too far apart, it does not seem skimpy. This is characteristic of the creeper, which does everything with a sense of measure. The flowers are bright pink, but not too bright; and they do not wait to fade on the vine, they drop when they are at their best, and they lie on the earth as clean-edged as if they were really made of wax. If you pick them up you see that special arrangements have been made to keep the colour from getting too bright, for the petals are covered with a very faint white network, which you cannot see at all from a distance, but which mutes the colour.

When Rosamund saw it she was so pleased that she could not speak at all, she was as silent as she had been all the first day we brought her to Kew.

'It shows that some things can be pretty and beautiful at the same time,' said Mamma. 'Like Mendelssohn. The Violin Concerto.'

'Da-da-dah-da, da-dah-da, da-da-da-da-da-dah, da-da-daha-da-da, dah-ah, da-daha-da-da-daha,' we all sang. It was nice being in the Gardens when there was nobody else there at all.

We stood in a circle and looked up at the lapageria, and Mamma sighed, 'I would like to stay and look at it for a long time.'

'Well, so you can, Mamma,' I said.

'But you must have your sandwiches,' she insisted, 'you must not miss your meals, you are still building up your strength, and all of you must go to bed earlier, we will start tonight, it is a disgrace, now we will go and eat.'

'Why should we not picnic in here?' asked Mary.

'That would never do,' said Mamma, timidly, 'we would be put out.'

'There is a gardener just round the corner, watering the Japanese rhododendrons,' said Richard Quin, 'I will go and ask him if we can.'

'And if we can,' said Mamma, while he was away, 'remember not a crumb must fall, not a scrap of paper.' She looked round on the neat sanded paths, the trimly towering ferns and shrubs, the bright immaculate domes and walls that contained us. 'This is as neat as anybody's home, neater than ours, must we always have so much lying about? But we are all working so hard. There is no time. How hard you children all work!' She looked round us with an assessing stare. 'At least you will be able to wear more sensible clothes than I had to at your age. This hothouse makes me think of it. When I was young and went to garden-parties in Edinburgh, the gentlemen always used to take the ladies round the hot-houses, and it was difficult for us to prevent our leg-of-mutton sleeves catching on plants, I knocked over a pot of primulas once, I have never forgotten it. But that sort of thing happens to everyone when they first go out. It will happen to you, you must try not to get too much upset. But anyway you will not be so cumbered. You will not have to wear big sleeves or bustles or high collars.'

Rosamund said, 'But you must have been able to wear heavy clothes. You move quickly, with a sweep.'

Mamma cast her mind back. 'Yes. I enjoyed wearing some of my dresses. I can remember them to this day. Oh, children, I am foolish to say that I am glad you will have sensible clothes, I hope you will have lots of clothes that are not just sensible.'

'Mamma has a photograph of you wearing a dress with a long train,' said Rosamund.

'Yes,' said Mamma. 'Slipper satin from Lyons. White, but it was a sort of pinkish grey in the shadows. Many, many yards of it.'

'Mamma says you managed the train so beautifully,' said Rosamund, 'it was always just where you wanted it to be.'

'Constance is a good friend to remember that,' said Mamma. 'Yes, I used to take such a pride in that train, in going across the platform in a straight line with it out behind me. Then when I got to the piano there it was, running in a neat fishtail down towards the audience, and my feet clear for the pedals.' She glowed, and then gave us a defensive glance. 'There is no harm in looking nice on the platform,' she said mildly, 'though, of course, the music must come first.'

We were all surprised at the idea that Mamma had ever cared about dress. We thought of her as an eagle, for this minute we saw a humming-bird.

With sudden bitterness she looked up at the lapageria. 'It is so unspoiled! To look at it you cannot believe the way things get spoiled in this world. But how stupid and ungrateful,' she cried, 'to forget that there was once something that had to be spoiled before it was worthless. When I married your father I was considered quite attractive.' She held her head high, and with a confidence that showed how utterly dazed and bludgeoned she was, beyond the point where she could have any exact perception of material objects, she stroked the shiny pelt of her old seal-skin jacket, as if it were a garment worthy of what she had been.

Richard Quin came running back, saying happily, 'The gardener says it is strictly forbidden to picnic in here, and that of course we can. And he says that we can move the potting-bench from over there for you to sit on, that is strictly forbidden too.'

He spread his coat for her on the bench, and we gathered round her and urged her to have a sandwich. 'Eat, eat,' we begged her, 'it cannot be good for you to live on so little, you had nothing for breakfast but tea.' Food was all we had at hand for an instrument of our tenderness. She took a sandwich to please us, and nibbled at it, her eyes on the lapageria, saying, 'Not even the best pictures in the old books give any idea of its trimness, the moderation of its prettiness.' But presently she sighed, 'If only I knew what was in the cupboard.'

We wished she would not speak of that. We could all see the open cupboard door sticking out over the mantelpiece, and it was hideous as the lapageria was beautiful. When Mamma had opened the door of the house in Lovegrove Place, that first day, we had thought a burglar was at work. Well, we had made no mistake.

'He must have had some reason for opening it,' she said, her eyes going from face to face among her children. 'There must have been some old story he remembered. Perhaps some of Mrs. Willoughby's jewels could not be found when she died, and perhaps he guessed that they were there, and left them untouched for a last reserve. If I could be sure that they were really valuable.'

We could not find anything to say.

It crossed my mind that perhaps my mother would have been a difficult wife for any husband, she was too brave about putting things into words.

'Do not look like that, my dears,' she begged us. 'I told you, I can only bear your Papa going away if he did not go empty-handed. You see, I have been very wicked, very wicked indeed.'

We pressed round her, telling her that she had never done anything wrong in her life, each holding a sandwich in one hand and caressing her with the other.

'You don't know what you are talking about,' she protested in a little, cracked voice. 'I have done something very wicked. I have kept something back from him, and I should have let him have it.'

'Mamma, what nonsense,' said Cordelia, 'what have we got that could be of any value to him or anybody else?'

'The portraits,' said Mamma. 'The portraits in your rooms. They are not copies.'

We looked to see which of our handkerchiefs was the cleanest, and gave it to her.

'That is a real Lawrence?' asked Mary. 'And a real Gainsborough?'

'But, Mamma, they cannot be, you must be mistaken,' said Cordelia. 'If they were originals they would be very valuable, and we have nothing that is worth having.'

'No, dear,' said Mamma. 'They are very valuable. I told you that you need not worry. I do not know what they are worth, but it will be enough to keep us all for a few years while you are all educated. I will write to Mr. Morpurgo, he has some lovely pictures, and I will ask him what dealer I should take them to, I think he will still help us though Papa has caused him so much trouble. He evidently admires your Papa very much. And what is so wicked is that I have always known that they were very valuable, and I did not tell your Papa. It was the first dealer who told us they were copies, and I did not trust him, he spoke with that dreadful accent Edinburgh people use when they try to speak like the English, a West End accent, they call it, the vowels are all clipped. I think he was trying to buy the pictures from us for nothing, because he had heard how badly the people at the newspaper were treating Papa. So I let another dealer come and see them, a nicer man, and he got another dealer from Glasgow, a Mr. Reid from Glasgow, and both offered me money for them, a great deal of money. But I did not tell your father. I let him go on thinking that they were copies and not worth selling. I felt I had to do it, or they would have gone like everything else. Richard Quin, one of the lapageria flowers has just fallen on the ground, just see if you can reach it for me without stepping anywhere you should not.'

She laid the pink bell on the palm of her hand and studied it, while we stood silent, astonished by the news, and by the terrible quietness of her remorse which lay so deep that we would never be able to get at it and destroy it.

Mary said, 'But, Mamma, it was not wicked. We all know that Papa cannot keep money, and that if he has it it becomes nothing, it goes away like snow.'

Mamma said, 'No, what I did must have been wicked, for it has put everything wrong. Try to be sensible and see that of course I would have felt all right now, if I had kept nothing from

343

your father, if I could say to myself that I had handed over to him all I had.'

'Mamma, Mamma,' I said, 'do not talk like that sickening beast Patient Griselda.'

'Rose, you must not use such disgusting language. Please try to understand that I have done wrong. Can you not see that perhaps I should have given your father one last chance by telling him about the pictures and letting him have this money too? It might have been that since they were portraits of his own people he would have felt differently about the money he got from them, and would have kept it all for you children and then there could have been respect all round. And maybe he has turned against me because he knew I was not being frank with him. Lately, when things have been getting worse and worse, I have often thought of the portraits, and how you were safe because I had them, and it may have been that he felt my lack of straightforwardness, and grieved because he had nobody truly with him. It might have been that that made him pass me in the street without speaking to me. Oh, I have failed your father.'

I tugged at Rosamund's arm, and we turned away from the group and walked down the sanded path till we were out of earshot and were sheltered by a projection of fretted palm-leaves. 'Rosamund,' I said, 'I know something about Papa that would make Mamma understand that really she could not trust Papa ever to think of her or of us. To get Mrs. Phillips reprieved he was willing to publish a pamphlet about the Judge which would have been contempt of court, and he knew that it would have meant he had to go to prison, and he never thought for a minute of what would happen to us. Do you think I ought to tell her?'

She stammered, 'Oh, but I do not think you could tell her anything about Cousin Piers that she does not already know.'

I hesitated. 'Are you sure?'

'Mammas know much more about Papas than we do,' she said, with what was for her unusual definiteness.

I rather wondered why she thought so. It often seemed as if they did not. When we went back Mamma was saying, 'You see, your Papa is driven by something that he cannot help, that wants him to go down and down. That is why he does such strange things, his great gifts and his power to please hold him up in the world, he has to make efforts to fall from the high place that belongs to him. That is why he has gone away He has not left you simply because he does not care for you, but this thing that wants him to fall is driving him on to do something which will bring ruin on him, and he does not want you to be ruined too, he has gone away alone, with nobody to look after him, simply so that you shall be safe. He cannot give you what other fathers give their children, it is not permitted to him, but what he can give you he has given you, and it is your safety. You must remember that all your lives. Since he is what he is, it is impossible not to love him. But look what I have had to do. Oh, children, if you love somebody, give them every chance. But no, I am not warning you of the real danger that is in front of you. I love your father and I have not been able to give him every chance. I would have found it so easy to do, it would have been no sacrifice for me to strip myself till I had nothing for I could get on with very little, I would not mind not getting on at all. But I could not do it because of you children. I had to keep some money safe for you, money which he could not touch. You do not know what he has got through. Gambling is worse than moth and rust, it does not even leave behind it rags and rusted metal, it eats up everything without remainder. If one of you got ill, and needed to have an operation or go to a sanatorium, what could I do if I had not kept those portraits? What would I have done tomorrow? I do not think there is five pounds in the house or in the bank. I had to keep the portraits for your sakes, but it has spoiled everything between your father and myself. This is not fair. Why should I have had to choose between treating you properly and treating your father properly? I know that all things will be right at the end of the time, if we do not stop working now and afterwards, but I cannot see how.'

'Mamma,' said Richard Quin, 'Mamma.'

But she did not listen to him. She said, 'As it is, it looks as if I would have been better off with either Papa or you, as if I should not have had both, and that is ridiculous, for I could not bear to be without you, and you are you because he was your father, he is in all of you, I had to have both. What is the answer to this riddle? But you see, it is only if I can think that he found

345

something valuable in the cupboard that I will ever have an easy mind again.'

She covered her face with her hands. 'Mamma,' said Richard Quin, 'Mamma.' But still she did not listen to him. It was extraordinary that she should not listen when Richard Quin spoke to her. We were right, her grief was so deep we could not touch it.

Rosamund stammered, 'Well, anyway, Rose, you need not be frightened any more.'

Mamma's hands came down from her face. She asked, 'Rose, were you frightened?'

Before I could say that Rosamund was wrong, she blurted out, stupidly, 'Yes, she was frightened. They all were, but they did not say so, for fear of upsetting you. But all the girls have been worried for a long time, they have always been quite envious when I said I was going to be a nurse, because it was so easy to arrange, and of course none of them know how they can be musicians if they cannot get a proper training, and Richard Quin has been wondering what he could do if he had to leave school so long before the proper time. And, of course, this morning it all seemed to have happened, what they feared.'

We could not have believed she would be so foolish. But she returned our angry stares blankly and said, 'Why should I not tell the truth?'

Under our eyes our mother was restored. 'Oh, my poor children,' she sighed, opening her arms to all of us. She let the lapageria flower fall to the ground, she did not even notice it.

'Of course one is afraid when one thinks that one is going to have absolutely no money,' said Richard Quin, who had in fact been afraid of nothing except that Papa might be dead. We all drew closer to her still, and breathed confessions of how abandoned and helpless we had felt, how we had feared that Cousin Ralph would not let us stay in the house if we could pay no rent, how impossible it had seemed that we should ever become musicians, how we too had dreaded the thought that one of us might become ill, how it had sometimes seemed to us that we might starve; and of how all that was over, because of what she had done about the portraits. The light that poured down from the high glass vaults through the green confusion

346

of boughs and vines made her look paler even than she was by habit; yet it could be seen that now she was well again, she was strong. 'You might have known,' she murmured, 'that I would manage for you somehow. But to think I did not know of all this you were feeling! Oh, children, you must always tell me when you are frightened.'

XVI

So when we woke next morning we did not feel ourselves to be deserted children, we simply lay awake a little before rising and wondered how our father was faring on this last adventure, at once so spectacular and invisible. We were also very much interested in the sale of the portraits. This we looked forward to, though we liked them, for we assumed that when we were rich we would buy them back, and it was amusing to let our possessions go out into the world for a time and be admired. We longed for the excitement to begin, and the first thing after breakfast Mamma sat down and wrote a letter to Mr. Morpurgo, in which, after due apologies for my father's strange behaviour, she asked him to recommend her a picture-dealer, and we all went together to post the letter. We wondered if Mr. Morpurgo would come down and see us, and if he would resemble the picture we had drawn of him as a Pasha with a face as big and jolly and yellow as a harvest moon. Then we dressed for church, but there was a knock at the front door. The little man from Papa's office who had come to see Mamma the day before was there again. Mamma got quite white, and took him into the dining-room, and Constance asked us if we would care to go to church with her, but we said not. We went into the sitting-room and waited. We did not mind being there, for while we had been at Kew the day before Kate had got the cupboard to close and had rehung the picture of the Spanish cathedral over the mantelpiece. Cordelia and Mary and I took off our Sunday hats and put them on the round table, making a pattern with them.

'I wonder,' said Mary, 'why Mamma thinks these hats are worthier of being our Sunday hats than our everyday ones.'

'I cannot think,' said Cordelia bitterly, 'they look far worse and cost as little.'

'Perhaps,' said Richard Quin, 'it is because on Sunday people are supposed to be good and kind, and may be expected to take a more charitable view of hats as well as everything else.'

While we were inventing charitable things people might find to say about our hats, Mamma came in and said, 'Really, your Papa is very thoughtless, though not so thoughtless as you children, not a day passes without your losing something. It seems he has taken away some keys from the office. Can any of you remember seeing three keys tied together with red tape? Well, then I will look in Papa's study.'

She was so relieved because the man from the office was not a dun that we all wanted to go to church, but it was too late. So Constance and Rosamund went to their room to finish some sewing; and Cordelia announced, knitting her brows and looking importantly into the distance, that she would go round and see Bayahtreechay, for so she still called Miss Beevor, about some things which had to be settled about next week's concerts; and Richard Quin produced three balls from the crevices of the sofa and went out into the garden, juggling even before he had got out into the air, even while he was going down the steps. Mary and I tossed who was to have the piano, I won, and she took her harmony note-book upstairs. Left alone, I found the room so full of Papa that I had scarcely the heart to start my scales. And before I had got to E major Kate showed in a visitor, telling me that he had come to see Mamma, but that she was still busy with the man from the office. I was sorry that Mamma had to see him. For whatever Papa had done to this sad man, he could not stand up against it. If it were his money that Papa had taken from him, he could not afford to lose it. If it were his trust that had been betrayed, he had been wounded too often before.

I tried to make him feel at home. There was a copy of George Borrow's *A Bible in Spain* lying on the table, and I asked him if he had read it. I explained that we had liked *Lavengro* and *The Romany Rye* very much, but we had never read this one, because the title sounded preachy, but Richard Quin had said there was no harm in trying, and we had got it out of the library, and it was the loveliest of all. I stopped there, because there did not seem anything else to say. He did not answer, but rolled on me a dark brown eye shining like a fried egg when it is not quite cooked. I did not think his health could be good. At length he cleared his throat and said, no, he had not read *A Bible in Spain*, but he had often heard of it. Then silence fell.

Suddenly he asked, 'Are you Rose or Mary?'

I said I was Rose and asked if Papa had told him about us. He said he had. Then silence fell again. It was odd, we hardly ever met people who did not talk to us. I supposed that what Papa had done had upset him so much that he could not think of anything else.

I was thinking I would go away and ask Kate to make the poor man some tea, when Mamma came in, carrying a small tin box. She smiled at the visitor and said, 'How do you do, I am so sorry that we must ask you to wait, but we were all hunting for some keys that are apparently very important to somebody.' She emptied the box over the table, and lots and lots of keys fell out. 'It really is most astonishing,' she exclaimed, 'I found this box with some keys in it, and our servant and I have put in it all the keys we could find lying about the house, and it turns out that I have many more keys than I have things that lock. Can you understand that?'

The little man did not seem to realise that she wanted an answer till she turned her eyes full on him, and then he cleared his throat, and smiled, and said that he could not.

'Of course you would not,' Mamma assured him. 'I am a bad manager. We are all careless in this house, we must clear things up, we must start tomorrow, fitting all these keys into the locks, and throwing away all that do not fit. But now I must find these office keys that are lost. There are three of like size, which were tied together with red tape when Papa got them, but who can tell now? Rose, help me to put aside those we know to belong to this house. These can go, they are all trunk keys.'

'And that is a clock key,' I said.

'And that, I think, is a key for some large piece of furniture, probably of the Empire period,' said our visitor, growing interested. 'But not French, Italian.'

'Yes,' said Mamma, hastily, 'I had some Empire furniture once, but I sold it long ago.' She passed her hand across her forehead and went on with her search.

The visitor's viscid eye rolled slowly round the room. 'He is thinking we have nothing left to sell and is afraid he will never get his money back,' I thought. 'I hope Papa did not owe him so much money that Mamma will have to give him all the money she gets for the portraits.' But his eye returned to the keys. 'May I help?' he asked, and drew his chair up to the table. 'And that is a key for a piece of furniture that must have been seventeenth-century Dutch. Probably a cupboard. You haven't got it now? No?' he sighed.

'This belongs to Cordelia's workbox,' I said, 'and this belongs to my music-case.'

'Oh, you are careless children,' said Mamma.

'It is not that,' I said, 'but what sense is there in locking up a work-box or a music-case? Nobody else in the world would want what one keeps in them.'

'Yes, but one often uses things for what they were not meant,' said Mamma. 'Some day Cordelia may find that she wants to keep something really valuable in her work-box and you may want to keep something secret in your music-case, and then where will you both be?'

For a moment we continued to turn over the keys. Then our visitor stopped helping us. He put his elbows on the table and rested his pale, lax chin on his clasped hands. 'Why,' he asked, smiling faintly, 'how could that be?'

'How could what be?' said Mamma absently. She had just picked up a key, looked hard at it, and murmured, 'Piers.' But our visitor was smiling into the distance, and did not notice. He repeated, 'How could it come about that this young lady and her sister should want to keep something valuable in a work-box and a music-case?'

He was asking Mamma for a story, as we had so often done when we were little, and she was glad to tell it, to prevent her weeping. She dropped the key that had reminded her of Papa and began, 'Well, they might have been walking in Hyde Park one Sunday and stopped to listen to the orators and been converted to Home Rule. . . .' But then there came a knock at the door, and Mamma said, wearily, 'Oh, the man from the office is growing impatient and I do not wonder. Forgive me,' she said to our visitor, smiling with a gentle kind of caution, to warn him that she might not be able to give him the satisfaction that he wanted, 'I will come back as soon as I can.'

I said, 'I will go on tidying the keys.'

He quietly went on helping me to sort them, but presently broke out into soft chuckling, that set the jowls of his small face shaking. 'That is a very delightful lady,' he said. 'Is she a relative of yours?'

'Why, she is our Mamma," I answered.

He let the key in his hand fall on the table and stared at me. 'Oh no,' he exclaimed. 'Oh no.'

'Why, did you know her before?' I asked.

'Yes, indeed,' he answered, 'indeed I did.' He took out a handkerchief and drew it across his lips and kneaded it in his clasped hands. Everything about him drooped. His egg-like eyes seemed about to slide down his face.

'She often looks much better than this,' I said, 'she is very much upset just now.' But I was angry, and doubted if I should have pandered to him by making that excuse. Mamma might have changed from being young and attractive to being old and bony, but he can never have been anything but funny-looking at any time of his life, so it was sheer impudence for him to be shocked at the way she looked.

'But of course it is Piers' wife,' the little man cried out, suddenly hitting the table and getting up and walking round the room. 'Of course it is she. She must come back at once. What is this business about keys?'

'Papa has taken away or lost the keys of the newspaper office where he worked,' I said, 'and they have sent a clerk round to get them.'

'That is easily settled. I will go and tell him to stop bothering your Mamma and get a locksmith on Monday,' said the little man, preparing to leave the room. But just then Mamma came back, and said to me, 'It is all right, Kate has found them, they were in his old Dutch tobacco box. Oh, the things he loves that he has had to leave behind him.' Then, remembering she spoke before a stranger, she sighed, and said to me, 'Now run away, dear,' and turned to him, squared her shoulders, and held her head high, and said, 'Now, what can I do for you?'

He asked, 'Do you not remember me?'

She looked bewildered and he was hurt. I thought how funny it was to be a man, he thought it natural and her fault that he had not recognised her, but unkind of her not to recognise him. Reproachfully, he said, 'I am Edgar Morpurgo'

She flung out both her hands, crying, 'Oh, you have been so good to us.'

'But you did not remember me,' he mourned.

'It is because you are so much thinner,' she pleaded.

'No, I am much stouter,' he said plaintively.

'Well, I knew there was no great difference,' said Mamma, and he was so glad to be with her that the answer seemed to satisfy him. They sat down side by side on the sofa, looking at each other happily.

'But how can it be you?' she asked, her voice quite young. 'We posted the letter to you only this morning.'

'I did not come because of your letter,' he assured her, 'but my wife and I got home from Scotland only last night, and it was too late to do anything when I read the message from the business manager of the *Gazette* saying he had gone.'

'It is so kind of you to have come,' she said, 'and so quickly. It is the kinder because Piers must have caused you so much trouble by going like this.'

'Never mind that,' he said. 'Do you know why he went?'

'No, no,' she said, 'if he had told me, I would have made him come with me to see you, whatever it was. Even though it might have meant that you decided to help him no more, you had a right to know.'

Mr. Morpurgo thought over this proposition, then sadly shook his head. 'A man like me has no rights over a man like him,' he said.

'I know what you mean,' she said. 'Even now there is no doubt about that, is there? We are all less than Piers. But to accept kindness from a friend and not be quite frank with him, that would be wrong if he were the greatest man in the world.'

'Yes, but we will forget it,' said Mr. Morpurgo. 'I mean that. I would have remembered if it had happened at any earlier time, for prudential reasons, to remind myself that there were risks I should not take in the future, for everybody's sake, even his own. But if, as everybody seems to think, this is the end of a chapter, I will not remember it. There are many other things about him to remember, as you know.' They were silent for a little, both looking out into the garden. 'Have you any idea where he has gone?' he asked.

She shook her head.

'He could be found, you know,' said Mr. Morpurgo. 'There are ways.' She said nothing, and he sighed. 'But no, you wouldn't care for that. And perhaps you are right. If he felt there was reason to go, he was probably right.'

'Yet I wish he could be found for his own sake,' said Mamma. 'I think he has some money. But you know what he is. It will be gone in no time. And then — and then — but there it is. If he felt there was reason to go, we had better not interfere.'

He patted her hand, saying presently, 'Now what about you? I have come to give you all the help that may be needed, and I want no argument. What is your position?'

'You can help me at once by telling me what art dealer would give me the best price for a Gainsborough and a Lawrence,' said Mamma.

Mr. Morpurgo took his hand away from hers, and rolled his expressive eyes up to the ceiling, as if he thought something would drop from it.

'Yes, they are up above us, in the children's bedroom,' said Mamma. 'How did you know?'

He took out his handkerchief and passed it over his lips as he had done before, and looked round our shabby room, as if to make quite sure. 'You have a Gainsborough and a Lawrence here in this house, in your children's bedroom?'

'Yes, and a Sir Martin Archer-Shee,' said Mamma. 'I know an Archer-Shee is of no value now, but it seems mean to him not to mention the picture, for it is very pretty. They are all three very pretty pictures, they are portraits of Piers' ancestresses, and you know how good-looking his family all were. It is strange he ever married me. They are in good condition and I think they should sell well, if I could learn the name of a reliable dealer.'

'Are you quite sure that these pictures really are by Gainsborough and by Lawrence?' asked Mr. Morpurgo.

'Mr. Alexander Reid of Glasgow said so,' replied Mamma.

'He did, did he,' exclaimed Mr. Morpurgo. A question then occurred to him which he tried to suppress. But after he had made an inconsequent remark about Papa's family it had to come out. 'How in God's name did you manage to keep these portraits from him?'

Mamma's hands fluttered. I said, 'Mamma is being very silly about this, she let him think they were copies, but she had to do that, hadn't she?'

354

He said, 'Certainly she had.'

'Please,' I went on, 'go upstairs and look at the pictures and tell Mamma how much she can get for them, and tell her if somebody could lend her some money now. I think there is hardly any in the house.' While they were gone I went on sorting out the keys, but it was hopeless, really. That box must still be somewhere in the ruins of the house.

When they came down again Mamma was saying to him, 'I want enough money to set the two younger girls on their feet, there will be no difficulty about them, they will be pianists and they have simply to get their training. And I must educate the boy, he will look after himself, he will be all right too. And I must do something about my poor Cordelia, though I cannot think what.' Mr. Morpurgo assumed a sympathetic expression, obviously prepared to hear that Cordelia was a dwarf or a cripple. 'She is not musical but does not know it. Well, you see, the sort of capital I will need to get them out in the world, after that it will not matter. Do you think the pictures will fetch anything like that?'

Mr. Morpurgo said, 'I think you will be quite comfortably placed,' and rolled his eyes up to the ceiling again, and again his pendant plumpness was shaking by a faint pulse of laughter. 'I came prepared to be so generous,' he murmured. But even now that I knew who he was, and he was amused and happy, he still appeared to me as a victim of melancholy need, and his voice continued to be plaintive as he promised us that we should have everything we wanted. 'I will take you to Mr. Wertheimer next week,' he said, 'and after that it will not be long before we have your affairs in order. Really, I think you will not have much to worry about, if you are reasonably careful. Now, is there anything else you have on your mind?'

'There is Aunt Lily,' said Mamma and paused.

'Whose aunt is she? Yours or your husband's?' asked Mr. Morpurgo.

'She is nobody's aunt,' answered Mamma, 'or rather, she is not ours. She is simply one of those people who, I do not know why, choose to be called Aunt by anybody they like.'

'Yes, yes,' said Mr. Morpurgo, 'the nannie class.'

'We have become very fond of her,' said Mamma, letting that comment go by. 'You remember the Phillips murder trial? Poor

Aunt Lily is Mrs. Phillips's sister. She stayed with us during the case.'

'You knew all these people?' said Mr. Morpurgo. 'Now that is remarkable. I have never come across the characters in a murder case. And I thought of you living so quietly. How on earth did you come across them?'

'They are quite ordinary people,' said Mamma defensively. 'No, not that. But then so few people are. They lived near here and the daughter, a delightful child, Nancy, was at school with my girls, and so it was natural to take in the child and her aunt. And really Aunt Lily is such a good creature, we all formed a great regard for her. That is why I am worried about her now.'

'But what is the worry?' asked Mr. Morpurgo. 'Is she in need of money? Or is it a question of finding her employment?'

'No, no, she is a barmaid at the Dog and Duck at Harplewood-on-Thames,' explained Mamma, 'she is happy there with some friends. But you see, she goes to Aylesbury Prison every visiting day to see her sister.' It was not Mamma's way to ask for favours directly or by hints. But if it had been any of us children that had behaved as she did, talking straight on in a level voice and fixing her eyes on a rosebush out in the garden, she would have said that we were hinting. 'Poor Aunt Lily felt the trial terribly; and Mrs. Phillips is in a very distressing state, she is not taking imprisonment well, though we cannot blame her, and she is quite cruel to her sister during the visits so they are quite an ordeal. My husband used to take her to Aylesbury and bring her back here. I will take her myself if nobody else will, but she attaches great importance to being escorted by, as she puts it, a gentleman. She is frightened of being in a prison, and she feels that the prison officials respect her more if she is with somebody whom they respect.' She paused, and after a second or two continued: 'It is not an easy undertaking. Poor Aunt Lily talks far too much, and what she says is not usually very interesting. Her appearance is unfortunate, too.'

Almost as if he were talking to himself, Mr. Morpurgo asked, 'Why should I not do that? I have never done anything like it in my life before. But really there is no reason why I should not be able to do it, if I make up my mind.' Again, he seemed amused as he said, 'I will certainly take Aunt Lily to Aylesbury.'

356

'That would lift a great weight off my mind,' Mamma assured him vehemently.

'And that is all the weight that you have on your mind?' inquired Mr. Morpurgo, smiling. 'All you want is a dealer to buy your Gainsborough and your Lawrence, and an escort to take Aunt Lily to her sister's prison? Is that really all?'

'No,' sighed Mamma, 'I want him to come back.'

'To come back,' repeated Mr. Morpurgo; and he suggested, 'just a little different, with that difference that would make him possible to deal with.'

'No, not different at all,' said Mamma, and wept, but only for a moment, since it was wrong that poor Mr. Morpurgo should be made unhappy when he came to do us a kindness.

When he had gone Mamma said, 'What a kind man! But did I ever meet him before? Still I felt at ease with him because he was so right about your father. But, how dull and flat it all is without him!'

All our lives just then were like that conversation, which was so pleasant, and was suffused with anguish. In the garden Richard Quin would throw into the air four or five balls (three were too easy for him now) and would keep them spinning, with misery on his upturned face. Once Mamma and I, coming back from a Bach concert, saw a shooting-star and while it still fell she gripped my arm and stood staring up into the glittering sky as if trying to trace where it had lost itself in the dark firmament, penniless, and then she went on with her comment on the *St. Matthew Passion*. As for Cordelia and Mary and I, we suffered wounds to heal. But it would be hypocritical to pretend that Mary and I did not enjoy it when Aunt Theodora, having heard about Papa's departure, but not about the Gainsborough and the Lawrence, called when everybody but us was out; and perhaps Mary went rather far when she assured Aunt Theodora that the only thing we three girls had now to fear was that men would marry us for our money. We also found, if not pleasure, at least distraction, in an attempt to stop gossip about the departure of Papa spreading through the school, by telling the other girls and the teachers all about the discovery that the pictures which hung over our beds had turned out to be a Gainsborough and a Lawrence. We got their attention easily, for at that time there were two works of art which were universally known; one was Sir Joshua Reynolds' Cherubs' Heads, and the other was Gainsborough's 'Portrait of the Duchess of Devonshire.' We never actually told lies, but we let it be supposed that Papa was taking part in the negotiations with the picture-dealers. There must have been some people in Lovegrove who knew that he had fled, and better than we did, why; but at least we contrived that some other people only slowly realised that he had gone and had a vague impression that he had made some money by selling some pictures, and had at some stage of the transaction found it profitable to go abroad.

There were indeed many practical matters to be arranged at this time. We children were faced quite early with the problem of the annihilation of Mamma's sealskin jacket. This first arose one evening when we were all in the kitchen helping Kate prepare the dried fruit for the Christmas puddings. Usually we made them about the twenty-first of March, but that year we had had no money to spare for buying the fruit and brandy; so one of the first things Mamma did when Mr. Morpurgo lent her money on the security of the pictures was to go out and buy raisins and currants and mixed peel, and we were all at work on them when Mamma came in and read a letter from Mr. Morpurgo telling her that he would call one day in the following week to take her up to Bond Street to talk to Mr. Wertheimer about the portraits, which by then would have been cleaned by the experts. We were excited by Mamma's intrepid entrance into a proud and glutted world where people with foreign names owned galleries full of masterpieces in the very same streets as the shops full of wonderful dresses where Constance and Rosamund sold their needlework. But when Mamma left the kitchen Kate said, 'We cannot have your Mamma going up to town with that poor Mr. Morpurgo and wearing her old sealskin jacket.' Everybody in our household spoke of 'poor Mr. Morpurgo' and put real pity into the phrase, though he was a millionaire and had two millionaire uncles, and had no apparent misfortunes in his personal life. 'You must all see what you can do to get her to let the old thing go to the dust-bin.'

We made some effort. That evening at supper Cordelia said, 'Mamma, what are you going to wear when you go up to see Mr. Wertheimer?'

'My black dress and my sealskin,' said Mamma confidently.

'Mamma,' said Richard Quin, 'that jacket is not sealskin any more, it is just a bit of a dead seal. There is a difference.'

'Nonsense,' said Mamma testily. 'Of course the seal died. Otherwise I should not be wearing its skin.'

'No, Mamma,' said Richard Quin, 'there have been two deaths. First the seal died, and then its skin went to the funeral and heard the will read, and of course it had been left everything, and then it sold the house and chose to make its home with you. But now in the fullness of time it too has died.'

'No, no,' said Mamma, 'do not be silly, children, any furrier will tell you that sealskin cannot wear out, and it is the best thing I have got, and where am I to get a new coat? These pictures, I do not yet know what they will bring us, and there are such a lot of you to put out into the world, and you are all bothering me, leave me in peace.' She covered her eyes, and it occurs to me now that she did not want to admit that the coat was bare because Mr. Morpurgo's visit had reminded her that she was a woman, and she could not bear to think that her poverty had forced her to go about for years looking like a scarecrow, and that what she had lost as a woman during those years was not now to be recovered.

Constance said, 'Perhaps Rosamund and I might take a look at it and see what we can do in the way of refurbishing it.'

Mamma sighed, 'How I wish we all had hands like you two! That would be very kind, Constance.' So we talked of other things, mild as milk, but with resolution steely in us. We were beginning to understand that Mamma would in some respects always be younger than we were, perhaps because she had not had as trying a childhood as we had had, and that for her sake we had sometimes to treat her with positive low cunning, to get round the fact that she was supposed to be older than us in all ways instead of just a few.

We met in the kitchen after supper to talk it all over, all us children, not Constance. She stayed upstairs with Mamma, by one of those accidents that often served our purposes to perfection though no hint of connivance ever coloured the blankness of her tone or disturbed her brow. Rosamund went and fetched the sealskin jacket from Mamma's room, because what had been said at supper gave her permission, and we spread it out on a chair under the light

'First of all,' said Cordelia, 'can she possibly get a new coat? I don't think she borrowed much from Mr. Morpurgo.'

'There are our money-boxes,' said Mary.

359

'There is almost nothing in them,' said Cordelia, contemptuously.

'What are you doing, Rosamund?' I asked.

'Why, this is a red-hot knitting-needle, and they make openwork patterns in leather with red-hot knitting-needles,' said Rosamund. 'Your Mamma knows that one must not wear anything that is moth-eaten.'

As the smell of burning grew stronger, Cordelia said, 'I don't know that we have the right to do this.'

'Your Mamma is very tired,' said Rosamund, 'let us get this out of the way for her.'

'And poor Mr. Morpurgo is very kind,' said Kate, 'but rich gentlemen are frightened of being stared at, you must consider other people's feelings.'

'I would not have the strength of mind to do this,' said Mary, doubtfully.

'Rosamund is like someone in Roman history,' said Richard Quin, 'and people in Roman history are much admired.'

Rosamund made three holes in the jacket, and pinched it to get rid of the charred edges. There was a horrible smell, and she opened the tradesmen's door into the garden, and stood shaking the jacket just outside in the fresh air. The moonlight fell on her and made her fair hair and tall body look as if they were covered with frost. All of us watched her unhappily, except Richard Quin who was laughing silently, and Kate who was washing the dishes. Rosamund came in after a few minutes and she and Richard Quin went upstairs, and came back alone, and gave the jacket to Kate, saying, 'Please give it to the dustman tomorrow. After I showed her the holes she began to turn it over and said it was far worse than she supposed, and I said it was so bad it ought to be put out of the house at once in case the moth got into other things, and now Richard Quin is telling her that he would like to see her in a cape, I looked at them in the Bon Marche this afternoon, they are not dear and are very plain and smart,' and she went upstairs again.

'Now do not be nice Nellies,' Kate told us, as we worked in silence, 'there are times when somebody has to do something quickly.'

But as we got older Rosamund and Richard Quin often struck us as formidable. It often seemed to us as if they were acting scenes from a play unknown to us, which they rehearsed in secret, but now their confederacy sometimes took a new and graver form, which always gave us some cause for feeling thankful and yet at the same time was alarming in kind. When our family found itself in a position from which there seemed no egress save by way of someone's pain, Rosamund and Richard Quin were always there to open another door, she with her calm stammering force, he with his conjurer's sleight of hand and patter, and they acted so neatly and quickly. But if one flagged and fainted in the street, and a nurse took one arm and an orderly the other, and whisked one into an ambulance and out of it into a hospital and on to an operating table, with the anaesthetic ready in the syringe, one would prefer them to act not too quickly or too smoothly, however urgent the need for operation.

We were as a rule, however, united in wonder at what was happening to us. Mamma's visits to Mr. Wertheimer went well, though the business was not concluded at once, and we were of course haunted by the fear which never left us till the cheque was actually paid into Mamma's bank, that the portraits were really copies after all. But there was much to distract our attention from that fear. Mamma had numerous callers. Some of them were duns, whom she could now refer to Mr. Morpurgo's solicitors, though even then the interviews were disagreeable. I still remember with a sharp pang of hatred a little yellowish man, looking up from the letter the solicitors had given Mamma to show to Papa's creditors, saying that they would consider all claims against him, and snarling at her, 'If this is a trick, you'll hear something from me you won't like.' Mamma pleaded for him that he was probably very poor, but it still seems to me that he deserved to be poor.

Most of the callers, however, were friendly. There was, needless to say, Mr. Langham, who came with boxes of Carlsbad plums, though it was not Christmas time, and paid long lugubrious visits, ostensibly to condole with Mamma, but rather to receive her condolences on the long betrayal of his devotion. His wife also called to offer her sympathy, but there again the purpose of the visit was executed in reverse, for it appeared that Mr. Langham's private life was not above reproach. Other admirers of my father came, after they had digested for some days whatever rumour of his flight had reached them, partly because they were still under the charm and sought the place where the enchanter had last been seen, partly because they had been drawn to him in the first place by political idealism and were too humanitarian to contemplate my mother's probable position unmoved. At any rate most of them offered her help, which she rejected in a manner that sent them away much happier. Laughing and speaking in a tone of rueful amusement, as if they might have offended her had it not been for her sense of humour, she told them of the sale of the family portraits. Papa was, she admitted, eccentric, and had perhaps been unusually eccentric, even for him, when he suddenly set sail to write his long book in peace, for some place unknown, whence he would return at any time with a like lack of the usual observances. But to leave his wife and children unprovided for, oh, no, her amused voice told them, he was not as eccentric as all that. And his worshippers went away in the happy belief that their worship had not all been error.

There came the wonderful day when the cheque was paid; and very soon afterwards there was an even more wonderful day. Mamma went to town early in the morning, and came back when we were at tea. It was plain that the day had gone well from her point of view, for she looked quite young for her, and held her head high, and had brought us a box of marrons glacés. She said, 'Mary, Rose, you must listen. You are to go to the Panmure Hall on Tuesday at three. I will tell them at school that you are to be excused.'

'Who is playing?' we demanded.

'This is not a concert,' said Mamma, bringing the rabbit out of the hat with immense gusto, 'and it is you who are going to play. You are to show Maurus Kisch what you can do and if you are good enough he will give you lessons till you go up for your scholarships.'

We could not speak. Kisch was the best piano-teacher in London who would trouble with quite young players. It was marvellous. Glory was about to begin: after this we were going to live a heavenly life of playing and doing nothing else, playing the best music with superb orchestras in halls big enough to give the music its due amount of room, to give the tone we got from the keyboard a chance to spread and show its quality. But it was also terrible. We might be no good after all. Mamma might just think we could play because she loved us. But Mary and I nodded at each other across the table, and said again what we had been saying throughout our childhood: 'It will be all right,' and we kissed and hugged Mamma.

'Now, for you, Cordelia,' Mamma went on happily. We drew back disconcerted. Was Cordelia to have lessons too? That would be a terrible waste of money. But after a shocked instant we quite saw that Mamma had to do this.

'And you, Cordelia,' Mamma went on happily, 'you are to go to the Regent Studios, in the Marylebone Road, on Wednesday at half-past two, to play to Miss Irene Meyer.'

Cordelia said nothing, and we knew why.

'She is an excellent teacher,' Mamma continued, pushing up her voice into cheerful curves. 'I have asked several people, and they all recommended her.'

'Did they?' said Cordelia coldly. 'I have never heard of her.' Then she burst out with the question which was, from her point of view, quite logical. 'If Mary and Rose are to be given the chance of being taught by Maurus Kisch, why am I not to be taught by Hans Fechter?'

We all saw her point. The two names were on the same level. But Mamma was more sharply pricked by that point than the rest of us. She cried, 'Oh, child, never think of Hans Fechter.'

'And why not?' asked Cordelia.

'He is a very cruel man,' answered Mamma. 'Never think of playing to him. I knew him when he was young, and he was terrible then, and now that he is older they say that he is worse, he has a tongue like a whip.'

'I wonder why you are so sure that he would want to use that whip on me,' said Cordelia, and soon after rose from the table and left the room, though we had not finished tea.

Mamma shook her head. 'Hans Fechter. God forbid.'

'Oh, poor Mamma,' we said.

'No, poor Cordelia,' she corrected us.

'She is like somebody in Shakespeare when they get an idea in their heads and go on and on,' said Richard Quin. 'You know, like Macbeth over the crown of Scotland.'

'Why do people make such a fuss about *Hamlet*, as if it was the greatest of all the plays?' Mary asked. 'Nothing in *Hamlet* ever strikes one as very like anything in real life, but people are always

363

behaving like Macbeth and Othello and King Lear. Our head-mistress is just like King Lear when she goes on and on about how we all lack *esprit de corps*, though really we behave reasonably well, and she should be contented.'

'I wish there was some more of Hamlet in all of you,' said Mamma. 'I would treasure a little indecision amongst you. He carried the thing too far, but I would like to see Cordelia unable to make up her mind about going in for a scholarship and the rest of you showing some hesitation in commenting on her. What a delight it is to have Richard Quin and Rosamund, who do not seem to want anything very much.'

'Oh, we do,' said Richard Quin. 'I want to be liked. And so does Rosamund.'

She threw back her head and exclaimed, 'Oh, yes, I must be liked,' with an earnestness that surprised us and made us laugh. But really she was very alarming. The firelight played over her face and made the barley-sugar curls lying on her shoulders a brighter gold, and there was a fullness about her like the Muscatel grapes we sometimes saw in shops, and all these things put together meant that she was more grown-up than any of us. It was tame to be a grown-up; and she engaged in none of our mental adventures, she was certainly stupid, nobody ever had claimed she was not. Also she was quiet, she was neat-handed and slow in movement, she looked forward to earning a staid livelihood as a nurse, she always told us what was the prudent thing to do. Yet it might be that she was going to be the least tamed of us all. Everything about her was contradictory.

'How I wish Hans Fechter wanted to be liked,' said Mamma; 'oh, children, I hope Cordelia will get Fechter out of her mind. But I will go and see Miss Beevor tomorrow evening, though it is very tiresome to have to argy-bargy about my own child with a stranger. I resent it that she is a stranger, I think of her as the strange woman that King Solomon wrote about, though he could not have had a more different type of woman in mind.'

But the next evening Kate ushered Miss Beevor into the room. Of course Mamma groaned aloud, as she was apt to do at the appearance of this harbinger of evil; and indeed the passage of time had made Miss Beevor's appearance even less pleasing to us. It was not that her taste in dress had worsened, she was still faith-ful to Pre-Raphaelite costume, and had abandoned her favourite violet and sage-green only for a dull rusty-red, and as usual she carried a white hide bag inscribed in pokerwork with the name of a foreign town. This time it was Venezia. We missed the mosaic brooch representing doves drinking from a fountain, but instead she wore an even less attractive trinket, a large heart-shaped gold locket, with a lute in repoussé work on it. But the alteration we really did not like was in her expression and bearing. She looked roguish and younger and plumper, and we knew that it was Cordelia's career that was nourishing her.

After the first groan Mamma regained her self-control and greeted Miss Beevor civilly, and said, 'Yes, indeed,' when Miss Beevor said, 'It is time we talked of Cordelia's future. Twenty-seven concerts last year.' It was apparent she thought of those idiotic occasions as a score over Mamma. 'I think we must all realise, mustn't we, that Cordelia's technique has improved immensely.' When my mother did not answer Miss Beevor touched the large heart-shaped locket on her bosom as if it were a cross and she were drawing strength from it. 'It had occurred to me that perhaps, as I understand you have a very lucky windfall, on which I congratulate you, we might hope for some lessons for Cordelia from someone worthier than myself. I've always known I'm not worthy, you know.'

My mother could still find nothing to say.

'We had thought,' said Miss Beevor humbly, 'of Hans Fechter.'

My mother shook her head.

'But why not?' asked Miss Beevor. She flushed suddenly, she trembled, her voice broke when she repeated, 'But why not?'

Mamma at last found her voice. 'Miss Beevor, I beg of you, never let poor Cordelia go near him. He is a terrible man.'

'Well, if it comes to that,' said Miss Beevor wildly, 'lots of people are terrible. Terrible in their refusal to see what's under their nose, terrible in their lack of natural affection. But what is terrible about Hans Fechter? Surely he has the highest reputation as a teacher?' But suddenly she clasped the locket. 'Or — can you mean — is he a Bohemian character? Do you feel that a beautiful girl like Cordelia would not be safe with him?'

'Fechter a Bohemian!' exclaimed Mamma. 'I should think not, Mrs. Fechter beats him. No, no, Miss Beevor, I do not mean that literally. And the case against Fechter is that he is a first-rate teacher who is bitter because he tried to be a concert violinist himself and could not succeed because he is not an attractive performer, and of course that is not fair, though fairness has nothing to do with the case, and he is too just to be harsh to his good pupils, but on the ones who are untalented he avenges himself cruelly.'

Miss Beevor said shakily, tugging at the locket, 'Cordelia is not untalented. I wish you would not call her "poor Cordelia!" "Poor Cordelia" indeed!'

Again Mamma fell into that silence which in fact proceeded from her love and pity for Cordelia, but which the other woman could not take except as a sign of craziness, or a deliberate and uncivil provocation, based on spite. 'Well, anyway,' she said fiercely, 'there is no use for you to worry. My old teacher, Signor Sala, has said he'll take Cordelia. He retired some years ago and went back to live in Milan, but his wife has just died, and he is returning to London to be near his daughter, who is married here. He heard Cordelia play yesterday, and he has offered to teach her for nothing until she goes up and gets her scholarship at the Victoria School of Music this spring. So there is nothing for you to worry about.'

'How hard you try to make things easy for Cordelia,' said Mamma, at last.

'Most people would think it a privilege to make things easy for Cordelia,' said Miss Beevor grimly. She looked at my mother as if she were trying to puzzle something out; then lifted her arms and began to scrabble among the ends of her hair underneath her Pre-Raphaelite bun at the back of her neck, for the clasp of the golden chain from which her locket hung. 'Look what I had made for me the other day,' she said. She held the locket out to us on the palm of her hand and pressed the spring. We looked down on a tiny coloured photograph of Cordelia playing the violin.

'I took the photograph myself,' said Miss Beevor, 'on the lawn one day, with my Brownie, and a friend of mine who is very artistic coloured it for me. He lives up in Scotland, and Cordelia cut off one of her curls for me, and I sent it up to him to copy. And I had the locket made for me by a cousin of mine who works for Liberty's. Isn't it lovely? Take it and look at it closely, I don't mind.'

Mamma took the locket in her own hand and murmured, 'What a charming idea.' She went on staring at it until Miss Beevor gave a little laugh and said, 'You know you're really quite proud of her in your heart of hearts,' and took it from her, and joined the chain again about her neck. 'If things go as well as I hope they will in the spring,' she announced, 'we must give you a locket just like this in celebration.'

'Thank you,' said Mamma.

'And things will go well,' Miss Beevor promised defiantly, 'Signor Sala is a wonderful teacher, and Cordelia will learn a great deal from him besides just music. He is a most cultured man. A great student of Dante. *Nel mezzo del cammin di nostra vita Mi ritrovai per una selva oscura.* Well, well, I must be going now, and I am sure that in a short time everything will seem much, much clearer before our troubled eyes.'

When I came back from letting her out of the house I found that Mamma was sitting on the floor by the fire, as we children did and grown-ups hardly ever did in those days. 'Well,' she said, 'I was wishing that your father was here. But even if he had been he could have been no help. Though would it not be wonderful, wonderful, Rose, to have him back, just for ten minutes, five minutes, sitting here. But I say he could have done nothing here. Oh, poor Cordelia, poor Cordelia, how that silly woman degrades her with her love. How queer it was to see your sister's lovely eyes painted the same blue as the sea in a coloured picture postcard. It is not fair, that you and Mary should be able to play, and that she should not. It is not fair that this fool should fall in love with her. Yes, we find ourselves in a dark wood.'

XVII

WHEN WE got to the Panmure Hall, Mr. Kisch, who was very old and had a grey pointed beard and wore a black velvet skull-cap, kissed Mamma on both cheeks and told two young men who were just going away that this was the great Clare Keith, who had retired far too young and had played the Mozart Concerto in C minor and Schumann's Carnival better than any other woman who had ever lived. Then he looked at us in a manner indicating that it had occurred to him also that perhaps Mamma thought we could play the piano only because she loved us. Then he took up the list of our repertoire which she had written out for him, and raised his eyebrows and asked, 'Have they really got all this music off the notes?' Quite disagreeably he told first Mary and me to play some Chopin Etudes. He asked Mary for the second Etude in F Minor, which puts you through the hoop of maintaining staccato and legato in the same hand, and he gave me the first of the Grandes Etudes, Op. 10, Number One, because it is a fiend to play at the proper tempo, and you need wide oscillation of the wrist. And he gave her the Revolutionary one and me the Black Key one, and after that it turned out that it was all right.

But neither then nor at any of the lessons did we get the sort of reassurance we had desired. It had seemed to us certain that if Mr. Kisch thought that we were really good he would burst out about it and be pleased. But of course in the practice room we said goodbye for ever to praise, which is the prerogative of the amateur. At every point of the professional's life it vanishes when it is within sight. A teacher must dwell on the faults and not on the merits of any pupil whom he recognises as an artist, and once the pupil becomes a public performer he develops a double personality and becomes teacher and pupil. The favourable notice, the flowers in the artist's room, the applause, the crowds, are evidences of success, but they are not praise. They cannot wipe out the self-censure for the lifeless cadenza, the smudged introduction of a theme. But there was some consolation as we found ourselves accepted members of a friendly tribe. There was a day when we stood with half a dozen of Mr. Kisch's other pupils while he played us passages from the Beethoven sonatas as he had heard Liszt play them long ago in Budapest, and nobody seemed to think we had no right to be there. Another day we went to hear Saint-Saëns give a recital of his own piano-music, and by chance we sat next to the red-haired girl who came to Mr. Kisch the hour after we did, and we had tea together afterwards, and she did not seem to be waiting to ridicule what we said. This was innocent living after the long criminality of school. It was not, of course, that our school-fellows and our teachers had belonged to an inferior breed of human being; it was that the horrid necessity of a general education must needs inflict on most children so many boring hours, when they are taught the subjects which do not interest them, that they must find refuge in spite, while their teachers grow irascible through teaching bored children. But here our studies were also gratifications of a passion. The young men and women standing round Mr. Kisch's piano had no time to think of malicious comment on each other because they were absorbed in watching the flail-like movements of his arms by which he drew from his piano a Dionysiac brilliance such as Liszt and his con-temporaries gave their audiences not to be achieved by the singing and relaxed technique of our time. The red-haired girl and Mary and I were not so much aware of each other as we were of the astonishing crystalline purity of Saint-Saëns' touch, which so denatured the instrument on which he played that the lush ornament of his own music vanished beneath his icy finger-tips and became austere as frost patterns on a window-pane. We were to learn, of course at a later date, that the world of music is not without its petty jealousies and resentment, since though musicians practice and contemplate a noble art, they are, like school-children, confined within a competitive world. But it is never so bad as school, and when we entered the world of happy apprenticeship we thought ourselves in heaven.

It was a pity, of course, that at home Cordelia was giving, with much more intensity, her performance in the character of a young genius preparing for a scholarship. Mamma was not alarmed by this. She had visited Signor Sala at his daughter's home in Brixton and had returned full of a persuasion that he was part of a comic dream of the Creator, and that laughter was to be his only effect. She found his musical attainments no better than she had feared, and she did not believe his story of having been a professor of Milan Conservatoire, but she was ready to forgive much to the old humbug because he had received her sitting in a high-back gilt throne, obviously part of an opera set, with two panels of machine-made tapestry on the wall behind him, one representing Verdi and the other Mascagni, rather larger than life-size, each at his country-house. She was not frivolous in her amusement. Because she thought him a rogue, she could not believe Miss Beevor's story that he was teaching Cordelia for nothing. She was sure that Miss Beevor was probably paying him substantial fees in secret, and while this set her the problem of how she was to sweep aside the pretence and repay her, it also made her certain that the bad old man would advise Cordelia not to try the scholarship that year, but to take lessons from him for another twelvemonth.

'It will be all right,' she said, in the words we children had so often used. 'And I do not know why you two, Mary and Rose, should get so angry with Cordelia. What harm does she do you, playing her violin with that old rogue? You are nowhere near her for the most of the day, when you should be working she is not even in the same house. When she is playing the violin in Brixton, how can it prevent you playing the piano in Lovegrove?'

'As I play the piano here in Lovegrove, or even in Wigmore Street,' said Mary holding her temples, 'I can feel Cordelia playing the violin in Brixton.'

'Yes, yes, I know,' sighed Mamma. 'It is like genius. Like the way that everybody all over Europe could feel Paganini playing or Rachel acting. Only it is the opposite of genius. But you should have pity on her.'

'Rose and I have a right to pity too,' said Mary.

'Do not be absurd,' said Mamma. She hesitated awkwardly. 'Something will happen,' she said faintly.

We realised that it had occurred to Mamma, as it had occurred to us at the Thameside Town Hall, that Cordelia was very pretty and might get married. But that now seemed to us a vain hope, her dedication had become so extreme. At school prayers we still stood on the floor of the hall, while she was with the highest class on the platform, ranged on each side of the headmistress's lectern; and we noted that she appeared among the other girls as a nun among the laity, so deeply was she disciplined by determination to polish her repertoire of Weniawski and Chaminade to the highest degree of perfection, so different from her companions' adolescent dreaminess was the precise anticipation in her neat small features. But in the spring we saw a sudden change. One evening she left the house with Miss Beevor, not so tense with the effort of impersonation as was usual when she was to fulfil a professional engagement, because the evening was to be something of a party for her. She was to play at a banquet held by a volunteer regiment in a neighbouring suburb, Ringwood, and the Colonel of the Regiment, a banker, had an Italian wife who had been an opera singer, a coloratura soprano, named Madame Corando, and she was going to be there. Mamma and she had known each other in their young days, and when she met Cordelia at local charity concerts, of which she was often a patroness, she always made a great fuss of her. So before this concert Cordelia had dressed with special care, and had gone away looking very lovely in a cherub style, with her pert nose looking perter because she was wearing a little wreath of white flowers and green leaves, set rather to the back of her head. At supper we spoke of her happily, knowing that she would be living part of that evening easily, not as the taut slave of her obsession, but as a pretty girl. But long before we expected her she was with us again; and it was a cab, not a car, that had stopped at our gate, so Madame Corando and her husband had not brought her home, as they usually did. She came into the sitting-room and stared at us absently, absorbed in some remote calculations, and we stared back at her in wonder, for she was not the same. She had taken off her wreath and was slowly turning it in her hands, and her face was heavy as if she were brooding on something with such fierce concentration that she had no energy left to keep her muscles taut. As she drew off her coat, she was thinking so little of what she was doing, so much of something else, that she might have been a sleep-walker, her sleep disordered for a great cause.

Mamma said mildly, 'Your dress looks very nice, dear.'

Cordelia started, looked down at her skirt, and ran a disparaging hand down it. She did not answer.

371

'Did it go well?' asked Mamma.

'Very well,' said Cordelia; 'they asked for a second encore, but I did not give it to them.'

'And how was Madame Corando?' asked Mamma.

After a pause Cordelia said, 'She talks too loud,' and added coldly, 'she is a very common woman.' A flash of triumph irrelevant to what she was saying passed across her face.

'So are many excellent musicians,' said Mamma. At this Cordelia made a slow, impatient gesture, and turned from us, and went out of the room, still moving like a sleep-walker.

'Now, what does that mean?' pondered Mamma, but without much anxiety. Cordelia had spirit, if something disagreeable had happened at the dinner, her sturdiness would have been up in arms to defend her pride. But it seemed more probable that she was entranced by some prospect which had opened before her, so novel that she did not know how to speak of it to us, who represented the familiar in her life. Mary and I spoke with perplexity of the change that night when we were undressing in our room, which we no longer shared with Cordelia, who had been given Papa's room. After we had put out the light, and were lying side by side in our beds, Mary said, 'Do you think that she can have fallen in love with someone at that dinner? We are almost old enough for that sort of thing, I suppose.'

The darkness seemed hostile and unexplored. I broke the silence by saying, 'Anyway she is, we might be too young, she isn't. Lots of people in Spain and Italy are married at her age.'

'But would she meet anybody at a Territorial Army dinner in Ringwood that she would want to marry?' Mary wondered.

'Well,' I said, 'if the Colonel of the Regiment was good enough for Madame Corando to marry, there might be someone else in it who would do for Cordelia.'

'Please God, please God,' said Mary, 'let it be that she has fallen in love with somebody, and let him fall in love with her, and let them get married soon.'

'No, no,' I said. 'Stop, Mary, please. Of course you wouldn't get a prayer answered if it was wrong, but still we ought to remember that Cordelia might not be happy, she is young to make up her mind, and she can't have seen him more than once.'

'Well, lots of people have fallen in love like that,' said Mary, 'and anyway she is sure to be happy for a time.' She was silent and I felt she was going on praying in the darkness; and was a little worried about it till I fell asleep. Cordelia took things, I realised, less passionately and more seriously than we did.

It appeared possible that Mary's prayers had been answered. Cordelia's aspect at school prayers, when she stood with the girls of her class on the platform beside the schoolmistress and we watched her from the floor, was now completely different. Now she no longer looked like a nun among the laity, she looked wilder and more passionate than the girls beside her, and she did not prevent herself from looking radiant even in the middle of the most melancholy Lenten hymn. But what was giving her that radiance had not happened yet, she had the bloom on her that comes of expectation. Also, if it had happened there would not have come those other moments when she forgot to bow her head in prayer, because she was staring straight in front of her, terrified lest what she hoped for would never be hers. All this corresponded with what we had read of love in books. But I was not so happy over this as Mary was, for it seemed to me that I recognised at times the bright falsity, the glittering misjudgment, which often shone about her when she played the violin.

But there was much to confirm our suspicions. One night at supper Cordelia asked Mamma sleepily if she could go up to London on Saturday morning with Rosamund to choose a new coat and skirt. She added, when she had been given permission, that it was going to be a grown-up coat and skirt. Mamma said, 'Well, I have seen things in the shops ready for Easter, though it seems early yet to buy for the summer, and all this summer you will still be at school. But it is your own money, and of course you will certainly be leaving school by the autumn, and if you get something really good it will last. But remember that it is not sensible to buy before you need, for you get interest on your money so long as it is in the Post Office.'

Cordelia did not reply, as we would have expected her if she had been the same as she used to be, by pointing out, impatiently, how little that interest was. She simply continued to live in a trance; and a few days later she walked into the sitting-room wearing the new coat and skirt. At this period the scissors had suddenly got to work on women's clothes. We were still not fully enfranchised from the load of textiles that our sex had been condemned to wear, but we were transformed, so far as the weight we had to carry and our agility, from cows to the heavier kind of antelope. Skirts were still long, but they were tubular, and were slit up the hem. The narrowness of Cordelia's skirt turned her into a walking pillar, slender and rounded and strong, built of some warm stone with the light shining on it, for the cloth was a pale golden fawn; and on her short red-gold curls she wore a round brown hat wreathed with creamy flowers. She was carrying her head high, her short nose, so exquisitely drawn, with its tiny triangular flatness between the point and the nostrils, was literally turned up and her pure rounded chin was raised. In her hand she carried her violin bow as if it were a sceptre. 'Do I look all right?' she asked carelessly, but she listened fiercely to our answer. Up till now she had always been confident that her appearance was good enough to help her win applause from her concert audiences, and that had been her only interest in it; but now she evidently hoped to buy with it some object on which she herself set a higher price. She stayed in the room for some time, standing upright, for narrow skirts crushed easily; but was far from us, even in another season of the year, for though Lent was still cold about us, she was carrying about her a private springtime, glowing in her thin clothes under some sun we could not see.

When she had gone Mary said, 'She has bought that coat and skirt because she expects whoever it is she is in love with to call on Mamma and ask to take her out somewhere.'

'But where could he take her?' I said doubtfully. 'It isn't summer, they can't go on the river.'

'Young men in magazine stories and novels take girls they want to marry to all sorts of places,' said Mary. 'Hurlingham and Ranelagh, oh, there must be places open at this time of year. People don't fall in love just in summer. Oh, please God, let it happen.'

'Don't do that,' I said, 'until we know that he is really nice.'

'I keep on telling you, she is sure to be happy for a time,' said Mary, 'and if it goes wrong, we will have got our scholarships and after that we will make money, and we can get her a divorce. The thing is to stop her playing now.'

Though no young man appeared in Lovegrove Place, Cordelia's behaviour continued to support our theory. She now took great interest in the post, which she explained as anxiety about the date of a big evening concert, which had been postponed because of a death, and might be fixed for some date when she was already booked. But such an anxiety would not have been burning, nor would it have given place to a burning satisfaction. And the day after she ceased to watch the post brought confirmation which even Rosamund had to admit was impressive, though she had never agreed with us that Cordelia might be in love, and had said that since we were always getting into states she did not see how we could fail to recognise that was all that was happening to our eldest sister too. 'Why, if she were in love,' she stammered, 'she would look different. Not like this at all.' But that morning Cordelia left for school early, telling Mamma that she wanted to speak to one of the teachers before prayers. But when Mary and Rosamund and I got to school she was not there at all. When we came home at one o'clock we learned that she had told Mamma that she was going to have luncheon with Miss Beevor. We felt a painful sense of crisis. We would never have dared to play truant from school, and Cordelia was more law-abiding than we were; also Cordelia was very truthful. Then Kate said to us, with an air of knowing nothing, that when Cordelia had left that morning she had been carrying a large cardboard-box and a big paper bag, and we went up and looked in her room, and the new coat and skirt and hat were gone.

'You see,' Mary said, 'she has gone to meet him, and probably his mother, and they will come back and tell Mamma that they are engaged.'

But I did not like it. The empty wardrobe looked wrong, as Papa's empty study looked wrong. And Rosamund shrugged an indifference I did not think she felt.

Anything might have happened. So Mary and I were not altogether surprised when, on our way back from school that afternoon, alone because Rosamund had gone to do some shopping, turning from the High Street into Lovegrove Place, we saw Miss Beevor ahead of us, hastening towards our home, and saw too that she was agitated. She was walking very fast, and sometimes trotted, till her long copper-coloured dress caught round her ankles, and her big feathered hat fell awry.

'Look, look,' said Mary, 'she is in a terrible state. I tell you it is not all imagination, it must be just what I thought. Cordelia has run away with someone and has written to tell Miss Beevor that she will not go on with her music. Come on, come on, let us ask her.'

When Miss Beevor heard our running feet she turned, closed her eyes on seeing us, and leaned against the railings. As we reached her, she breathed bitterly, 'I thought it was Cordelia.'

'What is the matter?' asked Mary. 'What has happened to her?'

Miss Beevor sobbed, and began to trot on again towards our house. We walked beside her, pressing her to explain, so that we could be prepared if there should be news to break to Mamma. We knew Miss Beevor to be very stupid and she might be making a fuss about nothing, but we had to be sure. But she only made sounds expressive of impatience and disgust, and waved us away. Her hands were bare, which was startling in those days; and as she made hostile gestures against us, she said in accents appealing for sympathy, 'I have lost my gloves, that too,' and bursting into tears again, scuttled on quite fast till she got to our gate.

There we saw at once that whatever bad news Miss Beevor had received, it had been heard here also. The front door was open and as we mounted the steps we saw that the handbag Mamma usually carried about with her was cast down on the mat. We hurried in, brushing past Miss Beevor, who was crying, 'I couldn't even get a cab, there is always a cab at the station, this day of all days there wasn't one.' She followed us into the sitting-room, which was empty. But the french window into the garden was open, and Mamma was standing on the lawn and looking up at the window of the little bedroom which had been Papa's, which was now Cordelia's.

We ran towards her, calling out, 'What has happened?' and Mamma took no notice, her eyes were fixed on the empty window. But when Miss Beevor was making her way down the iron steps into the garden, she slipped and fell to the bottom on to the gravel path, squealing as people do when they have reached such a pitch of misery that the inorganic world turns against them, and heels come off their shoes, and stones wait to bruise their knees. Mamma heard her, turned her great staring eyes upon her, and said to us, 'Pick that poor idiot up.' But Miss Beevor's frenzy had brought her to her feet before we could get to her, and she hobbled towards Mamma, crying out, 'I have lost Cordelia, I could not help it, she ran away from me.'

'She is here,' said Mamma. 'She is in her room. She has locked the door. What have you done to her?'

'I did nothing, she ran away from me,' said Miss Beevor, 'oh, thank God she is safe.'

'Safe?' said Mamma, 'what did you do to her?'

'I did nothing,' said Miss Beevor, 'what have I ever done to Cordelia but love her?'

'She has been with you, you tell me yourself, and she came home half an hour ago, older than I am. What did you do to her?'

'I know, I know,' said Miss Beevor. 'Oh, her face. Her lovely little face. She looked hard, cruel, just like you. Oh, Cordelia.'

'Well, what did you do to her?' said Mamma.

'I did nothing,' said Miss Beevor, 'it was that horrible man.'

'What horrible man?' asked Mamma. 'Stop clutching your hat, I cannot see your face.'

'Why,' said Miss Beevor, 'Hans Fechter.'

Mamma looked upward at the windows of Cordelia's room and stretched out her arms. 'My lamb, my lamb,' she said. Then she raged at Miss Beevor, 'Did I not tell you not to take her near him?'

'I could not help it,' said Miss Beevor. 'It was that vulgar woman, Madame Corando. She never should have been allowed to come near Cordelia. She has been married three times.'

'What, Giulia Corando sent Cordelia to Hans Fechter?' exclaimed Mamma. 'I do not believe it.'

'No, no, it was not like that at all,' said Miss Beevor. 'It was at that banquet. Cordelia played beautifully. She did, she did. If she did not, then there is no such thing as playing beautifully. And Madame Corando complimented her, and Cordelia thanked her, and told her what hopes we had for the scholarship, and then suddenly the woman was not nice any more. She said that being a professional was very different from being even a good amateur. And oh, then it became very unpleasant.'

'But all the same I cannot believe that Giulia Corando could have been ill-natured enough to send Cordelia to Hans Fechter,' cried Mamma.

'No, no,' said Miss Beevor, querulously, 'I keep on telling you it was not like that at all. But Cordelia always said it was impossible to tell you anything because you would not listen. It all happened because Cordelia held her ground and said that she was studying with Signor Sala. Then this dreadful woman said, "What, not old Silvio Sala?" and when Cordelia said yes, she burst out into the most vulgar laugh, everybody looked round, and she said he was an old rascal, and told a long story about how his father was a macaroni manufacturer who was mad about music, and he had determined to have a son who was a violinist, and he had pushed him as a boy, but he had never been any good, and the old father had left all his money to a nephew who really was a good violinist, and so the son had just had to get on as he could, and had swaggered about and pretended all sorts of things, and had said he had taught in Milan Conservatory, though he had never seen the inside of the place. Oh, the lies she told. Yet, after all, they may be true.'

'In the name of goodness tell me how Cordelia got to Hans Fechter,' demanded Mamma.

'I am coming to that,' said Miss Beevor. 'After that Cordelia would not stay any longer, she insisted on going home, and in the dressing-room I remember now, in the dressing-room she gave me such a hard look, I should have known that she was going to turn against me, though how she could, when she knew how I loved her.'

'Never mind that now,' said Mamma, 'go on, go on.'

'Then she told me that she did not believe what Madame Corando had said, but all the same she was afraid that she might lose her self-confidence because of it, and she asked me to arrange for her to play to Hans Fechter, and so I said I would, and we were so happy coming back in the train. And now we shall never be happy again.'

'What did Fechter say to Cordelia?' demanded Mamma, digging her nails into the palms of her hands.

'I do not know,' said Miss Beevor. 'Oh, he is a horrible man. And he was against us from the start. When we went in he looked at me in a most insulting way, and told me to go and sit in the hall while Cordelia played. Then——' she choked and stood wagging her head this way and that.

'Then what happened?' pressed my mother, shaking her, though not so violently as we had feared she might.

'How do I know?' said Miss Beevor. 'She came out of his room after about twenty minutes and walked through the hall and did not look at me. I spoke to her and she took no notice. She did not even wait for the servant who was coming up to open the door, she opened it herself, and went out into the street. And oh, her face. I could not have believed that she could ever look like that.'

'It was for you to follow her,' said Mamma. 'You had taken her to that house which I had warned you she should never go near.'

'I tried to follow her,' said Miss Beevor, 'but that horrible man came out and said the most dreadful things to me.'

'I told you he was cruel,' said Mamma. 'He would know the truth, but who else who knew enough to know it would also be low enough to tell it to you? Cruel, cruel. But why did you stay and let this brute jeer at you instead of taking care of Cordelia? You knew yourself that she was the only one of you three who mattered.'

'He stood between me and the door,' wept Miss Beevor.

'The brute, the brute,' said Mamma. 'But Cordelia?'

'When he said that people like me who encouraged children with no talent ought to be shot, I hit him with my umbrella,' wept Miss Beevor.

'I am glad,' said Mamma. 'But Cordelia, Cordelia.'

'That made him angry, and he opened the door and told me to leave his house as if that was not what I was trying to do, and all the time I had been hoping that Cordelia would be waiting for me outside, but she had gone.'

'She made the long journey home all by herself,' mourned Mamma, looking up at the bedroom windows.

'That was not my fault,' said Miss Beevor, 'I rushed off to Great Portland Street Station, and while I was crossing the bridge our train was coming in, and I saw her on the platform, and I called down to her, and told her to wait for me. But she looked up at me as if I were a stranger, and got into the train, and when I got down to the platform, it had started. Oh, Cordelia, Cordelia, I love her so.'

'Yes,' said Mamma, 'this is the worst of life, that love does not give us common sense but is a sure way of losing it. We love people, and we say that we are going to do more for them than friendship, but it makes such fools of us that we do far less, indeed sometimes what we do could be mistaken for the work of hatred.'

'Have I done so much harm to Cordelia?' asked Miss Beevor.

'Of course you have,' said Mamma, 'but you have no reason to blame yourself. You have only followed the general rule. But what matters at the moment is that Cordelia has locked her bedroom door.'

'To be alone, I suppose,' said Miss Beevor. 'Up till now she has always been able to come to me when she felt miserable. But now she has turned against me she will have nowhere to go.'

'Yes, yes, I must not forget that you have been very kind to her in her terrible discontent,' said Mamma. 'Children, children, Mary and Rose, you must always remember that Miss Beevor has been very kind to Cordelia, she gave her much that we could not have given her. But I am so afraid about Cordelia. When she came in she must have gone straight down to the kitchen, she had just come up the basement staircase and she passed me and went up to her room, and it seemed to me that she was carrying something in her hand.'

'She passed you too without speaking?' asked Miss Beevor.

'Yes,' said Mamma. 'But it has happened to me before. My husband once passed me in the High Street and looked at me like a stranger.'

'Your husband, yes, I suppose so,' said Miss Beevor, 'but Cordelia, I could not have believed that her lovely little face would look like that.' She burst into noisy tears, then suddenly caught her breath, and was rigid. 'Something in her hands? You mean, a bottle? Something that might have been poison?'

'You see how imperfect love is,' said Mamma. 'I said what should have indicated to you that she was in danger, and you did not notice it, you were absorbed in the pain she had given you by looking at you as if she did not know you. Yet your love for her is the best you can do. And my love for her is the best I can do, and both appear to be useless. And love makes some promises about being useful. But here am I, having beaten on her door and got no answer, and here are you, and neither of us knows what to do.'

'Shall I go and get the man who mended Kate's hair-trunk, just a few doors down the High Street?' I asked. 'He opened the trunk lock, he said he could open any lock.'

'That is the difficulty,' said Mamma. 'I do not know whether that would be wise. I do not really believe that any of you children will kill yourselves in any circumstances. I am sure you all have a dogged intention of living to the last possible moment, who would not? So I think it improbable that Cordelia will kill herself. But she lives by pride. What a gamble it is to have children! One can see it by the names one gives them. Here is Mary who is so fierce that she should have an Old Testament name, and Rose who is like a thorn-bush, and Cordelia who lives by pride. Well, if I get a strange man to break down her door, she will never forgive me. But on the other hand it is a heavy risk to take. She had something in her hand she did not want me to see.'

'There is a ladder in the stables,' said Mary. 'We can get it, and one of us will go up and get in at the window and open her door from the inside.'

'That is no use,' said Mamma. 'I have been to look at the ladder. The iron steps would prevent you from putting it near enough to the wall to reach the window. I will go back and knock on the door.'

We all moved towards the house, but halted as Richard Quin ran down the iron steps and crossed the lawn to us. He took Mamma's hands and said, 'Kate says that Cordelia has locked herself in her room and does not answer, what does this mean?'

'Cordelia has just been told she cannot play by Hans Fechter,' said Mamma, 'and she cannot bear it. She has locked herself into her room and we are afraid she may have taken poison.'

'I think not,' said Richard Quin, 'she will outlive you and me by many years. But she should have answered you, that is rude and inconvenient, and quite futile, for Mamma, you have not noticed it but I am now so big that there is not a door in this house I could not smash in with two minutes' gentle effort. And I will smash her door in now. Come along.'

We followed him submissively into the house. As we went through the sitting-room Miss Beevor moaned, 'She is all I have,' tottered, and fell over an armchair. As Mamma went upstairs she said, 'Poor idiot, it would have been so much kinder if that woman had been exposed at birth.' When we reached Cordelia's door she rattled the door-knob and called to her begging her just to say that she was all right. There was silence; and Richard

Quin put his shoulder to the door, drew back a moment to smile at Mamma and to shout, 'Cordelia, Cordelia, if you do not open the door I am going to break it in.' We heard a faint moan, and the panel split before his strength, he slipped in his hand and turned the key on the other side of the lock, and we all rushed into the room.

Cordelia was lying diagonally across the bed, her head on the extreme edge of the pillow, one shoulder right off the mattress, one arm hanging to the floor. Her long tight skirt made her look like a fallen pillar. It was not through ill-will that she had not answered. She was incapable of the smallest movement. The greenish colour of her skin, the stillness of her nostrils and her parted lips, and the motionless spread screen of her eyelashes on her cheeks, showed that the course of her life had very nearly stopped. 'Look,' whispered Mary to Richard Quin and me. Cordelia's right arm hung limp to the floor, but her right hand was not limp. It clasped the bottle of salts of lemon Kate used for cleaning the sinks and lavatories, and she was turning it round and round in her palm, while her fingers tried to get the cork out. But they were not trying very hard. They looked stubborn and sensible, as all of her had looked till now, and they were twiddling the cork with the intention of failure. But she was trying to force them to get it out. Richard Quin bent down and snatched up the bottle and was gone from the room in a moment, then was back to obey Mamma, when she cried, 'Oh, my poor lamb. Lift her up, she cannot lie like that, she will fall off the bed.' He raised Cordelia in his arms and set her in the middle of the bed, and held her up so that Mamma could kneel and look into her face and promise her, 'My dear, my dear, just wait and you will see that all this does not matter.' But Cordelia remained still as a doll in his arms, and with a rising voice Mamma implored her, 'Speak to me, dear, and tell me you are all right.'

At that Cordelia stirred, moved her head from side to side, opened her eyes, looked at Mamma, and at each of us in turn, then groaned, 'If I am not to be a famous violinist, how am I ever to get away from you all?'

Mamma was silent for only a second before she answered, 'We shall manage somehow, dear, do not be afraid. Perhaps you might like to have a year at school abroad. But we will talk of that tomorrow, now you must have some tea and take things

382

quietly. I will send Kate up to you and you must undress and go to bed properly. There is no place like bed when you are upset. Come along, children.'

Tenderly Richard Quin laid Cordelia back on the pillows, and we all left the room, as quietly as we could. Mamma was going into the sitting-room when she checked herself. 'Poor Miss Beevor may have come round, and we will not be able to talk in front of her. Oh, the wretched, generous woman, what is to fill her life now? But there is something I must say to you, I will just have to say it out here. Children, you must not be hurt because Cordelia put what she feels into words so badly.' Then our pallor, our stony horror, struck home to her. 'Why, did you not know this was how Cordelia felt! Oh, children, what a shock for you!'

'Have we been horrible to her? We didn't mean to be,' said Mary, and I said, 'We could not pretend about her playing because we knew it was going to lead to this some day. Somebody was bound to be awful to her sooner or later. But we love her.'

'Do not trouble yourselves about this,' said Mamma. 'You have been far better to her than I would have expected, seeing what you are. You must not think of it again. No, I am talking nonsense. You are not such fools that I can persuade you that what your sister said did not come from the depths of her heart, or that what she meant could possibly be pleasing to you. So try to understand it as if you were grown-up, and of course you nearly are. Cordelia wants to go away and leave us, and has been playing the violin furiously in an attempt to get the means of going away and leaving us, for reasons which cannot be laid to your charge. They bring an accusation against your father and me, and we cannot answer it. Yet again the fault is not completely ours.'

'Nobody in this family could possibly accuse you of anything,' said Richard Quin, 'and we all know that we could accuse Papa of various things but it would be a very silly and ungrateful thing to do.'

'Listen, listen, you must try to understand. You see, Cordelia and you alike have had a dreadful childhood. But you three, Mary and Rose and Richard Quin — I have not been wrong, have I? Children, you must tell me honestly if I am

383

wrong — but though I blush with guilt for having given you such a childhood, I think you have quite enjoyed it. Except for your father going away, I do not think you would choose to have had anything very different in our life.'

'Of course we have enjoyed every moment of it,' said Mary.

'Why wouldn't we?' I said. 'We are not soft.'

'The only thing is that it has been hard on you, Mamma,' said Richard, 'if we have to come back to earth, have me as your eldest child, I could be much more useful.'

'Yes, I think you three have been quite happy. But I doubt if Cordelia has enjoyed a single moment of her childhood. It has all been a torment to her. She is not selfish. It is not what she has lacked that is an agony to her, it is what we all have lacked. She has hated it that all our clothes have been so shabby and that the house is so broken down. She has hated it that I have always been so late in paying Cousin Ralph the rent. She has hated it that we have so few friends. She hates it that your father has gone away, but not as you hate it. She would have preferred a quite ordinary father, so long as he stayed with us. She wishes she could have lived a life like the other girls at school. Your father's writing, my playing, and whatever goes with those things, and the enjoyment we have had, are no compensation to her for what she has lost. Now, do not dare to despise her for this desire to be commonplace, to be secure, to throw away what we have of distinction. It is not she who is odd in hating poverty and —' she felt for the word — 'eccentricity. It is you who are odd in not hating them. Be thankful for this oddity, which has brought you safe through terrible years. But do not think you owe it to any virtue in yourselves. You owe it entirely to your musical gifts. The music I have taught you to play must have made you realise that there is a great deal in life which is not affected by what happens to you. Also the technique has been more help to you than you realise. If you are not soft, it is because the technique you have mastered, such as it is, has hardened you. If God had not made you able to play you would be as helpless as Cordelia, and it is not her fault but God's that she cannot play, and as God has no faults let us now drop the subject.'

She was about to turn away, but she was recalled by an anxiety. 'Richard Quin,' she desperately begged, 'I was speaking of

Mary and Rose when I said it was technique that had made them brave. You do not work hard enough! Promise you will work harder!'

He answered hesitantly, 'Mamma, it is not quite the same with me as it is with them. I wish I could explain,' but just then there was the sound of a key in the lock, and Rosamund came into the house, her satchel over one shoulder and her loaded shopping-bag on the other. The wind was strong that day, her golden curls were blown across her throat and breast, and she was flushed, she looked like a rose under a storm. Mamma said to her, 'My dear, poor Cordelia has been very much upset. That imbecile Miss Beevor took her to that monster Hans Fechter, and he was very rude to her, and she locked herself in her room. I have told her to go to bed. I think it better that none of us should be with her, and perhaps you could look after her.'

'She thought of committing suicide,' said Richard Quin.

'I told you,' Rosamund said earnestly, 'that she was in one of those states you all get into. Now I should not wonder if she had made herself really ill. I will go and get the thermometer out of my work-box.'

As she went upstairs my mother called her thanks to her, then sighed, 'Now I must deal with that calamitous Miss Beevor. Richard Quin, you will get her a cab and take her home. But in the meantime you three must go down to the kitchen, and get a tray for Cordelia and Rosamund, and have tea yourselves with Kate. And let us pray that some time we may again have peace and quiet.'

We always found the kitchen a kindly refuge in time of trouble, the glow from the coal-range was so warm and consoling, and Kate had such resources. Now she sagely said that for a long time it had been plain that all this rushing about to concerts had been far too much for a growing girl, and that there had been signs and enough that she was sickening for something, but that a few weeks' rest would put that right. While she boiled the kettle for Cordelia's tea we stood round the table and ate bread and butter with brown sugar piled on it, which we had liked when we were little, but had not had for a long time.

Richard Quin said, 'You two must not worry about poor old Cordy. Leave her to Rosamund. She has the advantage over all

385

of you that she isn't musical and isn't going to win anything on earth. She is the only one in this house who can see Cordelia without reminding her that she is no good at anything special.' And just then Rosamund came back and said, 'Cordelia has a temperature, I think. Richard Quin had better fetch the doctor. Tell him it is not urgent, but that he would probably prefer her to see him some time today.' When he had gone she said to Kate, 'She must certainly stay in bed, so may I have one of your white overalls? Then I will take over.' She fastened the garment about her with pins, for though she was tall, Kate was taller still, and bound a white cloth about her head to hide her hair. 'It is a kind of magic,' she explained to us, 'and Cordelia will obey me more.'

Richard Quin was back with us again, laughing. 'As I went through the hall, Mamma put her head out of the door and said she wants some tea for Miss Beevor, she told me she had been mistaken about her, that we all had been mistaken about her, she had many good points. I believe that in no time she is going to like her.'

'Oh, she will be another of those sitting downstairs when Aunt Clare is dying,' said Rosamund.

'So she will,' said Kate.

So Kate gave Richard Quin the tray she had been getting ready for Cordelia and he took it up to Mamma; and while Kate boiled another kettle we three girls went on standing round the table and eating bread and butter and brown sugar. I thought how strange it was of Cordelia not to like our life, which was so likeable, and not to like us, when we liked her all but her music, which nobody could like. But Rosamund was strange too. She had become a different person since she had put on the white overall and bound the white cloth about her head, and what was specially strange was that though she seemed unconscious of much that happened about her, she was perfectly conscious of this subtle change in herself and was going to trade on it in her relations with Cordelia. We had from time to time suspected she was stupid, and the teachers at our school had thought her remarkably so. But really this hardly looked like it. Another wonder struck me. I said, 'How did you know that Cordelia was just in a state and not in love?'

'Well, she did not look at all as if she were in love,' she answered.

'But how do people look when they are in love?' I asked.

'I could not tell you how they look,' she said, 'you know I cannot put things into words. But there is a look.'

I was baffled by her certainties. They were not the same as mine, and I began to suspect that they were more numerous and quite as well-founded. Even had Cordelia not spoken the words which paralysed the relationship between us, I could never have contrived the ingenious methods by which Rosamund brought her out of her humiliation during the next few weeks. She had read her thermometer correctly; Cordelia had had a temperature. It was the first intimation of the long illness, not severe, not feigned, which was to explain to the world, and in time even to Cordelia, why she had suddenly abandoned her musical career. It was fortunate that our old family doctor had just retired, and that the young man who succeeded him was unarmed against Mamma's dramatic powers and prescribed a course of rest and medical treatment probably not justified by the degree of Cordelia's anaemia and the functional disorder of her heart. But it was Rosamund who often assured him, with clumsy, stammering candour, and the artlessness of an overgrown schoolgirl so naïve in her enthusiasm for her future profession that she wore an imitation of a nurse's uniform, that Cordelia was manifesting symptoms he might otherwise have overlooked. It was Rosamund who impressed on Cordelia, without alarming her, that her physical state was so grave that it explained everything which had happened to her in recent months. 'B-b-but, C-c-cordelia, you c-c-cannot p-p-possibly get up yet,' she would say, her grey-blue eyes looking quite blind with earnestness. 'I have heard Doctor Lane say to Aunt Clare that though you will get quite well you have let yourself get so run-down that, oh, Cordelia, it really is not safe for you not to rest for quite a long time.' So it was established that what Hans Fechter had said to Cordelia could not have been of any importance and need not be discussed or even remembered, because she would not be able to practise for many weeks, or even months, or even years.

But Rosamund also reversed what had seemed bound to be a painful process. The rest of us had thought that, no matter what we did, Mary and I must go out into the world on our musical business, and leave our proud and ambitious Cordelia at home, humiliated by lack of occupation. But it was she who moved away from us and we who were left behind. Her bed was like a barge and we were on the quay. Rosamund was constantly with her, and did all her needlework in the sick-room, and Constance often joined her, and so did Kate when her work was done, and the three would sit sewing. It was as if the needles in their hands were oars, and they were rowing Cordelia away to the land where people were who are not musical. But of course this was music too. All these women worked in strict time, within a flowing rhythm. They imposed that time and rhythm on the room, on Cordelia. Soon there were pieces of stuff cut in queer shapes laid on the counterpane, and it appeared that Cordelia understood how they had to be put together to make something. We would be surprised to find by her bed all sorts of threads and silks we had never seen before, and queer-shaped needles, and Cordelia would tell us what they were as if she had been long familiar with their uses. Now she was always turning over magazines, which had never come into the house before, full of paper patterns and transfers, and talking as if there were many things to do, but no one thing that had to be done by any particular time or very well. Now she was as tranquil in her prettiness as the flowers we put by her bed.

We got our scholarships at different schools of music; Mary got into the Prince Albert College in Kensington and I was taken by the Athenaeum in Marylebone. Mary was to take my mother's maiden name, and become Mary Keith, while I stayed Rose Aubrey. We did not like either of these prescriptions; the separation made becoming a musician seem like having an operation or dying, one of those grim things one must do without company. But Mr. Kisch had insisted on them. He said it would not do for two concert-pianists to have the same surname; and he thought that if we were together we might dig ourselves into a hole and criticise our teachers by applying our family standards to them. He had told me too that it would be a pity if Mary and I were to compete against each other for awards. When I assured him that that would not matter for we would never be jealous of each other, he cleared his throat and told me that that was not what he feared. He had been afraid that it might be discouraging for me to be reminded too often that Mary played better than I did. This I had often suspected, but it had never been put into words by any of us, and I was astonished to find that his pronouncement brought tears to my eyes. I turned my head away and looked out of the window, so that he should not see them. But he had known they would be there, and he went on to explain that Mary played like an angel, as if she came straight from heaven, and if nobody else knew that that was not how I played, I would myself always know it. But I need not worry, because there was something in me which would carry me through, I would go on until I dropped, and in the end I would play, in a sense, as well as Mary. It was odd that when he told me this he showed more embarrassment than when he had told me of my inferiority, it was as if the quality which was to save me was something rough and coarse.

It was strange that we were not at home when we learned that we had got our scholarships, and heard the news in a strange house where we had never been before. Mr. Kisch had asked us to play at a private concert given by a man who lived in Regent's Park, a man who looked rather like Mr. Morpurgo, but who cared for music, whereas Mr. Morpurgo, we had discovered with regret, for it made paying back his kindness more difficult, cared not for music but for pictures. The purpose of the concert was to give a first performance to some songs written by a new composer called Oliver Something, and we had just to fill in time between the songs, and Mary was to play some Chopin and I was to play some Schumann. We were very pleased to go because Mr. Kisch said we were to be paid. We did not know how much, but it would be the first money we had ever earned. But he went on to say that he was sending us along because this man liked saying that people who afterwards became famous had played for him before they had made their names. That made us feel sudden terror.

The house was a nineteenth-century copy of an Italian palace, with lawns, at that time yellow with daffodils, dropping to a canal. Its rooms were high and splendid and the walls were painted with pale bright colours, against which Italian pictures of holy people and battles in full rage, tall Chinese vases covered with a tracery of flowers and huge, gross Buddhas, calm as if they had been small and shapely, and toy-neat French furniture, showed rich and solid and durable in beauty. We were not over-awed, any more than we had been by Mr. Morpurgo's house, for we had known Hampton Court Palace since we were small, and presently we had to switch our minds on to our music and notice

389

nothing. The concert was given in the ball-room, and we waited in what was evidently the music-room, there was another grand piano in there, and the panelled walls were inset with shelves filled by books about music. When I got back after playing my last piece we were both free, so we went round the shelves, wondering if we could ask permission to look at some of the books. I was wondering if I could own up how tremendously I had enjoyed the applause, and finally I said something about it, it seemed so dishonest not to admit it; and Mary winked at me, and said she had felt just the same. Then the butler came in with a telegram on a very big silver tray, and it was from Mamma to say that the letters we had been waiting for had come by the second post and we had both got our scholarships.

When I had read it I threw it down on the piano.

I said through tears that surprised me, 'I would give this scholarship up, I would never touch the piano again, if only Papa would come back.'

'Oh, yes,' said Mary, 'oh, yes.'

We went to the window and stood looking out into the garden, each with an arm about the other's waist. The sheets of daffodils were catching the wind, it looked as if the nap were being stroked the wrong way.

'But this will mean a great deal to Mamma,' I said, 'she had so little of the career that was hers by right.'

'Yes, it is a shame,' said Mary, 'so far as Mamma is concerned, all of it is a shame.'

'But she still likes a great deal of her life,' I said, 'there is always Richard Quin and she enjoys having Constance and Rosamund to live with us. But, I say, Mary, do you understand Rosamund?'

'Quite often, no,' said Mary.

'Of course, we would find it easier to understand her if she were a musician too,' I said.

'Well, she may not be a musician, but she is what music is about,' said Mary.

'What is music about?' I asked.

'Oh, it is about life, I suppose, and specially about the parts of life we do not understand, otherwise people would not have to worry about it by explaining it by music. But I can't say what I mean.'

What was music? I suddenly felt sick because I did not know the answer. I crossed the room and put my ear to the crack in the double doors which led into the ball-room. A song came through to me as a thin thread. I remembered how, when Cordelia had played the violin, her private thoughts, which were so contrary to the essence of music, had immediately become public property, audible to the deafest ear. The thoughts that this young composer had intended to make public had obstinately remained private. We had met him for a few minutes when we arrived at the house: he was a slender young man, with grey eyes clear as water, not so many years older than we were, gentle in manner, and from what he had said to us and from the character of his compositions it was plain that he was as essentially musical as Cordelia was unmusical. Yet even he was evidently finding it difficult to be a musician. I suddenly realised that for me it would be impossible. I looked round the room, lined with books on music, and felt that I was in prison, I had been shut up in a cube of music, and could not even have full use of my cell, so much of it was occupied by the grand piano, which seemed to me now not an instrument I had studied with results that till now had been successful, but an engine which throughout the years established tyrannous claims on my life, and was now enforcing them, and would enforce them for ever and ever, to my ruin.

For it was idiotic that I should become a musician. I had no musical gifts save those which had been transmitted to me by mother, and these must be pitifully diminished in the transmission, I was by so much a lesser thing than she was. If I played any composition well, it was because she had taught me to play it, and I knew that my performances, even considered as reproductions of hers, were always faulty. I did not want to be a musician. I did not want to grow-up. I could not face the task of being a human being, because I did not fully exist. It was my father and mother who existed. I could see them as two springs, bursting from a stony cliff, and rushing down a mountainside in torrent, and joining to flow through the world as a great river. I was so inferior that it did not matter if I should be prudent and escape the ruin to which my father had dedicated himself. His ruin, I saw, was nearer salvation than my small safety could ever come. I wished it was I, and not Cordelia, who had taken to her bed, and I realised that there was indeed no mere cowardice in her retreat, that indeed her stubbornness had risen to the heights of brave self-defence in her renunciation of the impossible task of living on the same scale as our father and mother.

'I would like to run away,' I said to Mary.

I have never known whether she heard me. At that moment the double doors opened, the dark, kind, smiling, eastern face of our host appeared, behind him there was the sound of subsiding applause, like a fan falling to silence in an exhausted hand. He said that Kisch had told him that we played some of Schumann's 'duets' very well, that he had mentioned this to somebody in the audience who was a specialist in Schumann's piano music, and who had expressed a great desire to hear us play them, and though he knew we had already done all that we had contracted to do, he would be so very pleased if we would play, say, 'Am Springbrunnen' and 'Versteckens.' Nothing could have stopped me from doing as he wished. Before he had finished speaking, Mary and I had turned to each other with our four hands spread; for the last month or two we had been fascinated by this suite, which we had never been taught, and which we had practised simply for our own amusement. We had also a sense that our host was disconcerted because the songs had been too faintly appreciated, and that he had thought it would be pleasanter for everybody, and certainly for the young composer, if the audience took something away with them other than the lassitude excited by his work. I was a musician in my own right, though I could not yet say to what degree, I was a human being and I liked my kind, so I went with my sister back into the concert-room. Or perhaps I was swept on by the strong flood of which I was a part.

THE END

VIRAGO MODERN CLASSICS

The first Virago Modern Classic, *Frost in May* by Antonia White, was published in 1978. It launched a list dedicated to the celebration of women writers and to the rediscovery and reprinting of their works. Its aim was, and is, to demonstrate the existence of a female tradition in fiction which is both enriching and enjoyable, and to broaden the sometimes narrow academic definition of a 'classic' which has often led to the neglect of a large number of interesting secondary works of fiction. In calling the series 'Modern Classics' we do not necessarily mean 'great' – although this is often the case. Published with new critical and biographical introductions, books are chosen for many reasons: sometimes for their importance in literary history; sometimes because they illuminate particular aspects of women's lives, both personal and public. They may be classics of comedy or storytelling; their interest can be historical, feminist, political or literary.

Initially the Virago Modern Classics concentrated on English novels and short stories published in the early decades of this century. As the series has grown it has broadened to include works of fiction from different centuries, different countries, cultures and literary traditions, many of which have been suggested by our readers.

Other titles by Rebecca West available from Virago

THIS REAL NIGHT

'*Rebecca West's novel touches the very essence of life . . . Reviewing Rebecca West is like trying to review Michaelangelo. Perhaps we have become afraid of acknowledging contemporary greatness*' – Sybille Bedford

The Fountain Overflows (1957), with its evocative portrait of the Aubrey family, is acknowledged as Rebecca West's fictional masterpiece. In this novel, published a year after her death, she continues their memorable story.

It is the early 1900s. With the disappearance of Piers, her feckless and gambling husband, and the sale of some valuable paintings, Clare Aubrey has a firmer hold on the purse strings. The three girls are now taking tentative steps towards adulthood: Rose and Mary are at music college, struggling for artistic perfection; Cordelia, characteristically self-assured, has fallen into the role of art dealer's assistant; Richard Quin, their beloved younger brother, is contemplating Oxford. Rebecca West describes their coming of age, with its gradual acceptance of love and loss, one which will become all the more poignant with the events of the First World War.

THE THINKING REED

'She dazzled her audience by the precocious ambition of her voice and its barbed brilliance' – Marina Warner

Isabelle is beautiful, immensely rich and a widow at the age of twenty-six. In 1928 she leaves America for Cannes and Paris in search of high society – and love. For though outwardly she has everything women dream of, inside she craves the peace of a lasting marriage. To find the kind of love she needs Isabelle must choose between three men: her violent, fascinating lover, the aristocrat André de Verviers; a reserved plantation owner from the Deep South, Laurence Vernon; and the eccentric millionaire Marc Sallafranque . . .

First published in 1936, this is Rebecca West's most popular work of fiction: at once a masterful portrayal of the brilliance and decadence of high society in the 1920s, and a poignant and compassionate portrait of one woman's life and loves.

THE RETURN OF THE SOLDIER

Rebecca West – highly intelligent, highly gifted, vital, original, combative, formidable and kind – was a great woman'
– Victoria Glendinning

The soldier returns from the front to three women who love him. His wife, Kitty, with her cold, moonlight beauty, and his devoted cousin Jenny wait in their exquisite home on the crest of the Harrow-weald. Margaret Allington, his first and long-forgotten love, is nearby in the dreary suburb of Wealdstone. But the soldier is shellshocked and can only remember the Margaret he loved fifteen years before, when he was a young man and she an inn-keeper's daughter. His cousin he remembers only as a childhood playmate; his wife he remembers not at all. The women have a choice – to leave him where he wishes to be, or to 'cure' him. It is Margaret who reveals a love so great that she can make the final sacrifice . . .

In Rebecca West's first novel she powerfully explores the nurturing and life-sustaining force of woman in a world governed by the destructive powers of man.